"*Reluctant sleuth and Miami developer John Deal is the last of his kind—a builder who appreciates his craft. His friend Arch Dolan was the last of his kind, too, a Miami bookseller who sold books because he loved them. Now someone has killed him for it. And he's only the first body to fall. In quick succession the CEO of a huge bookstore chain and a local lawyer meet violent ends...and Deal starts finding connections.*

Still, it's not easy for Deal: his estranged wife Janice, is still emotionally and physically scarred from mishaps the last time Deal stepped into the path of the wrong people. But Janice was close to Arch and she's as eager to find the killer as her husband. Working together, they discover that Arch's sister, lately employed by a charismatic revivalist, has disappeared. With the clues pointing north, Deal and Janice set out on a journey to a distant and frigid climate, one that threatens to chill them out for good."

"*The best installment in a first-rate thriller series.... Standiford serves up crackerjack action and memorable characters.*"

—*Publisher's Weekly*, starred review

Book Deal

Also by Les Standiford

Spill
Done Deal
Raw Deal
Deal to Die For
Presidential Deal,
Deal With the Dead

Book Deal

Les Standiford

Poisoned Pen Press

Library of Congress Catalog Card Number: 2001098485

ISBN: 1-59058-012-5 Trade Paperback

Poisoned Pen Press
6962 E. First Ave. Ste. 103
Scottsdale, AZ 85251
www.poisonedpenpress.com
info@poisonedpenpress.com

Printed in the United States of America

This is for Mitchell and Rachelle
and for good book people everywhere.
And, as always,
for Kimberly and the Three Muskatoots.

Deal and I would like to extend grateful thanks to
all those who have aided in the shaping of this
book, among them:
our close reader, Bill Beesting,
our editor, Eamon Dolan,
our agent, Nat Sobel,
our partner in crime, James W. Hall,
and our eagle-eyed booster of boosters,
Rhoda Zelda Kurzweil.

Author's Note to the Poisoned Pen Press Edition

Though the mists of time grow thick, I can still remember clearly the day that Jim Hall called to tell me he'd finished reading the draft of the fourth in the Deal series. "And I've got your title," he added. I could tell he was as proud of himself as all the others who had tried proposing titles for the series along the way (*"No Deal; Shut Up and Deal; Have I Got a Deal For You,"* etc.)

"So?" I asked. *"Book Deal,"* he told me. And—surprise—I was as tickled as he was. I banged the phrase onto the title page and shipped the beast off to my editor, sure that he would be just as pleased.

Alas, it did not turn out to be the case. Not threatening enough, came word. Okay, I said, how about *"Killer Book Deal."* That brought the explanation that mystery readers would not be interested in a crime novel having to do with books. I countered that John Dunning was having fair success long about then with a title called *Booked to Die,* and suggested some other possibilities: *"Hardback Deal"* is one that sticks with me, though the list numbered in the twenties, at least.

Finally, I was taken aside, where it was patiently and carefully explained to me that there were no conceivable circumstances under which my book was going to be published bearing a title that had anything whatsoever to do with books or publishing. The reasons for this were laid out to me in a scene that—in my memory at least—was not unlike that wonderful moment in *Network,* where corporation mogul Ned Beaty explains the facts of media life to his wretched anchorman Peter Finch. Though I would love to pass along the various unvarnished truths that were conveyed to me during my own heart to heart, it was the agreement between my mentor and myself that in return for his forthrightness, such would remain confidential.

So I will have to leave it to the reader to have a look at the story that follows and venture a guess as to what considerations might have superceded such paltry issues as what I wanted to call my book.

In any case, *Deal on Ice,* is what was settled upon way back when, and only after considerable more whining on my part was this compromise reached: the silhouette of a pistol, overlaid upon the cover art as printed on the advance readers copies, would be replaced, upon publication, with a rendering of a book. Those who saw the finished product must still be wondering what a book was doing floating through a snowstorm.

Suffice it to say, then, that I am greatly pleased, not only to see this book back in print, but with its original title restored, and a dead-on cover design by Tom Corcoran. For this, and for all their many kindnesses, I would like to thank Barbara Peters and Robert Rosenwald most sincerely. As I would like to thank Mitchell Kaplan once more for giving me the idea to write it in the first place.

Les Standiford
Miami, February 20, 2002

Foreword

"This isn't just a business, it's a way of life."
—*Arch Dolan, proprietor of Arch's House of Books*

It was the mid 1990's. The go-go years of the big box bookstore expansion. A Barnes & Noble or a Borders envisioned for every corner. Independent booksellers, once enjoying over 50% of marketshare, were finding themselves in some serious trouble. Closings were common, and by this time, the ramifications of a book retail market dominated by two or three large, centralized players were being debated, not only at bookseller conventions, but on the pages of *The New York Times, Harper's* and *The Wall Street Journal.* Publishers who knew, felt it dangerous to have a distribution channel that lacked diversity, and civil libertarians were worried about what would happen if the large chains had so much influence that they could actually control what did get published. Closer to home, a large chain bookseller had decided to open one of their boxes, 25,000 square feet worth, about a block away from my store, Books & Books, which had been in business for over ten years in Coral Gables, Florida, and I was nervous.

My good friend Les Standiford had the answer to my nervousness. He put John Deal on the case. John Deal, the contractor with a heart of gold, had already taken on corrupt developers, greedy sugar farmers, and seedy Hollywood producers. And like Travis McGee before him, he did so with much critical acclaim. *Done Deal, Raw Deal,* and *Deal To Die For* all received boisterously rave reviews. And *The Miami Herald* likened Les to "a poet in a trench coat." The *bookstore wars* would be a piece of cake; John Deal would prevail. I told Les everything I knew about the business: my hopes, my fears. He was and is a quick-study, and *Book Deal* was born.

And Les got it right. The feel, smell and nuance of bookselling infuses *Book Deal* with uncanny authenticity. Les' love for books and bookstores makes this a celebration of all the great, good places which are home to independent bookstores. As we cross into the new millennium, there are still challenges. Market share has been further eroded, and a new threat to the independent bookstore has emerged with the growth of on-line retailing, yet there remains a vibrancy to the great independent bookstores. They are still the heart and soul of so many communities across this country. Don't count them out. John Deal didn't. Neither did Les Standiford. And on behalf of all the Arch Dolan's who are keeping all the House of Books afloat, I thank them both. I also thank Poisoned Pen Press for making *Book Deal* available once again.

If you, the reader, have found your way to *Book Deal* for the first time, you're in for a treat.

—Mitchell Kaplan,
Books & Books

Note

While I love South Florida just as it really and truly is, this is a work of fiction, and I have taken occasional liberties with the landscape and place-names involved. May they please the innocent and guilty alike.

Chapter 1

She paused outside her office door, carefully checked the long, dimly lit hallway in both directions, then hurriedly slid her key into the lock—so quiet now, she could hear the tumblers click—and entered. Not that she didn't belong here, not that she wouldn't have a reasonable explanation for returning, even at this hour, and if it came to that, she might be ready for a confrontation, some opportunity to explode into righteous indignation that would provide the perfect excuse to quit. But if she met someone, if she encountered Security, there would have to be that explanation, and she was already late: her pulse had begun to race, and her throat was thick with anticipation.

She moved inside, shrugged out of her coat, tossed it aside, traced her way to her desk by feel, nudging her way past the conversation area and the vague nimbus of the sofa, skirting the stone-slab coffee table and the huge puff of the down-stuffed chair, gliding the notch of her hip along the edge of her desk, quite aware of the sleekness, the teasing heat of that motion through what she wore. She kicked her heels off, dug her toes into the thick carpeting, felt a tingle rise from the flesh of her insteps to the back of her throat. She paused, closed her eyes. She could see the room in the ghostly light of her mind, every last detail of it. She ran her tongue over her dry lips, reached out to press her palm to the cool marble of the credenza behind her desk. She found the switch she wanted, pressed it down. She opened her eyes and waited.

The screen came alive first, with a tiny pop and crackle, and then a soft blue glow of light that spilled out into the room like mist, and she heard the grinding of the processor soon after. She realized that these sounds, so familiar to her by day, had taken on a new, almost human tenor, as if the machine itself knew what she was about. Illogical to think so. But it was night and even the muscles of her jaw were like tiny coils, quivering with a current of their own, and she felt as though she could be forgiven for thinking of this collection of microchips and circuitry as something approaching flesh and blood.

She waited impatiently as the machine cycled through its initial sign-on procedure, entered the password that gave her access to the master computer, an unfathomable bank of cards and boards and micro-circuitry lodged somewhere beneath her in the bombproof bowels of the building. When the machine had finally settled, she reached into her pocket, withdrew what anyone else might have assumed was a calculator, or some strange sort of television remote. She aimed it at the screen and pressed a series of numbers—her numbers—which the device would encrypt.

Prompted by this transitory code, the bland graphic painted by her organization's master computer vanished, and a series of vague images flittered across the screen, each one colorful, but too quickly gone to be discerned. She listened to the hiss and cries of the machine's electronic dialing, closed her eyes again as she waited, felt the flashes of color washing out over her, cleansing her in electronic light.

When the pulses had stopped again, she opened her eyes to find that the machine had squirreled its way along, as it had been taught, through the many points of choice offered in cyberspace, dropping her out precisely where she had left off her normal work only hours before. *I don't work in this room*, she thought. *I work out there, somewhere. Out there, in the vast infinity of machine space.*

Her machine sat quietly now, its screen bathing her in a film of deeper blue, and she imagined that she could feel the light's cool touch as she pulled the ties of her robe loose and sat down before the machine to take a different path.

"You feel more comfortable here?" he asked her, and she found herself nodding in response.

But it was a question pulsing before her on the computer screen, after all. She glanced across the dimly lit room to the door of her office. Locked. Yes, she had locked the door. Of course she had. She smiled at herself as she hurried to tap out her response.

"Is 'here' in Norway?" She watched her own message unfurl below his question, tiny electronic characters laid out against the dark blue of computer space.

"Yes, I think Norway," came his answer.

"Well, it seems very warm in Norway," she typed. It was true. She felt a thin trickle of sweat inching its way down the flesh just in front of her ear. Another time she might have brushed it away in annoyance. Now it felt like a tiny finger tracing its way down toward her throat, toward the plane of her chest. She willed it on its way, and her breasts tightened in response.

"...and how is the situation of your work?" she read.

A tick of sound from somewhere, she thought. But it was just nerves, her imagination.

"I am still deciding," she replied. "Such disillusionment. Maybe the best thing is to leave. But time will tell." Then she added, "I don't want to talk about work tonight, please. I am feeling too comfortable now."

"Ah, good," was his response.

She murmured a prayer of thanks. In fact, she was greatly distressed about "the situation of her work," but she was determined to bury her feelings, for tonight at least. As their scheduled day and time had neared, she'd found herself burning with anticipation, and she did not want anything to spoil it. The suspicion that her passions might possibly have risen in direct response to the greater urgencies in her life had occurred to her, but she did not care. Comfort was where you could find it, she had decided, and nothing was going to deter her from that tonight.

Besides, the fact was that she did feel more comfortable here, in this new meeting place. They had met in a much different arena: "on line," as it was referred to, in one of the chat groups on the Internet, nothing like alt.sex.bondage, of course, but one of the more innocuous ones, where she had been lurking quietly in the background, keeping an eye out, not for cybermates, but for lost souls who might profit by what her organization might provide. She had read about all these groups. What better source of converts? How patronizing she had been, she thought now.

Torsten, his name, and though it bespoke of Scandinavian open-mindedness, even sexual brazenness and amorality, she'd been touched by the innocence of the messages he had sent when he'd first appeared on-line: "I am new to this," he'd said. "I am alone...but not lonely," these messages popping onto her screen interspersed into the chat of three women complaining about the rudeness of men they'd met on-line.

"...I am being amazed at how the world has changed to allow such a thing as this...," she'd read that and more and finally felt somehow so taken by this Torsten, whom the other three steadfastly ignored, that she'd found herself tapping out her first truly "personal" message in response, surprised by how her fingers trembled as she pressed the keys.

Things had progressed rapidly with Torsten, and beyond her wildest imaginings. She knew it was partly to be accounted for by her own loneliness. She hadn't had what might be termed a "date" for more than a year, having come to prefer the predictable, low-grade boredom of her own company to the inevitable disappointment she'd become accustomed to in her relationships, the last, of course, worst of all.

There were men around, other men in the organization, of course, and she hadn't sworn off them, but the organization was growing so rapidly, and the responsibilities of her position had increased, and she felt that she'd needed no distractions, not for a while at least. And somehow the weeks had become months and those had strung together into a year or more...and then, suddenly, there had come Torsten, from nowhere, or from out of cyberspace, to be more exact.

They had discovered common interests in reading (biographies and histories, primarily), in cooking (the *medium*-fat diet and a little wine never hurt anyone), in thinking (how vast the world had become with these machines leading the way, how difficult it seemed to feel an important part of things). She could have him on her terms, or on equal terms at least, no more at the mercy of his whims as to when to be together than he was at hers.

Though they had shared vague physical descriptions (she had subtracted a few pounds from her true weight and five years had somehow vanished from her age; he, on the other hand, had called himself a better-looking Sigmund Freud), she was free to imagine him physically as she preferred (these imaginings becoming steadily more intense), and she was free to speak with him without fear, for she was ultimately just a few letters and symbols, as ultimately untraceable by him as he was by her. And though it had been Torsten to guide them gently out of the common group where they had met and into a private "room" where they could talk more intimately, she'd soon discovered a latent desire to speak openly of things she'd barely allowed herself to think about, much less express.

At first, he'd questioned her about her work (he was an accountant, in a large city, and though he'd never said, something in his odd syntax suggested it was in some European country), her upbringing (his a pastiche of anonymous boarding schools, exact locales unnamed; hers inconsequential, in a city of the American South, she'd told him, and never said how far south, nor how misleading that expression was, in her case). In the beginning, she'd been extraordinarily cautious, as if any chance detail she might let slip would lead to this unknown man tracking her down, across continents, perhaps…she'd come home late from work one night to find a sex fiend, a killer slavering in the bushes by her doorstep.

But little by little she'd lost her reserve. He had become her friend, after all. And she had begun to confide in him. At first she'd shared the vaguest hints of her unease about her job, and then, at his gentle prodding—"We all have passed through these periods of doubt about what we do"— she'd confessed graver concerns. She'd told him nothing specific, of course, but spoke of matters she had discovered that, if not outright criminal, at the least seemed at odds with the very mission of their organization.

"In this new world order," he'd tried to reassure her, "perhaps what seems untoward is just the way of business."

No, she'd told him. She knew the difference between matters of simple exigency and what was downright wrong.

Was there no one she could talk to about these matters? Torsten had asked. No, she told him. There was no one. Of course that was not exactly true. There was one person, and she had taken certain steps, but she had not seen fit to tell even Torsten that.

Besides, by then they had begun to speak of other intimate matters, discussions of things that had swept her into utter dizziness as she tapped and read, tapped and read. It had started with his admission that he had found himself thinking of her lips as he read the words she typed, how her mouth would move as she formed the words, and she'd quailed at first, but then thought, well, yes, they had the words between them but not the sounds, not the lips...

...and then discovered as she typed her timid response that her thighs were bathed in warmth. They'd somehow passed on from lips to skin to hands and what those might do...

...and had anyone suggested to her a month ago that she would find herself admitting to a total stranger that yes, she had in fact touched herself in those ways, and found it intensely pleasurable, she would have called it unthinkable. But now, what would have been a flush of embarrassment or shame had become a heady, heart-pounding rush of exhilaration as she responded to his inquiries: "Tell me how...tell me how it feels...tell me that you can feel me there with you, in your office, my hand with yours..."

Even now, her hand had moved to her breast, was squeezing the knotted flesh of her nipple to the very edge where pain took over pleasure. She swallowed thickly, saw that her robe had fallen entirely open, that she was fully bared before the glowing machine. She closed her eyes and arched her neck up to the blue light, and thought that some soft sound had escaped her throat.

I am in Norway, she thought...*in Tibet...in Oz...I am floating in clean, clear space where nothing can hurt me, nothing can trouble me, where I can be just as I wish to be...*

Glorious freedom here, then. And thanks be to Torsten, who had told her of the need to move their meeting place again. He read the magazines, the specialists' reports, kept up with such things, it seemed. When he'd discovered that others had invaded their "room," to "lurk" invisibly while they spoke of such intimate matters, he'd been not so much incensed or embarrassed as saddened. While she had felt a sudden pang of fear—imagine if the others with whom she worked were to ever learn or overhear—he had reassured

her. The two of them were just as anonymous to those electronic voyeurs who "watched" as they had ever been.

Still, the dynamics of their meeting had been altered
dramatically. Certainly, there had been no more discussions
of her work. And even their sexual conversations became
awkward, truncated, interrupted by signals that others had
slipped into the "room," or by Torsten's manipulations to
check for such intrusions.

Then he had discovered the safeguards. First, the device
she'd used when she logged on, a tiny computer itself, actually,
which converted her password into a different, encrypted
code each time she used it.

And now, as a double safeguard, this new place, this
Comnet. A "remailing" service. In reality, a computer somewhere in Scandinavia, where their messages would arrive,
after leapfrogging along the Internet, to be stripped of their
original identifying codes, and receive new, randomly assigned
names. Here, in some room within a room within a room of
an indifferent Nordic machine, they could converge, safe
from any prying eyes.

Insulated now. Insulated and insulated again, disem-
bodied spirits trysting in some mythic ice cave of the future.
In real-world space, she might find herself confused,
doubting, uncertain, but here in the place the machines had
created, she could come to be with Torsten, and for now at
least, be free.

"...something different...something you have never
done...," she read on the screen before her now. Her hand had
moved to her thigh, then slowly up to a fold of flesh that
seemed almost agony to touch. She felt her ankles lock
against the spokes of her chair, felt her pulse thudding in
her ears.

"...my hand is your hand..."

Her lower lip was caught in her teeth, her fingers truly were
another's as they probed and stroked...and yet something

was nagging at her, fighting for attention: in your office, he had said. Had she slipped, had she told him where she was? She'd been so careful all these weeks, no clues, no hints…but perhaps he'd just assumed. It was natural, wasn't it. He was in his office, so she'd be in hers…

She threw off the thoughts, silly, silly, found herself urging upward now, lifting herself out of her chair toward an avalanche of release as great as any she had ever known. She knew that she was speaking aloud now, any thought of typing a distant memory, but it did not matter, for Torsten would have joined her in his own turn, and they were connected over the vast, impossible stretches of ether…her very being had disintegrated, spread across this unknowable space, her consciousness filling with one explosion of light after the next.

"Oh, dear God," she said, and might have spoken the words again, had she not heard from somewhere the sounds of the door lock clacking, the rush of feet upon carpet, the spoken reply.

"Harlot," came the voice. "Blasphemer. Jezebel!" The words hissed in her ear.

At first the words meant nothing. They might have been elements of her fantasy, imagined sounds that barreled out of the tunnels of the ethernet along with the images of light and color that rocketed about her brain…

…and then she felt the arm about her throat, and realized that she was being pulled backward, brutally lifted from her seat, her ankles raking the spokes of her chair.

She would have screamed, but the arm was pressed too tightly against her throat, her chest burning, her strength so suddenly sapped that her kicks and thrashings seemed pitiful, even to her.

"Such a disappointment," she heard, a voice, familiar now, ripe with bitterness. "Did you think I wouldn't learn what you'd done? Did you think I'd let you threaten everything?"

She felt her heels fly over the back of the chair, felt them bounce against the soft carpet. He was holding her upright, pressed close to him now, and the pressure at her throat seemed even tighter. She fought to get a look at him, but the grip that held her was unyielding. She saw a shoulder, the shadow of a face, the glint of a poster on her wall, a train rolling through the heartland with a message that assured her that life was a journey and not a destination, and then her eyes had come unfocused, were rolling back in her head. The little ticks of sound, the untoward phrase, "*there, in your office,*" how had she let herself ignore the warnings?

"I trusted you," he said, and his voice was nearly a sob. "I trusted you!"

He squeezed more tightly, and as she began to lose consciousness, she thought his voice had become mocking, echoing the words she had read moments before on her computer screen: "...what is the situation of your work," he hissed. "...my hand is your hand!"

He was beyond outrage. "...godless...ungrateful... abomination..." The words cascaded in an unintelligible litany, and the words no longer mattered.

How had he known, she wondered? How could he have possibly known? And then, in the next terrible instant, though her mind thundered with agony, she knew the very worst.

That this very man, the man who held her, who squeezed the life from her body, who would kill her now...

...he was the one...he was the only one who could have known...

...*he* had sent those words...

The outrage of it burned through her, galvanized her into one final act of resistance. She drew up her foot, slammed it down hard on his instep. She heard him gasp with pain, felt his grip loosen. She brought her head forward, found the soft flesh of his hand, bit down as hard as she could. She shook her head violently, her teeth still fastened, until she heard him howl, and his hands flew away. She felt blessed air rush into her lungs, swung her elbow back, felt a satisfying crack as it struck his face.

She heard him cry out again, saw his shadow, cast by the glow of the computer screen, flash across the wall in front of her as he went down, tumbling over her desk, scattering files, the pictures of her family, the spray of summer flowers she'd learned to dry herself. She was already running for the door, her hands grappling for the handle, the metal slipping in her hands like some object from a dream you just can't hold…

…until mercifully she had it, the door opened, slammed behind her, and she was out in the long hallway, alone. She glanced at the door helplessly—no way to secure it—then bolted away down the hall, her bare feet slapping the cool tile, echoes that died behind her as she run. Door after door flashed past her, bland titles, no comfort in any of them: Media Research, Communications Services, the several portals into Archives. She reached a broad intersection, hesitated, heard a door slam down the hallway behind her.

She drew a kind of sobbing breath, turned left, ran down the wide hallway toward the Convocation Center. A huge arena, two dozen exits there, out to the vast parking lot, her car…and then she remembered with a pang that nearly took her legs from under her: the keys. Yes. Still in the pocket of her coat, back in her office.

Her lungs were burning now, her side ached, her throat was raw. Footsteps pounded behind her and she had to keep going. Going somewhere.

She fastened her gaze on the big double doors fifty yards away and forced her rubbery legs to move. She could make it to the hall. And then she could get outside. And somehow she'd find help.

She glanced behind her, found her pursuer had not yet reached the turn. She turned back, thinking she had thirty yards, twenty-five…

If she could just make it through those doors before he saw her, perhaps she'd have a chance. She was gasping when she reached them, clawing at the handles, the first door unyielding, but the second—yes, yes, thank God—swinging open at her touch. She glanced back to see the hallway still empty, then she was through the doors and closing them quickly behind her.

She paused inside the silent cavern of the arena, steadying herself against a stand that held a marble baptismal font, a stack of collection plates, an usher's candle damper in a notched sleeve. A series of life-sized saints, figures from biblical lore, and some characters who were the outright invention of the Reverend James Ray Willis seemed to stare down at her from their niches along the walls of the vast arena. All the accoutrements of salvation, she thought, none of them much good to her now. She'd lost her claim to grace, that was plain enough. She'd been found out, discovered wallowing in sin and degradation, proven herself unworthy, never mind that she'd been tricked. And damn it, that was still no reason to die.

Her breath thundered in her ears, and she forced herself to rest another moment, savoring the silence that surrounded her, the familiar tang of new carpet and bindery glue and whatever vague residue of beingness still hovered in the air from last Sunday's visit: 10,000 faithful souls who'd come to hear James Ray Willis proclaim God's word and would come again the next and the next.

She edged herself up to the tiny window set high in the door, used the breaker bar to balance on her tiptoes until finally she could see. There was a gold-filigree mesh that reinforced the glass and tinted it somehow, giving an undersea cast to the light that streamed through from beyond, but there was no mistaking it: the hallway lay glistening and empty. Perhaps she'd lost him after all. Perhaps he'd lost his nerve, was even now retreating...

She was almost dizzy with the possibility of safety when the face shot up before her, the twisted features no more than an inch away from her own. The snarl he gave when he saw her vibrated the glass between them, and she fell back screaming as the door began to buck in her hands.

She felt herself being pulled outward, into the hallway, and leaned back with everything she had, digging her toes into the carpeting for purchase. She managed to get the latch engaged again, and, still hanging desperately to the breaker bar, pulled the lock switch down by dragging her cheek painfully over it. She was still hanging to the bar when she heard glass shatter above her, and looked up to see his bloodied hand groping wildly her way.

She fell back, felt herself emitting little grunts that were as much expressions of rage as of fear. He gave up trying to reach her then, and began to paw about the inside of the door. *The latch*, she thought. *He's going for the latch.*

She watched him grope about for a moment, feeling mesmerized, as if she were some poor bird caught in the gaze of a snake…and then her gaze landed on the baptismal font. She staggered to the stand, unsheathed the brass candle damper, and found it satisfyingly heavy. She measured herself, drew back then, and swung, closing her eyes at the moment the thing struck home and his scream echoed down the long hallway outside.

She listened to the curses and moans issuing through the broken window for a moment, realizing that she'd managed to peel away a layer of skin on her own cheek, but the pain and the trickle of blood were nothing to her now. She tossed aside the heavy candle damper and ran up one of the broad aisleways toward a glowing exit sign.

She banged through the swinging doorways into the atrium, and stifled another scream when she saw the figure standing in front of her, hand extended in a gesture of fellowship. A cardboard cutout of the Reverend James Ray Willis, welcoming all who approached into the blessed fold. She slammed the thing aside with a swipe of her arm, sent it tumbling into the always babbling Stream of Mercy that coursed the granite inlay of the entry.

She hurried across the chilly slabs, banged against the breaker bar at the central bank of glass doors and staggered out into the crystal-cold midwestern night. She nearly wept at the sight of her little red sedan, nestled under a vapor light at the edge of the nearby parking lot, for she had remembered something in there as she completed the arc of her candle damper swing: her father's practical voice echoing in her ears as he handed her another of the gizmos he was fond of bestowing on his children. "You put yourself a key in this magnetized little box here, stick it up under the fender like so, you'll never have to worry about locking yourself out again." No matter that she'd never done such a thing in her life, and that he never had either, better safe than sorry his motto, and wasn't she happy for that now.

She ran across the strip of brittle grass, her bare feet going fiery with the frost that lay there, the pain easing as she reached the warmer asphalt. Moments later, she was kneeling at the rear bumper, her hands groping through a crust of dirt and road grime coating its under edge. Five years since she'd stuck it "just so," but magnets didn't wear out with time, did they?

Right beneath the license plate, wasn't that where she'd left it? Or was it the gas cap? Or the trunk lock? She'd nearly given up, was ready to run on across the lot, not more than a mile out to the highway and there would surely be someone to help there, even at this hour…when her hand found the little case under a mound of dried mud and she wrenched it free, shearing off one of her fingernails in the process.

She tried to open the rusted case without success, banged it a couple of times against the asphalt, tried again. She held the thing to the light, realized she was pushing the top of the case in the wrong direction. This time pried it back at the cost of another nail. Key in her palm now—*safe, safe, I'm going to be safe*—she rose and, seeing the lights of a car approaching across the vast expanse of parking lot—it couldn't be him, no way it could be him—and ran to the door of her faithful sedan and felt her feet strike a patch of ice on the asphalt.

She fell so quickly she hardly had time to brace herself. One hand struck the ground, sending a bolt of pain up her wrist, her cheek bouncing off the ice. She lay stunned for a moment, blinking as the lights of the approaching car washed over her. *Key*, she thought, *key*! And felt the key still clutched in her good hand. She tried to scramble to her knees, but her wrist crumpled and she was down again, her face, her lips, dragging the asphalt as she desperately scooted and clawed.

A car door opened and slammed closed. "Here, here," she heard from somewhere above her. A woman's voice, soothing, kind. She caught a glimpse of sensible black shoes, stockings that ended at the knee, a hemline of dotted Swiss. It might have been her grandmother, someone's grandmother, she was thinking…and then felt hands lifting her up.

"What's all this?" the woman's voice came to her. She stared at the woman, who propped her against the door of her idling car. It *was* a grandmother: felt hat, crumpled veil, spray of flowers. And there was another figure coming out of the driver's side and through the glow of headlights: a tall, gaunt, balding man in an ill-fitting dark suit, the very uniform of a farmer-parishioner, and that was the stock in trade of the Reverend James Ray Willis.

She felt a surge of relief, safe now among the salt of the earth. "I'm all right," she managed.

"Of course you are, dearie," the woman said. She turned to her husband then and smiled. "She says she's all right, hon."

"Why, heck, yes, she is," the man said, and he was wearing the same smile.

"Wait," she said. "Are you…?" But she would never finish the thought. For there was an arm about her throat once again. And a terrible pressure. And a bombshell of light that loosed her across the skein of space at last.

◉◉◉

The next service, a Saturday, they arrived early, found seats in the vast center section of the Convocation Center, on eye level with the pulpit. These were the best seats, they'd decided, trial and error over the past several months. Sitting elsewhere, you could get the effect, sort of, but it was a lot like trying to watch a big-screen TV from the corner of a room.

"It's a waste of time getting here so early just to sit," the tall man told his wife.

"Did you have something better to do?" she asked him.

"We got us traveling on our agenda. We could be at the airport, watching this on TV."

"We've got plenty of time," she said. "Besides, what if it was the Reverend himself today?"

He glanced at the stage. "It hasn't been the Reverend himself for over a year now. Why would it be today?"

"Just a feeling," she shrugged. "All that's going on."

She turned her gaze back to the stage, where dozens of people in black skirts and white blouses or black trousers and white shirts were bustling about, armloads of flowers here, little settees and couches there, all the cables, and the cameras, the lights coming up for testing and then dying away, and all the while the people filing into the vast hall, the hundreds turning into thousands. How many of them wanting the same thing, he wondered, that the Reverend himself would come to them on this day.

All the bustling, and the wondering, and the filing in, and the waiting, and then, finally, the lights went down, and a hush descended upon the crowd, and he felt her hand on his arm, her grip growing unconsciously tight, almost painful in anticipation. *She wishes he would come so bad,* he thought, and it was a wistful feeling that grew in him as well as the lights got dimmer and the ghostly cone of light that illuminated the pulpit grew brighter.

It was amazing, he had to admit, watching the light surrounding the pulpit grow milky and opaque, something swirling around in that beam as if creation itself were under way. Creation it was, of a certain kind, for what it must take to pull off the illusion was well beyond his reckoning.

But still…but still…he thought.

The swirl had become a sinuous twist of smoke, the crowd humming now, the smoke a vague shape, the shape a form, and the form finally revealed itself: the Reverend James Ray Willis standing there, or at least a version of him. Ten feet tall, maybe twelve, maybe more, hard to tell at this distance, his arms lifted in benediction, his smile promising everything good and everlasting. Once upon a time, the man himself had stood in that pulpit, he'd beckon the unwashed forward, lay on hands, heal the sick, soothe the sick at heart. But times had changed.

"Hallelujah," called the shimmering, holographic image to his flock.

"Hallelujah," the flock roared back, a sound that would rock them bigger than any cheer out of the football stadium at the college down-state.

"Hallelujah," his wife called along with them. And so did he, just a moment late, and all the while the man was thinking, still, wouldn't it be better if it was the Reverend himself? Just once? The devil with all this, all this technology. Was that so much to ask?

Chapter 2

"...corporate chain saw killers," the voice, dripping condemnation, boomed about Deal's sleep-filled head. "Worldwide conspiracy of bankers and merchants..." The voice impossibly loud, a crackle and humming filling the pauses between the words.

Deal found himself awake, groggy, his eyes blinking in the blinding, apocalyptic light of his television set. "...soul-rotting mire of materialism and excess..." the voice blasting, shaking the glass of the sliding glass doors in his den. A man's face filled the camera's lens, the jaw set, the lips a thin line, the eyes piercing, Paul Newman blue.

Deal swung his legs over the edge of the couch, sat up, groped around for the remote control. He was beginning to put things together. He'd fallen asleep on the couch, had probably rolled over onto the remote. He found the thing wedged between the cushions, fumbled with the buttons until the volume mercifully decreased.

The camera had pulled back to reveal more of the man who'd been speaking. Where Deal might have expected a shot of a spittle-spraying wild man pounding a podium before a mob, what he actually saw was a man seated on the sofa of an interview show set, carrying on conversation with a host who looked vaguely like Pat Boone. The man who'd been speaking was wearing a softly draped three-piece suit, wore his gray hair close-cropped but stylish, had one leg crossed casually atop the other. Deal checked his watch: 3:30 A.M. What channel, what kind of talk show had he found?

"Handsome fella, isn't he?"

The voice came out of the darkness at Deal's side, stopping his breath. Deal spun about, saw the vague lump that was his neighbor, Vernon Driscoll, laid out nearly supine in the recliner there. His memory bank was kicking in now. They'd been watching the Miami Heat game, a telecast from the West Coast that hadn't started until eleven. Deal was pretty sure he'd caught most of the first quarter, but after that, all seemed vague.

He rubbed his face with his hands. "Who won?"

Driscoll shifted his bulk in the recliner. "I'm not sure. It was either all the guys who used to be the Warriors now playing for the Heat, or maybe it was the other way around. You get sleepy, that kind of stuff's hard to keep straight."

Deal tried to laugh. "Couple of die-hard fans we are."

Driscoll cranked the seatback of the recliner into an upright position. "Yeah, I woke up to old James Ray Willis there, I thought maybe we'd died and gone to hell after all. How come you had it on so loud?"

Deal shook his head. "I must've rolled over on the remote."

They were silent then, Deal feeling his thoughts falling into order. Saturday night, really Sunday morning now. He would have to drop by one of his construction sites later, talk to an architect, but that wasn't until noon. Plenty of time for a decent rest. Send Driscoll home, fall into the sack.

Driscoll, however, had leaned forward, turned the volume up on the set again. Maybe he'd forgotten whose apartment he was in, Deal thought.

"We're moving toward the One World government," James Ray Willis was saying. "...the demise of Communism, the rise of the Global Plantation." The Pat Boone look-alike was nodding as Willis rattled off the phrases breezily.

"And we all know what the plantation owners have in mind for the little man," Willis said. He was staring meaningfully into the camera lens now. Applause erupted as the camera drew well back from the set to a high shot from the rafters. The set where Willis and his host chatted lay in a pool of light on the stage of an arena that could have housed the Heat game or a major convention. Hard to tell for certain, but the place seemed packed. When the cameras cut in for a reaction shot, the look of rapture on the wildly applauding audience was unmistakable.

"Willis wants to be the new Father Coughlin," Driscoll said. "Fascist pastor of the worldwide airwaves."

Deal glanced at the screen. "You watch this stuff?"

Driscoll shrugged. "I saw a piece in one of the news magazines. Father Coughlin's views were mild compared to this guy's."

"...which is what the international media has set out to accomplish, my friends." Willis was leaning forward, ignoring the host, peering intently into the camera as if at Deal and Driscoll. "Anyone who doesn't wear Calvin Klein, live in a gated community, drive a Cadillac car, you watch the television long enough, you'll start to feel like a failure. We know better, but it's a difficult struggle. We need to readjust our conceptions of the truly decent life. We need to stand up and reclaim our lives and the promise of this country from the bond traders and their allies on Madison Avenue and in Washington..."

Applause, applause. The pitch was mild but relentless, Willis's voice soft, yet urgent, almost hypnotic in its rhythms, Deal thought. Or maybe it was just the hour. He pressed a button on the remote, and James Ray Willis imploded into a brief dot of light.

"I need to stand up and go to bed," Deal said.

Driscoll had not budged. "So many of these guys out there," he said, staring dolefully at the darkened set as if Willis's visage were still etched there. "I worry one of them's going to take hold someday, lead us right back into the Stone Age."

"'The best lack all conviction, while the worst are full of passionate intensity...'" Deal said, quoting.

"Excuse me?" Driscoll said, staring at him.

"It's from a poem I read in college," Deal said. He was at the doorway of the den now. "Your guy's a nutcase," he pointed at the darkened set. "A nutcase in a good suit. You're welcome to sleep in the chair, Driscoll, but I'm going to bed."

Driscoll sighed, heaved himself up from the recliner. "I wish I had your outlook on life, Deal. All the things that've happened to you, I'm surprised you can still sleep nights."

Deal led the way down the hallway without reply, paused at the doorway to Isabel's room. He glanced in at his daughter's sleeping form, sensed Driscoll looking over his shoulder at the five-year-old with the Mickey Mouse PJs and a hammerlock on a teddy bear. Deal turned to him, clapped his arm about the ex-cop's shoulder, led him on to the front door.

"I've got plenty of things to worry about, Vernon."

Driscoll nodded. Deal opened the door, admitting a draft of cool January air. The breeze was out of the north, the sky clear, suggesting a fast-moving front on the way through. High fifties right now, he guessed, maybe seventy tomorrow. Perfect Florida winter. If the weather held through the week, he'd have all his crews back on the job after two weeks of rain.

Driscoll was ambling across the breezeway toward his own apartment when he suddenly stopped, holding a finger straight up as if he'd remembered something suddenly. He turned to Deal. "I read a book once myself," He squinted one eye, thought, then brought his finger down to point at Deal. "'He who cannot remember the past is condemned to repeat it.' How's that grab you?"

"Good night, Vernon," Deal said. He was willing himself back to sleep even before he'd closed the door.

◙◙◙

Deal had to circle the block twice before he saw a spot open up, a panel truck with a caterer's logo pulling away from a meter on the opposite side of the street. Sunday afternoon on a downtown Gables side street, he would never have expected this problem. Any other time, he'd have given up, come back to Arch's store another day. But he'd spotted Janice's car, angle-parked in her characteristic spot in front of the shuttered bus station around the corner. He'd circle a dozen times, whatever it took.

He glanced ahead, saw a line of oncoming traffic stymied by a red light down at Camino de la Vaca, checked his mirror, saw a clear lane behind. He hit the accelerator hard enough to jolt him back in the seat, felt a little sheepish at the squeal of the Hog's tires.

He swung the car into the entrance to the municipal parking lot (full, he'd been through there twice already as well), then reversed quickly, the tires yelping again as he bounced through the gutter and came back out, headed in the opposite direction. He glanced in his mirror again, saw that the light had turned green, saw the traffic muscling toward him.

He hit the accelerator more carefully this time, quickly guided the Hog ahead, into the open spot nose-first, finishing even with the meter, his wheels flush with the curb, all of it in one unbroken swing. Not bad for a vehicle this size and weight, he thought, allowing himself a smile as he switched off the ignition.

The Hog, which had started off life as a Cadillac sedan, had long ago been modified by its original owner into a gentleman's El Camino, half its roof cut away, its rear seat and trunk transformed into a pickup bed. Deal, who'd picked it up years back, in lieu of payment for a job, had threatened to get rid of the thing a hundred times, once had even seen it go full-fathom five all the way to the bottom of Biscayne Bay. How it had been resurrected from that watery grave was another story. But the fact was, he was still driving the beast, and he'd come to develop a grudging affection for it, as if it were some old, ungainly dog that just wouldn't go away.

All that history with a car, he thought with a self-deprecating snort. Had he still been there to say it, his old man would have told him sentiment was the sort of thing that, added to a dollar, might get him a cup of coffee down the street at Doc Dammer's. His old man, Deal thought. Philosopher to the end. What would he have to say about his son's present moonstruck state?

Make it a buck and a half, Pops, he thought, and roused himself from behind the wheel. He was intending to get out, hurry across the street, when he realized that a car had stopped beside him, so close he couldn't get his door open.

"You are a very bad man!" he heard as the passenger window of the car glided down. There was an angry dark-haired woman at the wheel of the car. Cream-colored jacket, a flash of slender arm, tasteful gold, manicured nails. She'd have been a knockout except for the scowl on her face.

He noticed that she had one hand on the wheel, the other digging into an expensive-looking leather bag on the seat beside her. Horns were sounding from the cars backed up in her wake.

Christ on a crutch, Deal thought, already envisioning the headlines. "DRIVER STEALS PARKING SPOT, PERISHES IN HAIL OF FIRE." It *might* make Monday's *Miami Herald*, if it had been a slow weekend in paradise.

He was considering his options—try for his passenger door, dive onto the floorboards—when she continued.

"I'm going to *write* your license down," she cried, whipping a sizable notepad out of her case. "I will *report* you!"

Deal stared speechless as she scrawled furiously at the pad. She gave him a last angry glance, then sped off.

He fell back in his seat, waited for the rest of the traffic to clear. He supposed it was heartening, encountering a loony

who actually intended to employ some imaginary system to
vent her rage. But then, she'd had a noticeable accent. Maybe
she was just new to South Florida. Give her a week or two,
she'd be carrying antitank missiles in her purse.

He got out then, about to cross the street, then started
when he heard the blast of a horn. He turned, found a late-
model Cadillac inching toward him, one with all its parts
intact. There was a round-faced matron at the wheel, an
apparition from his childhood in straw hat, white gloves,
and neck scarf, the woman actually waving him on across
the street. Deal stared at her, uncertain, noted the guy in
the seat next to her, a ramrod type in a three-piece woolen
suit and high sidewall haircut staring out at him impassively.

They looked like a pair out of Grant Wood, he was
thinking, like maybe they'd turned a corner in Des Moines
a second ago, suddenly found themselves in a fancy automobile somewhere else…then the woman tapped the horn
and waved again, and he hurried on across the street. From
the crazed to the serene in one parking job, he thought,
acknowledging the couple with a wave.

He came up onto the opposite sidewalk and hesitated
outside Arch's shop, checking his reflection in one of the
display windows—a sign there, an author coming to read
from his work—Deal wondering suddenly if he looked too
spiffed up. White shirt, pressed jeans, wool sports coat, and
his ancient lizard boots. Nothing fancy, really, but for Deal
it was tantamount to dinner dress. He'd had his meeting
with a client earlier—a home he was building in Gables
Estates—and had been on his way from the site back to the
fourplex on the edge of Little Havana when he spotted
Janice's car and decided to stop. Now he found himself
worrying she'd think he'd dressed up for her.

Crazy. Guy with gray showing in his hair fussing like a
schoolboy. It was his wife in there, damn it. He smoothed
his hair against the cool January breeze, had another

unsettling thought. The way the sun blanked out the windows, she could be standing inside there looking out at him, he'd never know. Jesus! He turned away, made his way for the door like a man exuding purpose. He'd say he'd been looking at the author's books stacked up there. If he could only remember what they were.

He yanked on the door handle once, twice, checked his watch and then the door sign—they couldn't be closed at 2:30, could they, even on a Sunday…then stopped, cursing his stupidity. How many times had he been here, anyway? He took a breath, pushed, felt the door give easily in, heard the familiar tinkle of the old-fashioned bell that announced visitors to Arch's House of Books.

He blinked, adjusting his eyes to the dim light as the door swept shut behind him. He inhaled the familiar perfume of bindery glue, slick cover stock, dust, the many marriages of paper and wood. It was a reassuring smell, one he associated with knowledge and reason and culture, of course, but more important, with peace. No matter what was wrong with the momentary world, he could walk into Arch's, start wandering the rooms, in a couple of minutes he'd start to relax. *It's all happened before, Deal*, the jammed shelves seemed to whisper to him. *The worst and more. And we're still here. Bearing witness. Read all about it.*

Such thoughts had always managed to comfort him, sure. But now there was something new in the mix. Janice. Working in Arch's store, if you could believe it.

Or presumably she was. No one behind the front counter, no trace of her perfume in the woody air, no one at all in the anteroom, for that matter. Though that wasn't really surprising. The store was a rabbit warren of interconnected rooms, each of which had had former lives: travel offices, barbershop, five and dime. Their fortunes had declined, along with the general atrophying of most downtown shops, but from the moment Arch had left teaching and opened the first serious bookstore in the Gables, his traffic had risen steadily, astonishing nearly everyone, especially his bankers, and far overwhelming his original space.

A furrier next door goes belly up, no problem. Arch assumes the lease, blasts a passage in the adjoining wall and, voilà, instant children's books section. Law offices upstairs flee to Broward, where there's a more moneyed class of criminal, Arch drills a hole in the ceiling, installs a spiral staircase that winds up to the new rare books annex, presided over by Uncle Els, retired attorney and dedicated bibliophile.

The best thing about the arrangement, in Deal's mind, was the utter Topsy-like quality of the growth. Now you could wander from hard-cover fiction (the anteroom) in two different directions: right, into children's (a dead end), or left, into architecture and photography. religion and philosophy were further along in what had been the furrier's vault. At the far end of that track, in the former five and dime, were paperbacks, magazines, and all the poetry publications, along with an open space where Arch sometimes hosted touring authors or invited the local aspiring writers to read. He'd stuck a freestanding fireplace in there (Deal had helped find a way through the labyrinthine Gables building code for that one) and had been threatening to add a coffee bar (you're my builder, right, Deal?), but he finally admitted he would need more space for that, had told Deal he was biding his time until a designer of swimwear vacated the next premises in line.

Deal heard the murmur of distant voices, thought of something, checked the sign in the display window he'd been using as a mirror a minute ago. Sure enough: Diego Quintero. Reading from his new novel, *Calculation of Dreams*. Sunday. 2:00 P.M. Deal nodded, moved on toward the reading room.

Whatever had caused the parking problems outside, it was clear that Diego Quintero had little to do with it. Arch had set up two dozen or more folding chairs in the common area of the big back room, but fewer than half of them were occupied: Arch sat at one end of the first row, beside him a middle-aged woman Deal recognized as an author's escort, Regina something or other, spoke with a British accent though she told Deal once she'd been born in Mobile. The two of them had their eyes on Quintero, who stood gripping a music stand cum podium, head bent and sweating, his gaze fervent, his voice booming as he read from a passage about a group of Cuban peasants fleeing an approaching horde of pigs.

At the opposite end of the row was another guy he'd run into at the bookstore several times, Reed or Reeves or Rheem, an inveterate book collector, that much Deal remembered. That one sat with a stack of *Calculation of Dreams* balanced in his lap. There was a copy of the poster advertising Quintero's reading propped at the side of his chair, a pile of *Miami Herald* issues at his feet. It meant Quintero was a growth stock in Reed/Reeves/Rheem's eyes: Deal had stood in enough autographing lines to know. Not only would he be getting Quintero's signature on the books, but also on the poster, and on whatever ads or reviews he'd come across in the newspaper. Deal tried to imagine some scene in Sotheby's, twenty years in the future, "And now, what am I bid for two dozen signed 'Cultural Calendars,' advertising the author's inaugural publicity tour..."

Deal nodded acknowledgment at Arch's welcoming smile and edged on into the room, took a seat in the back row, glanced down the aisle at another member of the audience. If Janice noticed his arrival, she didn't let on. Her gaze was fixed on Quintero, as if intensity in this audience might make up for what it lacked in size.

For his part, Quintero seemed undaunted. He had added sound effects to the proceedings, stared out at them now, rocking the podium side to side, making what Deal thought to be remarkably lifelike snortings. "Pigs," Quintero called.

He let go of the tottering music stand, waved his hands in a dramatic circle, his eyes wide. "The entire world become pigs!" Two more great snorts, and then Quintero was dramatically still, his hands pressed to his sides, his head bowed to his chest like a singer whose aria had ended. Deal glanced around, joined in the applause, wondering how a dozen people clapping, however enthusiastically, sounded from Quintero's end of the room.

◎◎◎

The question was still with Deal some time later as he made his way back through the store toward the children's section, where Arch suggested he might find Janice. Though he wasn't sure that a world turned into pigs was going to be of great interest to him, Deal had picked up one of Quintero's books, as much out of admiration for the man's game performance as for the vividness of his bizarre vision. That was one thing about coming to Arch's store for a reading, he thought. You never knew what you might discover. He'd joined the line waiting behind the book collector (Cleese, actually, the man reminded him) as Quintero dutifully signed the books, the poster, and five copies of last Sunday's arts column that mentioned Quintero's appearance in a sidebar.

By the time Deal had shaken hands with Quintero, had his book signed, "To my new friend, John Deal," and listened to a rendition of other striking barnyard sounds (*Calculation of Dreams* was a kind of Latino *Animal Farm*, the good-humored Quintero told him), Janice had disappeared, and he'd had to interrupt Arch, who was apologizing earnestly to Regina for the disappointing turnout, to ask where his wife might have gone.

He found her finally, in the deserted children's section, squatting before one of the kid-sized bookcases, her back to him, reshelving a pile of tumbled hardcovers at her feet. Or at least that's what she was supposed to be doing. At the moment he came in, she had a book balanced on her knees, was turning one of its sizable pages.

"You recommend that one, would you?" he said.

She whirled, the book tumbling to the floor, and caught herself from going over with an outstretched hand. She had her mouth open to say something, but closed it when she saw it was him. Her salesperson's smile vanished, was replaced with something even more inscrutable. Not displeasure, exactly, but then again, he might have settled for the practiced smile.

"Good grief, Deal," she said, staring up at him.

He put out his hand. She hesitated a moment, then softened, let him hoist her up.

She gave him a real smile finally, shook her hair back from her face. "You scared me," she said.

He nodded. "It's a good thing you weren't in the crime section." When she didn't say anything, he pointed back the way he'd come.

"So how'd you like the reading?"

"He's good," she said after a moment. "A shame about the turnout, wasn't it? Sunday afternoon and all."

Deal nodded. "He seemed to take it in stride."

She was studying him now. "I was surprised to see you," she said. "I didn't know you were into magical realism."

Deal thought about it. What could it hurt, letting her think that's why he'd come in. "He's really something on those animal sounds," he said.

She smiled. He probably hadn't fooled her at all. That was one of the many things he liked about her, of course, that she'd never been fooled by him. He gestured at the fallen book. "So, how's that one?"

She glanced down, seemed to consider the question. "It's a Christmas book," she said. "About a little girl who just wants her big brother to be nice to her." She paused. "We sold a lot of them during the season, but I hadn't really looked at it. I was just thinking Isabel might like it."

"She doesn't have a big brother," Deal said.

She stared at him. "What does that have to do with anything?"

He shrugged. "It was just an observation."

Less than five minutes, he thought, they were already into dangerous waters.

"The way your mind works," she said, shaking her head.

"But I have many positive qualities," he tried.

She cocked an eyebrow at him, seemed to relent. "How is Isabel?" she said finally.

"Fine," Deal said. He paused, weighing his words. "She's happy you're back in town. She told me this morning, 'Every Saturday I get to see Mommy now.'"

She nodded, her eyes averted. "I'm happy, too," she said.

"That makes three of us, then."

She glanced up at him, and for an instant, he saw the old Janice behind the careful facade. The woman he'd fallen in love with, so many years ago.

And then, just as suddenly, the moment passed. No one else would have noticed, of course, not even if they'd been standing right beside him. Only he could see the shadow that was back in place.

"Why don't you bring the book by the fourplex after you get off," he said.

"Deal..." she began, but he cut her off.

"I don't have to be there," he said. "You can just drop by, she's so excited..."

"I can't, Deal."

She stared at him, her lower lip trembling the way it always had when she was truly upset, and he held up his hands in surrender. If anything, he was thinking, she had become prettier than ever. She'd had her hair tinted in a shade of auburn that suited her tanned face, had it stylishly cropped though still long enough to cover her ears, he noted. A few lines had deepened in her face, but they simply served to define the planes and angles that he'd always loved. See this woman across a room, you'd make for her in a heartbeat, he was thinking. No matter what.

She glanced over his shoulder to make sure no one had wandered into the anteroom. "We talked about this," she continued, struggling to get her voice under control. "I told you what Dr. Rascoe said, and you agreed. Everything by stages. I thought you understood…"

"I do," Deal said. "I really do. I'm sorry."

She sighed, shook her head. Maybe it meant she accepted his apology, maybe it meant simply that he'd behaved in just the inappropriate way she'd expected. Deal had the sudden feeling he was being subjected to a test, one to which no correct answers were possible.

"So you found a place and all?" he said.

"The Mariner," she said. "Right around the corner from the Mayfair House."

He nodded. The Mariner was a landmark building in Coconut Grove, a wood-framed apartment building with a lot of smoked glass overhung with banyans and massive tangles of bougainvillea. Studios and one-bedroom units, mostly. The kind of place you'd want to live if you were single.

"You decided to live in the Grove, you should have said something," he told her. "Terry Terrell would have let you have his gardener's cottage."

"I don't think so, Deal."

"It's a nice place," he said.

"Is this how it's going to be, Deal? I tell you something about my life, you try and revise it?"

Her expression was neutral, but he knew he'd been pushing it again. "It's a nice place, that's all."

"Free rent, sex at eleven?"

"Jesus, Janice," he said. "Terry's not that kind of guy."

"He's recently divorced, his parties make the society pages all the way over in St. Pete," she shrugged. "What kind of guy is he?"

"What's all this talk about sex?" a voice behind them said.

Janice's face flushed suddenly, and Deal turned to see Arch coming down the passageway toward them.

"We have a couple of sexology books, sir," Arch continued. He was smiling, had his arms outstretched to welcome Deal, "but we keep them in philosophy." He paused and mimed the coming of a sudden thought. "Of course there was the Madonna book, but I'm sorry to say we sold out of those."

Arch flung one arm around Deal's shoulder. "Now, did you want to buy a book on sex, or are you just coming on to my new assistant manager?" he said, nodding at Janice.

It was Deal's turn to blush. He was trying to think of something to say when a horn sounded from outside. A white car had pulled up to the curb in the loading zone, a man at the wheel, his face obscured from Deal's view.

Janice glanced at her watch, then back at Arch. "I'm sorry, Arch. I lost track of the time," she broke off, sweeping her hand at the pile of books still littering the floor. She started toward them, but Arch held her back.

"It's OK," he said. "You've done more than your share today."

"I feel terrible," she said.

"Go on," Arch said. "The place is empty. I'll finish up."

She gave him a grateful look, then hurried behind a counter and scooped up a sweater and a purse. She stopped on her way out, put her hand on Deal's arm.

"Thanks for coming by," she said. "I'm happy to be back, Deal. I am." Her gaze rested on his momentarily. "I'll see you Saturday. Bright and early."

Deal felt his features arrange themselves into a smile, felt his head bobbing in response. "Bright and early," he managed.

Janice turned to Arch. "And I'll see you first thing in the morning?"

"Blue Monday," Arch said. "Slowest day of the week."

"Come off it," she said. "This place is a gold mine."

"Right," Arch said. "Look around. Books marching out the door."

"It's Super Bowl Sunday," she said. "What do you expect?"

Deal felt another surprise, though it took him a moment to force his mind off the man in the car outside. The Super Bowl? He'd forgotten all about it. Who was playing, anyway? How his life had changed. When they'd lived in the house in Miami Shores, Super Bowl Sunday was one of the highlights of the winter social calendar. Every year a massive block party. A neighborhood betting pool. Halftime show by the neighborhood kids, though they'd never had a child to join in, and now that they did, look what had happened.

He turned to glance out the window again, but the white car had inched on ahead, and all he could see was the license plate, one from Sarasota County.

"That's the art collector?" he said.

She gave him her bright smile, the one that said, Lay off my rear, Deal. "Richard helped me bring some things over, that's all."

Deal felt himself nodding again. "I'd like to meet him," he said.

"Calm down," she said. "He's sixty-five."

"Then he's lived long enough," Deal said mildly.

She gave him a wider smile this time, then turned to Arch. "Tomorrow," she said. "And thanks. You don't know how much I appreciate this."

"We're just happy to have you back," Arch said. "Right, Deal?"

"You bet," Deal said. But she was already down the hall, and he wondered if she'd even heard.

◎ ◎ ◎

He was watching through the window, saw her open the door of the white car, saw her get in, lean across the front seat, offer a peck on the cheek to the man who was silhouetted inside.

Sure, he thought, she would do that. A polite gesture, that's all it was.

"You want to be careful with the blinds," Arch said. "I just had them installed last week."

Deal looked down, saw that he had a handful of wooden slats bunched in his fist. He let go, turned to Arch, who was bent over, stuffing the last of the books back in the shelf. "Sorry," he said. He pointed. "I meant to tell you, I wanted one of those books."

Arch gave him a look. "You're sorry you want a book? You don't have to be sorry. I like to sell books."

"The Christmas book," Deal said. "About a little girl and her big brother."

"It was big for us," Arch said, nodding.

"So I hear," Deal said. "So I hear."

They were at the front counter of the store now, Arch running the register through its final sales tally, Deal sipping a beer Arch had produced from the back room refrigerator. When the machine finally stopped its whining, Arch ripped off the tape, glanced at the figures, shook his head.

"Poor Diego," Arch said. "I was worried about the date, but it was the only time he could come." He gave Deal a smile. "It was good of you to come, though."

Deal held up his palm. He was getting a lot of mileage out of this, it seemed. Maybe he'd make a habit of it, every six months or so, come to a reading where he'd never heard of the author, couldn't pronounce the title of the book.

"All the trouble I had finding a place to park, I figured the place would be jammed," Deal offered.

Arch nodded, glanced outside. Even the loading zone across the street had filled up. Deal thought one of the illegally parked vehicles might have belonged to the lady who was going to shoot him with her memo book.

"Yeah, that's probably the Colombians," Arch was saying.

"What are you talking about?"

"There's some big Super Bowl bash at the Colombian consulate down the street," he said.

Deal stared at him. "The Colombians give a rat's ass about the Super Bowl?"

Arch waved his hand at the jammed street. "I guess they do. I have an invitation around here someplace if you want to go."

Deal held up his hand. "I'll pass," he said. "Who's playing, anyway?"

Arch laughed again. "You are an original, Deal."

"Because I don't know who's playing in the Super Bowl?"

"That's one reason," Arch said. He was stowing cash and credit card receipts into a zippered bank bag.

"Look," Deal said. "The day the Browns go to the Super Bowl, I'll be there. In fact," he added, "you'll be my guest. Seats on the fifty. Doesn't matter where it's played."

Arch zipped the bag shut, tossed it in a drawer beneath the register. "The Browns, huh? I guess that'll give us twenty years or so to get ready."

"Could be a couple of years, smart guy."

Arch nodded. "Let it never be said you are a fair weather fan, Mr. Deal."

Deal shrugged. "It's really Janice's fault," he said. "She got me into rooting for them. That was our first date, in fact. Browns and the Dolphins. The Orange Bowl."

"You asked her to go to a football game on your first date?"

"She asked *me*," Deal said. "I mean, I asked her out, and she said sure, as long as I didn't mind going to this football game."

Arch stared at him, bemused. "Janice is a football fan?"

"She'd just moved down here from Ohio," Deal said. "I think she was kind of homesick or something. Anyway, the place was packed, Kiick and Csonka were playing then, the crowd was crazy, beer was coming down from the upper deck like a rainstorm...we had a great time."

Arch shook his head, still trying to comprehend it, apparently. "So who won?"

Deal gave him a look. "I did," he said. "I always thought so, anyway."

⚉ ⚉ ⚉

They both were drinking beers now, the front door had been locked, its shade drawn down. They were sitting in sling chairs in the magazine *cum* reading room with their feet up on a big wooden coffee table that looked like a thick cross section taken from a huge banyan trunk.

Arch, who had been staring off at the ceiling, turned to give Deal a look. "My father wanted me to be a doctor," he said.

Deal nodded in commiseration. "My old man wanted me to be an attorney."

"There's something to be said for the helping professions," Arch said.

Deal nodded again. "They help you get rich," he said.

Arch laughed. "I've always liked your take on things," he said.

Deal saluted him with his beer. "Speaking of attorneys, where is Uncle Els? I thought Sunday was a big day in rare books."

"He was in earlier." Arch shrugged. "He probably went home to watch the game."

"Sure," Deal said. He doubted Els knew what the Super Bowl was. After all, this was a man who had retired from the legal profession because, in his words, it had grown "too combative and tawdry." Els, inveterate reader and longtime widower, had salted away most of what he'd made in his realty law practice, had backed Arch's plans for the store from the beginning. He'd probably had the rare books annex in mind all along, Deal thought.

He stared at the ceiling, imagining himself up there, burrowed into the leather Morris chair Els had installed, feet propped on the matching ottoman, fringed reading lamp burning at his shoulder, nose in some edition of Dumas or Dickens, untrimmed musty pages and color plates by the score...not such a bad life, he was thinking, pirates, dungeons, derring-do in the shadow of Old Bailey...then blinked, realizing he'd nearly dozed off, that Arch was speaking to him again.

"...admire the way you hang in there, Deal. All the crap that's come down on you the past couple of years..." Arch paused, shaking his head. "...now what's going on with Janice..."

Deal sighed. It brought him back from romance and adventure with a vengeance. "Who could blame her," he said. Not himself, certainly.

Arch nodded, waiting for him to say more.

"I appreciate your offering her the job," Deal added after a moment.

Arch rolled his eyes. "Are you kidding? Janice is great. She gets things organized around here. Besides, you and I went to high school together. You set me up with Lilia Estaban. You dated my sister. You put my fireplace in, for God's sake..."

Deal held up his hand again, trying to smile. He was also remembering Sara, Arch's sister. A truly lovely girl. Sweet, doting, kind. They'd gone out a few times in high school, some fewer times once Deal went off to college. He'd developed a taste for more complicated women, or so he told himself back then. Well, he'd sure gotten what he'd hoped for, no question about that, not where Janice was concerned.

"How is Sara?" Deal asked. "Still in Chicago?" Last he'd heard, she was working for a publishing house, some outfit that churned out inspirational pamphlets, the occasional Dale Evans memoir, weekly readers for various denominations.

Arch shook his head, glum now. "She took a new job, marketing for one of her clients." He sighed. "It's good money, I guess."

"Hey, Arch," Deal said. "Sara's a sweetheart. She's happy…"

Arch nodded, unconvinced. "My sister, out there spreading the gospel."

"She could be here in Miami, going broke in books and construction."

Arch glanced at him. "You're right, I guess. It could be worse. She could have married you."

Deal laughed and they clanked their beers together. Back to good times, Deal thought. But a moment later Arch was staring at him solemnly.

"If I could do something, put you and Janice back together, I'd do it in a second," Arch said. "It breaks my heart…" He trailed off again, and Deal thought he saw a trace of moisture in his old friend's eyes.

That was Arch for you, of course, heart on his sleeve, aching for everyone else in the world. He'd always been that way. If there'd have been a Most Decent award in high school Arch would have gotten it, hands down.

"'A year, ten years from now, / I'll remember this…not why, only that we / were here like this together.'" Arch was reciting now, waving his hand like an orchestra conductor's to mark the lines.

"And what is that?" Deal said.

"A poem," Arch said. "By Adrienne Rich. About this couple who've been having their troubles."

Deal lifted his eyebrows. "Sounds cheery."

"The point she's trying to make," Arch said, "they're going to get through it. It's a bad time, but they're going to make it, talk about it together years from now."

Deal nodded. "It would be nice to think so," he said.

Arch watched him a moment, his enthusiasm seeming to ebb. "Yeah, what do I know?" he said. "Me, the grizzled bachelor…" He lifted his hand, began again in a softer voice this time, "…'but there's got to be somebody / Because what if I'm 60 years old and not married / all alone in a furnished room with pee stains on my underwear / and everybody else is married! All the universe married but me!'"

Deal glanced at him. "Adrienne Rich again?"

Arch laughed. "Hardly. That's Gregory Corso. They had slightly different esthetics."

Deal thought about it a moment. "Maybe that's the problem with Janice and me," he said. "Maybe our esthetics don't mesh anymore. Maybe I should take that up with her shrink."

"Like she says, Deal. One step at a time. At least she's back in town, right?"

Deal took a deep breath, as if that might drive out the ache in his chest. What Arch said made sense, if you looked at the matter logically. But if love were a matter of logic, there'd be a hell of a lot fewer problems in the world, wouldn't there?

If he were able to turn a clear mind upon the matter, he might want to suggest to Janice that she take a flying leap at the moon while he went on about his life. But that was assuming he could look at her and not feel the same god-damned tidal-strength pull in his gut that he'd felt since the day they'd met. And even if he could drown it out, there was the tiny matter of their daughter, Isabel, wasn't there? Didn't he owe it to his daughter as well, to go along with his estranged wife and her one-step-at-a-time notions?

And of course, there was the guilt that never really left him, the nagging, irrational voice that insisted that all the terrible things that had befallen them were, in the final analysis, Deal's fault. Janice might have always been wrapped a little tight, but as Arch had made clear, who could blame her for buckling under the stress: two different attempts on her life, and either one of them could have taken Isabel as well. Crazed men who wanted Deal, but didn't care who else got in the way. The first time, she'd nearly been drowned by a psychopath who tried to make her miscarry, the second time, after Isabel's birth, it had been fire—you'd have to look close to notice, but the scars from the many skin grafts were still there, and in Janice's mind they were a lot larger than life.

Two different teams of psychiatrists had attempted a diagnosis of her condition—the abrupt mood swings into depression, despair, and anger, the inability to cope with what she called her "former life." The best the doctors had come up with was to describe it as a form of post-traumatic stress reaction, not unlike that experienced by combat veterans, a psychological distress that endured long after any signs of physical trauma had vanished. Be patient, they advised him, endlessly. Offer love and support. It had taken a long time for such complex symptoms to manifest themselves, they were not going to go away overnight. Logical, perhaps. But to Deal, it sometimes seemed a lot more clear-cut than what the doctors wanted to make it.

Think of it this way: Hang around Deal, someone tries to drown you, then burn you to a cinder. What would anyone expect next? Earthquake? Avalanche? Most guys, when they pissed somebody off, at the worst you'd have to duck a hay-maker, maybe get a call from a lawyer. Deal, on the other hand, seemed to have a knack for attracting psychotics and assassins.

He laughed mirthlessly and shook himself from his thoughts, turned back to Arch. Decent, sensitive Dylan Archibald Dolan. His friend through thick and thin. The shy kid from high school who'd grown up to be tall, dark, and as exotically attractive as the poets his mother had insisted he be named after.

"You're the one who ought to be married, Arch," Deal said. "I see all these women in here, running you around the sexology stacks. If there was anybody who could keep from screwing it up, it'd be you."

Arch laughed. "It comes back to my basic human decency," he said. "I look into the limpid pools of a woman in love and I remind myself how that fervent expression is going to change when I show her the bank statement at the end of every month."

"Come off it," Deal said. "One slow Sunday and you're going to sing the blues?"

"I wish that was all I had to worry about," Arch said, his voice growing more somber. He finished his beer, used the empty bottle as a pointer. "You know what's coming across the street?"

Deal turned in his seat. The view out this set of windows was not particularly remarkable. A bank building on one corner, the abandoned Trailways station on the other. The VW convertible Deal had earlier taken for Janice's was gone now, replaced by a Cadillac as new and shiny as the Grant Wood couple's. The traffic seemed to have died away, everyone in place before the consulate's big screen by now, he imagined.

"What am I supposed to see, Arch?"

"The bookstore that ate the Gables," Arch said.

Deal turned. "What are you talking about?"

Arch reached into the wastebasket they were using for a cooler, found another beer and opened it. "Eddie Lightner called a few weeks back. You know Eddie, don't you?"

Deal nodded without enthusiasm. Lightner was a commercial real estate broker with a penchant for the offshore client. He kept one office in Miami, another in Grand Cayman. A goodly number of his stateside business associates had fallen into misunderstandings with one governmental agency or another, and Deal's father had once threatened to make him part of the foundation of a condominium tower when Lightner came scavenging around the DealCo offices at a difficult time. But while so many others around him had gone down in flames, Lightner had endured unscathed for decades, friend and confidant to a dozen successive, wildly disparate city administrations.

"Well, Eddie was just calling me as a friend," Arch continued. "He wanted me to know that someone had finally picked up the lease on the Trailways station."

"The pedestrian mall people?" Deal said. That had been a much ballyhooed possibility for the property, which consisted of an entire city block, ever since the bus company had pulled out more than a year ago. Turn the whole thing into an inviting plaza with fountains, lush plantings, boutiques, and upscale shops that would lure Gables shoppers back downtown.

"I wish," Arch said.

"The cineplex?" Sixteen theaters, a couple of restaurants, on-site parking, it was another proposal favored by Gables city fathers and business leaders.

Arch shook his head, still glum.

"Okay, the governor wants to build a prison there," Deal said.

Arch tried to laugh, but there wasn't much joy in it. "I'd be the first to sign a petition for that," he said, taking a healthy swallow of his beer. "The fact is, Lightner called to let me know that my new neighbor was going to be a Mega-Media store."

"Mega-Media." Deal shook his head. "What's that? Discount electronics?"

Arch nodded. "I'd forgotten, Deal. You don't get out a whole lot."

"I get out. I just don't go shopping."

"Mega-Media is that new super bookstore chain," Arch said, wearily. "It's been written up in *Time*, the *Wall Street Journal*, and so on. It's more than books, actually. Movies, music, interactive texts, associated computer software, some peripherals." He glanced out the window as if he could see customers already flooding through the competition's doors.

"Their stores average thirty thousand square feet," he said. "This one will be twice that, according to Lightner. They're going to make it their flagship operation, maybe move some of their U.S. operations down here along with it."

"Their U.S. operations?"

"It's a fairly far-flung enterprise that a guy named Martin Rosenhaus put together," Arch said. "He's created a kind of media holding company. There are the stores, of course, but he's also got newspapers, magazines, and broadcast outlets worldwide. He's been going after independent cable operators, too."

Deal took a breath, put his beer down on the table. That was one thing about the way the world turned. Just start figuring you have a corner on the misery market, somebody else comes along, tries to knock you right off the game board.

"So our good buddy Lightner put Mega-Media into the lease, huh?"

"He says if he hadn't done it somebody else would have."

"Eddie has a way with words," Deal said.

"He's probably right," Arch said.

"Bullshit," Deal said.

"No," Arch said. "It's true. They like to target guys like me."

"Target you? Why would real estate developers want to target you?"

Arch shook his head. "It's not the developers…" He started to say something else, then broke off. "Hold on a minute," he said, struggling up out of his sling chair. He went behind the counter, pawed through a stack of papers, came up with a folder that he carried back to Deal.

"Here," he said. He pulled a magazine out of the folder, put it on top, handed the packet to Deal.

The magazine was a copy of *Publishers Weekly*, opened to a feature story with full-color illustrations: "THE BOOKSTORE WARS" went the legend, accompanied by some cutesy art depicting a number of mom-and-pop, cottage-styled bookstores sprouting arms and legs and done up as Western settlers. The "little" stores were diving for cover as a multi-storied structure the size of an office building and labeled CHAIN STORE strode down the street, six-shooters blazing.

"Take it home," Arch was saying. "If I try to explain it to you, you'll think I'm paranoid."

Deal folded the paper away. "Arch, I'm your friend. You tell me somebody's after your butt, I'm not going to doubt you." He raised the paper between them, tucked it under his arm. "Now what's this all about?"

Arch took a breath, sat back down in his chair. "Targeting," he said. "That's what we—we little guys, that is—call it when one of the major bookstore chains moves into a town where there's a thriving, locally owned store already."

Deal nodded. "We have that in the construction business," he said. "We call it competition."

Arch waved his remark away. "Competition's one thing, this is something else altogether. One of the chains'll come in, buy up property right across the street from a store like mine, one that's been doing well." He paused to pick up his beer and wave it in the direction of the bus station again. "They'll discount bestsellers forty percent, hardcover fiction twenty or thirty percent, give you a card for ten bucks, you can buy anything in the store for ten percent off for the whole next year. They'll put in a café, a music bar with live entertainment, stay open until midnight seven days a week." Arch broke off, took a slug of his beer.

Deal glanced at him, hearing the skepticism rising in his voice. "I don't see how they could do all that."

"Oh, they'll do it, all right," Arch said. "You can sit right here and watch."

"But where's the profit in it?"

"That's just it," Arch said. "We've found instances where they're able to squeeze a bigger discount on the books they buy from the major publishers, of course, and our trade association has instituted a lawsuit over that. But the fact of the matter is there isn't going to be any profit, for them." He jabbed his finger angrily at the windows.

"Not unless they drive the little guy out, at least, because the market's not big enough to support the independent and this huge store with all its overhead. That's their strategy, you see. Look around, find a thriving bookstore, drive a stake into its heart, then take over once the corpse has been buried. You can stop giving away your big discounts then, trim your hours back to whatever's reasonable, cut your staff to the bone, cut your list of titles to the bone, forget about your bands and all that, and run your big hairy store like a supermarket. Somebody comes in to ask for a copy of the *Paris Review*, the kid at the counter says maybe it's in the travel section, go have a look!" Arch threw up his hands.

"Everything we've tried to do here would be wiped out. What you'll be left with is books by the pound."

Deal stared at him. "You're telling me you're just going to fold your tent and leave?"

"Of course I'm not," Arch said. "Even though our friend Eddie Lightner suggested it'd be the smart thing to do, unload the subleases before I'm down to the short hairs." He gave Deal a disgusted look.

"But I own the main building. I just refinanced last year, took out a new thirty-year mortgage so I could do this section over." He waved his arm about. "I told Eddie to buzz off. After all these years, the store's finally coming into its own, now here come these guys for the spoils. Well, forget it. We're going to fight."

He sat back in his chair, turned his gaze out the window again. "This isn't just a business," he said, his voice softer now. "It's a way of life."

The way he said it, Deal thought, he might have been talking to himself as much as to him. Deal nodded, glanced around the spacious room, took in the magazine racks with their offbeat, exotic titles, some of them in Spanish, one in Russian, another in Chinese ideographs. He noted the inverted funnel of the fireplace, remembered the August night they'd christened it, the temperature outside about ninety, the A/C going full blast inside. Not long after, he'd stood in the back of the room with Janice and at least fifty other people who couldn't get seats, listening to Isaac Bashevis Singer read his nouveau Yiddish folk tales. Frail, pushing ninety at the time, the old man had worked the crowd like a master, then evoked the biggest laugh when he took his seat on the podium and crushed the straw hat he'd left there earlier.

"Dybbuks," the old man had said, raising the smashed hat. "Devils made me do it!"

Deal had also listened to James Baldwin here, had been as mesmerized as everyone else by the incantatory power of the man's words. Drawn by Janice or by Arch's entreaties, and sometimes by his own interest as well, he'd heard poets, fiction writers, artists, reporters, photographers, social commentators, and crime writers, all of them connected in the common cause of books. It was an impressive array, and he wondered if Arch was right. Even the monthly readings by the local students and aspiring artistes had their charm. Would Mega-Media really mean the end of all that? No more Diego Quinteros. Usher in an endless run of famous ex-generals, first lady poets, and retired actresses come to hawk their fitness books? Anything was possible, Deal supposed, and still…

"This kind of thing you're talking about," he said to Arch. "It really goes on?"

"It's no picnic for the little guy," Arch said. "Not anymore. Read the articles, you'll see for yourself."

Deal nodded, but something else had occurred to him. "Look," he said. "Maybe it'll be good for business, like, one antique store moves in beside another, it makes for more traffic, helps them both out."

Arch fixed him with a disbelieving stare. "Deal," he said. "This is a serious problem. Who's going to come into my store for a book they can buy for eight bucks less just across the street?"

It stopped Deal, and he sat staring at Arch for a moment. "Me," he said finally.

Arch made a sound that might have been a laugh, but it was hard to tell. "I wish everybody were as stubborn as you. I wouldn't have to worry about these guys."

Deal glanced around. "Like you say, you offer personalized service. People like that. And there's the rare books. I don't expect Mega-Media is going to get into those, are they?"

Arch sighed. "The rare books are wonderful, but they can't support the whole store."

"I'm just trying to help."

"I know you are," Arch said. He mustered a smile then and rose, tossing his empty beer into the trash. "Hey, we've spent enough time wallowing. We've got a new assistant manager, we've got that fireplace, we've got a community here. We're not going anyplace."

He gestured toward his office in the back. "Now, I've got some paperwork to do. Maybe I can get out of here in time for the second half."

Deal put his own half-finished beer on the table, nodded. "You're welcome to come by the fourplex," he said as he stood. "I suppose I ought to tune in, see what all the fuss is about."

"It might be good for you," Arch said. "I'll see when I can get loose."

"And if there's anything I can do about all this…" Deal trailed off, nodding out the windows toward the abandoned bus station.

"I know," Arch said, moving toward the front now. "But don't worry. Nothing's going to happen overnight. They could always change their minds, go after some poor bastard in another city. Besides," he added, "I might have a trick or two up my sleeve. Something for Mega-Media to think about, anyway."

Deal studied him for a moment, waiting for more, but Arch seemed to have finished what he had to say.

"I'll keep my fingers crossed," Deal said. "For all of us."

They were at the front door now, and Arch nodded as he turned the key to let Deal out. His smile was genuine this time. "'For poetry makes nothing happen,'" he said. "'It survives / in the valley of its making where executives / Would never want to tamper...it survives, / A way of happening, a mouth.'"

"Corso?" Deal asked.

"Auden," Arch said.

"Right," Deal said. He was outside now, turned in the cool evening air toward his friend. "What's it mean?"

"It means you don't get involved with books if you want to make a lot of money," Arch said. And then he closed the door.

Chapter 3

His bookkeeper had been on vacation for the week, and it took a good hour for Arch just to sort the mail that had accumulated in her absence. He'd spent the first fifteen minutes after Deal had gone wondering whether he should call Eddie Lightner, see if what the man had suggested to him yesterday were really true, but in the end, he'd decided against it. How could you trust a guy like that? Sentence the House of Books to heinous assault one month, show up a few weeks later with dirt for sale on Mega-Media. He should have talked to Deal about Lightner's claims, he thought. Deal was in construction, he might have known what to make of it, how to check out the value of Lightner's information. But it all seemed too sleazy, too pathetic, admitting he'd even think about turning to Eddie Lightner for help of any kind.

Maybe tomorrow, Arch thought. A good night's sleep, maybe he'd go see Deal after all. Deal would understand, he had a practical mind. If they could use Eddie Lightner, then use him. But first find out if Lightner was simply peddling another come-on.

Bury yourself in minutiae meantime, Arch, he told himself. "I spent the entire day at the desk / and it nearly pulled me down like all the rest..." Lines from Machado rattling through his head. Furiously, he tossed circulars, magazines, and assorted junk mail into the trash can, and then, when that had filled, began what had become a mountainous pile on the floor beside him. Bills went into a sizable stack of their own on the left side of his desk. And there was a much smaller pile of personal correspondence on the right side of his desk, most of which would turn out to be drum-beating hype for new books from their publishers, along with an occasional letter from an author, or note of complaint or thanks from a customer. In front of him, in a spot all its own, sat the thick white envelope, addressed to him in a florid hand and bearing the return address of his sister in Nebraska.

By the look of it, he could assume what was in that envelope as well: another wad of the tract material she was fond of sending along to him, more of the Reverend James Ray Willis's press releases, full of glad tidings and exhortations to join the multitudes who had already seen the light.

Sara was his older sibling, three years his senior. She'd fussed over and protected him as much as his own mother had, and, and, while they were close enough in age for that relationship to endure, there had always been sufficient distance to insulate them from the petty squabbles and rivalries that might have developed otherwise.

He had idolized her in his early years, admired and respected her later on—when she went off to college in New Orleans and later landed an impressive-sounding job with a publisher of inspirational books in Chicago. Though her visits home had dwindled over the years, they had maintained an earnest correspondence that flowed equally in both directions, at least until the last few years, when she had left her job in Chicago for a position as executive assistant to James Ray Willis, one of the few televangelists who had not been sullied in the era of the Jim and Tammy scandals.

Though Arch still loved his sister dearly, it had become increasingly difficult for him to conceive of a member of his own family, certified agnostics all, working for a self-righteous egotist like Willis, who had seemed to gloat as his fornicating peers were picked off one by one. Nowadays, Willis seemed to cut less of a public figure, but Arch suspected that was because the man didn't have to. With his high-profile competitors out of the picture, tithes by mail to the Willis compound had probably grown astronomically. Willis likely had to spend most of his time supervising his investment portfolio, his real estate holdings, and his growing business empire, lucky to carve out time for a Sunday sermon.

Arch's sister was fond of sending him copies of press releases from the Willis mill, announcing this and that new enterprise: the construction of a ten-thousand-seat "tele-chapel" designed by Arquitectonica; the development of the largest privately owned broadcast and production center in the U.S., on a sprawling site just outside Omaha; a series of planned Christian-living communities, actual little cities to be constructed on various sites around the Midwest; and on and on. She meant it as testimony to the vitality of her boss's vision, Arch knew, but each fresh packet of material only sent him into a deeper funk concerning his sister.

Cursed with the combination of a certain sweet but prim countenance and a growing career interest that was daunting to many less confident men, she had passed through a series of quiet and unsatisfying relationships into middle age, never coming close to marriage, or so it had seemed to Arch. Now, he was convinced, she had sublimated whatever earthly passions she might have still possessed into a near-obsession for Willis. How else to account for the breathless quality of her letters: "The kindest, most generous, most gifted and visionary person I have ever known...," a phrase he could still see burning on a not-so-long-ago page.

In reply, Arch had, by his own lights, lost it. He'd run off a copy of Yeats's "The Second Coming," highlighted selected passages in yellow marker, had sent it off Express Mail without a covering letter. There'd been no reply from Sara.

Now he stared doubtfully at the fat letter, wondering what exercise of Christian charity it had taken for his sister to respond. How had she finally overcome his invitation to imagine the Reverend Willis in Yeats's context: "...what rough beast, its hour come round at last, slouches towards Bethlehem to be born?"

Still, curiosity gnawed at him. He could tear open the letter, pitch the Willis crap without even looking at it, force himself into his sister's letter far enough to where he'd begin to sound her soft voice in his head, forgive her for whatever claptrap Willis was responsible for seducing her into. Soon enough, she'd leave off with that part of things, say she forgave him, and get into how she was doing, what she'd been reading of "worldly" literature, he could love her once again. That's how it usually worked with her letters, after all.

He took another glance at the formidable stack of bills, and nodded. No contest. Commerce would just have to wait. He flipped open his Swiss Army knife, slit open the fat envelope with a blade he knew he'd ruined cutting paper, then watched a typewritten sheet flutter out onto the floor. Strange, he thought, bending to retrieve it. His sister almost always wrote her letters in longhand, just another of the old-fashioned traits that endeared her to him. He tossed the fat part of the packet aside and turned to the letter.

"*Dear Dylan,*" he read, wincing at the name he'd managed to drive from everyone's usage but hers. "*I am sure that you suppose I have not written sooner out of spite, though that is not the case at all. I know you don't approve of my work, nor of my employer, and, though, you've never come right out and said so—don't worry, little brother, I read you like one of your beloved books—you think I've squandered my life. The poem you sent along speaks eloquently in that regard. The fact of the matter is, your letter (not really a letter, though, was it?) arrived at a time of some crisis for me—and don't worry, I am not ill, though I am confused, perhaps somewhat sick of heart. I might have contacted you sooner, but to tell the truth, I am not sure that the interpretation I find myself wanting to place on the materials I have enclosed is the proper one. But I have kept my own counsel long enough and know that I can trust you to read these documents and tell me if what I sense is of true concern. I love you, and I know, despite the miles and the many barriers that have seemed to distance us over the years, that you care for me just as dearly. I will be eager to hear from you. Your devoted Sara."*

Arch put the letter back on his desk, closed his eyes, leaned back in his chair with a sigh. Just what he needed. His sister suffering some kind of midlife spiritual crisis and turning to him for help. Worse yet, she must have seen some intention to undermine her faith in his sending her that poem, but his target had been that oaf Willis, not her whole way of life. God knows he didn't have any corner on the way to enlightenment. What was he supposed to say now? Great. You finally came to your senses. Let's nuke your whole past and start all over again? He'd be plenty happy if she just shitcanned the Reverend James Ray and went back to the publishers of *Inspirational Thoughts for Moderns.*

He shook his head and opened his eyes, glancing around for what he'd done with the fat part of the packet. He was curious, at least, trying to imagine what she'd run across that could have her doubting Brother J.R. and the promise of joy and Christian zoning covenants all of a sudden. Tibetan mysticism? Secrets of the Rosicrucians? Tammy Faye's letters to a prisoner?

He swiveled about in his chair, spotted the packet on top of the pile on the floor, bent to pick it up. He ripped off the cover, unfolded the wad of papers inside. As he had anticipated earlier, there was a glossy brochure from Willis's PR mill atop the stack, this one with a headline about a Christian cable service soon to be up and running. The God Squad cometh via satellite. Arch scanned a couple of more paragraphs, pitched the flyer over his shoulder.

The second sheet was a Xerox of some crude spreadsheet, a series of inked or penciled figures with categories that didn't make sense to him. This he stared at for a moment, until he was sure that it wasn't his sister's writing, then put aside. Beneath that was a typewritten letter to the Reverend Willis in what he thought might be German, and he put that aside as well. It was the fourth piece that caught his attention. he scanned the memo once, then a second time, to be sure he had not misconstrued. He flipped quickly through the rest of the papers, feeling a sense of sadness and despair descending upon him as he went. *Sara*, he found himself thinking. *Oh, dear Sara. No wonder you feel those foundations quaking.*

He put the papers carefully aside, reached quickly for the phone. Though they hadn't talked since Thanksgiving, and he kept almost no phone numbers in his head, he dialed hers without hesitation. There was a maddening pause until finally the call went through, then another frustrating period as the rings echoed futilely in his ear. He had almost returned the receiver to the hook when he heard the connection make and what he took for the sound of a voice on the other end.

"Sara?" he called, snatching the phone back. "Is that you, Sara?"

There was a hissing silence on the other end.

"Sara," he repeated, trying to keep his voice even. "It's Arch. In Miami."

"She's not here," he heard a male voice say suddenly, and it startled him so that it took him a moment to answer.

"Who is this?" he managed, finally. When there was no response, he tried again. "Listen. This is her brother, in Miami. Where is Sara?"

There was another pause, and then the voice came again: "She's in church," the man said. And then the connection broke.

Chapter 4

Arch was staring at the phone, about to dial again, when he heard the knock at the rear door of the store. He glanced at his watch, puzzled. The rear entrance was deliveries only. He kept his own car in a tiny space back there; his accountant sometimes used that door; and a few of the staff who opened might come in that way in the mornings. But it was a narrow pass that led in from the alley in back, past assorted detritus and the foul Dumpsters of a restaurant that fronted the other side of the block, nothing a customer would want to use.

Could it be Janice back for something she'd forgotten? Maybe she'd tried the front door and he hadn't heard. Or maybe it was Deal, back to drag him off to the Colombian Superparty. The knock came again, more insistent this time, and he hesitated, put the phone back in the cradle. He needed to think about that next call for a moment, anyway.

He came out of the windowless office into the room where he and Deal had been talking, noted that the sun was a red ball sinking behind the buildings to the west. Maybe it was the mood he was in, but he could swear the fiery light bounced from the deserted bus station windows like megastore neon already installed.

The knock came again and he called out, "All right! I'm coming." He'd see who this was, head on home, try his sister from there. The more he thought about it, the person who'd answered Sara's phone must have meant she was in her office. But still, who was it who'd answered? Not the Reverend Willis, certainly. Not even a smidgen of that man's suffocating ebullience. A friend? But they all tended to be members of the congregation. And if she was at work, it seemed a bit too intimate for one of the anointed to be hanging out in her house unattended.

Given what he'd just read, he was concerned, but he wasn't quite sure what to do next. If it was Deal at the back door, he thought, pushing into the tiny rear foyer, maybe he could take up the matter with him, make sure he wasn't overreacting.

He flipped on the bare overhead light, found the knob, pulled the heavy steel door open as far as the safety chain would allow. It took a moment for his eyes to adjust; then he realized there were two people standing there in the narrow passage, a tall, dour-looking older man in a suit that seemed a size too small, and a sturdy woman, a head shorter, wearing white gloves and a veiled hat, a patent leather bag clutched under her arm. *These are not Miami people*, he found himself thinking.

"Mr. Dolan?" the woman asked.

"Yes," Arch said, puzzled.

"Is this the bookstore?" she continued, trying to peer over his shoulder.

"The House of Books," he said, nodding. "We're closed, though."

"Oh, darn it," she said, turning to her husband in despair. "I told you."

She turned back to Arch. "Dexter was hungry," she explained, a mournful expression squeezing her round face. "So of course we had to eat." The man glanced at her neutrally, as if she might be speaking some foreign tongue.

"We open tomorrow at ten," Arch said, trying to be polite. That was the Gables for you. People like these two could be holed up in a secluded bungalow in the woodsy Miami suburb, have their groceries delivered, watch the Nickelodeon channel on cable, pretend time had stopped right about the time *The Brady Bunch* went into syndication.

"We're from Nebraska," the man said finally. He stared at Arch as if it explained everything.

"We're flying home tonight," the woman chimed in. "We can't come back tomorrow."

"Well, there's a good bookstore in the airport," Arch said. "We don't stock so many bestsellers, anyway."

"Oh, but that's just it," the woman said. She had a white handkerchief out of her purse, was pulling it anxiously from hand to hand. "We took a tour over on Miami Beach earlier today. We just fell in love with all those Art Decoupage buildings. The lady who was taking us around said you had a wonderful book we could take home and put on our coffee table, didn't she, hon?"

"Art Deco," the man said.

"What?" she said, turning to him.

"Art *Deco*," the man repeated, clearly out of patience with her. "For God's sake, Iris. At least get the words right."

"I don't know what he's talking about," the woman said, turning back to Arch. "We wanted to get that book, Mr. Dolan. The lady said you'd be the only one to have it."

Arch hesitated. It was true that his was one of the few stores around to stock much in the way of architecture. And there were actually a couple of new books featuring the Beach's Deco district. One sold for seventy dollars; the other, a slipcased edition, went for a hundred. He took another look at the pair.

"These are fairly expensive books…" he began.

"We could pay cash," the woman said. "If you've closed up your register and all, I mean." The man stared at her as if the suggestion outraged him, but finally he nodded his agreement.

Arch took a deep breath. What the hell, it hadn't been such a great day. He could help these folks out, ring everything up in the morning. "Just a minute," he said finally, pushing the door closed so he could slide the chain lock free.

He swung the door wide open then, and motioned the couple inside. He had turned to lead them through the cluttered foyer when he saw a band of something white flash past his eyes. In the next instant he was face down on the gritty floor, a knee driving painfully into his back, something digging tightly at his throat.

The handkerchief, he found himself thinking, his hands flailing helplessly at his sides. There's a fat woman on my back and she's trying to kill me with her goddamned hankie.

🌀 🌀 🌀

Els had been dreaming when the noise awakened him, and it hadn't been a pleasant dream, either. It had started off well enough, him selling a first edition of *Huckleberry Finn* for $700, one of a pair he'd picked up at an estate sale in Mount Dora a couple of years ago. Then the same fellow had returned later for the other copy and, when Els had hesitated, offered a thousand for it. When Els had given in, the man handed over the cash, snatched up the book, and waved it in Els's face, cackling madly. The man revealed himself as a rival rare books dealer, and wanted Els to know the books he'd just sold were so-called devil's apprentice editions, each with its final plate defaced by a renegade printer: Huck arrived at the Phelps farm, Ma Phelps staring down at Huck, and by her side, Farmer Phelps, only in this case, with an erection the size of a silo bursting from his drawers. Though 250 were estimated to have run before the "joke" was discovered, none had ever surfaced. Until this moment in his dream, that is. The man flipped the book open to the final plate and Els found himself staring at

Farmer Phelps' massive penis that in fact turned a $1,000 book into one worth half a million. The rival dealer's laughter echoed so loudly that the walls of the bookstore reverberated and shelves full of books came crashing down...

Els came gasping up out of his Morris chair, his hand already digging in his pocket for the key to the Americana case. He blinked awake, saw that it was dusk—good Lord, he'd slept through the entire afternoon—and couldn't help but glance at the case, where the two copies of *Huckleberry Finn* were still nestled safely on the top shelf, pressed tightly between a set of crystal bookends cast in the shape of planets. He'd bought the bookends in another estate sale, and the inscription etched into the base of each had served as the inspiration for their store's name: A World of Books.

Els was fighting the urge to unlock the doors, pull the two volumes down, double-check the final plate of each— but that was ridiculous. Dream or no dream, he knew they were standard first editions, and whatever he got for them, *if* he could ever be persuaded to part with them, would be a hell of a sight more than the two hundred dollars he had paid.

Still, the dream had seemed so real, the cackle of the rival dealer's laugh so similar to Marion Eberhart's, a real dealer from Fernandina Beach whom he knew and despised, that Els thought that it couldn't hurt to check...which was when he heard another crash from down below and realized that he hadn't dreamed everything, not at all.

He hurried to the top of the stairs, heard violent cursing, stopped when he realized it was a woman's voice.

Els stopped, looked about the darkened landing at the top of the stairs. Could he still be dreaming? He ducked down, craned his neck past the cranny where the top of the staircase joined the landing, but it was too dark to see much below.

He thought he saw Arch's shape dart from the passageway that led from the reading room—someone tall and thin, at least—and angry shouts coming down the passageway after him...and then Arch, if that was who it was, had turned and hesitated, leaning his weight against one of the tall freestanding bookcases that housed hardcover fiction and shoved, toppling it toward the mouth of the passageway.

There was a heartrending cracking noise, the top of the shelf meeting the wall, the weight of the books splintering the wood, then books cascading to the floor in a mountainous pile. Oak, Els thought. Red oak. That section of shelving had cost a fortune all by itself, but they'd wanted to be free to move things about, change the arrangement of the room as circumstances might dictate.

Els glanced frantically over his shoulder, knowing he was not dreaming now, but wishing fervently that he were. He felt a breathtaking thudding in his heart, the noise from below and the hammering within his own body too much for him suddenly. He sat heavily on the landing, his fingers going numb, his lips, his tongue numb too, his mouth gaping open, popping closed, stupidly, automatically, as if he were some beached fish.

He could see clearly down into the store. Arch was at the front door now, his features clearly outlined by the light drifting in from a street-light outside. He was yanking frantically at the deadlocked doors, cursing under his breath, glancing over his shoulder at the passageway where there was the sound of wood grinding and books thudding as whoever it was tried to make way into the front.

Els knew what the problem was. He'd mentioned it to Arch more than once. "What's going to happen when there's a fire?" he'd wanted to know. "You deadbolt yourself inside and forget where you put the key, you'll burn to a crisp." Little consolation that he'd been right, Els thought. Someone down there whom his nephew was running desperately from, himself with a front-row seat, dying of a heart attack.

He tried to call out to Arch, felt a strangled cry escape his throat, but it was nothing that could carry over the tumult of splintering wood, the angry curses, the rattle of the unyielding doors. Els had a thought then and stared down at his feet: one leg was splayed out on the landing, out of reach, out of the question; but the other had tucked itself up under him. He willed his hands to move, stared in some surprise as one hand obeyed. He grasped his leather moccasin, pulled, flung the shoe down the steps in one backhanded motion.

The shoe struck Arch on the shoulder. He started to ignore it, glanced down in the light from the street, then up the staircase at Els.

"Good God," Arch said. He glanced back at the commotion by the toppled bookcase, then cursed again and bounded up the stairs.

"Els," he said. "What are you doing here?"

"Asleep," Els said, or tried to. He felt Arch's hands circle under his shoulders, lift him up. Arch was dragging him back up into the reading room, he realized. He waved the hand that still seemed to work in the direction of his desk. "Phone," he said. "Nine-one-one. Nine-one-one!"

Arch propped him in the Morris chair, stared in the direction of Els's gesture. He shook his head abruptly. "They've cut the wires, Els."

Els stared at him mournfully. More splintering sounds from downstairs, more thuds of books flying about.

Arch stared about wildly, then seemed to think of something. He ran to Els's desk, swept the top clean, dragged it into a corner of the room.

Els watched as his nephew clambered onto the shaky nineteenth-century piece, another artifact he'd carted home from the estate sale in Mount Dora. Arch groped about the molding where the shelves met in the corner, pulled. He staggered back, jumped down from the desk, bringing a spindly attic ladder down out of a hidden ceiling panel with him.

In seconds he was back, lifting Els under one arm, pulling them up the rickety ladder with the other. There was a pause and Els felt himself being boosted up through the ceiling panel into musty darkness. Arch gave a final heave and Els felt himself go wholly into the darkness. His shoulder crunched down onto the ridge of a rafter, and his face buried itself in a scratchy pillow of insulation. He expected Arch to join him, but instead felt the ladder spring back into place, banging his legs, levering his face up out of the insulation momentarily before it fell back against the ladder framework with a painful crack, and he knew he was alone again.

He heard angry shouts, the sound of footsteps pounding up the stairs, then more splintering of wood and another crash from the room immediately below him. A bolt of light struck him then, and his instinct was to recoil in fear. All he managed was a slight lolling of his head, however. In a moment, he'd flopped back to his original position, found himself peering through a seam where the attic stairs had not quite realigned when their spring-loaded mechanism snapped closed.

Someone had snapped on the overhead light in the rare books room. One narrow shaft of light leaked into the attic just in front of his nose, another rose straight up into the dusty air from the back of the light fixture, a truncated cylinder that projected into the attic a few feet away. He used his chin to lever himself forward a fraction of an inch, blinked away the tears in his eyes, stared down to see Arch, a good part of him, anyway, backing away from someone, a leg of the broken desk upraised in one hand, his Swiss Army knife in the other. There was a vague blur of motion just out of Els's range of sight, and Arch swung the table leg, and staggered back.

There was an unfamiliar cry, a smashing of glass, and Els knew that it was the Americana case, gone. Someone, or something, gone through those panes. He saw another blur of motion, heard Arch cry out terribly, felt a pain inside him that went deeper than anything physical. He heard thudding sounds, saw a fluttering of brilliant color plates fill the air below: the first-issue Audubon? The N.C. Wyeth folios? Impossible to know, and tears filled his eyes anyway, and not for any book, no matter how rare, how irreplaceable.

He heard a heavier thud then. Heard a gasp unlike any sound he'd ever heard before. More heavy blows, each one ending with an awful sound like a heavy stone falling into mud, until finally there was silence. Something hit the floor then, and tumbled, and Els realized that he was staring down through the crack in the staircase at one of the crystal book-ends from his Americana case. Half its heavy globe sheared away now. The other half bathed in blood.

"All these goddamned books," he heard a voice say. And then the lights went out.

Chapter 5

It was Monday morning when Deal got the call. He was back on site in Gables-by-the-Sea, going over yet another series of changes on the house he was building there, this time with the architect.

"We decided we want to go with marble out here on the portico floor," the architect was saying, pointing at a spot on the plans. For lack of a better place to work, they'd unrolled them on the hood of the Hog. There was a breeze coming in off nearby Biscayne Bay, and Deal had tucked one corner of the thick sheaf of prints under a windshield wiper.

He stared down at the elevation sheets, which were rattling in the rush of the wind. He had one hand braced on the hood, could feel the heat of the engine seeping up through the metal. "Marble," Deal repeated. "On the floor of the porch."

The architect nodded without meeting his gaze, staring off over the skinned half-acre before them, as if he could see the portico already in place. Deal straightened, surveyed the site himself. It was situated on a narrow spit of land that jutted out into Biscayne Bay, had an amazing view. You could see six miles or more south along the ragged coastline, all the way to the stacks of the nuclear power plant at Turkey Point. To the east, across five miles of bay, was Key Biscayne, its low-lying silhouette punctuated here and there by condo towers and, at its tip, in Bill Baggs Park, the old lighthouse, a structure that looked as though it might have been plucked from a site somewhere off the coast of Maine, tossed to stick like a dart from the distant coral outcroppings of a tropical paradise. To the north of the Key, another mile or farther, lay the skyline of Miami and the glistening half-moon of the bridge on the Rickenbacker Causeway. The bridge connected the mainland and the Key in a graceful arc that seemed at this distance about what a marlin running at full tilt might manage.

With this view, you were talking land value about a million, maybe a mil and a quarter, Deal thought, as he simultaneously felt an urge to be out there, cutting a wake across the cobalt water, trailing that grand imaginary fish. Add another million and a quarter for the house, and that estimate going up every time he and the architect met.

Of course there had been a perfectly good house here, until a month or so ago. One of the first built out this far on the point maybe thirty years ago, it had taken a direct hit from Hurricane Andrew, seven feet of tidal surge that came in through the front doors and windows and went straight out the back, sweeping everything inside along with it. Though the structure itself had held fast, the owners had not. They'd ventured back from whatever refuge they'd found inland, had one look at their doorless, windowless, newly-divested-of-furnishings place, then taken their insurance settlement and lit out for the mountains of North Carolina, well above the storm-surge line. The house had sat boarded up and untended ever since, until it finally sold to a South American distributor of tapes and CDs, and the architect had called Deal out to estimate a redo of the original.

Though no work had been done since the storm, the place had been sealed up dry, and Deal had thought the concrete-block shell salvageable. But the new owners, a childless couple in their fifties, had somehow determined that they were in need of more room, so the original three-bedroom, two-bath Bahamian-styled bungalow had been razed (add another thirty-five thousand just for demolition) and was going to become the six-bedroom, six-bath colossus laid out on the plans heating up on the hood of the Hog. Not what Deal would have done, but then he was about two million and a half shy of the price tag for the project, so what did it matter what he thought? He was going to build this house, and put a nice chunk of the proceeds into his daughter Isabel's college fund, and then he was going to go on to the next project, that is, if they ever got off ground zero here.

Fonseca was the architect's name. A slender kid in his late twenties, thin little mustache, manicured nails, drove a three-year-old Buick that looked like it had come off the showroom floor yesterday. Just standing next to him made Deal feel untidy. Still, he wasn't a bad kid, never gave Deal that supercilious attitude some architects liked to hand builders, as if they were brain surgeons patiently explaining things to a scrub nurse.

"This wasn't your suggestion, was it?" Deal said finally.

Fonseca shook his head, still staring off.

"First time it rains," Deal said, "that marble porch floor is going to turn into a skating rink. Did you mention that to the missus?"

Fonseca turned back to him. "I pointed that out."

Deal took a deep breath. "But she likes the look of marble."

Fonseca nodded. "She thought maybe we could put some kind of coating on it, something nonskid."

Deal stared at him. "Right," he said. "We could cover it with a couple inches of roofing tar. Of course, that'd take something away from the appearance."

Fonseca shrugged. They'd already had a half-dozen of these change conferences and the footings for the house hadn't been poured yet.

"Okay," Deal sighed. "I'll refigure it for marble. But why don't you suggest shellstone or something. Plant the suggestion, anyway. Marble is never going to work. First person that sails on through the stained-glass entryway is going to be suing you and me both."

Fonseca nodded. "We're five months away from the tile work. I figure we'll have worked our way well beyond marble by that time."

There was a pause and they shared a smile then, and Deal was about to ask him what other changes were on the agenda when he felt the chirping of the beeper at his belt. He checked the number on the read-out, wondering if it mightn't be one of the men he had waiting for materials to be delivered to the endless Terrence Terrell project in the Grove this morning, but this series of digits didn't register. Someone to get back to later, he was thinking, and in fact had turned to Fonseca, was about to make some wisecrack about the burden this job had turned out to be for them both, when it finally sank in.

He checked the beeper again, and this time saw what he'd nearly passed over before. An unfamiliar Gables exchange, all right, but preceded by the three-digit code he had formulated to identify emergencies. He'd shared the code with only two people, and one of them was dead.

"I'm sorry," he said to Fonseca. He was already jerking open the door of the Hog. "I've got to get to a phone."

Fonseca looked at him oddly. "Here," the architect said without hesitation, reaching into his jacket pocket. "Use mine."

Deal hesitated, halfway into the Hog. He stared at the cell phone Fonseca extended to him. A tiny clamshell of plastic, about the size of a ladies' compact, if a bit fatter. There was an expression of puzzlement on Fonseca's face, as if he were waiting for Deal to explain where his own cellular had been left. Deal glanced around, calculating how far he'd have to drive through this residential area before he'd find a pay phone.

"Thanks," he said finally, and took the tiny phone.

Fonseca waved it away and strolled off toward the portico-to-be, giving Deal his privacy.

Deal unfolded the phone, took a moment to find the right switches, finally punched in the number he read from the beeper. There were two rings before the connection made and a voice said something in what might have been Spanish.

Deal covered his ear against the rush of the breeze. "I didn't understand you."

More of what sounded like Spanish, ending with what sounded like, "...*a cleaner.*"

"Look," he said impatiently, "this is John Deal. Somebody beeped me..."

"*Oh*," he heard, the person breaking in. "*Momentito!*"

He heard clattering at the other end, as if a wall phone had been left to dangle, the sounds of a cash register ringing, then, finally, "Deal?" It was Janice's voice, pained, breathless. The sound of trouble on the way.

"It's me," he said. "What is it, Janice?"

"The store," she said. "The bookstore..." Her voice trailed off as she struggled to get her breathing under control.

"You're at the bookstore?" He felt his own pulse thudding in response suddenly. He glanced at Fonseca, who was on the other side of the lot, gingerly digging the toe of his shoe at something in the loose earth near one of the foundation markers. "What's wrong?"

"I'm at the dry cleaner's, down the street," she said, her voice straining. "The phone in the store doesn't work. Deal. They must have cut the lines...Wait, just a minute..." He heard a siren in the distance, excited voices in rapid-fire Spanish. He glanced northward, out over the water where a pair of frigate birds hung motionless against the incoming breeze, pointed toward the shimmering skyline of the city. *I can see very nearly to where she is,* he thought…and it only made him feel more helpless.

Then she was on the line again. "I called an ambulance, Deal. And the police…" she broke off, her voice nearly lost in her sobbing. "Oh Deal…I have to go…"

"Janice," he shouted, his head light, his ears ringing with dread. More sirens in the background, the thudding of the phone as it bounced along the wall.

"I'm on my way, Janice," Deal cried, already sliding behind the wheel. He fired up the Hog, dropped it into gear, and mashed the accelerator, fishtailing across the building lot in a billowing cloud of dust. He leaned out the window to toss Fonseca his phone, and caught a glimpse of the architect's astonished expression as the thing bounced off his chest and out of his clumsy grasp.

The Hog took out a line of blue-ribboned marking stakes along one side of the property, and then Deal had to grab the wheel with both hands as the big car launched itself off the back side of the building pad, hurtled through space for a second or two, then slammed down hard, chewing fill dirt and powdered coral into a plume that raced with him all the way out to the street.

◉ ◉ ◉

"I know who did this, Deal," she said, her voice flat, hollow. He'd had to steady her, hold her upright while they were loading Arch's body into the coroner's wagon. Now that the van had pulled away, now that it was disappearing down the street, she had steadied. She'd stepped away from his grasp, stood with her arms wrapped about herself, staring after the departing vehicle with a frightening intensity.

Deal glanced through the propped-open door inside the ruined store, where a team of investigators combed through the wreckage. Vernon Driscoll was in there somewhere as well. Deal had called him from the same dry-cleaning shop Janice had used earlier, and the excop had turned up at the store inside ten minutes. Driscoll was a good four years off the force, but still had his connections. There'd been a moment of hushed conversation between Driscoll and the lead detective on the scene—burly, hangdog Driscoll in his rumpled coat and baggy slacks, and a wiry counterpart twenty years his junior wearing a close-cut Italian suit—and then Driscoll had ducked inside, under the crime scene tape that fluttered in the breeze at the door.

"Are you okay?" Deal said, turning back to Janice. He had begun to feel lightheaded himself. "Do you want to sit down somewhere?"

She turned, studied him for a moment. "He wanted to build a café, did you know that, Deal?" She waved her hand aimlessly. "He'd have made it a sidewalk café, if they would have let him, the zoning and all."

Deal nodded, reached a comforting hand her way. "I know, Janice."

"This town," she said, her mind flipping somewhere else abruptly, the way your TV cable company might toss you right out of the world you thought you were in. "You own a pickup truck, you can't even park in your own driveway." She turned back to him, her eyes blazing. "Everything's about appearances. How everything looks."

"Janice," he said warily, stepping toward her. His stomach was hardening into a knot. He'd lost her down such a path before, had watched the Janice he knew and loved dissolve before his very eyes, vanish from his life as surely as if she'd been whisked away inside some alien space beam.

She stepped back, just out of his reach. "Arch didn't care all that much about cafés, though." She glanced at him as though she were explaining something to a stranger. "He just felt he had to, you know. Because all the big stores have them now. Cafés and croissants and stages where a band can play…" She broke off, shaking her head. When she glanced at him again, her eyes were glistening. "Damn it, Deal. All he ever wanted to do was sell books. To people who loved to read. And they *killed* him, for *that?*"

One of the detectives inside glanced out the open doorway, then went back to his work, carefully stacking book after book, shaking each one as if some message might come tumbling out from between the pages. Deal stepped forward, caught her shoulders. "Janice, is this something you've talked about with the police?"

She glanced inside, shook her head. "No," she said, and suddenly her voice was calm again. She glanced at him, somber, but composed. A different person, somehow, as though the things she'd just said were thoughts that had never been uttered. "They think it was a robbery."

Another detective inside had cleared a pathway to a tumbled set of shelves blocking the passage to the magazine room, was dusting the edge of the wood for fingerprints. Just a bunch of guys doing their work, Deal thought, images of hurricane cleanup flitting across his mind. Disaster strikes, and you carry on. "Being not the ones dead…" The words echoed in his mind. Some fragment from a poem Arch had quoted to him once, that much had never left him.

"And you think it wasn't robbery?" he tried again, gently.

She glanced up at him as if he'd made an accusation. For a moment she seemed ready to snap at him. And then, suddenly, her expression shattered and she collapsed against his chest. "Oh, Deal," she sobbed. "It was awful. It was terrible."

"I know," he said, holding her tightly, patting her back. "I know."

The words came hesitantly at first, then began to pour. "I came in the back door," she paused, gulping a breath. "…and when I found it unlocked I started to worry. And then when I walked in and saw the mess…I mean, if the door had been forced open I'd have thought, okay, someone broke in, in the night…" She stopped to look up at him.

"But I knew Arch would never forget to lock that door, and I started walking through the rooms, calling his name, because his car was outside, and I had to crawl over those shelves to get into the front, and by that time I knew something terrible had happened..."

"Janice," Deal began, trying to soothe her, but she pulled away from him again, wiping at her eyes with the back of her hand. "I *have* to tell you this, Deal. All right? I have to *tell* you."

He put his hands up, nodding in reassurance, and she went on.

"I saw the cash register open, and the cash box," she said, "and the checks and credit card receipts scattered all over and I had to force myself to look behind the counter and he wasn't there and I was saying 'Thank God, thank God,' but then I saw the front door was still locked and bolted, so I went back into the children's section..."

She faltered again and Deal reached out for her, but she held up her hand, gathering herself. When she turned to him again, her eyes were blazing. "They'd destroyed it, Deal. The children's room. Ripped it apart. Not just the books. The displays, the artwork, the little tables and chairs. You wouldn't believe what it looks like in there,"

He shook his head helplessly. "Maybe it was kids..."

"*Kids?*" she said incredulously. "Kids aren't capable of doing what happened in there." She paused. "Animals, maybe. Not kids."

"Janice, we don't know what might have happened yet..."

"I know what I saw, Deal. I know what I found upstairs. Do you know what that felt like? Walking up those stairs, knowing what I was going to find? If you'd seen what I'd seen. Oh, dear God," she said, crumbling again. "Oh, Arch. Oh, poor, dear Arch..."

He caught her in his arms, pulled her close, imagining despite himself what it must have been like, finding Arch there in the airless room. He'd had a glimpse as they'd brought the body out…it'd been like taking a blow, the one you never saw coming. Everything normal enough, but then suddenly your head is snapping back and there doesn't seem to be any more oxygen in the air around you and you're gulping and staggering, your legs full of sand…

Another wave of lightheadedness swept over him and he had the sudden feeling he was clutching Janice against an awful gale, that the sidewalk beneath their feet was not a sidewalk at all, but the deck of some pitiful boat that could pitch them over at any instant. His hand went to the back of her neck, pressed her face close to his chest. He could smell her shampoo, the same woodsy scent she'd always used, could feel the dampness of her cheek on his shirt, the heat of her against him…he felt something giving way inside him, an immense longing swelling up, threatening to crush the wall he'd so painstakingly constructed over these past months— if you don't let it, it can't hurt you, be safe, be safe, be safe—these pitiful voices of reason flying away in the face of the welling emotion that threatened to crash down upon him like one of those huge breakers the surfers dare to fall…

"Janice," he murmured, might have been about to add, I love you, nothing can change that, nothing can be too terrible if that holds…

And that was when he heard the voice at his shoulder.

"Mr. Deal?"

Deal glanced up to see an older man in a white suit and Panama hat standing beside them, an expression of concern on his face. A jewelry salesman, Deal found himself thinking. An undertaker's front man.

"I'm Richard Levitt," the man said quietly as Deal continued to stare. He seemed apologetic for interrupting, yet made no move to step away.

Deal shook his head, uncomprehending. He felt Janice pulling from his grasp.

"Richard," she said, her voice weak, still choked with emotion. Her gaze went to him, then back to Deal.

Deal glanced across the street then, saw the car drawn up to the curb, in front of a crowd of curious bystanders that a uniformed cop was keeping at bay. The front of the car was angled toward him this time, so that no plate was visible, but it was the same Japanese luxury car he'd seen yesterday, gliding up in front of Arch's to take his wife away. There was a moment of silence, the three of them exchanging glances, a piece of very bad theater, or so it seemed to Deal.

"You're the gallery owner," Deal said finally. "From Sarasota."

Levitt nodded, cut his glance at Janice. "I'm terribly sorry," he said softly. Then he added, "Are you all right?"

Janice nodded.

Levitt seemed uncertain, compelled to move toward her, yet wary of Deal's presence at his side.

He turned to Deal. "I'm really not certain…can you tell me what's happened?"

Deal shook his head. "Arch Dolan was killed," he said, gesturing at the mess inside. "It might have been a robbery."

"My God," Levitt said. His hand went automatically to his head. He pulled his hat off, gazed in through the open door in dismay.

Levitt's hair was snowy white, but thinning. Deal could see liver spots dotting his scalp, noticed them on the back of the man's hands as well. Well kept, but sixty-five if he was a day. Deal shook his head, confused at the welter of thoughts that coursed through his mind. Did he need to be jealous of this man? He glanced at Janice, who had moved away a bit, held a hand against the store's facade to steady herself.

"Janice discovered it," Deal continued. "She didn't tell you?"

Levitt shook his head, still reeling himself, apparently. "No…I got a call that there was trouble…" He broke off, turned back to Janice.

"I'm not feeling very well," she said, her face pasty.

It was enough for Levitt. "Come sit in the car," he said. He glanced at Deal, but he was already moving toward her.

Deal fought an irrational urge to step in his way. But what was he going to do, shove the old man away? Deck him? Shout, foot atop his silk-shirted chest, "Hell, no, she can't sit in your Japanese car!" The whirl of emotions within him seemed beyond what any reasonable person should be asked to contend with. Arch murdered, Janice here beside him, in his arms one moment, being whisked off by a man he'd fantasized beating to a pulp more than once…

"Yo, Deal." He heard the gruff voice behind him then, and turned to see Driscoll in the doorway of the store, beckoning.

Driscoll seemed surprised at Deal's hesitation. "Come on, it's okay," he said, impatient.

Janice was already moving unsteadily across the street, one of Levitt's hands on her arm, the other wrapped about her shoulders. Levitt was bent at her ear and seemed to be whispering encouragement. Anyone else might see a gentle, elderly man comforting a distraught woman, might be heartened by the thought of loving kindness. What Deal saw incited a sickening mixture of rage and despair. When he turned back to Driscoll, he felt so weary, and even guilty himself.

"I gotta warn you, it isn't very pretty up here," Driscoll was saying. The two of them had to step aside as a uniformed cop came down the staircase, a clear plastic bag full of loose book pages in his hands. Deal thought he saw a smear of blood across one page, then realized it was a plate, some lush illustration—red drapes fluttering behind intrepid swordsmen—torn from one of the old volumes Arch and Els housed in the upstairs annex.

The cop nodded at Driscoll, let his gaze linger on Deal a moment. "He's with me," Driscoll said, and the cop went on by without a word.

"Come on," Driscoll said, leading the way up the narrow staircase.

What had been up there were two pleasant rooms, the first a kind of library where a dignified reading area had been set up—a pair of burgundy leather chairs, each with its own tasseled lamp, a coffee table atop a faded oriental rug in between. Deal remembered it as the kind of place you'd sit in for five minutes, find yourself sliding right out of the world into whatever you happened to be reading.

He still had the picture of it in his mind when he made the landing. But now the chairs were upended, the lamps tumbled over, brass standards twisted, shades flattened, the rug kicked into a wad in a corner. The old coffee table was on its back nearby, its four curved legs thrust up like a wooden animal begging for mercy. The ceiling fans were unmoving, the air thick with a smell he didn't want to identify.

Driscoll pointed through an open doorway into the adjoining room, where a couple of technicians busied themselves. The imposing glass-fronted bookcase that had held the rarest of the rare had toppled to the floor and shattered. Pieces of the case's wooden shelving were stacked like kindling beside a shoal of glass fragments. Here and there a shred of paper or binding poked from the wreckage like scraps of clothing. There was a taped outline of a body on the floor nearby, a grotesque yellow cartoon surrounded by massive dark stains.

That's the smell, Deal thought, his stomach churning. *Butcher, baker, candlestick maker. That's what dying smells like.*

Driscoll gave him a closer glance. "You okay?"

Deal managed a nod. "Did anyone call his parents?"

Driscoll shook his head, his eyes helpless. "They're someplace in Asia, chasing the butterfly migrations. One of those kind of trips where you follow your nose. No itinerary, no reservations. The housekeeper says they call in every week or so."

Deal nodded. Arch's father had been a neurosurgeon. One day he'd been scratching the back of his neck, found a lump there. A week later he was under the knife himself. The tumor on his spinal column had been benign, but that's all it had taken to readjust his priorities. A week in intensive care, six months of physical therapy until he could walk again, the man had retired.

"He's got a couple of sisters," Deal said. "Sara lives in the Midwest somewhere. Arch was just telling me. And there's a younger one in New York. Deidre."

Driscoll nodded. "The one in Omaha wasn't there when they called. The one in New York is seven months pregnant, already on bed rest because she went into false labor last week. They're trying to figure out how to tell her."

Deal closed his eyes momentarily. "How about Els," he sighed. "This is going to kill him."

Driscoll shook his head. "He wasn't home, either."

Deal stared. "You mean he's just going to walk into work, find all this going on?"

Driscoll shrugged helplessly. Deal turned away, thinking. Maybe he should go downstairs, post himself on the street. If he saw Els coming…he thought, then stopped. If he saw Els coming, he'd do *what?*

He turned back to Driscoll, who pointed into the adjoining room at one of the technicians who busied himself dusting down a green glass bookend bearing a globe the size of a grapefruit. "There were a couple of those bookends," Driscoll said. "The other one was all busted up." His normally flat expression twisted into a scowl. "It looks like that's what they used." He cleared his throat.

"Multiple fractures of the skull, that's what the report is going to read. But that's the pretty way to put it."

Deal turned away from the inner room, trying to draw a decent breath. He had the sudden sensation that he was sucking down air freighted with Arch's blood, and for a moment he thought he might be sick. Finally, mercifully, the feeling passed, leaving him drained, his stomach tight as a fist.

"What happened here, Driscoll?" he managed.

Driscoll gave his characteristic shrug. "The register was cleaned out, Dolan's wallet emptied, the office was tossed, like maybe they thought there was more to find..." Driscoll turned up his palms. "Looks like he was killed resisting a robbery."

"A bookstore," Deal shook his head. "Why would someone pick a bookstore to rob?"

"Maybe he was the only place open."

Deal glanced at him.

"Hey," Driscoll said. "Crackheads aren't exactly known for their powers of logical reasoning. Some dickbrain needs a rock, he'll do whatever it takes to get it."

Deal swept his arm about the ruined place. "That's what you think this was? A crackhead robbery?"

Driscoll shrugged again. "I don't know what it was, Deal. You asked me a question, I'm talking about what I see so far."

Deal felt himself relent momentarily. No point in taking out his feelings on Driscoll. It was true enough. While the Gables might like to parade its safe and glittery side to the rest of crime-weary South Florida, it still had its share of losers and drifters and grifters haunting the streets. They moved like smoke, from a shuttered shop entrance here, to an alleyway there, to a dim office corridor somewhere else, and the only time you paid any attention to their existence at all was when you reached for your purse or your wallet and found it gone...or you came back to the place where you'd parked your car and found the windows spread across your seats in a sheet of little diamonds...or maybe you didn't find your car at all and just walked around in a circling daze for the fifteen minutes it took you to realize you really had parked it exactly there, and that it really had disappeared.

So that was what had become of his friend Arch Dolan? *The shadow of one of those faceless people passes over him and he's gone, that's it, Arch is just one more statistic and the person responsible is about as possible to find as the guy who turns your new car into spare parts in twenty-five minutes?*

"The coroner figures he's been dead since last night," Driscoll continued. "No signs of a forced entry, so he either let whoever it was in, or he forgot to lock the back door."

"I left him about five," Deal said absently, his mind fighting to regain that last picture of Arch, sending him out into the cool evening with his reassuring grin…

He forced himself away from the memory, turned back to Driscoll. "I went out the front."

"Yeah," Driscoll said, nodding down the stairs. "You're probably the last one who saw him before this happened. They'll want a statement from you."

"Sure," Deal said, feeling leaden and groggy. Why hadn't he come back, dragged Arch out of the store, forced him back to the fourplex to watch the goddamned game, or down to the Colombian Super Bowl bash, for that matter? They could have gotten good and drunk, explained American football and quoted poetry to diplomats and sleek, ill-tempered women who drove expensive cars.

"You want to go down, I'll introduce you to Stearns? He's the detective in charge."

Deal glanced up at Driscoll, nodded. He wanted to add something like. "Sure. Being not the one dead, I will gladly do that," but he doubted Driscoll would understand, and he was in no shape to explain.

His attention had been drawn to something on the floor nearby, the corner of a yellowed book page poking out from under the bottom of one of the bookshelves in the anteroom. He bent, caught the page between his fingers, pulled it out, bringing along some dust balls and associated crud that had probably been under the shelf since they'd added the room on three or four years ago.

It was another loose bookplate, this one of a fearsome pirate looming over a frightened boy, cutlass upraised. The two were on the deck of a schooner, and a plank stretched out to starboard over a yawning, heaving sea. A gang of thugs, their faces glowing in lush, Wyeth-like brushstrokes, watched the drama eagerly from the wings. There was a caption, but Deal didn't bother to read it. "Talk or walk," the picture made it clear.

But it didn't matter whether you talked, he wanted to tell the kid in the picture. It'd come to the same thing anyway, they'd make you walk. And if Captain Blood didn't get you, Captain Crack would, or the guy waiting in the wings after him. Forget all that crap about luck or pluck or fairy dust. Take your best shot at the pirates while you still had the chance, make them throw you overboard. You could get that much satisfaction out of life, at least.

He lay the plate aside, was about to stand up, go downstairs with Driscoll, give his useless statement to a cop, who might or might not find the excuse for a human who'd done this terrible thing, and whether that happened or not, it sure as hell wasn't going to bring Arch Dolan back to life, back to his beloved books.

He thought of Arch's mother and father, and his sisters. Of Deidre, lying quiet a thousand miles a way, holding her breath and doing her best to bring a life into this world, and then, at the other end of the vale, of Uncle Els, short for Ellsworth, who was going to discover this dreadful business and likely fold up his tent right then and there...and though he would not have thought it possible, Deal's spirits sank another notch.

He found himself fingering something then, something he'd picked up absently from the skiff of carpet hair and dust tangles and whatall he'd pulled out with the bookplate, and noticed that he was twirling a tiny red apple between his thumb and forefinger. Tiny red apple, tinier green stem and leaf attached to it, part of the brown branch it had been dangling from still hooked on and waving at nothing.

Something from a kid's toy, he guessed, but it stirred some chord inside him and he might have thought more about just what that mental jangling was, but he'd also noticed something else nagging at him, some repetitive scratching sound, grating, annoying, the way a ceiling fan will sometimes list off-kilter or bind up against a bad bearing and grind on…he'd had to change out a hundred of them in his home-builder's career, something anyone with a screwdriver, pair of pliers, and the brains of a goose could accomplish, though why complain if it made Deal's occupation all the more necessary…

He broke off his surly thoughts then. The fan wasn't working in here, was it? He remembered that now and glanced up at the ceiling, where the sound seemed to be emanating from. He stared at the stationary fan blades, all four of them hanging placidly, a fringe of feathery dust on the leading angle of each unmoving edge.

And still the rasping sound came.

Driscoll seemed lost in thought, staring out the window as he waited for Deal to go downstairs. "You ready?" the ex-cop asked absently.

Deal stood. The sound still there. Clearer at altitude.

"You hear that?" Deal asked him.

"What?" Driscoll said.

Deal's eyes roamed the ceiling, finally caught it, the little telltale seam in the ridges and fissures of the pressed faux-tin ceiling. He traced the seam to an intersecting angle, then another, then back to the molding where ceiling and plastered wall were joined.

"Help me with that table," Deal said, stepping around one of the ruined lamps toward a library table pushed against one wall.

Driscoll was puzzled but still joined him, helped lift the heavy thing.

Deal maneuvered them to what seemed like the proper spot, jumped up on the tabletop, found he could reach far enough to press his palm against the ceiling. His fingertips traced the outline he'd seen from below, but found nothing, no hidden catch, no handhold to give at his touch.

"What the hell are you doing?" It was Driscoll's voice, reverberating oddly at this height.

Deal glanced down. He must have jostled the fan climbing up. Two blades listed up, nearly touching the ceiling, while another pair pointed down, framing Driscoll in their dust-shedding angle.

Deal turned back, craning his neck, staring at the puzzle of the ceiling. He realized that the rasping sound had stopped. He raised both hands above his shoulders, braced himself, popped his palms up sharply against the panel he thought was there.

And it was. Hidden, though he should have known how. A spring catch, he was thinking. He'd seen one like it—an old-fashioned attic entry—in Terrell's place in the Grove. The memory flashed through him in the same instant that the hidden panel released and rushed down upon him with a force he could not have expected. There wasn't time to duck. The edge of the door hurtled by, clipping his forehead painfully, sending him over backwards. It happened so suddenly, it might have seemed funny, in a cartoon.

He cried out as he felt his feet go off the coffee table, shooting out from under him. He was heading for a backflop on the floor. Actually, he was going to be laid straight out when he landed, and it would be more like a backbreaker, wouldn't it? And then he felt Driscoll's hands beneath him. Not catching him, exactly, but enough to break his fall.

For an instant, at least. Until the panel had swung fully open and Deal saw what had driven the panel down with such sudden force.

Els. Els hurtling out, leaden, flying down upon them like some terrible afterthought. Deal had time only to throw up his arms. And then everyone went down.

Chapter 6

"Why don't you just throw the damned thing away?"

She ignored him, checked the hat, fluffed the spray of berries at the brim, reset its angle. If you didn't know it had been stepped on…, she thought. Last night, after they'd got back, she'd wet the straw, blocked the crown with a couple of towels, used the blow-dryer to try and reset the shape. Once you found something that fit, you hated to give it up. Besides, she'd chosen the sweater with the red embroidery to wear on the plane, and she liked the way the berries on the hat picked up the color.

She turned from the mirror, left off her primping. He was sitting at the table of their hotel suite, paring his fingernails with his pocketknife. It crossed her mind that her husband was probably the first person who had ever done such a thing in this place—it was the Grand Bay, a monument to splendor that Dexter had insisted upon after reading an ad in a magazine. Most people, if you could afford four hundred dollars a night for a hotel room, you'd have yourself someone to pare your nails for you.

"Since when did you become a fashion consultant?" she asked mildly.

He swept shavings off his lap—a little flurry of white flakes that fell through a band of sunshine and disappeared—

and smiled up at her. "You don't have to know a whole lot about fashion to figure that hat was a mistake."

She saw movement out of the corner of her eye and glanced over his shoulder, out the window. There was another one of those tiny green lizards that had hopped off a flowering hibiscus onto the sill outside, puffing its obscene neck sack out. Shaky little lizard, bright red throat. She didn't know anything about the tropics, but she could tell when something had sex on its mind.

She turned away, considered Dexter's own outfit: lime green beltless slacks, white loafers, a white golfer's shirt with green piping around the collar. Earlier, he'd come back from the men's shop in the hotel with three such outfits, the way he liked to treat himself once they'd finished a task. The pink version and the powder-blue version were in his suitcase.

"You look like some old fart who died and came to Florida," she said.

"You got the Florida part right," he said. "I saw that Porto Rikkan golfer, Chi Chi Rodriguez, wearing this very thing on TV. Natty little guy. He was collecting a big check from some guy in a suit. They both looked real lively to me."

"Is that what's next?" she said. "You're going to take up golf?"

"Why not?" he said. "They got guys playing on this Senior Tour, one of 'em was a farmer until he turned fifty."

"Dexter." She shook her head sadly. "You're fifty-three. You've never swung a club."

"Oh, I've swung a club or two, don't worry about that."

"I'm talking about on a golf course."

"I've got a natural athletic ability," he said, "and I keep myself fit. How many of those old fat guys could do five hundred sit-ups, a hundred of push-ups, you suppose?"

"I don't know that's what's important to hitting a golf ball," she said. It stopped him, sent him staring glumly down at his new white shoes for a bit.

Finally he looked up, back on the offensive. "I've taken notice what these women down here wear, Iris." He pursed his lips, shook his head. "Some of 'em 'll wear a hat, all right, but nothing like that."

"I've heard just enough about my hat," she said.

"Not just hats I'm talking about," he said. "We're in a rut. I got clothes in my closet back home have been there for twenty years."

She fixed him with a stare. She'd read about midlife crisis, but Dexter seemed to be picking it up a little late in the game. "You want to stay down here in Miyama, get yourself some hot-pants sweetie, just come right out and say so."

He grinned. "You're plenty enough woman for me, Iris. I was just making a suggestion, that's all."

"Next time you come up with a suggestion, write it down, put it up your suggestion box," she said.

He rose, encircled her waist with his arms. "I like a woman who gets testy," he said.

She elbowed him in the ribs—not the way she would if she really wanted to hurt him, of course—then stepped out of his grasp.

"You going to get on the plane like that?" she asked, scanning his costume once again.

"And why not?"

"Because it's about twenty-eight degrees where we're going," she said.

"I was thinking about that," he said. "Maybe we ought to take another day or two down here. Nobody's going to mind."

"And do what? Take golf lessons? Run up a big hotel bill so you can stare at the big hats jiggling past that swimming pool?"

"We came all the way down here. This is where normal people go for a vacation. We might as well enjoy ourselves."

"We came down here on business. Business is over and done with."

"Iris…" he said, reaching for her.

"Idle hands are the Devil's playground," she said, swatting his hand away.

"Nothing says a man and his wife oughtn't to take their pleasure," he said. He feinted one way, moved in on her.

She sidestepped, caught him by his new white shirt and flipped him onto the gigantic bed. It would've worked, except he'd caught hold of her sweater on the way over. She felt the heavy fabric bunch under her armpits, felt herself being pulled right onto the bed after him. Fifty-three or not, Dexter was still quick with his hands.

She tried to roll away, but he was already atop her, smiling. "You better get off, you don't want to get hurt," she said, gasping for breath.

"I'm already hurting, just looking at you," he said.

She glanced down, realized he'd managed to unsnap her brassiere in the tussle. She felt her face flush. "Dexter," she said, trying to project a semblance of outrage.

"Hey," he said. "Don't be ashamed of all what the Good Lord gave you."

She felt him move against her, felt herself respond. She raised on one elbow, rammed the heel of her palm against his chest. She'd pulled the punch, but the blow still sent him over. She rolled onto her hands and knees, was scrambling toward the opposite edge of the bed when she felt his hand catch the hem of her slip. The garment whisked off her like slick water, disappearing along with her panties. That was a size 12 fanny waving at him, she thought, shooting a kick behind her. If it were an 8, would all this amuse her more?

He had a grip like iron, had it on one of her ankles, was dragging her back across that enormous bed. She kicked again, felt her heel bounce off his shoulder, but her resolve was weakening. And when he grunted it wasn't a sound of pain at all.

She was trying to keep herself from smiling as he levered his arms, turned her over. There was a moment there where she saw an opening, could have sent her fist to the soft cartilage of his throat, could have used her hands to stun, even finish him, but this wasn't some enemy of the truth and the light and the way, this was her husband and they were mercenaries together in the necessary war.

He straddled her now, working his way up. She sent her hands to his throat, grabbed, pulled, split the godawful golfing shirt from neck to navel. Dexter looked pained for a moment, but must have noticed the color rising in her cheeks. He was shrugging out of the remains of the thing when she caught hold of his beltless waistband and popped it like tissue.

"Go ahead, sweetie. There's plenty more where those came from," he said.

"Oh, Dexter," she said. She had her arms about his neck now and squeezed him. Maybe he was right. Maybe they'd spend just one more day. Nobody would begrudge them that, not after all they'd accomplished. She squeezed harder, wriggled herself down into the bed-covers.

"Whoo-eee," Dexter cried, and came home to Mama.

Chapter 7

"...that his vital signs have stabilized."

"But isn't there..."

"...a man his age...we'll just have to wait and see."

The voices drifted to Els as if down a dark, deep well. Though he could not see, he knew he was huddled at the bottom of that dark well and that awful dark-dwelling things were crawling about him in the hidden seeps and nooks and crannies and were just waiting for the voices to go away so that they could finish their work. There was no pain, but there was the fear. A freezing, paralyzing terror that numbed him, and robbed him of his will. He could not see. He could not speak. He was alone in the darkness, as helpless as a child. And there was nothing he could do to keep the horrid things away. Nothing he could do but lie and wait and hope.

🐚 🐚 🐚

Deal stared down at Els, saw a tremor in the hand that lay atop the snowy sheet. He turned to Driscoll, whose eyes followed the departure of the nurse who'd warned them: "Just a moment more, now."

"His hand moved," Deal said.

Driscoll turned back. Els's hand quivered again. Driscoll nodded. "Maybe we can bring in a Ouija board, he can talk to us that way."

"Christ, Driscoll."

"Hey, you told me the guy had a sense of humor. Maybe he can hear us, it'll perk him up."

Deal started to say something else, then broke off. Bedside machinery beeped softly, regularly, vital sign printouts scrolled and tumbled quietly to the floor. Els was alive, that was something positive, wasn't it? He turned for the door, caught the nurse on her way from the central station toward another room.

"His hand moved," he told her.

She glanced in, nodded. "That's good," she said.

"That's all?" Deal said. "Shouldn't you call the doctor?"

She paused, put her hand patiently on Deal's arm. "It's not uncommon. He's had a severe stroke. The movement could indicate he's regaining some function, or it could simply be Parkinsonian."

Deal stared at her. "Parkinsonian?"

"An involuntary tremor."

"Like a frog twitch," Driscoll chimed in.

The nurse glanced over Deal's shoulder. "Excuse me?"

Driscoll shrugged. "Like in biology. You zap a frog, it twitches."

The nurse bit her lip. "If you mean an unconscious response, then yes."

Driscoll nodded, satisfied. Deal had spent enough time around the ex-cop, knew not to be offended. Stimulus-response, that was Driscoll's view of the world, all right. Forget the bedside manner. Observe much, assume little. What turns out to be, is. What doesn't, isn't. The gospel according to Vernon.

The nurse had turned back to Deal. "I don't mean to be unkind. It's something we see a lot of."

Deal nodded. "I just thought you should know."

"We'll call you the moment anything changes," she said.

Deal nodded again, moved along toward the elevators, haunted by the vision of Els, his frail figure lost amidst the machines and the tubes and the snowy linens. How suddenly and terribly the world had turned. Arch gone. Els, who must have served witness to his nephew's death, hanging on by a thread. And Janice, whom he'd hoped had come back, seemed as good as gone herself.

Take stock, Deal, he told himself. *You have your daughter, you have your health, you have the work you love...*but it seemed a sham, the pitiful ramblings of a man whose glass was without question three-quarters empty, not even a quarter full.

"Mr. Deal?" Deal glanced up, saw a man rising from a bench in the small waiting room opposite the elevators and the nursing station. He noticed also that the elevator doors were opening, though he didn't remember pressing the call button.

"I'm Martin Rosenhaus," the man said. Deal took in the soft drape of his suit, the artwork on his tie, the buttery glow of the shoes he wore. Deal could probably buy a serviceable pickup for what Rosenhaus had spent on the day's wardrobe.

"I don't mean to trouble you," Rosenhaus added, glancing down the hallway, where Driscoll lingered in conversation with the nurse. "But there doesn't seem to be anyone else. No family member, I mean..."

Deal began to wonder if Rosenhaus might be an attorney, some Gables ambulance chaser sensing a score. "What can I do for you?" he said. He'd have simply stepped away into the elevator, but he'd driven to the hospital with Driscoll.

Rosenhaus was in fact extending a business card his way now. "I'm the chief executive officer of Mega-Media International," he said. "I've come to Miami to supervise the opening of our store and the transfer of certain corporate offices. I was to meet with Arch Dolan today, but..." he broke off, gestured down the hallway.

"The authorities told me that Ellsworth Dolan had survived," he continued. "But I didn't realize how serious his injuries were." Rosenhaus paused. "I wanted to extend my condolences to the Dolan family. I understand you were a close friend…"

Deal nodded, finally took the card. Tasteful, everything embossed, thicker than average, as if there were two cards stuck together. Deal fought the urge to disdain the man on principle.

"Arch was telling me about your store," Deal said. "He thought you were going to run him out of business."

Rosenhaus looked pained. "I'm sorry to hear that. I think ours would have been a mutually beneficial coexistence."

Deal paused. Rosenhaus had a way with syllables, all right. "That's not the way Arch described the prospect," Deal said. "I read some of the clips he gave me. Suits, Federal Trade Commission complaints…"

Rosenhaus nodded as if they were discussing unfortunate family gossip. "It's an extremely volatile time within our industry, Mr. Deal, but the fact is, nothing but good would have accrued to Arch's store by our coming in. Studies show that most of our customers aren't the traditional bookstore shoppers at all." He glanced at a nurse who glared from behind the station counter, then lowered his voice.

"We bring new buyers into the marketplace. Arch's House of Books would have profited right along with us in that regard. We could never have hoped to duplicate the ambiance of a store like his. Arch Dolan would have kept all the customers who appreciated his way of doing business and acquired some new ones as well."

Deal thought it sounded like someone from General Motors inviting everyone who wanted to drive a horse and buggy to keep right on doing so. "You're using the past tense," Deal said. "Why is that?"

Rosenhaus lifted his hands in a placating gesture. "I simply meant with Arch's tragedy, and Ellsworth Dolan incapacitated…"

"You'd have clear sailing," Deal finished for him.

"Not at all," Rosenhaus said. "I'd be thrilled to see Arch's House of Books survive. Arch Dolan made this a book town single-handedly. His store is a cultural icon. Just as DealCo stands for something in your own industry. It would be wonderful for the entire community to see that bookstore continue."

Deal stared at him a moment. "Who told you what I did?" he asked.

Rosenhaus flashed his ingratiating smile. "Everyone knows about DealCo Construction," he said. "I'm sorry my people didn't talk to you about our plans for renovating the space to begin with."

Deal stared at him in amazement, trying to imagine it: Hey, Arch, don't roll over in your grave, but I'm just going to do a little remodeling work for Mega-Media International.

He glanced away, noted that Driscoll had finally finished up with the nurse and was moving down the hallway in his shambling way. "Well, Mr. Rosenhaus, I appreciate your sentiments," he managed. "I don't mean to be short with you, but it's been a pretty lousy day." Deal pushed the elevator button again and the doors stuttered open.

"Not at all, Mr. Deal. You've been most kind. And I'm very sorry about what has happened." He had his hand extended again.

Deal glanced at Rosenhaus's hand. He looked up, raised the card in his fingers in answer, stepped on into the elevator.

Driscoll joined him, gave Rosenhaus a curious glance as the doors closed behind them.

"Looks like a lawyer," Driscoll offered as the car started down.

"A lot worse than that," Deal answered, and turned to watch the numbers fall.

Chapter 8

"Perhaps that's a good place to begin," Dr. Goodwin said. "Exploring why it is you feel uncomfortable about coming to see me." She wore an easy smile, had come around her big blond desk to sit in a chair closer to him.

Deal sat at the angle of an expansive sectional sofa, feeling at something of a disadvantage. It was comfortable, the sofa, and the view out the windows of Goodwin's corner office was grand, but maybe that was part of the problem, the disarming illusion of ease. Or maybe he just wanted to be the one ramrod straight in the upright chair, gazing down on the poor sap sunk in the cushions.

Deal shrugged. "I like your new digs," he offered, waving at the windows. "Very light, nice and airy." They were a dozen stories up, high enough to afford a view from downtown Gables all the way west to the expensive, oak-and ficus-and palm-blanketed suburbs, where antebellum mansions and Mediterranean villas circled a couple of golf courses and the unlikely soaring spire of the Biltmore Hotel, a neo-Renaissance holdover from the glory days of the Gables.

Goodwin followed his gaze, then turned back, appraising him, waiting.

"Ball's in my court, right, Doc?" Deal threw up his hands. "I don't know if uncomfortable is the right word, really…"

Goodwin nodded, noncommittal, encouraging. She was a handsome woman in her forties, tall, big-boned, with straight blond hair that fell nearly to her shoulders. A no-nonsense woman, an Aussie who'd been in Miami a dozen years. Deal had met her a couple of years back, when he'd brought Tommy Holsum in for a checkup. *Poor Tommy*, he thought. *Poor, simpleminded Tommy.* The doc had been on the money about Tommy, and even if it hadn't done his former tenant much good in the end, Deal had come away feeling a certain trust in her abilities. Enough to call her, make this appointment, anyway.

"I'm not used to it, that's all. It's a new concept for me," he said.

"And what's this 'it' you're talking about?" she said.

"Admitting you've got problems," he said, after a moment.

She nodded, as if reserving comment on the simple-mindedness of his remark.

"That you can't get straight yourself," he added. "That's just the way I grew up. Stiff upper lip. Something happens, that's life. You just deal with it."

"Sounds pretty hard-nosed," she said.

"My father came from the old school," Deal said. "He worked hard, played hard, we didn't see a lot of him. He'd have told you it was all business, of course, one way or another, and I suppose he did set up more projects at the track or over a card game or on the golf course than he ever did in his office." He broke off, thinking for a moment. He'd come this far, no point in holding back now.

"He was always good to me, you know, but he was mostly absent. And when he was around, he was usually in the sauce. My mother accepted it, pretty much, just looked the other way. Most of the other women she saw at the country club did the same, I guess, so after the kids got older, the wives'd just start getting blasted themselves. It was like there was this enormous goddamned void that they tiptoed along every day, but nobody ever wanted to say anything about it. Nobody talked about what troubled them. They just coped as best they could."

Goodwin nodded. "And you seem to sense how frustrating that would be, feeling bad about a situation and never speaking out?"

Deal stared at her. *Christ, yes*, he was thinking, *who wouldn't sense it*…but then he realized he'd never uttered these thoughts to anyone before, and certainly not to his own mother or father. He was also aware of how vehement his tone had become, and how quickly it had happened. He glanced down at the low table between them, at the coffee he'd brought in from the waiting room. The good doctor hadn't slipped him something, had she?

"You know what I think it is," he said, scooching forward on the cushions until he felt a firm edge under his seat. "I think it's having the sense that it's no damn good complaining about things you just can't fix."

"And you're feeling that way yourself?"

Deal opened his hands. He glanced at Goodwin again. This was probably not a person he wanted to play poker with.

"I'm not a fixer, John," she said. "But I don't think that's the point. If the only person you talk to about the things that bother you is yourself, you can get caught in a circle, lose any hope of objectivity. That's a role I *can* play, helping you maintain an honest dialogue with yourself."

He reached for his coffee, sipped thoughtfully. "What I like about the building trades," he said finally, "you go out in the morning, you take out your hammer or your backhoe or your bulldozer, and you whale away. At the end of the day, whether you've been knocking one down or putting it up, something's different. Something's changed." He looked up at her. "Good, bad, or indifferent, you've accomplished something. There's a lot of satisfaction in that, you know."

"But people are more complex than buildings," she said.

"That's the shame of it," he said, nodding.

They shared a brief smile; then Deal was staring out the broad windows again, realizing that he could see the roof of the abandoned Trailways station from where he sat, that the gray, flat-roofed building just catty-corner would be Arch's House of Books.

"I've had a fair amount of difficulty these last few years," Deal said. "My old man died, and my mother right after. Then we found out the business had pretty much gone down the tubes and the little bit that was left someone tried to kill me for." He finished his coffee, put the cup back on the table. "A couple of times, Janice ended up in the way, and nearly died. She was burned in one of the incidents; there are scars the doctors are still working on."

"I'm sorry to hear that," Goodwin said.

Deal nodded. "If you saw her on the street, you'd never know anything ever happened, not now," he said. "But she doesn't feel that way. She feels…" He broke off. "Disfigured, I guess. Like she's not attractive anymore, not to me at any rate."

"And have you discussed this between yourselves?"

"Somewhat," Deal said, feeling uneasy. "I wouldn't say we'd ever gotten very far."

Goodwin nodded, as though to admit it were some kind of victory in itself.

"We're separated right now," he said.

"And how do you feel about that?"

Deal stared at her. He wanted to shout, *How the hell do you think I feel?*, but realized Goodwin had no way of knowing about the little imps that danced around inside his head chanting their various mantras of pain and guilt. "Your fault, your fault, nah-na-nah-na-na-ya," like the hyena chorus in that Disney movie he'd taken Isabel to see.

"I'm not very happy about it," he said. "I love my wife. We have a five-year-old daughter. I'd like to see things work out."

"Have you considered couples counseling?" Goodwin asked.

"I don't think that's an option right now," Deal said. "Janice is willing to keep the lines open, but we're moving kind of slowly."

"That must be frustrating for you," Goodwin offered. Deal glanced at her again. If someone else had made the comment, he might have bristled. But there was something about Goodwin's manner that disarmed him. Not to mention the fact that she was dead on in her assessments.

"Even remodeling is a hell of a lot easier," he said.

Goodwin smiled, made a note on a pad she kept on the arm of her chair. "How about work?" she asked. "How is that going?"

"Okay," Deal said. "Good, in fact. DealCo was principally a commercial contracting firm when my father was alive: he did a couple of the grand hotels on the beach, some condos on Brickell, a couple of the bank towers downtown. But like I said, that was all over by the time I grew into the business. Mostly I've been doing custom residential work ever since the hurricane. It's a word-of-mouth business, but it's been picking up, slow but sure."

"And this is more interesting?"

"Say you had your choice, Doc: put up an acre of mini-warehouses, or do a makeover on Terrence Terrell's coral rock mansion."

"I don't even know which end of a hammer to use," she said, "but I think I understand the point."

"You ever need something done, you know who to call," he said.

"I'll keep it in mind." She gave a fleeting glance at her watch and Deal checked the clock on the wall. He'd very nearly run through a hundred dollars' worth of chat, and he'd scarcely noticed.

"Another thing that's been bothering me," he said, clasping his hands together. "This thing that's happened to Arch Dolan." He gestured out the window in the direction of the store.

"Yes," Goodwin said. "That was terrible. It was a wonderful store."

The past tense again, Deal thought. "Arch was a good friend of mine, I even did some work on his place."

"I didn't realize," Goodwin said.

"The room with the fireplace, that's mine," he said.

"Very comfortable," she said.

"I didn't design it or anything," Deal said.

"It is a very nice room," Goodwin said.

"We spent the afternoon there, the day before he was killed."

"Oh my," Goodwin said, and the tone of her voice sent a pang through him.

Deal looked at her. "Janice had been working for Arch. She's the one who found him."

Goodwin shook her head in amazement.

"The cops think a crackhead did it," he said.

"Is that what you think?"

Deal turned his palms up in a gesture of helplessness. "I don't know," he said. "But I know what I want to do to the person who did it."

"These are normal feelings," Goodwin began.

"No, Doc, there's more to it. I've been thinking about it a lot. Maybe even obsessing," he said. "The fact is, I think it's why I called you."

She sat watching him intently. The hour chimed on the wall clock, but Goodwin's gaze didn't waver. "We have a moment," she said. "Go on."

"Like I was telling you before," he said. "I've lived all my life believing a person is in control of his own destiny. Take responsibility. Screw up, take the medicine. Do good, take a bow. And I've handled all the crap these past few years the same way: put your head down, don't complain, just stay the goddamned course."

"And...?"

"And I don't think I can do that anymore," he said calmly. "I think I've had it up to here. I went over to the video store last night, I rented that Charles Bronson movie where they rape his wife and daughter, he goes around the bend, turns into a vigilante like that guy on the New York subway?"

"Maybe I've heard about it," Goodwin said.

"I watched it twice," Deal said. "Piece of morally bankrupt shit I would have walked out of before, all of a sudden I'm sitting there cheering. I went to bed, I dreamed I was hiding in Arch's store waiting for the bad guys to come back, I even left the front door open to make it easier."

Goodwin nodded.

"There was a noise, I picked up a shotgun, turned on the lights."

"And?"

"It was Janice," he said. "In my dream, it was Janice standing there. I knew she wasn't the one who did it, but I had this feeling that I had to do something. That I was going to shoot her anyway."

"Did you?" Goodwin's voice was quiet.

"I woke up," Deal shook his head. "But I woke up wanting to shoot."

A light was blinking on a wall panel near the office clock. Another patient out there pressing the call button just as he had, Deal was thinking. Time to get one fractured teacup out, bring in the next.

"I find myself thinking I've had my share now, Doc. I'm not going to take anymore."

Goodwin nodded. "It's good that you express these feelings, John. More than that. It's about time, I'd say."

"You don't think it's a little irrational?" he said. "I mean, I find myself with this feeling I owe someone a boatload of pain."

"That's hardly irrational," she said. "Everyone has a certain frustration threshold and I'd say yours is unusually high. Besides, feeling is one thing, doing another. If everyone who had a sexual fantasy acted it out, for instance, it'd be a pretty kinky world."

He nodded, considering it for a moment. "People have sexual fantasies?" he asked, straight-faced.

It brought a hearty laugh from her, and she rose from her chair. She extended her hand. "I think we've accomplished something, John. If you're comfortable, I'd be happy to see you again. I think there are a number of issues, things we should take our time working through."

He stood, too, and the fact was, he did feel a little better. He'd barely managed to enumerate the various imponderables that plagued him, it was true, but it did seem that the mere act of cataloguing his feelings meant something. And Goodwin didn't seem to want to sign commitment papers for him.

"Sure," he said finally. "Same time, same station?"

"The spot is yours," she said. "I'll see you in a week."

"A week?" he said. "I could get in a lot of trouble in a week."

"Do you really think you will?" she said.

He stared back. They shook hands then, and he felt the strength in her grip. *Good*, he thought, a bit giddily. He'd had a hand on the controls for long enough. Let someone else share the worry for a while.

Chapter 9

Deal left Goodwin's office, plugged the meter where the Hog was parked, walked a half-block to the Pig & Whistle, a pub tucked away in a Bahamian-styled bungalow on this once-residential street. It was a suitably dark place, dead empty except for himself and a waitress/bartender. He'd intended to order lunch, but the quietude did something to him. He went straight to the bar, had a beer and a boiled egg instead.

He rarely drank beer during the day—it made him sleepy—and he'd never before had one of the disgusting-looking eggs that bobbed in a pink-vinegar jar. He gnashed it down, ordered another, and a second beer. The waitress asked him if he wanted anything else.

"An angioplasty," Deal said. She looked at him strangely, and he decided against repeating his little joke.

When he hit the street again, his pulse rate had slowed, though it still struck heavily enough to echo in his ears. He saw a meter cop putt by on his little three-wheeler cart, peering suspiciously at every parked car. Deal saw the guy finally stop beside the Hog, get down with his ticket pad in hand.

Deal checked his watch: he hadn't been in the pub more than twenty minutes, he'd hit the meter with two quarters, enough for an hour. He found himself sprinting down the sidewalk, his legs heavy from the beer.

"Hold up," Deal called, out of breath.

The cop glanced up at him, bent back to his pad.

Deal was at the meter now, his pulse thundering. "I just paid this meter."

The cop looked up at him again, nodded. "I'll bet the dog chewed up your homework, too."

"What did you say?" Deal shook his head. Maybe the heat had gotten to him. Maybe this was another dream.

"Meter's expired," the cop said, pointing at the bubble, at the little red "Violation" disk that poked up like a buoy from a metal sea.

"Like hell it is," Deal shouted. He slammed the meter with his forearm, sent it shuddering on its standard. There was a clanking of coins, followed by a ratcheting sound as the red disk disappeared. The indicator needle whined, flipped up, steadied itself at one hour.

"You're abusing public property," the cop said mildly. Deal noticed he was wearing a portable CB in place of a side-arm. What was the worst the guy could do, shoot him down with radio waves?

"I put money in this thing a minute ago, it didn't register," Deal said. Some part of him seethed, reveling in this insane confrontation, while another watched in mild amusement: "LOCAL MAN GOES TO MAT OVER PARKING TICKET, LEAVES BEHIND WIFE AND DAUGHTER."

The cop thought about it a minute, finally flipped his pad shut. "Okay," he said, magnanimous now. "You paid up in time, lots of people do that."

Deal fought back his anger. "Two quarters," Deal said evenly. He checked his watch. "Twenty-three minutes ago."

The cop shrugged. "Then you got some free time, didn't you." He was turning away when he stopped to point at Deal's chest. "For a minute there, I thought you were bleeding."

Deal stared down, saw a trail of bright red egg juice drops across his shirt. He looked back up, ready to say something, but the cop had already gotten back in his scooter and was putting off.

❀ ❀ ❀

Deal reached the abandoned Trailways station from the west, having circled a block out of his way to avoid passing Arch's House of Books on the way. He'd learned from Janice that the store was still closed—it'd take days to sort out the mess—but the thought of simply walking past those blanked-out windows was more than he could bear.

On the way, he'd gone back into the Pig & Whistle to do what he could about the stains on his shirt. He'd used a handful of paper towels, some pink soap from the dispenser—all he'd accomplished was to spread the egg juice drops into a wider pattern. He looked at his reflection in a window, turned away, shaking his head. He looked like a guy who'd taken a spray of automatic fire, was walking around and sweating through it.

Head still swimming a bit, he paced on down the frontage of the building that was going to house the MegaVille or Universe of Books or whatever it was to be called. He paused, calculating, then turned at the far end of the building and stepped off down the side. Forty thousand ground-floor square feet inside the building, give or take. He guessed Arch's at about a tenth of that. On-site parking, a second story for offices or expansion, he supposed you could create a "Universe" of a sort here, after all. The windows had been smeared opaque with glass wax, but a few bulbs burned inside, enough for him to get a sense of things.

It looked like all the interior walls had been gutted, but the plaster-board was still raw and unpainted, and there were no signs of racks or fixtures yet. It'd take at least a month to be up and running here, Deal estimated. Or maybe Rosenhaus intended to bring in one of those kamikaze crews like those he'd seen work over other chain outlets: a commando corps of laborers who descended on enormous virgin space like locusts with hammers, could transform something the size of an airplane hangar nearly overnight into a fully stocked K Mart, Wal-Mart, Appliances-R-Us Mart, a latter-day circus crew or all-for-profit Habitat for Inhumanity contingent.

He circled on to the back of the building, where there was an alleyway and a sizable parking garage opposite. There were several bays there, originally used for housing buses, now blocked by huge containers used for holding construction debris. Shards of old ceiling support struts, partition studs, and assorted detritus jutted from the big steel sleds, but there was something wrong, all of it covered with that film of abandonment, the look he'd seen often enough around a construction site where something had interrupted the process longer than it should have.

He glanced around, moved closer to one of the sleds. He jumped up, caught the rim of one container, hoisted himself in a chin-up over the edge. He had a quick look, then had to turn away quickly from the rancid smell that rose up from inside. He'd caught a glimpse of sodden wallboard, discarded rags and cans, oily green pockets of rainwater, swirling clouds of insects. Nothing disturbed in there for weeks, or so it seemed. Bad enough as it was, but had it been summertime, the whole thing would have already festered into one indistinguishable mountain of fungus in this climate.

He dropped down, started toward the other container, stumbled over a chunk of two-by-four, and sent it thudding against the steel side in front of him. He heard scrabbling noises and glanced up in time to see a huge rat launch itself off the edge just above him. The thing landed on a smashed cardboard box, then hit the ground and scuttled across the alley and into the recesses of the parking garage. Deal patted the side of the second container. "Good enough," he said, and turned back in the direction he had come from.

@ @ @

It took him another ten minutes to walk to the Gables City Building, most of it along Miracle Mile, the main shopping drag. Midafternoon on a Thursday, the streets busy with shoppers, never mind the score of malls within twenty minutes' driving. Maybe the Universal Book Purveyors knew something after all, Deal thought, glancing at a Gucci'd-out mother and daughter struggling out from a shop door just in front of him.

The pair had half a dozen bags each, big plastic things dangling from their arms like heavy fruit about to drop. The woman was in her forties, slim, deeply tanned, wearing a short linen culotte ensemble that showed off a nice pair of legs. Her daughter wore a similar outfit, cut a couple inches shorter up an identical pair of legs. She might have been twenty but had the same hairstyle and insouciant expression her mother wore, hardly out of her teens and desperate to be bored with it all.

Deal saw heavy gold flashing at ears, throats, wrists, thought they might as well be wearing signs for muggers: "KLONDIKE. MOTHER LODE. FOLLOW US HOME!" The girl's glance swept over him, caught sight of his juice-stained shirt, flicked away without reaction. She'd seen plenty of droolers on the street like him. He watched the two turn down a narrow access path between two buildings, headed for the parking lots in back. He imagined spotters on the roofs up there, a flurry of CB communications, so many crooks trying to get on the airwaves all at once there'd be nothing but spaghetti to hear. Miracle Mile, he thought. Sure. It'd be a miracle if those two made it home unscathed.

He turned away, saw a panhandler approaching him, a guy with several days' growth of beard and hair that had been worked on by three different barbers, all of them insane. He had a car radio in hand, wires trailing out its back. "My car broke down," the guy was saying. "I took my radio out so it wouldn't get stolen. I just need some money for gas."

Deal kept walking, but he'd made the mistake of accepting eye contact. The guy fell into step beside him. "I'm over there on LeJeune," the guy said. "Blocking traffic."

Deal glanced at him. "The radio's a dumb idea," he said. "Just get an empty gas can. It's been done, but it still works."

The guy stared at him. "I just need a couple of bucks, man."

"Take a look at my shirt," Deal said. "You think I'm going to give you money?"

The guy looked, said nothing. They had approached a curb now, had to stop for the light. The guy watched Deal closely, started to turn away when the light changed.

"Wait," the guy said.

Deal saw the guy's hand go into his pocket. He tensed. *Right here in broad daylight*, he thought. *Here it comes.*

"Take care of yourself, pal," the guy said. He pressed something into Deal's hand, scurried off down the street after a guy in a suit, waving his radio. Deal turned his palm up, stared at the well-worn visage of Washington that peeked up from a fold in the bill. A panhandler had taken pity on him, he thought. What would Dr. Goodwin have to say about that?

🌑 🌑 🌑

"Long time no see, Deal," Custer said. He was a little man with a concave chest and wire-rimmed glasses, wearing a white short-sleeved shirt with a pocket protector full of pens. He stood to shake hands, then sat back down behind his battered desk and picked up what was left of his sandwich.

"You don't mind, do you?" he said, taking a bite. "It's the first chance I had all day."

Deal shook his head, turned away from the sight of the egg salad working in Custer's mouth.

"So how's business?" Custer said. "Been a while since I shuffled any DealCo papers."

"It's been a while," Deal nodded. He could hear the wet sounds of Custer chewing and kept his eyes out the window, waiting. In addition to any number of homes in the Miami suburb, his old man had built a couple of condo towers, the Miracle Mall, the Colony Hotel. DealCo had even been in line for the reconstruction of the Biltmore Hotel, that long-idle but glorious relic left over from the 1920s and the heyday of George Merrick, visionary, inventor of Coral Gables.

It was a job that Deal, just coming into the business in a serious way, had coveted. The hotel, a massive white elephant from the day it had been constructed, sat west of the city in a residential district, an unlikely high-rise done up in the cornball and now-crumbling neo-Renaissance style that was Merrick's trademark. As a matter of fact, the very peak of the hotel—a false bell tower capped with a needlelike spire—was visible to Deal from where he stood in Custer's office.

He'd been up there once, years ago, had stood on the viewing platform to survey the whole of the city laid out before him. A golf course, still operated by the city, sprawled about the hotel's base, its layout stitched through by a canal he'd often fished in his youth. Several bridges that looked as if they'd been barged over from Venice spanned the canal, and it was said that in the golden days guests floated aprés-dinner beneath those graceful arches, lounging in gondolas that *had* been imported from Italy.

And such guests they had been: a panoply of jazz-era legends, old rich and new, the legendary and the freshly famous, some attracted by the merits of the newly developed paradise, others come down on the cuff, willing shills for Merrick's fervent pitch. Paul Whiteman, Amy Lowell, Scott and Zelda, the Babe, Lucky Lindy, Al Capone, all larger-than-life figures from history class who took on even greater proportions in Deal's adolescent fantasies, even though the Biltmore's life as a glitter dome was brief: in fact, the place had gone into receivership less than a decade after it had opened. The building had had a brief second life as a veterans' hospital after World War II, and there'd been a number of plans for revitalizing the place over the years, but it had been long shuttered by the time Deal discovered it.

Originally drawn by the Deal family gardener's tip that the fishing was unparalleled in the canal that cut through the course, Deal would sneak in off nearby Coral Way, skulk down the short thirteenth hole, early, before the greens-keepers were out, or late, after the last foursome had made the turn toward home. At the canal, he'd toss a line baited with shrimp into the crystalline water, sit waiting for whatever fresh- or saltwater fish might be cruising the tidal currents up from or down toward the Coral Gables Waterway, which eventually hooked up with Biscayne Bay itself.

Bass, snook, snapper, sheepshead, mudcat, after a while it really didn't matter to Deal, for he never kept what he caught anyway, and besides, the place had begun to work its magic on him. Evenings, he'd sit in the vast silence, the homeward traffic out on Bird Road a distant hum, and watch, mesmerized, as the setting sun ran a ruddy line up the hotel's deserted tower until it finally winked out against the graceful spire.

Rumor had it that Capone had once kept a suite high up in the tower's second tier, that a woman had died under mysterious circumstances in those very rooms, that her plaintive wails still coursed the hallways, sang through the rails of the balconies in those distant reaches. At thirteen, Deal and Flivey Penfield had spent one evening up there in an effort to learn the truth, but all they'd heard were the scratchings of the rats in the walls and the mutterings of a drunk who'd taken up residence in the gallery that overlooked the enormous swimming pool far below, a long-empty yawn of concrete where Esther Williams had once performed aquatic ballet. Of course, it wasn't even fully dark when he and Flivey had fled their musty lookout, so the question of haunting was still moot in Deal's mind.

Still, he'd never abandoned his fantasies: the vast pool filled again with sparkling water, the cavernous ballroom alive with sophisticated music, guests in tails and glittering gowns, a gangster's flashy entourage in one corner, an industry titan's equally garish coterie in the opposite. How could you have a nostalgic yearning for a life you'd never experienced? he'd asked himself when he was older. But he'd never really gotten over that yearning—how could you *not* want such a marvelous thing reincarnated, that was his best response to his practical self. Who wouldn't want to see the Titanic rise up and steam gloriously into port? Who wouldn't want the Crystal Palace to materialize from its long-buried British ashes, who wouldn't want to stroll the hanging gardens of Babylon, for that matter? Just because a good thing was impossible didn't mean he shouldn't want it, not in Deal's book. "Ah, but a man's reach should exceed his grasp…" and all that sort of thing. Did that make him a fool?

He turned back to Custer, who'd finally finished his sandwich, was pointing at him with a pickle spear. "Last paperwork I saw of yours was the preliminary plans for the Biltmore," Custer said. He turned the pickle around at himself, bit hungrily into it. "Too bad about your old man," Custer said.

Deal wasn't sure if the expression on Custer's face was a show of commiseration or a reaction to the sour taste of the pickle. DealCo had landed the job, all right, a twenty-million-dollar contract, but more important, work Deal had looked forward to, he'd get to raise the Titanic after all…and then the scandal: Deal's father indicted, two Gables commissioners unseated, the city manager fled. He nodded, gave Custer the benefit. "Yeah, thanks."

Deal had tried to imagine his father's feelings, had tried all these intervening years, in fact, ever since the evening his mother had called him to the house, met him with her blitzed but shell-shocked face at the door and pointed him toward his father's study. Deal had seen the blood on the walls and the ceiling from twenty paces down the hall. "Enough," said the note his father left. And, as though it were an afterthought: "I'm sorry."

Half a glass of single malt, a couple of Valiums, and his war-relic Walther for a kicker. That's what had happened to the Biltmore job, to DealCo, to his father, to Deal. A couple of months later, his mother finished off the package, though in a more tidy fashion. She'd gone for the booze and pills alone—no Walther, thank you very much. A pretty serious jolt to the old power of positive thinking, all right, but hey, just because a good thing was impossible...

"The place looks good, doesn't it?" Deal said. "The Biltmore, I mean."

Custer looked at him blankly. "Does it? I don't know. I never been out there since it opened."

"You haven't been out there?" Deal heard the incredulity in his voice.

"Bottom line, it's an old hotel," Custer shrugged. "I hear they're losing money, even with that Swiss outfit running things."

"That's too bad," Deal said.

"Should have told everybody something when the Japs backed off the deal," Custer said. "The Japs don't want it, then it's gotta have problems."

Deal nodded, stared at the little man. Maybe he should check in with Custer on a regular basis, keep his expectation levels under control. "What's your take on Christmas, Custer?" Deal said.

"What?" Custer had the rest of the pickle working in his mouth.

"Nothing," Deal said. "It was a joke."

Custer shrugged, swallowed the remains of the pickle. "So what brings you over here, besides old times?"

"Just curiosity," Deal said, keeping his tone offhand. "I was wondering about the Trailways project."

"The bus station? What about it?"

"I went by, it looked like it was on the stall," Deal said. "I thought maybe you'd have heard something."

Custer pursed his lips. "Nothing I know of," he said. "We didn't shut them down, if that's what you mean."

Deal nodded. "So who is it?"

Custer opened his hands. "Some bookstore chain."

"I know what's going in the space," Deal said. "Who's got the job?"

Custer lifted his shoulders almost imperceptibly. "We let that permit a while ago. I'd have to check the files for the name of the builder."

Deal stared at him. Custer sighed. "What, you think some schmuck builder's in trouble, you want to horn in on the action?"

"Just curious," Deal said, but he wasn't trying to sound convincing. If it pleasured Custer to think he was trying to steal business, Deal would let it play.

Custer stared at him expectantly. Deal opened his own palms. "Just checking, Clyde."

"Something for nothing, that's what you mean," Custer said.

Deal sighed, reached into his pocket.

Custer held up his hand. "Forget it," he said. "I'm just yanking your chain." He twisted his features up into something that might have been a grin. "You guys," he said, pushing himself up from his chair. "Glad I'm not in the business."

But you are, Deal thought as the man turned toward a bank of battered file cabinets along one wall. *You are in the business.* There wasn't a job in Coral Gables that didn't go through Clyde Custer's office for approval, that didn't leave a chunk of its budget right here on this shabby little desk. Hard to say how much DealCo overhead had been checked off in the form of little brown-bagged bundles of cash "forgotten" on the desk, on the side table, beneath the very chair where Deal was sitting.

And to look at a guy like Clyde Custer, you'd have to wonder how crime did pay. Sit in your cubbyhole office with some fifty-year-old furniture, wearing clothes that looked like they came out of one of the file cabinets, eat egg salad, don't go out on weekends, what the hell was the point of graft?

Custer came back to his desk, fell back into his chair as if walking across the room had exhausted him. He flipped open a file in his hand, scanned a page, then another. Finally, he closed the file. He scribbled something on a notepad, tore off the sheet, and shoved it across the desk.

Deal picked up the paper. "Carver Construction? Is that what this says?"

"I never heard of them either," Custer said. "Out of Omaha, Nebraska." He pointed at the slip of paper.

"Is this how you normally write?" Deal said. "How would anybody understand it?"

"That's the point," Custer said. "Nobody knows where you got the information."

Deal looked at him. "What about the Gables seal up here in the corner, Clyde?"

Custer shrugged. "Lots of people work for the city," he said.

And plenty of them on the take? Deal thought, but didn't share the thought. He folded the paper away, stood up. He reached for his wallet, handed Clyde a card, ignoring his show of disappointment. "You hear anything about the job, I'd like to know about it," he said.

"I'll ask around," Custer said.

"And go out and have a look at the Biltmore," Deal said from the doorway. "It turned out really nice."

"I'm glad to hear that," Custer said, waving his hand vaguely. He was unwrapping a package of Twinkies as Deal went out.

Chapter 10

"It's a privately held company," the secretary was saying. "We don't have an annual report, anything like that. I could send you a list of clients—Nebraska Rural Electrification, IBM, the Worldwide Church of Light, the Oglala Nation…"

"How about the city of Coral Gables?" Deal asked. He heard the shuffling of papers on the other end of the phone line. He was sitting at the desk in his "office," a battered trailer set up on a strip mall site just off Old Cutler. His gaze drifted out the window, over the skinned, rain-puddled lot, over the ten-foot bank of swamp grass and Florida holly that bordered the site. There was a squadron of buzzards circling the sky in the distance, working the updrafts over Mount Trashmore, the pile of waste that constituted the highest point in South Florida.

"Is that in Nebraska, sir?" The secretary's voice cut in.

"No," Deal said. "That'd be Coral Gables, Florida."

"Oh," the voice said, a bit distrustful now. "I'm not showing that."

"Well, maybe I could speak to someone else."

"In reference to what?"

"You've got a project going down here," he said. "I'd like to talk to someone about it."

Another pause. "In Coral Gables, *Florida*," she said.

"The only one I know of," Deal said cheerily.

"I'll ring Mr. Kendricks," she said curtly, and Deal heard the line switch to hold. So what if he'd pissed her off? At least he knew where Omaha was, so now she had some geography of her own. He fiddled with the phone cord, noted idly that the phone itself was a rotary model. He'd used that wheel to dial out—he'd had to—but hadn't even noticed. Weird. Something twenty years old in Florida. Most of the other rotaries probably formed a geological layer about five hundred feet below the surface of Mount Trashmore.

There was a click on the line, then a voice. "This is Kendricks," Deal heard. The secretary hadn't mentioned Kendricks's title, but Deal caught it from his tone. *I'm the one who handles assholes.*

"This is John Deal, DealCo Construction, down in Miami," Deal said affably. "I understand you've got a project in Coral Gables?"

"I don't know anything about that," Kendricks said. "We have a rather large operation."

"This is a pretty big job," Deal said. Kendricks said nothing.

"With Mega-Media International," Deal continued. "Converting an old Trailways station into a retail store and corporate offices."

Kendricks paused. "We've done some work for Mega-Media," he said. "I don't know anything about a project in Florida. What's your interest in this, Mr...."

"Deal," Deal said. He pondered a moment, decided to go ahead with it. "I ran into Martin Rosenhaus down this way," he said blithely. "He mentioned some problems on the job, I told him I might be able to help."

There was another pause. Deal imagined his words sailing across the continent, Kendricks assimilating them, some bullshit detector on Kendrick's desk flashing in big red silent letters: "LIAR, LIAR PANTS ON FIRE."

"Martin Rosenhaus referred you here?" Kendricks's voice had risen a notch.

"I made the offer," Deal said. His hand was sweaty on the phone handle. *Never play poker, Deal.* Janice's oft-repeated words ringing in his head.

"Deal, you said your name was?"

"That's right."

"And the name of your company?"

"DealCo," Deal said. "Makes it easy to remember."

"I'll check into this," Kendricks said. "Someone will get back to you."

"You need the number?" Deal asked. He rubbed at the plastic dial wheel. A five-number exchange? In Miami? Where had this thing come from? He was still puzzling over the question when he realized the connection with Kendricks had gone dead.

⦿ ⦿ ⦿

Driscoll shook his head as Deal finished his account of the conversation. They were was sitting at one of the tile-topped cement tables in the side yard of the fourplex, Driscoll drinking a Red Stripe, Deal with a plastic glass bearing the remains of an Alka-Seltzer in front of him. He belched, but the sour feeling in his stomach persisted. How many of those pickled eggs had he eaten at the Pig & Whistle, anyway?

"Why'd you give him your name?" Driscoll said, finally. He took a swig of the Red Stripe, wiped his lips with the back of his hand. He was dressed in what he liked to call his "lounging attire": outsized Bermuda shorts, a Pig Bowl T-shirt, and $1.49 rubber flip-flops from K Mart.

"I guess I'm not used to this line of work," Deal said. He followed Driscoll's gaze to the corner of the yard, where Mrs. Suarez, another of his tenants and now his steadfast baby-sitter, patiently pushed Isabel on the wooden swing set Deal had built.

Deal felt an unaccountable chill pass over him. He glanced back at Driscoll, who gave his typical shrug.

"It's no big thing," Driscoll said. "Best case, the guy starts talking to you about whatever's going on. Worst case, somebody calls Rosenhaus, he tells them you're full of shit. They'll just figure it like Custer did: you're trying to horn in on a construction job that's gone sour."

"I don't know," Deal said. "It all depends on what they're trying to hide."

Driscoll gave him a look. "Who says they're trying to hide anything?"

"It's just a feeling I have," Deal said. "Nobody wants to give me a straight answer."

Driscoll finished his beer, put the empty on the table. He stood, stretched. "That's the way people are," Driscoll said. "It's their job not to give straight answers."

"Custer knows something; Kendricks, too," Deal insisted. "I heard it in their voices."

"Better be careful," Driscoll said. "You're starting to sound like a detective."

Deal nodded absently. "I was reading some of the stuff Arch gave me," he said. "This isn't some abstract issue. Mega-Media grossed about two billion dollars last year, but their profit margin was about half a percent, less than what some supermarkets make. It wouldn't take much to send that empire tumbling."

"Is that so?"

"One of the articles made it sound like some huge pyramid scheme. You keep opening huge new stores, painting this rosy picture of expansion, it all looks good until there's no place else to build, you're faced with actually running a business."

"Sounds like a stockholder's lookout to me," Driscoll said, shrugging.

"Vernon, if Rosenhaus is really hanging on by his finger-nails, anything might be enough to send him over the edge."

"Mmm-hmm," Driscoll said. He'd begun his loose-parts amble toward the swing set, his eyes on Isabel and Mrs. Suarez. "What do you propose, write off to Rosenhaus, ask him for a copy of his Dun and Bradstreet?"

Deal stared after Driscoll in frustration. "Billions of dollars, Vernon. That's what we're talking about here. You're the one who always says it, 'Two reasons why people kill other people. Love and money.'"

Driscoll nodded distractedly. He sidled up beside Mrs. Suarez, gave her a smile, held his finger to his lips. When Isabel's arc brought her close, Driscoll dug his fingers into her ribs. Isabel shrieked with laughter, leaned back to see who the culprit was.

"Do it again," she cried, gripping the ropes, kicking her heels out. Driscoll obliged, and the cycle repeated itself half a dozen times. Simple pleasures, Deal thought, and felt a momentary ache.

When she'd finally tired of their game, Isabel hopped down from the swing and ran to throw her arms around Deal's neck. "Mrs. Suarez says I have to take a bath," she said.

"Mrs. Suarez is right," Deal said. "Get your PJs on, pick out a book to read.

"*Two* books," Isabel said.

"Two," Deal agreed.

"*Three*," she said.

"Go on, now," Deal said, and watched her run happily off toward the house. *She's grown*, Deal thought. *I turned my back for a minute, she's grown a foot.*

"Quite the negotiator, she is." Driscoll had come back to the table to join him.

"Yeah," Deal said. "It's what my old man used to call the 'flinch' system."

He turned to find Driscoll eyeing him curiously. "You go out, give a bid on a job, a brick driveway, let's say. You measure everything, figure your costs, add in what you need to make the absolute bare minimum, you tell the guy, 'Well, that'll be four thousand dollars.'"

"Uh-huh," Driscoll said, more interested now.

"If the guy says okay right off, then you're supposed to say something like, 'Of course that's just for materials. When you add in labor...'" Deal trailed off, smiling.

"You keep on going until the guy flinches," Driscoll said.

"To hear my old man tell it." Deal nodded.

After a moment, he continued. "I think it's just an old construction man's joke. Like this. Know what's just as good as a parachute if your airplane goes down?"

Driscoll shook his head.

"A fifty-foot extension cord. You bail out, toss one end of the cord off into the clouds, hang on tight. You don't have to worry. The cord's bound to get tangled up in something before you hit the ground."

Driscoll made a sound deep in his chest that might have been a laugh. "Must get pretty boring out there on the job."

Deal shrugged. "That was my old man. He had a million of them."

Driscoll nodded. His eyes had acquired a far-off cast. "My old man was never much of a joke-teller," he said.

"You been up to see him lately?" Deal asked. Driscoll's father lived in a nursing home in Ocala, in the north central part of the state.

"July," Driscoll said. He turned to Deal. "I go up there, it's a nice place and all, but there doesn't seem much point in the trip. He thinks I work in the home. Sometimes he tells me about his son the cop, down in Miami." Driscoll turned away again, released a stream of breath. "But still he's my old man. He doesn't know it anymore, but I do."

Deal nodded. He wondered what that would be like, his own father still around, sitting rocklike in a home somewhere. He could go in every now and then, ask him point-blank how it felt to piss a life away. He turned to Driscoll.

"Uncle Els," Deal said.

"Yeah?" Driscoll said, eyeing him. "I give up. What's the question?"

"It's the same thing. I mean, who else is there to give a shit? He had to witness what happened in that bookstore, now he's lying in the hospital like a vegetable, all by himself. His brother is chasing around Afghanistan with a butterfly net, one niece is stuck in ICU, trying to have a baby, the other one's off to the four winds somewhere..." Deal stopped, shaking his head.

"Where'd you say Sara was, anyway?"

Driscoll stared at him, uncomprehending.

"Arch's sister Sara," Deal said impatiently. "She had a job in Chicago the last I heard, but Arch told me she moved. At the store, you said the police tried to call her. I'm thinking I ought to try."

Driscoll shrugged. "They called her house and the place she works now, some Jesus freak outfit. In Kansas City, I think. Or Omaha."

"Omaha," Deal nodded. "City of the week. That's where this Carver Construction is headquartered."

Driscoll rubbed his meaty face with his palms. "They also play the College World Series there. Maybe the umpires are in on it."

"Come on, Driscoll...I just want to call the woman."

"So call her."

"You don't remember where she works?"

Driscoll shrugged. "I'll get you the name first thing in the morning."

"I appreciate it."

"Sure," Driscoll said. "But there's one more thing about this detective work you're doing."

"What's that?"

"First thing you have to consider when somebody gets whacked—pardon the term—is motivation. You told me yourself Rosenhaus and his mega-bookstore, they don't have to worry about Arch Dolan. They don't have to kill him. They just let him drown in red ink."

"Yeah, but…"

"Leads to one other rule of the profession, Deal," the ex-cop cut in, pointing one of his thick fingers across the table top, "you have to keep your feelings out of it. Same reason a surgeon doesn't take out his wife's tonsils. Of course it's a damn shame what happened, and looking at Uncle Els doesn't make it any easier. But you start *needing* to find who did this, then maybe you start making connections that aren't there, just to make yourself feel better. You know what I'm talking about?"

Deal stared back at him silently, not trusting himself to speak. He counted to ten, using the thousands method.

Driscoll sighed. "That's what I like about you, Deal. I'll bet all your teachers used to say the same thing. 'Listens carefully. Takes advice.'"

Deal managed a laugh. "Give me a break, Driscoll. I'd like to see your conduct grades."

"Places I went to school, they didn't have conduct," Driscoll said. "We had combat."

Deal laughed again. "You wouldn't mind getting me that information?"

Driscoll stood. "Okay, already. Probably won't be until the morning, though." He stretched, glanced at Deal, who had also risen.

"She's off on some weekend shackup, Deal. Whenever she gets back, finds out what happened to her brother, it'll be soon enough."

Deal tried to put the thought of Sara Dolan and "weekend shackup" together, but it didn't seem possible. No point in getting into it with Driscoll, though.

"Maybe you're right, Driscoll. But it might as well be me she talks to."

Driscoll finally nodded. "You need any help, just let me know, I'll try to work it into my busy schedule."

"I appreciate it," Deal said. "How are things in the private detection business, anyway?"

"Not so bad." Driscoll checked his watch. "I got a regular gig Sunday nights, now, at the Zaragosa Drive-ins. Couple of them been knocked over, both late Sunday night. I put on a funny paper hat, wear an apron over my piece, pretend I'm flipping burgers. Guy shows up at the drive-in window with a shotgun, we're going to have us a ketchup squirt."

"Are you serious?"

"That's what the owner would like, I'm pretty sure. Me, I'm gonna give the guy the money in a paper bag, ask him if he wants onion rings with that. I'll get his license number, do it the sensible way."

"Sounds like a lot of fun, Driscoll."

"It's not so bad, and we're not exactly talking minimum wage. Plus, I get all the burgers I can stand."

"Da-dee," Isabel's voice drifted from an upstairs window.

Deal clapped Driscoll on the shoulder. "Thanks for the advice, Driscoll. I'm just going to make a couple of phone calls, that's all."

"Sure," Driscoll said. "Do what you gotta do. Just be careful, okay?"

Deal gave him a smile and turned toward the house.

"Read her *The Little Engine That Could*," Driscoll called after him. "I always liked that one myself."

"Yeah, me too," Deal said. And it was not such a bad idea, he thought as he went on inside the house.

Chapter 11

"Let's go! Let's get moving!" The voice drifted down the darkening fairway to where Dexter Kittle was squaring himself above the glowing yellow ball at his feet. He glanced over his shoulder in the direction of the voice, saw a cart similar to his own parked in the fairway a couple hundred yards behind. A man in white slacks and a straw boater stood beside the cart, his hands held to his hips in a gesture of impatience. The guy was wearing a polo shirt done in alternating horizontal bands of black and yellow, a poor choice for a fat man, Dexter thought. At this distance you saw mostly gut. It make him look like a bee.

Dexter was learning about golf fashion. He had found a pair of soft magenta-colored slacks in the hotel's pro shop. With the help of a young woman salesclerk, he'd complemented the slacks with a plain white shirt and a navy V-neck sweater that felt as buttery as cashmere.

"The pocket of the shirt's on the wrong side," Dexter told the clerk when he'd come out of the dressing room, his old clothes under his arm.

The clerk had smiled. "That's what they do with golf shirts," she said. "So the pocket's out of your way on your backswing." She folded her hands together, gave him a demonstration. "See?"

He watched her left arm brush over her pocketless breast, wondering about that. What the hell was a pocket to get in the way compared to what looked to be a 36C cup, but he decided not to ask. Iris had stayed out of the shop, but he'd been with her so long, she could tell when he'd even *considered* untoward thoughts.

Right now, for instance. He glanced up from the ball again. There she was, sitting in the passenger's side of his cart, fooling around with her knitting. He wouldn't put it past her to hear the thoughts clanging around inside his brain: C cup, breast, nipple.

Iris glanced up from her knitting. "Like the man says, Dexter. Get a move on. It's cold out here."

"It's the seventeenth hole," Dexter said. "If he don't like it, let him turn around and go the other way."

"I don't imagine that's permitted," Iris said, back at her needles.

"I paid for eighteen holes," he said. "I intend to play them."

"That man probably feels the same way," she said.

"He'll get finished," Dexter said. He turned back to the ball, waggled his club, drew the club back, paused at the top—just like Dennis, his instructor, had said—then, trying to banish all thought of breasts, C cups, and nipples from his mind, brought the club down. The clubhead tore a dark gash in the turf and the ball shot off to the right, a screaming blur of yellow that disappeared into the canal just ahead with a thunk.

"Throw me another ball," Dexter said. He'd had two lessons earlier today. A hundred and twenty dollars, he ought to be able to get one ball over a goddamned creek.

"Come on, Dexter," Iris said. "You've knocked half a dozen in there already."

"Throw me another ball," he said. "I'm going to do this."

Iris sighed, reached into the open compartment of the cart, tossed three balls out onto the ground at his feet. "That's the last of them," she said. "Let's get it over with."

"Hey! Jerkwad!" The man's outraged voice rolled down the fairway toward them.

"That'd be the downside of having one of these houses," Dexter said, gesturing at one of the mansionlike structures where the back lawn ran fifty yards or so down to join with the green of the fairway. Ten or twelve rooms, it looked like, lots of windows overlooking the course, a formal dining room with a set of french doors and a glittering chandelier all lit up, ready for dinner.

"Imagine," he continued. "Live in a place like that and have to listen to such language all the time."

"I don't see a bunch of people being offended," Iris said. "I don't think these folks spend a lot of time outdoors, if you want to know the truth."

"If I lived there, I could sneak out on the course anytime, get in all the practice I wanted."

"If you had the money to live in that place, you wouldn't care about sneaking, Dexter."

He started to answer her, then gave up. It'd go on that way forever, his trying to get the last word on Iris. That much he had learned. It was simply more trouble than it was worth. He turned back to the ball, steadied himself. He willed Iris's comments from his mind, banished Dennis's advice as well. He forced himself to forget about the bee with a hat and white legs behind him. He thought briefly of the perfect breasts of the pro shop clerk, and then he erased that image as well.

He thought only of the golf ball, and swung.

"Well, I'm a sonofabitch," he said, watching the ball soar up into the nearly dark sky. He almost lost sight of it as it reached its apogee, but the fact that it was headed where it was made it easier to follow.

It arced gracefully out over the canal, cut across the wake of a pair of squawking parrots returning to their nest for the night, then dropped to the green up ahead with a satisfying *thump*. The ball skipped once, and there was a clanking sound as it disappeared.

"Iris," he called, his breath caught in his throat. "Did you see that? Did you see what just happened?"

Iris looked up from her knitting. "See what?" she said.

"GET A FUCKING MOVE ON!" the man behind them bellowed.

Dexter closed his eyes momentarily, reliving what he'd just accomplished. "Nothing," he said finally, and slid his club back in his bag. He bent and pocketed the two remaining balls. "We're going to eighteen now."

◉ ◉ ◉

He guided their cart over the high-arched bridge that spanned the canal, stopped where most people did when they had to putt out, stepped smartly, clubless, across the grass to the seventeenth green. He reached the flag, glanced down into the cup, smiled. He jerked the flag up with a snap, just like he'd seen a caddie do on television, watched the little yellow ball shoot straight up like it'd been goosed. He dropped the flag back in the cup and caught the ball all in one motion.

He was heading toward his cart when he heard something, felt a *swoosh* of air past his face. He jerked back instinctively as a golf ball thudded into the green a few feet away. The thing took a hop, then skidded on into a high collar of grass near a sand trap.

Dexter turned. The fat man stood in the fairway not far from where Dexter himself had been minutes before. The guy had his hands on his hips and stood staring up at the green as if daring Dexter to say anything.

The two of them looked at each other for a moment, then Dexter turned away. He walked back to his cart, got in, drove a dozen yards to the tee box for the eighteenth hole. He unsheathed his driver, pulled off the fuzzy head that had come with it, tossed it on the cart seat.

The driver was an unusual-looking thing, had a black graphite shaft with yellow striations molded into the material. It had cost him two hundred and seventy-five dollars, but the clerk assured him that he'd see twenty-five yards added to his drives. As twenty-five yards was about the sum total of what he'd been getting, Dexter had considered it a bargain.

He teed up the ball, stared off down the fairway toward the spire of the old hotel, the Biltmore, they called it. Its lights were fairly glowing now, twilight fully fallen, and it looked like nothing you'd ever see in Nebraska. He was glad their work had brought them out this way. Coconut Grove had its pleasures, but this was something else.

He attempted to duplicate the same emptying of his mind as before, but certain things just wouldn't let him go. He felt a sudden, irresistible force claim him as he brought the club down, and he knew that was wrong. A swing you could use to chop off the head of an ox, he thought, that was nothing you could use out here.

"Where'd that one go?" Iris called out of the darkness.

"I'm not real sure," Dexter replied.

He was walking away from the cart, back toward the seventeenth green, where a vague blur of yellow, white, and black was moving through the gloom.

"Where are you going?" Iris called.

"Be right back," Dexter said. And he was.

◎ ◎ ◎

"What happened to your new golf stick?" Iris asked him, later. She had the headless shaft in her hand, was examining the shattered stub.

"Busted it with that last swing," he said, shaking his head.

"That was an expensive item," she said. "Maybe you ought to ask for your money back."

"They don't make stuff like they used to," he agreed.

"You can say that again," she said. She took another look at the striations on the shaft. "Funny-looking piece of equipment. It had a name, didn't it."

Dexter glanced up at her. "It did," he said. Some things just seemed to've been destined. "Guy in the pro shop was calling it the Killer Bee."

Chapter 12

It was almost eight-thirty by the time Deal had finished *The Little Engine That Could*, for the third time. Driscoll, childless ex-homicide cop that he was, had been right. She'd loved it. And Deal's delivery of the various train engine voices had improved dramatically with each reading. On the final pass, she'd started to nod, and by the time the Little Blue Engine was once again chuffing down the hill toward the ecstatic, expectant children who lived in the valley, "Ithinkican, ithinkican, ithinkican…" Isabel was fast asleep.

At least she'd been distracted enough not to ask him for the thousandth time when her mommy was coming home, he thought. How would he have told *that* story? How mommies get sick sometimes, a different kind of sickness, how they have to go to special hospitals and not because they're hurt but because they can't think so clearly…and yes Mommy still loves you and you'll surely see her soon…

He pulled the comforter up around her shoulders, fighting another pang, even deeper than the one he'd felt earlier when he'd noticed how she'd grown. Children have worse lives, Deal. Much worse. She is happy. She is with people who love her…He turned off her bedside lamp, brushed his hand against her cheek.

"Is a nice story," Mrs. Suarez said as Deal eased out of the room. How long had she been listening, he wondered?

"It's an old one," he said. "My father used to read the same book to me."

Mrs. Suarez nodded. "Isabel, she likes."

Deal answered with a nod of his own.

"Maybe they have *en español*, in the bookstore..." she said, then broke off, clapping her hand to her mouth. "*Madre de Diós*," she said, her face blanching. "I am sorry..."

"It's all right, Mrs. Suarez," he said. "Please."

He knew what she was feeling: his friend the bookseller murdered, his store devastated—it was bad luck and, as far as Mrs. Suarez was concerned, an unforgivable breach of manners to call the tragedy to mind, however unintentionally.

He put a hand on her shoulder, squeezed gently. "It's a good book," he said. "I think I can find a Spanish edition somewhere."

Mrs. Suarez nodded gratefully at him, and her gratitude had nothing to do with his promise to find the book. She had erred, he had noticed, the matter had to be forgiven. In her cosmos, even the smallest transgressions were to be accounted for, and if they were not...well, seventy years old, maybe a hundred pounds dripping wet, she was as formidable a defender as he could want on his side. Lock this Cuban expatriate up in a room with Fidel, he thought, it'd be even money the one to walk out would not be smoking a cigar.

"I feel very bad about your friend," she said. "Is a terrible thing."

"Thanks, Mrs. Suarez."

"They going to find who did it and—" She made a wrenching motion with her hands that left little doubt as to her picture of a just punishment.

"I hope so," he said.

Mrs. Suarez nodded and turned her gaze away, to where Isabel lay, illumined in the ghostly glow of a Kermit the Frog nightlight. "This life, it is not always so easy," Mrs. Suarez said.

She'd lost her husband in Cuba during the revolution, her son in an automobile accident on a rain-slick Hialeah street, a sister in the Jackson Memorial cancer ward. Now she was worried about Isabel, about him, Deal thought. Whatever sadness he felt about Janice, Mrs. Suarez internalized it in turn. At first he'd taken her for a gloom-monger. Now he knew better. She'd become his witness, and his friend.

"Yes," he said finally. "It's tough, but it sure beats the alternative."

Another one of his old man's favorite lines, Deal thought. Was that what happened? Get to a certain age, you lapse into these patterns? He wasn't sure Mrs. Suarez would understand, and glanced up, ready to explain his departed father's witticism.

In fact, he found her smiling wistfully.

"*Es verdad,*" she said, and reached to squeeze his hands in her leathery pair. "We are the lucky ones, eh?" If it hadn't been for the moisture he saw ringing her eyes, he might even have believed her.

❀ ❀ ❀

He tried Omaha information first, was not surprised when he discovered no listing for a Sara Dolan. The days were long gone when a single woman had the temerity to list herself in the phone book, he supposed, even in Omaha. He'd have to wait on Driscoll to provide the numbers in the morning. Meantime, there was another possibility that had occurred to him, one a little closer to home.

He had to dig deep into his storage closet, dig out the Rolodex from the salad days to find the phone number of Eddie Lightner, the smooth operator who'd arranged the lease for Mega-Media. To his surprise, the number, a Coconut Grove exchange, was still good. He wasn't surprised at all, however, when Eddie's machine voice picked up.

Deal hung up in the middle of Eddie's recorded assurances that the call meant everything in the world to him, and sat pondering things for a moment. He ought to go to bed, get a decent night's sleep, start over in the morning. But he felt like the little blue train, over the hump at last, and picking up steam. No way to stop now.

He tapped on the door of the bedroom Mrs. Suarez had been using often these days, told her he was going out for a few minutes, asked if they needed anything from the Farm Stores minimart, an all-night place that Isabel had named the "cow store" for the dairy animal on its sign. Mrs. Suarez came to the door in a housecoat, assured him they needed nothing, and added, in Spanish, that he should go with God.

A couple of minutes later, he was guiding the Hog down Seventeenth Street on his way toward the Grove. A light rain was falling, just enough to glaze the streets, and even though he had the light he took it slow going across Coral Way. Going with God or not, the neighborhood attitude toward traffic signals got a little flexible as the hour advanced and traffic thinned out. Oh, they would *want* to stop, if they saw the Hog in the intersection, but with a head of steam up and a slick roadway, maybe throw in a set of bald tires...intentions and actions did not always mesh.

He made it across safely, however, passed the old Citgo station that had kept its same corny Deco architecture from the thirties, thinking that the building was another reason never to move back to stylish Miami, where anything older than last week automatically went onto the developers' hit lists. He wound his way on down through the modest residential neighborhood, had soon swung out onto South Dixie, where the traffic was a little heavier—maybe a Heat game letting out of the Arena downtown, or a concert, maybe

Eddie Lightner was in a car ahead or behind him, or in a bar putting the moves on another in a long line of bimbos and what the hell was he doing out here driving around anyway?

He edged into the left lane, made the turn into the Grove at Douglas, heading due south now. He turned again, then a second time, was deep down one of the leafy tunnels that served as roadways in Coconut Grove, before he was ready to admit what had really brought him out. He guided the Hog to the side of Tigertail Avenue, brought his headlights down, sat staring up at the Mariner, the exotic conglomeration of wood and glass angles that Janice was now calling home.

There were a couple of dozen apartments in the building, many of them with lights ablaze, and he had no idea which one might be hers. He didn't want to know, for that matter. He already felt like some high school kid cruising his girlfriend's house, hoping…hoping *what*, exactly? That she'd walk out of the building, on her way to the E-Z Quick for some Häagen-Dazs, he could say he'd just pulled over to check his tire pressure?

Shape up, Deal. You want to talk, call her up on the phone. He pounded the wheel, disgusted with himself, dropped the Hog back into gear, pulled back onto the street again.

It took him a couple of minutes to find Lightner's street, a tiny cul-de-sac off Tigertail, but the reward was finding the place blazing with lights, an Acura angled in at the verge with its personalized plate clearly visible: EDDIE D.

Deal squeezed onto the margin behind the Acura, got out of the Hog, noticed a tall, gaunt man in the shadows on the opposite side of the lane, attached to a tiny dog on a leash. Deal nodded, but the guy moved along without comment, apparently absorbed in the dog's agitated dance along the shrubbery. "Yeah, well, have a nice dump," Deal said as he turned away, but he doubted the guy heard him over the distant thunder of music coming from Lightner's house.

The rumble had grown into a physical force wave as Deal reached the entryway of the house, a low-slung block building overhung with ficus trees and surrounded by an eight-foot wall that hid most of the property from the street. He'd been in the place a couple of times, back when DealCo was a major player in South Florida development. Though it was all invisible from where he stood, Deal knew that there was a pool on the other side of the wall, a small but lushly landscaped yard, a house with a lot of floor-to-ceiling glass that opened out onto various angles of the exotic surroundings. A typical Grove house—nothing special on the outside, a real box of chocolates inside.

He tried the bell, but the music throbbed on, unabated. Deal shifted his feet, heard a squishing sound, glanced down to find water pooled on the floor of the entryway. Strange, he thought. The rain that had misted his own neighborhood seemed to have missed the Grove. Maybe Lightner's sprinklers were on? He glanced into one of the planter boxes beneath the doorbell, but it seemed dry. Then he noticed the rivulets oozing out from under the doorjamb.

There was an iron gate that was supposed to serve as security, but it swung away easily at Deal's touch. When he hammered at the door itself, the thing, done up like a massive ship's hatchway and encased in about an inch of glossy resin, fell inward as if it turned on rails.

The music hit him like hot wind, an unintelligible blare of human screams and distorted instrumentation that was blaring strongly enough to vibrate a framed print just inside the doorway. Deal stared down the brightly lit hallway, stunned momentarily by the sound, by what he saw. Water poured onto the floor tiles from an elevated passageway down the hallway. Some of it splashed over a Giacometti-like wooden sculpture that had tumbled there, then rushed on down a set of steps that led to a sunken living area. Another tributary had formed that led down the hallway and over the doorjamb at his feet. The force of this stream had picked up now that he'd opened the door.

He glanced over his shoulder at the Hog, thought about going for a phone, then found himself hurrying inside, trying to sidestep the stream of water, making for the passageway on his right.

He saw the woman first. She was face down on the floor of Lightner's den, long hair fanned about her head and shoulders, a flimsy kimono pushed up over her bare buttocks, her hands and feet splayed, the water piling against one thigh before it coursed on toward the hallway. Deal should have guessed where the water was coming from.

The aquarium was Lightner's exhibition piece, something he was fond of showing visitors. It was a huge tank, several hundred gallons, that ran nearly the length of the room, set into some highly burnished cherrywood cabinetry that also housed the sound system and a television monitor that even now displayed a live video image of the room, like some floor display from an electronics store of the damned.

Deal saw it all in a glance, a miracle of technology: One dead woman with long red hair, one stunned intruder staring dumbly over her lifeless form, and there, Lightner himself, head and torso crashed through the cabinetry and submerged in the massive tank, legs dangling over the lip, water jetting from cracks in the shattered front.

Deal turned from the ghostly image to the tank itself, saw a cloud of tiny, needlelike silverfish swirl like smoke from Lightner's face, felt Lightner's pop-eyed, sightless gaze lock on his own. An orange fish the size and shape of a throwing knife bumped its way down Lightner's jawline, mouth popping as if it were delivering a series of kisses. A huge angelfish brushed through the wavering fan of Lightner's thinning hair. Something iridescent and wormlike lashed from the cavern at Lightner's lips, as if he'd acquired some new aquatic tongue that was flailing about, trying to explain all this.

Just an eel, doing an eel-like thing, Deal told himself, but still he felt his knees weaken, felt himself reeling backward, out of the room. One foot caught at the edge of the step, his other hit the slick tile of the hallway and went out from under him. He went down hard, his shoulder, then his head, slamming the tile. He came up on his hands and knees, stunned, his vision blurring in and out. The music was still pounding at a deafening level, seeming to suffocate him now. His stomach heaved mightily, then again. He steadied himself, then began to move crablike toward the entranceway, thinking that if he could just get outside, into the cool quiet air, he could maintain.

He managed to drag himself upright, push himself along the wall, his shoulder tracing a wet course along the plaster. He felt more than heard the sound of something far off in the house, a shudder that passed through the wall and into his shoulder. A door slamming? he wondered.

He staggered out into the night, where, blessedly, the power of the distorted music was muted. He bent over, bracing his hands on his knees, gasping for breath. Just the wind knocked out of him, he assured himself, as his head began to clear.

Something moved in the corner of his vision and he jerked his head sharply, throwing up his hands in a defensive posture, though anyone could have done him in at that moment. What he found was a tiny dog—some blend of terrier and God knows what, trailing its leash, whining, dancing frantic circles, darting toward the street and back again. Deal had a flash of memory: the dog snuffling the bushes, its gaunt-looking master trailing behind.

He heard the sound of a car engine starting somewhere, gravel popping against a garbage can. He caught another breath and, still gasping, reeled on toward the street after the dog. The animal was yapping now, its movements more frenzied, tangling itself in its leash, dancing backward toward a dark canopy of undergrowth opposite the Hog.

Deal hesitated, fumbling for his keys. He'd call 911, then see what the dog had in mind. But the animal was back at him, actually growling now, an absurd, pipsqueak sound that was muffled even further when it grasped Deal's pantleg in its mouth and began to tug, digging its claws into the loose gravel at the verge for purchase.

Deal shook his leg loose, fought the urge to kick the dog into oblivion. "All right," he said, and followed the animal into the shadows.

The dog had calmed finally, sinking to its haunches as Deal ducked under an overhang of branches and approached. He saw a pair of tennis shoes sticking out of a thick planting of lariope, bent down, expecting to find trouser legs, the body of the gaunt man there. Instead it was a muscular pair of calves, heavy thighs, someone clad in running shorts and a T-shirt. Deal leaned closer, saw a young man with a sweatband around his forehead lying motionless, his chin tilted up at an impossible angle.

"Good God," he said, staggering back.

He ran for his car then, expecting the dog to be yammering at his heels, but the thing stayed by its master. It had set up a mournful howl by the time Deal made his way to the Hog and went to place his call at last.

◉ ◉ ◉

"You going to be okay?" one of the cops asked him. "A glass of water, maybe?" Deal glanced up. It was a blond woman, her hair pulled back in a ponytail. Mid-thirties maybe, trim, a businesslike set to her movements. But she looked at him with concern.

Deal nodded. "Thanks."

"I've got a message for you," she said. "From Vernon Driscoll. He said he's on his way."

Deal looked at her. "You know Driscoll?"

She gave a short laugh. "Everybody knows Driscoll," she said.

Deal nodded again, sank back against the soft leathery upholstery of Lightner's living room couch. The lady cop gave him a last glance, then turned away as attendants maneuvered a gurney into the hallway from the den.

"Who the hell puked?" one of the attendants complained.

"Somebody want to get that dog out of the way?" another called.

Deal glanced up, saw the ratty terrier dodge the grasp of the lady cop. It bounded into the sunken living room, made a beeline for Deal, still trailing its leash. The thing dove onto the couch, huddled against him. He could feel it trembling, the thud of its heartbeat. Deal felt his hand go to the dog, begin to stroke it automatically. He wasn't fond of small dogs, not at all, had owned a series of black Labs until they'd had to sell their house in the Shores. "Shark bait" was what he called the little yappy ones like this. And yet this one…well, it had displayed a certain form of guts.

The lady cop came back into the room, bent down on her haunches, gave the dog a pat. She glanced up at Deal. "The guy in the bushes," she said, "he didn't make it."

Deal nodded.

"His neck was broken, that's what it looked like to me."

"The guy I saw earlier with the dog," Deal said, "it wasn't the same guy who was lying in the bushes."

She nodded. "The detectives'll talk to you about it," she said. "I got an address off the dog's collar earlier," she said. "Just around the corner. A little place, like a gardener's cottage, you know? Nobody else there. Maybe he lived alone."

Deal glanced down at the dog. "Maybe," he agreed.

"You want to hold on to this guy for now?" she said. "Otherwise, I'll have to call Animal Control."

Deal shrugged. Somehow he'd been thinking of the dog as some piece of evidence, a clue to be handled with kid gloves. Now he understood the creature was basically a nuisance. "Sure," he said finally. "I'll watch him."

She nodded, stood. "Too bad he can't talk," she said. She lifted the corner of her mouth into a Driscoll-like gesture that said, "So whaddaya going to do," then turned back toward the activity in the den.

Deal watched her go, moving with the economical grace of a gymnast, her hips as slender as a boy's. But, a woman of substance, he was thinking, and then he saw Driscoll's bulk appear in the hallway door.

❀ ❀ ❀

Driscoll gave him a wave, motioned for him to stay put, disappeared into the den, where several plainclothes detectives had been at work for some time. Aside from the female cop who'd taken his preliminary statement, no one had spoken to Deal. It seemed odd. Sure, he'd found the bodies, made the emergency call, but even Deal could figure that didn't mean he hadn't done it. Maybe they were in there drawing straws right now, seeing who'd be good cop, who'd be bad, let's grill the Deal guy. A couple of minutes from now, he'd find himself under a naked lightbulb, head swiveling back and forth as the questions rattled at him.

The dog whined softly, put its chin up on his thigh. Deal looked down, gave it a reassuring pat. "You're my only alibi, pal," he said. The dog blinked, tucked its head away again. Not a promising gesture, Deal thought. When he glanced up, Driscoll was in the hallway, beckoning him with a thick finger.

"What's that?" Driscoll said, pointing at the dog as Deal approached. He had thought about what to do with it, ended up tucking the creature under his arm.

"It belonged to the jogger," Deal said, nodding toward the outside.

"What are you doing with it?" Driscoll said.

Deal stared at him. Driscoll was wearing a rumpled sport coat, but underneath was a T-shirt with a hamburger emblazoned on the chest. An odor of meat and grilled onions emanated from the ex-cop, and the dog had lifted its nose to check it out. "I don't know," Deal said.

Driscoll gave the dog another doubtful look.

"So what's going on, Driscoll? Nobody's asked me anything."

Driscoll nodded. "They'll get around to it," he said. He glanced back inside the den, thought about something, finally motioned for Deal to follow him. "You're not going to believe this," he said.

Deal took a breath, followed after the ex-cop. The bodies had been removed, and a narrow walkway had been described through the room with crime scene tape. Most of the water was gone from the big tank now, though there was still enough seepage to keep the floor dangerously slick. The shallows inside the ruined tank were alive with leaping, shuddering fish. With Lightner's body gone, Deal could see a starburst the size of a dinner plate in the tank's glass front. Smears of blood radiated out from its center. Deal felt his stomach constrict again, and turned away.

"You don't have to see this, you know," Driscoll said.

"I'm okay," Deal said.

Driscoll gave his characteristic shrug, and drew him along toward a knot of plainclothesmen who had gathered around the TV monitor Deal had seen earlier.

"The guy is hung, I'll have to say that," someone was saying.

"*Was* hung," someone else said. "Come on, Lonnie, get to the part where the doorbell rings."

Deal glanced over one detective's shoulder. The image showed Lightner and the woman on the den floor. Lightner was on his knees, shucking out of his robe, the woman poised before him, also on her knees, her backside up in the air, her robe bunched around her shoulders, exposing her breasts.

"The lady had a set," someone said.

"Shut up, Dewhurst," the lead detective said.

Lightner's companion had placed her head on her hands, and though her face was turned toward the camera, her hair had tumbled free and Deal could see only her parted lips. Lightner glanced up as if checking the position of the camera lens, and Deal found his head swiveling toward the bookcases that lined the wall behind him. The camera had to be hidden up there somewhere, but he couldn't see any evidence of it. He wondered briefly if the woman had known the act was being filmed.

When he turned back to the monitor, the figures were moving in accelerated fashion, actions that might have seemed erotic now reduced to Keystone Kops herky-jerky.

"Hold it," one of the cops said, and the image froze. "Yeah, there. Now back up a couple of frames, right where her head comes up."

The woman's face blinked clearly into focus via a series of still images. "Okay, now go," the lead detective said.

The woman was still staring toward the camera when the doorbell rang. At first Lightner paid no attention, but then the chime sounded twice more, in rapid succession.

Deal heard a curse, then Lightner was getting to his feet, throwing his robe on, moving out of the room toward the door. The woman rearranged herself into a sitting position, drew her robe closed. She glanced in the direction Lightner had taken, shrugged, reached to pick at something on an eyelash. She examined whatever she'd found, flicked it away, plucked again. Deal thought she looked like an actress whose scene had been put on hold while the crew hashed out some technical problem.

"Can you give us that security camera image now?"

"Just a second, it's a little complicated." There was a plainclothes cop on the far side of the room, a guy with a weight lifter's build wearing jeans and a T-shirt, fiddling with one of the components in Lightner's setup.

"You see anything yet?" Artie called.

"No...yeah, wait a minute, there it is," the lead detective called back.

A cutout had appeared in the lower corner of the monitor, a blurry black-and-white image of Lightner at the doorway, talking through the security gate to an older woman wearing a floppy hat, white gloves, big tinted glasses. She was saying something to Lightner, making dithery motions with her hands, out toward the street.

Lightner said something back, threw up his hands, disappeared. In a few seconds he was back, handing the woman what looked like a cellular phone. Deal tried to imagine what was going through Lightner's mind at the moment. Just about to get off, some loony shows up at your door at 11:00 P.M., wearing garden party attire.

"We got any sound with that?" the lead detective called.

"I don't think so," Artie said. "You won't get it in PIP, anyway."

The woman in Lightner's den, meanwhile, had stood up, found her purse, lit a cigarette. She glanced around, dropped the match in a plant container, blew a stream of smoke toward the camera, checked her watch impatiently. Deal felt an immense sadness overtake him. This woman had spent the last moments of her life smoking, waiting impatiently for Eddie Lightner to return and finish a trick?

Meantime, in the insert, the woman in the floppy hat had dialed, listened, banged the cellular phone against the side of her hand. Her demeanor seemed to have taken a sudden change. Her face twisted into a scowl and she shouted something angrily at Lightner. "...piece of shit," Deal caught, thinking, *The loony really is a loony after all.* Lightner's head bobbed as if he were shouting something in return.

The woman in the floppy hat spun about, started away from the house, still carrying Lightner's cellular phone. Lightner fumbled at the security gate, then hurried out after her, worried about his property. Don't do it, Deal thought, rooting against hope as if it were some horror movie where you shout at the heroine not to go down to that basement.

But Lightner did do it. Twisted the key, swung open the grate…and in that instant, when the gate was finally free, everything changed. The woman in the floppy hat tossed the phone aside, spun about, advanced on Lightner in two quick strides. Her fist shot out, knuckles extended oddly, and Lightner went down, out of the frame. The woman moved after him, sending what looked like karate kicks at the fallen Lightner.

Lightner was up then, moving toward the security camera, a smear of blood on his upper lip. His face bloated up momentarily, distorted into fish-eye perspective as he swept past the camera. But there was no mistaking the look of terror in his eyes. In the next instant, his face was replaced by the image of a huge, misshapen hat, flapping after him like some surreal creature of the night.

The tiny picture was a static shot of the entrance and the action shifted back into Lightner's den: Lightner running into the room, shouting, pointing at the startled hooker.

"Hey, where's the sound?" the lead detective yelled.

"No sound at all now?" Artie called. "Shit!" He turned back to the console he'd been fiddling with, began pushing buttons.

The woman in the hat was on Lightner's heels, clipped him at the base of the skull with a chopping motion of her hand. Lightner went down like a rock, tangling into a cluster of carved African sculptures that occupied a corner of the room like miniature wooden Indians. The hooker made a beeline for the doorway, but she wasn't quick enough. The woman in the floppy hat reached out, caught her by a length of her long hair, jerked her backward.

The woman in the hat raised one foot, planted it at the base of the hooker's spine. She twisted the hooker's hair into a rope, and, using both hands, jerked down savagely. The hooker's arms shot straight out from her sides as if she were being electrocuted.

"Fuck me," one of the detectives said, his voice little more than an awed whisper.

Thankfully, Deal thought, the hooker's face was averted from the camera. In the next instant, she was crumpled on the floor, back broken, just the way Deal had found her.

Meanwhile, Lightner had struggled up, was coming at the woman in the hat with one of the sculptures upraised like a baseball bat. He roundhoused the thing at the woman, who ducked it easily. He sailed past, losing his grip on the sculpture. The thing must have tumbled out into the hallway at that point, Deal thought, reliving his first glance into the house.

Lightner turned, came at her again, nothing but his bare hands this time. Fast Eddie Lightner. Big-time player, hustler, cocksman extraordinaire. Not a decent bone in his chiseling, hump-your-crippled-grand-mother body, Deal thought. And still felt a wave of despair and sadness as the woman in the flowered hat caught Eddie by the lapels of his two-hundred-dollar silk robe and slung him face first against the thick glass front of the aquarium.

The sound came back in time to render the sickening crunch, the hiss of the water as it began to spray from the tank. Deal turned away, hurrying quickly out of the room then. He knew how this movie ended, after all.

☺ ☺ ☺

Driscoll caught up with him outside, where he'd stopped to put the dog down in the little patch of grass between Lightner's house and the street. The roadway had been sealed, the area where the jogger's body had lain now another beehive of activity. Driscoll turned and motioned to a detective who'd followed them to the door that everything was all right.

"Yeah, tell 'em I'm not fleeing the scene," Deal said, a bitter edge in his voice.

"They gotta talk to you, that's all," Driscoll said. "You ought to be happy they got that video. Otherwise, they'd be all over your ass right now."

Deal nodded. "Next time I find bodies, I'll keep that in mind. I'll walk out backwards, let the paperboy handle it."

Driscoll ignored him, worked his shoulders under the jacket he'd put on. "I presume you had some thought in mind, coming to see the deceased at this time of night," he said mildly.

Deal stared at him, defiant.

Driscoll shrugged. "You don't have to talk to me, but you'll sure as hell have to explain yourself to those guys." He nodded toward the house.

Deal let out his breath, allowed the dog to nose toward a clump of bushes. "I thought maybe Lightner would know something about why the Mega-Media project is stalled."

"Yeah?" Driscoll said. "Why would that be?"

"Because he put the deal together. He called Arch Dolan up to tell him about it."

"How nice of Eddie," Driscoll said.

"Eddie was a sleazewad of the first water," Deal said, "but he was the kind of guy who knew things."

Driscoll nodded. "So now you're a detective, huh?"

Deal shrugged. "Something's going on with the Mega-Media project," he said. "I'm going to find out what it is."

Driscoll glanced back toward the house. "Seems to me like you're running out of people to ask."

Deal was ready to agree when the dog gave a jerk on its leash that pulled him off balance. He turned as the thing made a four-pronged dive into a thick bank of artillery fern, burying its head into the greenery and snarling. "Get out of there," Deal said, pulling on the leash. "Come on."

The dog came out unwillingly, dragging something in its mouth.

Deal bent down. The dog was trying to avert its head, but he gathered up the slack in the leash, pulled it around. "Look here," Deal said as he gently tugged the object from the dog's mouth.

He handed the cellular phone to Driscoll, who took it by its stubby antenna. "Dog slobber'll ruin the prints," he muttered.

"She was wearing gloves, remember."

"Oh, yeah," Driscoll said.

"Good dog," Deal said, patting the terrier.

"You want to go back inside now, tell the boys your story?" Driscoll said.

Deal glanced up at him. "Does this bother you, Driscoll? Me wanting to run this matter to the ground?"

Driscoll sighed. "You can run matters wherever you want to," he said. "But from the looks of this mess, you better be careful."

Deal stood. "So you think maybe I'm right, somebody didn't want Lightner talking?"

Driscoll threw up his hands. "Kind of guy Lightner was, a whole bunch of people might want him dead. You just can't make these giant leaps, Deal. The point is, you start nosing around dirty people, you never know what's going to happen, that's all I'm saying. Now go tell the boys you came to see Lightner about a job you were trying to get and let's go home."

Deal stared at him. "You're telling me to lie?"

Driscoll gave him a droll look in response. "Forget it, Deal. Handle it your own way."

⊚ ⊚ ⊚

"So Lightner arranged the lease for this giant bookstore that was going to run your friend Arch Dolan out of business, is that right?" The detective, who'd said his name was Flynn, had a notebook out, a pencil in one hand, but his eyes were on the backside of the female officer Deal had met earlier.

She was bent over in front of the still-dripping tank, staring sorrowfully at the dying fish. One of the big angelfish spasmed up out of the shallow puddle that was left, flashed briefly in the light like a twirling coin, fell back again.

"That's right," Deal said.

The detective turned to him, waved his arm around the room. "But your friend Dolan is dead. It would have been pretty hard for him to do all this, wouldn't it?"

Deal gaped at the detective. Driscoll, who stood a few feet away, inspecting some of the titles in Lightner's bookcase, gave Deal an I-told-you-so glance. "Of course he's dead. That's the point," Deal said.

The detective scratched behind his ear with his pencil. "If there is a point, it seems to elude me." He glanced back at the female officer, then consulted his notebook again. "Your pal Dolan was a pillar of the community, an unfortunate victim of crime. What we got here," he paused, glancing around the room with distaste, "is your basic scumbag hit. Lightner's a player, Mr. Deal. He's got markers spread all over town, he's screwed more people than Linda Lovelace, what happened isn't hardly a surprise. I go around on this, people are going to tell me, nah, I didn't do it, but when you find who did, give 'em my congratulations."

Deal sighed, exasperated. He opened his mouth to respond, then closed it again. Faced with Flynn's bluff certainty, his own suspicions seemed far less substantial, even to himself. Mentioning the difficulties at the Mega-Media site seemed impossible suddenly, an airy nothing. Flynn would consign him to the conspiracy theory brigade, along with the Jim Garrison Fan Club and the UFO Spotters of America, if he hadn't already.

"It seemed there could be a connection," he heard himself mumble lamely.

"Uh-huh," Flynn said. His eyes were on the female cop again. "Is that what you came over to talk with Lightner about?"

Deal thought he saw a new light appear in Flynn's eyes. Maybe considering him as a suspect, Deal thought, imagining Flynn measuring him, trying to figure out what he'd look like in women's clothes and a floppy hat.

"No," Deal said, hiding the resignation he felt inside. Driscoll had pulled a book down from the shelves, was thumbing through it, but the expression on his face told Deal where his attention was. "There was a project I was interested in bidding on," he continued. "I thought maybe Lightner had some information that could help."

Flynn nodded, flipping his notebook shut. "That was Eddie's stock in trade, I understand. Always ready to lend a hand."

If the price was right, Deal finished Flynn's message in his mind.

"You think you'd recognize the guy with the dog if you saw him again?" Flynn asked.

"I don't know. It was dark. He was tall, thin." Deal shrugged. "I couldn't see his face."

Flynn nodded again. "Yeah, well, we'll be in touch. Thanks for your help, Mr. Deal."

He tipped his notebook at Deal, then ambled off toward the female officer. "Hey, Sylvia," he said. "Where you been keeping yourself?"

She turned, glanced at Flynn with something less than enthusiasm, drew herself up. "Out of trouble, Floyd," she said, and walked on out of the room.

🌼 🌼 🌼

"Floyd Flynn's a piece of work, isn't he?" Driscoll said.

"Floyd Flynn, that's really the guy's name?" Deal said.

Driscoll shrugged, motioned to the bartender that he wanted a refill on his draft. "Frigging Floyd Flynn is what we used to call him," Driscoll said. "Five bucks if you can say it three times."

"He seemed more interested in the lady cop than anything else."

"I tried to tell you," Driscoll said. "Curiosity is not Floyd's metier. Tends to complicate things, often results in thought, even hard work."

Deal shook his head, took a sip of his own beer.

At Driscoll's suggestion, they'd driven on toward the fringes of the Grove's business district, stopped at a tavern called the Ruptured Duck, a hangout for locals that Deal had passed by a thousand times. No European tourists, no kids in Calvin Klein, no yups from the affluent Miami suburbs. Here the atmosphere was red Naugahyde and shagcarpeted walls, heavy on the smoke, Sansabelts, and mascara. There was a stuffed mallard mounted above the bar, a mocked-up surgical truss wrapped around its mid-section.

"They get the live-aboard crowd," Driscoll remarked, following Deal's gaze. "Houseboaters and sailboat people, mostly." He tipped his full beer at the bartender, a blond woman with a formidable bustline, a tight smile, and a leather skirt cut halfway up a shapely thigh.

"She's either forty, carrying sixty thousand miles, or sixty carrying forty," Driscoll said. "What's your guess?"

"Have another beer, Driscoll."

"I like this place," Driscoll continued. "It's gone downhill a little, but then again, so have I."

Deal laughed despite himself.

"So what's your next move, Sherlock?" Driscoll asked.

Deal shook his head. "I don't know. Maybe it *is* crazy."

Driscoll shrugged. "Frigging Floyd is no measure of what's worth looking into."

Deal glanced at him. "A minute ago, I would have sworn you were trying to discourage me."

"Hey," Driscoll continued, "you have a hunch, you might as well play it out. All's I'm trying to tell you is, don't expect somebody else to work your own wavelength, Deal. Me or Floyd or anybody else."

"Sounds a little mystical, coming from you."

"No mystery to it," Driscoll said. "More like common sense, the way I see it." He drained his beer. "I gotta go to the can. Order me another beer, will you?"

Deal nodded, watched Driscoll move off into the dark reaches of the bar. Work his own wavelength. Sure. If he only knew what that meant. There was something going on at the Mega-Media site, that much he was certain of. Whether it had anything to do with Arch's death or Lightner's, that was another matter. Impossible to know unless he found out what the problem was. He could always go back to Custer's office, try to find out if the little bastard was hiding something, but that would be tough. Custer had made a career out of playing the angles. It'd take hanging him out his office window by his heels to get him to talk. That or a significant amount of cash.

But what choice did he have? Lightner was out of the picture. Carver Construction seemed like a dead end...but still, somebody had to know what the hold-up was...

He was staring off into space, shredding his cocktail napkin, wadding the strips into little balls that he fired off the bar top with flicks of his finger, when the bartender slid into his line of vision. She glanced down into her cleavage, plucked something out with her fingers. She dropped the paper wad on the bar in front of him, gave him a smile.

"Lose something?" she said.

Deal felt his face redden. "I'm sorry..." he began.

She was laughing at his discomfort.

"Get you anything?" she asked.

"My partner needs a beer," he managed.

"How about you?"

Deal thought there was something in the way she said it. He took another look at her. The skin at the top of her breasts smooth, the flesh of her neck taut, her jawline firm. Closer up, her eyes, unwavering on his, almost soft. Not an unattractive woman. Not at all. And then he heard the laughter.

A while since he'd heard that sound, of course, but just as unmistakable as the sound of his daughter's middle-of-the-night cry. He turned away from the bartender, was off his stool in an instant and heading toward the sound with a backward wave.

There was a little room off to the side, a place you couldn't really see from the bar. Electronic dartboard, jukebox, half a dozen tables around a parquet dance floor the size of a dining room table. Most of the tables were empty, but a couple had been pulled together. A group of younger people there, three women in casual dress, two late-twenties guys in T-shirts and jeans, tanned muscular arms and sun-bleached hair—rough carpenters, Deal thought, or maybe pleasure-boat crew-men—but he really didn't focus, because his gaze had locked in on the woman at the end of the table. She was wearing jeans, a white shirt, its sleeves rolled up, a scoop-necked T-shirt underneath. Too old for the crew she was with, but just right for him, he found himself thinking. She looked as lovely as he'd ever seen her, except for the bleary look in her eyes, which were focused somewhere a million miles away until he was almost over top of her.

"Janice," he said, his voice sounding like it was full of rusted springs and gears that didn't mesh. "What are you doing?"

She glanced up, a look of surprise there for a moment, then vanishing quickly. "Deal," she said. A faint smile crossed her lips. She waved idly at the others about the table. "Meet my neighbors."

Deal glanced at the group, turned back to her. "What are you doing here?"

She turned her hands up on the table. "There must be an echo in this place."

The larger of the guys was giving Deal the once-over. "You know this person?" he said to Janice.

Deal didn't trust himself to look at the guy. He could feel the pressure building up inside, another few seconds there'd be cartoon whistles hooting steam out his ears. "It's okay, Rem," she said. "I know the gentleman."

Rem gave Deal another look—just don't get any ideas, Buster—then turned back to his companions. Deal sighted in on a spot right behind the guy's ear—sunburned flesh, a fringe of bleached-out curls—felt his hand clench into a fist.

"Have a seat," Janice said, her hand falling on his. He turned, found the loopy smile still playing about her lips. "Have a beer, Deal. Chill out."

Deal looked at her hand on his. "Chill out," he repeated. He barked a laugh. "Sure," he said. And finally sat down with his wife.

"Something else?" the waitress who was handling the room asked, her pad poised.

"Two coffees here," Deal said. "Another round for the table."

He gestured at the adjacent places, empty now. Rem and one of the women, a redhead in a form-fitting Speedo top and baggy khaki shorts, were at the dartboard, firing away. The other couple was on the dance floor, locked in a near-catatonic two-step as Otis Redding wailed in the background, old man trouble just wouldn't leave him alone.

"Coffee?" Janice said. "What fun are you?"

"Irish coffees, then," Deal said to the waitress. She nodded was about to turn away when he added, "hold the Irish."

The waitress gave him a look, then moved on. They watched her switch her way back toward the bar, silent for a moment.

"I used to have a butt like that," Janice said, over the brass changes of Otis's backup.

"You've got a better one now," Deal said.

"Is this a come-on?" Her loopy smile was back.

"Just a statement of fact," he said. "You never answered my question."

She stared at him for a moment, finally drained what was left in her glass. "I guess Mrs. Suarez didn't tell you," she said.

Deal stared at her blankly. "Tell me what?"

"That I came by the fourplex earlier."

Deal shook his head. "I didn't hear about it."

Janice shrugged. "About six. I thought maybe I'd catch you, see Isabel…" She trailed off, drew a breath. "Anyway, you hadn't come home. I told Mrs. Suarez I'd come in, talk to Isabel."

"Yeah…?" Deal said, puzzled.

"Mrs. Suarez said she didn't think that was such a good idea."

"Mrs. Suarez said that?"

"She said she wasn't going to let me in."

Deal stared at her. "Janice, I never said anything to Mrs. Suarez…" There was an unspoken agenda here, suddenly, a specter of memory that haunted them both: a year or more ago, Janice checking herself out of the clinic where profound depression had landed her, coming home while Deal was away to carry Isabel off for a day and night, a manic spree of spending and shopping that ended harmlessly, save for several thousand dollars in credit card charges that Deal was still pecking away at. But that was a long time ago. Janice was better now, he reminded himself. She was okay. She was going to be *fine*. But still…

Janice waved her hand. "I know you didn't say anything to Mrs. Suarez, Deal. It's not your style." She focused on a plastic straw she'd knotted in her hands momentarily, then lifted her gaze back to him. "She was just doing what she thought was right, taking care of Isabel. I wasn't going to make a scene..." There was moisture gathering in her eyes, and she trailed off, turning her attention back to her straw.

Deal started to say something, then stopped, watching Janice's fingers work: loop, loop, snap; loop, loop, snap. If anything, her tears only incited him. Now's the time, Deal. Jump in with both boots. What did you expect, a brass band? The prodigal wife's return. Nice of you to drop by, say hello to your daughter...

His indignation boiled up, nearly overwhelming him, a wave so thick and hot from his gut, he didn't trust himself to speak.

He sensed her reading the emotions that must have been pulsing out of him like blips from some emergency beacon: hello out there and all the ships at sea, Johnny Deal is mighty pissed...

"I asked her to tell you I'd stopped," Janice said. "I went on back to my apartment. I waited a while, I thought maybe you'd call."

She shrugged. "Rem saw me out on my balcony, asked me to come along." She mustered her smile again. "So here I am, Deal. That's what I'm doing."

She stared at him, a challenge in her gaze. Deal took a breath, let it out, opened his palms on the table. "Yeah, well, I never got the message."

Janice laughed mirthlessly. "I'm not even going to touch that line."

He stared at her, finally understood, granted her a laugh of his own. "Lot of water over the dam, huh?"

"Like, maybe, Niagara Falls?"

He nodded. "So, where's Richard," he said after a moment.

She measured him before answering. "Back in Sarasota, Deal. He has a business there. A woman he sees. A life."

Deal lifted his chin to acknowledge it. "It's a nice town, Sarasota. Peaceful. Pretty streets. Hardly anything ever happens there."

She sighed. "I came by, Deal. I came by to see you and Isabel."

He nodded again. "I'm sorry I wasn't home," he said. He paused. "I'm sorry about Mrs. Suarez."

Janice's lips pulled into a brief smile that might as well have been a grimace. "It's okay," she said.

They sat quietly for a moment. He could step in here, Deal thought. This was the time. Put his indignation, his anger, aside. It was the moment he'd fantasized about for God knows how long. One day, she will realize. The old Janice will come back. *Deal,* she'll say. *Deal...*

Sure enough, he thought. Sure enough. And still he waited. And waited. And somehow, the words would not come. He stared across the table as though Janice sat in a different dimension, as if nothing he spoke or shouted or willed could cross the foot-wide chasm between them.

On the far side of the room, Rem lasered a dart into the bull's-eye, turned to see if Deal had noticed.

"That guy's gears grind a little tight," Deal said, hearing himself break the silence.

She gave him a look: anger? sorrow? a little of both?

"Can it, Deal," she said finally. "He lives with Linda there, the one with the boobs. He's just looking out for me."

Gone, he thought. The moment gone, gone, gone. "Since when did you need taking care of?"

She folded her arms on the table. "I was having a nice evening, Deal. You came in here just to piss me off, why don't you go build a shopping center or something."

He took a breath, held it a couple of counts. So many thoughts whirling inside him now, he felt light-headed. "I'm sorry," he said. "It's been a night."

"Yeah?" she said. She looked him over more closely. Her gaze had softened again. He saw that little tremor at the corner of her lips, a tic that always signaled concern growing in Janice's mind. "Come to think of it, what are *you* doing here? That's the real question, isn't it?"

He opened his mouth, about to attempt some explanation, or maybe to hell with that, just take her hands and speak what's really on your mind, Deal...

...then broke off when he saw the expression that had swept over her face: her eyes had widened, her mouth in an O. Perfect charade pose of surprise, or even alarm....Deal swung about, expecting maybe he'd find Rem, barstool or ball bat or dartboard upraised, ready to deliver Deal's apt reward for hesitation...but instead it was Driscoll, the big ex-cop coming their way with the dog from Lightner's house tucked under his arm.

"Vernon," he heard Janice call.

"Hey, darlin'," Driscoll said. He swept her to him with one of his great arms, holding the dog aside with the other.

Janice stepped back from him, glanced at Deal. "So this is boys' night out?" She turned back to Driscoll, who swung his gaze at Deal.

"What are you two doing with a dog?" Deal, his mind still spinning, heard the question as if from miles away.

"Two Irish, hold the Irish," came the waitress's voice then, and they all were moving awkwardly aside to let her put the drinks down.

"Better make it three," Deal managed finally, and motioned everyone to a seat.

෴෴෴

It took Deal a good half-hour to tell it all. By the time he'd finished, Rem and company had decamped, leaving the back room to the three of them, or four, counting the dog, which had polished off a couple of leftover hamburgers provided by the waitress and was now snoozing, its snout laid across one of Deal's Topsiders.

Deal gave Driscoll a glance as he wound the story up, turned back to Janice. "So I didn't even tell this detective why I'd gone to Lightner's. It seemed like a waste of time."

Janice nodded glumly, her gaze turned inward. She turned to Driscoll abruptly. "That's what you think, right? First Arch, now Eddie Lightner. Just one big coincidence."

Driscoll held up his hands in protest. "What do I know? I'm working the case of the daring burger bandits, okay?" He made a goofy face, plucked at the Zaragosa Drive-in T-shirt. "Matter of fact," he said, downing his coffee, "I'm headed home. Got the 6:00 P.M. to 2:00 A.M. shift tomorrow."

He stood, put his hand on Janice's shoulder. "Next time I run into you, why don't we make it a happier occasion, what do you say?"

Her expression softened and she put her hand atop his. "You smell like onions," she said.

"It's that new cologne," Driscoll said. "Gets 'em every time."

He waved goodbye then, was out the door of the place before Deal felt a nudge beneath the table and remembered the dog.

"Hey," he said, starting up, but the thing was sprawled across both his shoe tops now and somehow he couldn't bring himself to disturb it.

He fell back into his chair, glanced across the table at Janice, shrugged.

"You went into therapy, you got yourself a dog…that's a lot of changes in your life, Deal."

He shrugged again. "No pets allowed at Casa Deal," he said.

"So call a meeting of the tenants' board," she said. "Amend the bylaws."

"Maybe."

The waitress passed the doorway into the back room, gave him an inquiring glance. Deal shook his head.

"That must have been a big thing for you," Janice persisted. "Going to a shrink."

"I'm not close-minded, Janice. Is that what you think?"

"It's just not your style, to ask for help."

He took a breath. "And what is my style?"

"To get a bigger hammer," she said.

"Whatever works, Janice."

"You think I'm weak, though, don't you?"

He felt an ache coursing through him, a pain that seemed to trace an old fracture running from his toes to the top of his head. "Of course I don't. If I'd gone through what you had…"

"But you have," she said, cutting him off. "That's just it. You lived through the very same things. But you just step over the bodies and keep on trucking. I'm the one who can't maintain…"

"Janice…" he said, reaching for her.

She waved him off. "Stop it, Deal. Stop looking at me like that. God. You should see yourself."

He sat back in his chair, shaking his head.

"Something's funny?"

He threw up his hands. "Trying to have a conversation with you. It's like taking a test that there's no right answer to," he said.

She considered it a moment. "It's not a test, Deal," she said.

"No?" he said, meeting her gaze. "Then what is it?"

She opened her hands. "Our life," she said. "That's all it is."

The waitress went past the doorway again, her apron slung over her shoulder now. The place was quiet, Deal thought, only he and Janice holding up the parade. He glanced at his watch, turned back to her.

"I'll just say one thing, Janice. Everything that happened to us, to you…well, how I used to take it was, it really happened to *me*. It was something *I* had to address."

She started to say something, but he motioned her silent. "But I'm not the one who was kidnapped, and I'm not the one who was burned." He saw her hand go automatically to her cheek, pull a lock of hair forward, still covering scars no one else could see. "I can't know what you felt, Janice. I can't know what you feel now. But I don't think you're weak." She glanced at him, then away, began toying with her coffee cup.

"I can't change the past," he said. "But I'm willing to do whatever I can now. That's all. That's all I wanted to say."

She nodded, her eyes following a design of wet circles she fashioned on the tabletop with the cup. "The worst thing's been about Isabel," she said, softly. "You know what that's like, keeping yourself away from your own daughter?"

He could only shake his head.

She set the cup away, clamped her hands between her thighs, stared up at the ceiling. "Because you know you're so screwed up you don't want her to see you?"

"Isabel wouldn't..."

Janice whirled on him, her eyes flashing. "Don't say it, Deal. Don't tell me she wouldn't know. I had a mother who was crazy as a barn owl and I thought, oh, I made it out okay, I escaped, I'll never be like her, and look!" She broke off to stare at him defiantly, sweeping her hands about her.

Deal knew about Janice's family, of course: her father a once-successful farmer whose slide into alcoholism mirrored the decline of the sugar beet industry in northern Ohio, her mother a classic enabler who finally joined her spouse, neck-deep in the sauce. They'd finished it off with that head-on collision with an eighteen-wheeler, headed the wrong way up a freeway exit on a snowy afternoon. The highway patrol had called it an accident, but Janice always added: "Yeah, the accidental part was, my old man intended to smash into a bus."

She was staring intently at him now. "I'm better now, Deal. I'm on the road back, at least. I'm ready to see Isabel, for Isabel to see me. But it's still hard, it's still one foot in front of the other, one step at a time."

And what about us, he wanted to say, where do you and I figure in? But he didn't. He met her gaze and nodded his understanding, and that was all he could manage. "Isabel wants to see you," he said. "Whenever you want."

She bit her lip. "Thanks," she said.

"It's late," he said. "I think they're ready to get us out of here." He eased one foot out from under the sleeping dog, then the other. Maybe he could just leave it there, he thought. A new mascot for the Ruptured Duck.

"What about Arch?" Janice said. She hadn't budged.

"What about him?"

"This thing about the Mega-Media site. You're just going to give up on it?"

"Of course not."

"So what's next?"

"I don't know," he said. "I could go back to Custer, try to find out if he knows anything..." He shook his head at the prospect. "If I could find somebody who worked for the contractor, it might be easier, but since they're from Omaha..." He broke off.

"Where Arch's sister Sara is from," Janice added.

"Probably just a coincidence," Deal nodded.

"Maybe," Janice said. "Tell me again who this outfit did work for."

"The Sioux nation, IBM, the Worldwide Church of Light..."

"That's the one," she said, stopping him.

"The one what?" Deal had his eyes on the waitress, who stood at the end of the bar, cutting glances at them as the cash register chunked out the spools of the nightly report.

"Arch's sister worked for that big-time televangelist in Omaha, the International Church of something or other. Arch was embarrassed about it. He told me Sara was always sending him reams of stuff about what this guy was doing, spreading the word and all. If that's the outfit Carver did work for…"

"Then Sara Dolan could put me on to someone at Carver."

"It's a shot."

Deal considered it. "The trouble is, nobody's been able to get in touch with Sara. I tried Information earlier, just wanted to tell her about Arch, but she's unlisted…" He trailed off, frustrated.

Janice shook her head. "Amazing, isn't it. Arch gets killed, his family doesn't even know about it."

"More than amazing," he said. He sat a moment, running it all through his head. Finally he turned to Janice. "You've got a key to the bookstore, right?"

Janice nodded, her expression uncertain.

Deal checked his watch again. "Maybe you'd be willing to go over there with me."

She shook her head. "I don't know, Deal…"

"Look, you said Arch's sister sent him literature from this outfit. At the very least, we can get her phone numbers. Maybe someone in her office can help out."

She closed her eyes for a moment. "The thought of going back there…"

"Janice, you'd do anything you could to find out who did this to Arch, wouldn't you?"

She opened her eyes, shook her head wearily. "That's the thing about you, Deal. Start swinging that big hammer, everybody else get out of the way."

He smiled, bent to pick up the dog. "In and out in fifteen minutes, tops."

Chapter 13

The ringing of the phone had insinuated itself so neatly into Rosenhaus's dream that for a few seconds he was lulled even further into what had become a rare emotional state for him: the gratifying illusion of being loved and sought after by other human beings once again. The hordes who hated him for his success, gone. The hordes who toadied up to him wanting to feast off his success, also gone. Here, in this dream, he could simply be and be valued for his essence, or so it seemed.

Specifically, he had discovered that he'd written a novel, a Tom Wolfe-like chronicle of political, sexual, and economic machinations in American publishing, a work that turned out to have made Michael Korda's ruminations on power seem sophomoric. A *Times* review had said he'd not only outdone Wolfe, but Wolfe's own idol, Dickens himself. Redford's company had already bid twenty million on screen rights. He suspected the ringing phone signaled a call from Bob himself—how would Rosenhaus feel about an older guy playing the lead…

…but before Rosenhaus could press the button that would put Redford onto speakerphone, the dream evaporated, leaving him tangled in the bedsheets and flailing about to find the source of the incessant, wretched ringing that had disturbed his sleep.

"This better be good," he barked into the phone. He read the glowing numbers on the bedside clock—2:07 A.M.—vowing to see that whatever hotel operator had allowed this disturbance would be fired.

"Don't go getting testy with the help now," Rosenhaus heard his new business partner's voice. "I explained how important it was, they had to put me through."

Rosenhaus struggled to an upright posture, his back against the padded headboard. Had he grumbled his intentions out loud? He tried to calculate, but he was still too groggy. "What the hell time is it where you are?"

"This is unusually spiritual talk from you, Martin. God. Hellfire and damnation. You've been sitting up late, peering into the deeper recesses of the soul, have you?"

"I was sleeping," Rosenhaus said irritably as another veil of irrational pleasure whisked away from his waking self: in his dream, he remembered, Mega-Media had committed to a million-copy laydown of his new novel, a record order by a long shot. It hadn't occurred to him as he slept that being CEO of the company might have had something to do with that extraordinary vote of confidence; but now, awake, the businessman in him not only saw that commitment for the hollow gesture that it was, but also felt a chill at the prospect of the hundreds of thousands of returns he would surely have had to handle. Thank God he hadn't actually written the book, he thought.

"I was sleeping, too," Rosenhaus's caller said. "Ten to midnight. Then up for three to four hours, then a couple more of sleep. Observation of the animal world, Martin. A horse, for instance. A horse will do its horsy thing in the field, eat a little bit, have a snooze right there on his feet, then he'll wake up and go about his business, eat some more, take a nap…he'll go on like that around the clock, left to his own devices."

"Is that what this call is about," Rosenhaus asked, "the diurnal cycle of the horse?"

"A city person such as yourself ought to reconsider what might be learned from a closer observation of the animal kingdom."

"Dog eat dog," Rosenhaus said. "How about that? There's also one about minks I admire."

It brought a response that was either gruff laughter or a snort of derision. "I just wanted you to know we were able to help you out on that zoning issue."

"Zoning issue…?" Rosenhaus began, then realized. Eddie Lightner. Guy with his ferretlike grin offering to smooth over the problems at the Miami building site. For a price. When he heard Lightner's figure, Rosenhaus had placed a call to his new partner. Lightner was a minor irritation, really. But they were already well over budget, and they'd hoped to get the store, the largest in a chain of enormous stores, open before South Florida's season had slipped entirely into the summer doldrums. There was a substantial supplemental stock offering planned. Glowing news from Miami would help.

Rosenhaus switched the phone to his other ear. "Well, that's good. I'm glad to hear it."

"Glad to help when I can, Martin. But we can't make a habit of these things, you know."

"So what did it cost us?" Rosenhaus asked. *Us*, he thought, still uncomfortable with the thought of a partner. He'd been leery when this merger had been proposed, but someone waves a hundred million dollars in your face…and besides the money, it appeared there would be other advantages, aligning himself as he had. In this instance, apparently, how easily a more experienced "negotiator" had swept aside a bothersome matter. He figured it might have required half the sum Lightner'd been asking.

"You don't want to know."

Rosenhaus heard the finality in the voice, felt a sudden jolt of concern. "Wait a minute…"

"The matter has been dealt with, Martin, that's all you need to know."

"But…"

"A man like that, once he's seen a person pay him off, you don't know what he'd turn around and do. What he came to us about didn't amount to a hill of beans. But some of the things he said suggested he knew about our arrangements, Martin. He was insinuating several insane threats. With that new telecommunications bill passed, there'll be any number of people trying to do what we're doing, the price of business is going to go way, way up. We simply can't have that."

"How could he have known about us?" That was one of the conditions of the partnership. Absolute secrecy. Let the word get out, it could drive up the price of pending acquisitions, wreck an intricate plan it had taken them nearly a year to hash out. But once everything fell into place…well, it would create an entity unprecedented in the media world. They'd not only make a fortune, they'd have power beyond politics, beyond borders, beyond reckoning. Rosenhaus understood the need. It was in his interest, too.

"I've been wondering about this man's source myself, Martin…"

Rosenhaus heard the innuendo. "Come on, now," he said. "Surely you don't think I'd say anything."

"My name isn't Shirley," his new partner said. "But loose lips sink ships. So let's just cross this item off the list and move along, what do you say?"

"Well, of course," Rosenhaus said. "Absolutely." He was trying to affect certainty, but his hand felt sweaty on the receiver now and his voice sounded strained in his own ears.

"By the way," the voice on the other end said. "You ever hear of someone named Deal? John Deal?"

Rosenhaus ransacked his memory. "I've met him briefly."

"Uh-huh. What did you two talk about?"

Rosenhaus sat up straighter. "Nothing. He was a friend of Arch Dolan's. I bumped into him briefly, that's all. What's this about?"

"Nothing," the voice came. "Just wondering."

There was a pause on the line. "You sound a little nervous. You're not getting weak-kneed, are you, Martin?"

"Absolutely not," Rosenhaus said. "Don't worry about anything down here. I'll be in touch."

"I hope not, Martin," his new partner said. "Not for a long, long time." And then the connection broke.

Chapter 14

"This is a little like Nick and Nora, don't you think?" Janice spoke over her shoulder, her voice determinedly light, echoing off the storefronts of the deserted street. Deal trailed behind her, waiting as the dog sniffed one parking meter, then another.

They'd parked in back of the store, but while Janice's key had opened the rear door, a chain lock barred their entry, and they'd had to come around to the front. Though the dog's leash had disappeared at some point in the evening, Deal had found a length of electrical cord in the back of the Hog, fashioned a stiff lead so he could bring the animal along. A good thing, too, he mused. The amount of piss the thing had left on the meters, he could have turned the front seat of the Hog into a lake.

"Nick and Nora who?" Deal asked. He rummaged through his memory bank, trying to sort out which ex-neighbors, which set of long-estranged friends.

Janice was at the front door of the store, had her key in the lock. "Nick and Nora Charles," she said, sounding exasperated.

Deal stared at her blankly.

"For God's sake, Deal. William Powell and Myrna Loy," Janice said. "*The Thin Man*, movie detectives from the thirties and forties. They drank a lot of martinis, they had a dog. They always caught the bad guys."

Deal nodded, finally with it, his mind suddenly full of flittering black-and-white images of ease, wit, and sophistication. High-rise apartments, cocktail shakers, villains in tails and cutaways.

"That's the movies for you," he said.

"It came from a book," she said.

"Dashiell Hammett," he said. "I've read them all."

"Then why didn't you say so?"

He shrugged. "I've been trying not to think about mysteries lately. It seems like tempting fate."

She gave him a look, pushed open the door. "Come on," she said. "We've only got a few seconds to bypass the alarm."

She found the little blinking panel in the dark, pushed a series of buttons. Several frantic red dots of light fell into placid, steady green.

She paused then. He stood behind her, heard her slow intake of breath, the even slower release. He imagined reaching out to take her shoulders in his hands, to steady her, pull her close…but somehow his arms would not move from his side. This mental push and pull, he thought. If anyone asked him, did he want her back, he'd wonder at the stupidity of the question. And yet, this close, some force, some fear perhaps, held him still.

"I can do this," he heard Janice say, though it seemed as if she were talking to herself more than him. In the next moment, she'd flipped another switch, and the room was bathed in light.

The shelves were upright once again, the books aligned in what seemed like orderly rows. Janice moved forward, pulled down a pair of volumes. "Philosophy," she said with a sigh. "Right next to Robert Waller." She turned to Deal. "I've got to get in here, straighten things up."

Deal nodded. "Sure," he said. "That'd probably be good."

She dropped the two books on the sales counter, motioned him through an archway. "The office is back here," she began, then gave him a distracted smile. "I don't know why I'm telling you, though. You built the place."

"I didn't build it," Deal said, following her through the passage. "A guy named McClelland did. I just traced over some of his work."

She was into the third room now, flipping another light switch, moving down a book-lined corridor of shelves, shaking her head here, throwing up her hands there. "It's a mess. It's going to take forever."

She stopped in front of the door with the joke-shop brass plate: Nerve Center.

"That's important to you, isn't it, Deal?" she said, turning to him.

"What's that?"

"You didn't build it, you just remodeled it."

"Sure," he said, shrugging. "It'd be like me putting out a new edition of Shakespeare, then claiming I'd written it."

She paused, gave him what seemed a wistful smile. "You're good at what you do, though. Did I ever tell you that?"

"I seem to remember," he said, trying for a smile of his own.

There was another moment then, the place hissing with quiet, her eyes steady on his, him noticing the worry lines about her eyes, the mole that dotted the flesh between the corner of her lips and the bold line of her chin, the quiet scrabble of the dog's nails on the parquet flooring at their feet...

"You okay to go in there?" he said finally.

She closed her eyes briefly, bobbed her head up and down.

"I can do it by myself," he offered.

"I'm all right," she said, turning from him, swinging the office door open wide.

❀ ❀ ❀

They'd been at it nearly an hour, Deal at Arch's desk, the drawers, the pile of mail on the accountant's side table, Janice

at the files. He'd found Sara's Omaha phone and address on
the Rolodex and, under the desk blotter, a yellowing birthday
card to Arch signed "your loving sis." Janice had taken down
a photograph from a bulletin board to lay in front of him:
Arch standing before the lighthouse at the tip end of Bill
Baggs Park out on Key Biscayne, one arm slung about Sara's
shoulders, another about his younger sister Deidre's.

Deal stared into Arch's guileless eyes. A guy he could say
anything to, ridiculous or sublime—the price of two-by-
fours is up, my life's gone to hell—didn't matter, he could
always expect a reasoned answer. Decent, selfless Arch. And
Deal getting old enough to count the rare value of the loss.
You make true friends so easily when you're young—and
with equal difficulty later on.

He turned the photo onto its face, turned in the desk
chair as Janice rolled another heavy file drawer shut.

"Nothing?" he asked.

She shook her head, sank into a cross-legged posture on
the floor, pulled the bottom drawer out toward her. "The
cops have been through all this stuff," she said glumly.

"Yeah, but I don't know how interested they were," he
said. She nodded, but her enthusiasm had clearly waned.
Deal knew how she felt. It was late and they were both tired
and the longer they spent, the more hopeless it seemed.
Driscoll'd said it plenty of times: detective work was the
most boring activity in the world, 99 percent of the time.

They sat facing each other for a moment. "You really
think it was all about books?" he said finally.

She stared at him, brushed her hair back over her ear,
then pushed it forward again quickly. He felt a pang, found
himself wanting to lean forward, take her hands, tell her
gently how her ears were fine, how the doctors did a flawless
job, how the scars were hardly noticeable…but it had been
an unconscious gesture, something so deeply embedded in

her by now, how much good was his earnest meddling going to accomplish?

"I know what you mean, Deal," she said. "I was pretty naïve about the book business myself. You see it as this labor of love, a mom-and-pop kind of enterprise, and it was really, until big business got involved. Then you find out what the stakes are, the kind of money that's riding on stock offerings, on making bestsellers, it turns you around." She broke off, gesturing out toward the store. "I was at the front register the other day, a publisher's rep stopped on his way out, he wanted to know how much we got for displaying books in the 'Staff Recommendations' racks. I didn't know what he was talking about. I told him we each displayed the books we cared about, thought other people should read, too. He told me how the chains get paid thousands of dollars by publishers for doing the same thing." She threw up her hands. "I told Arch we should at least make up a sign, 'Staff has received no promotional considerations for the display of these books.'"

"It's scummy, all right," Deal said, "but I'm not sure what it would have to do with someone killing Arch."

She closed her eyes for a moment, nodding. "I know," she said. "I know how I must have sounded right after..." She broke off, waving her hand upward, toward the room where Arch had been found. "...right after it happened. Faced with something like that, your mind just fixes on what's convenient. I heard what Driscoll said, how it doesn't makes sense some monster corporation would be involved when they're going to steamroll you anyway..." She broke off for a moment, then fixed him with a stare. "But you must think there's something funny, too, or we wouldn't be here, not unless you're just humoring the distraught wife."

"Janice..."

"You're a nice guy, Deal. Nice guys do things like that."

"Not in this case," he said, his voice firm.

She shrugged, seeming to buy it, but whether he'd really convinced her was hard to say. Finally she sighed, turned back to the open drawers, began a determined rifling through the hanging folders.

"It's all a mess, Deal." Her voice was doggedly upbeat. "Old P&L statements next to Author's Agents, Possible Vacations—that's a laugh, he *never* had a vacation..." She turned back, shaking her head. "He's even got *books* in here."

She reached into one of the bulging folders, pulled out a volume with a battered dust jacket, held it up for Deal to see. *The Court of Last Resort*, Deal read. *Shocking stories from the files of* True *Magazine*, went a subtitle. He reached to take the book from Janice, wondering what Arch would be doing with such a book as that in his personal files.

"What else is in that folder?" he asked as she handed it over.

She glanced down, shaking her head. "Nothing."

She was looking away when she let go of the book, and Deal missed the exchange. He caught a corner of the lurid dust jacket, felt the book itself slipping free, opening a jagged tear across the cover illustration: a man strapped into an electric chair, an executioner about to throw the switch, an intrepid reporter dashing pell-mell down a hallway with his hand upraised, trailed by a crowd of cops and prison officials. Before Deal could bring his other hand up to catch it, the cover gave way altogether and the yellowing volume shot downward.

The corner struck the floor between his feet with a cracking sound. Pages shot free from the shattered spine, and Deal felt an illogical flash of guilt—dumbhead book or not, for some reason Arch had felt it worthy of safekeeping. Now he'd ruined the thing. It'd probably turn out to have some great arcane value, he thought, sweeping the pages up hurriedly. Deal the fumbling detective, diminishing Arch's estate by a major factor.

He glanced sheepishly at Janice, who rolled her eyes. Then he felt something...a difference in textures at his fingertips, a slickness, a weight...he glanced down, realized what he was holding was not one of the rough-cut pages that had split from the book's binding, but something of much heavier stock, card stuff, almost. The piece had been folded in half, must have been tucked inside the volume.

He laid the ruined book aside, turned the card over, unfolded it. It took him a moment to comprehend what he was looking at, but then, even as he stared at the bold block letters printed there, all the loose shards of thought that had been jiggling inside his mind began to mesh, pieces of a stubborn puzzle finally falling into place.

"Look at this," he said, nudging Janice, who had squatted down to resume her digging through the files.

She took the card in both hands, scanned it, shaking her head. "Asbestos...stop order...," she said, her voice puzzled.

"Check the address that's written in the blanks," he said.

She glanced at the card again, and this time her mouth formed an O. "It's right across the street."

"Check the handwriting in the corner."

He pointed to a hastily scrawled note: "A—You may be amused. Call me.—E.L."

"E.L.," she said. "Eddie Lightner?"

"Arch's trump card," Deal said, reaching to take the card back from her. "He told me he had a couple of tricks up his sleeve. This must be one of the things he was talking about."

He reached across the desk for the telephone. "If you were a hotshot CEO, what Gables hotel would you pick?" he asked her, already punching numbers.

She stared at him, still puzzled. "The Biltmore, I suppose, but why...?"

"I'll explain it in a minute," he said, then motioned her for quiet. "Miami," he told the operator. "The Biltmore Hotel...and the Grand Bay, just in case."

As it turned out, he didn't need the second number and it wasn't really that much of a surprise. Any other city the size of Miami, there'd be half a dozen choices at the very least—but here, where thirty years ago there'd been a hotel glut, there was the Biltmore in the Gables, the Grand Bay— and maybe the Mayfair House—in Coconut Grove, a few miles away, and then there was everything else. In addition to the steadily decaying mainstays, there had appeared some pleasant enough chain hotels catering to business travelers, and a few renovated Decostyled inns on South Beach, but investors had steered clear of lavish hotel building for a good long time.

Too bad for big-bucks travelers, Deal thought, good luck for him. Yes, there was a Mr. Rosenhaus registered. No, he could not be disturbed. It was 4:00 A.M., after all. Which led to their being in the Hog at this moment, headed toward…well, toward some sort of confrontation, although Deal hadn't figured out the precise shape of it yet.

Deal swung the Hog off Coral Way at Granada, sped down the two-lane road that here seemed more like a leafy-roofed tunnel than a city street.

"You're going to get a ticket," Janice said, clutching at her armrest.

"Probably," Deal said, pressing the accelerator down. "They do tickets pretty well in the Gables."

He was at seventy now, the Hog's motor settling into a purr that seemed ever more contented the faster they went. The thick trunks of the banyans, oaks, and ficus that canopied the street flashed past in a blur, clouds of leaves whirling up in a glowing wake he could make out in his rearview mirror. It was like a dream-drive, Deal thought: the car hurtling like some capsule out of time, Janice on the seat beside him, her face pensive, reflecting the ghostly green light from the dash…

He turned back to the road, saw a car edging to a stop on a side street up ahead, caught sight of the familiar flasher rack on the roof. His foot flew to the brakes, knowing he'd be late, late, late...

Then his headlights illuminated the lettering on the vehicle's side, the logo of some home security outfit, a Beagle Boys burglar with his hands upflung, a rent-cop drawing down on him.

Deal hit the accelerator again, blew past the intersection, shooting a skiff of oak leaves over the rent-cop's hood. "You're lucky," Janice said.

Deal shot a glance her way. "In this instance, yes," he said.

"Would you like to remind me why we're doing this?" She pointed out the window in the direction they were traveling.

"Sometimes you just need to shake the tree, see what might fall out." He could see himself in the reflection of the window behind her: his shrug, his deadpan expression lit in the glow of the dash lights. It seemed the sort of thing Driscoll might have done, he thought.

"Why don't we just take the thing to the police?" Janice said. At Deal's request, she'd folded the stop order, put it in the purse that rested on the seat between them, beside the sleeping terrier.

"And what do you think Floyd Flynn would do with it?" Deal asked. His eyes were forward now, locked on the luminous spire of the Biltmore, which rose up in the distance like a beacon. "Thanks very much, Mr. and Mrs. Deal, we'll take this information into account just as soon as I study Eddie Lightner's sexual technique a couple more times."

"Still...," she said. "I don't see what you hope to accomplish."

Deal shrugged, turning off Granada onto a side street that led to the hotel's entrance. "I'm not sure, either. But if nothing comes of this, I can always go see Floyd Flynn, right?"

She shrugged, then gasped, pointing at something in front of them. Deal had stopped at a cross street, was about to pull on through, but now stared as a grayish-hued animal the size of a dog, trailing a huge, bushy tail, trotted gracefully across the intersection in front of them, giving the Hog a sidelong glance as it mounted the opposite curb and disappeared into the darkness.

"That was a wolf," Janice managed, her voice a mixture of fear and surprise.

"A fox," Deal said, thinking how glad he was the dog at his side hadn't been awake to see it. "They're just a little smaller."

"It's the same thing," Janice said. "What's a fox doing in the middle of Coral Gables?"

Deal shrugged. "It probably lives on the golf course. I used to see them out there, years ago. I had no idea there were any left."

"You say it like it was a good thing," Janice said, her voice still reflecting amazement.

"Well, it is, isn't it?" Deal turned to her. "They don't hurt people. They eat rabbits, possum, raccoon. Maybe a house cat every now and then."

"It's the city, Deal. There aren't supposed to be wolves running around a city."

"Yeah, well, I guess somebody forgot to tell him."

They stared at each other in silence until Janice finally turned away.

"It's the same thing with Arch, you know," he found himself saying.

At that, Janice turned back to him, her face a mask of disbelief.

"I'm serious," he said. "Arch and his bookstore. Some people would say he was like that fox, some creature out of time and place. World's changed, so close down your mom-and-pop operation, Arch, go burrow somewhere else, leave retailing to the big boys, they know how to move those bestsellers."

"You have a very strange way of seeing things, Deal."

"You disagree with me?"

Janice sighed in exasperation, but something like a smile crossed her features.

"Are we really going in there?" she asked, turning to point at the massive hotel that rose up before them like some fairy-land palace: spires, bell towers, cupolas, and curlicues, Gothic archways, and cantilevered balconies everywhere, all of it lit up golden against the night. His boyhood dream, finally come to life.

"We gotta go in," Deal said, and guided the Hog up the long, elevated incline that led to the second-story entrance of the hotel.

◙ ◙ ◙

"That valet looked at you a little strangely," Janice said. She kept her voice low, trying to keep it from echoing as they crossed the immense tiled lobby. Deal wondered who she was hiding it from. The bellhop stand was deserted, the public rooms empty, even the reception desk was unoccupied.

"He doesn't see too many cars like the Hog," Deal said. "Not to mention it's 5:00 A.M." He gave her a smile. Even though his adrenaline was pumping, he was beginning to feel a bit light-headed. His eyes roamed the lobby automatically, taking in the heavy furniture—all of it original, or seeming so—the decorated columns, the gilt-work on the vaulted ceiling, the antique pieces in the dim recesses. Amazing. As a kid, he'd peered through the grimy windows into this room, it had looked like the kind of place where winos would hold a convention, and had. Now it was a show-piece. A museum. Not only had it cost a fortune to restore, he thought, it would cost another fortune to maintain. He wondered idly how long it could last.

On their way to the reception desk, they had to work their way past a pair of sizable aviaries, both of them draped to keep the birds quiet for the night. "These are the hundred-dollar rooms," Deal said, gesturing at the big cages.

"Funny," Janice said.

"Other people have laughed at my jokes," Deal said.

She gave him a look, headed on to the vacant counter. Deal joined her there, gazed through an open door into an operations area where a young woman in a navy suit, her hair pulled into a tight bun, sat at a desk, vacantly sipping at a cup of coffee. When Deal cleared his throat, she started, sloshing coffee onto her hand. She stood quickly, started to wipe her hand on her skirt, then stopped.

She hurried out toward them, waving her hand dry at her side. "I am sorry," she said, her accent vague. German, Deal wondered? Or Dutch? "I did not see you."

"It's okay," Deal said.

"You are checking in?"

"No," he said. "We came to see Mr. Rosenhaus. Martin Rosenhaus." He nodded at the computer monitor behind the desk.

She hesitated, glancing at her watch. When she looked up again, she was wearing a practiced smile. "Yes, well, the house phones are around the corner…"

"I know," Deal said, checking the girl's nametag. "I've already spoken to the operator, Mette. There's a block on Mr. Rosenhaus's phone."

"Ah," she said. "Well, then…" She opened her hands to show him that nothing could be done. "I will be glad to take a message," she added.

Deal nodded reassuringly. "I know it's late, Mette. But it's important." He turned his hand up on the marble counter between them, showed her the bill that he had folded there. Before she could protest, he had clasped her hand in his. "All I need is for someone to call upstairs, let Mr. Rosenhaus

Book Deal 189

know I'm here. Tell him it's Mr. Kendricks, from Carver Construction in Omaha. He'll want to see me."

The girl looked at Deal, then at Janice, who smiled pleasantly. "We were supposed to meet Marty for dinner last night. Our plane was delayed."

"The airline flies so late?" the girl said.

"Our own plane," Deal said. "We had a little trouble, had to set her down in St. Louis awhile."

The girl lifted her chin in acknowledgment. She glanced down at the counter, withdrew her hand from Deal's grasp, smoothed the front of her suit jacket. Even someone standing at Deal's shoulder wouldn't have been able to see her pocketing the bill.

"One moment," she said, picking up a phone. She turned her back to them, spoke softly into the receiver, using a language that Deal could not quite discern.

"Ya, ya," he made out, and the name of Kendricks and Carver, and then there was silence. After a moment, he saw the girl's head bob, and then she had turned back to him once again. She glanced quickly around the lobby, then opened a drawer beneath the counter. She withdrew a key and slid it across the marble to Deal.

"It's the thirteenth floor," she said, pointing across the lobby toward a bank of elevators. "Use the first car. You must use the key to make the elevator stop there."

Deal palmed the key, smiled his thanks, extended his arm for Janice. "Good old Marty," he said. "I knew he'd be happy to hear from us."

⊗ ⊗ ⊗

"You gave her a hundred dollars?" Janice said. She'd let go of his arm the moment the elevator doors had closed behind them, moved into the opposite corner of the car.

Deal found the key slot beside the button for number 13, inserted it, twisted. As the car began to rise, he turned, gave her a sheepish look. He reached into his pocket, opened his palm, displayed the same folded-up bill with a sliver of Ben Franklin's grin showing.

"But how...?" She began, as Deal clasped her hand between his own. She gave him a look, withdrew her hand, glanced down at the bill in her hand, unfolded it.

"This is a five," she said, protesting. "How did you do that?"

"Actually I gave Mette a ten," he said. "I figure that's fair. Besides, you fold a ten the right way, it can look like a hundred at a quick glance."

"Deal..." Janice said, still aggrieved.

"Blame my old man," he said. "Work as a building contractor long enough in this town, you get pretty good at passing bills around. It's one thing he taught me that still pays off, no pun intended." He nodded as the elevator car began to slow and the number 13 lit up on the burnished brass panel. "You can keep the five," he added.

"Forget it," she said. She was stuffing the bill in his shirt pocket when the elevator doors slid open and she stopped with a gasp. "Oh my God," she said, staring out into the opulent room that opened directly before them.

"If it was good enough for Al Capone," Deal said, taking her elbow to guide her out, "it ought to be good enough for Martin Rosenhaus."

🅐 🅐 🅐

They stood in the vestibule of the suite for a moment, caught by the other-era splendor of it all: Persian carpets, crystal chandeliers, the kind of fussy antique furnishings that Deal would never want but knew would cost a fortune. Even more impressive was the view: floor-to-ceiling windows that gave a 180-degree panorama, the streetlights of the still-sleeping Gables just below, the skyline of downtown Miami five miles to the east, all of it backlit by the barest hint of dawn edging up from the Atlantic in the distance.

"What was it Arch used to say, 'Don't get involved with books if you want to make money?'"

Janice shook her head. "Rosenhaus isn't 'involved with books,' Deal. He's basically playing the stock market, positioning himself for a big public offering."

They heard slapping footsteps then and turned to find Rosenhaus, still clad in pajamas and slippers, hurrying down a staircase that gave out into the vestibule behind them. He hit the bottom landing, was cinching the belt of his robe tight about his waist when he saw them. He stopped short, his expression of annoyance faltering momentarily. Shake the tree, Deal thought. You never know.

"What is going on here?" Rosenhaus said, his bluster back.

"Sorry to wake you," Deal said. "I'm John Deal…"

"I remember you," Rosenhaus said, his face dark. "What is this? I got a call saying the project manager was here, some kind of an emergency…"

"Maybe there is an emergency," Deal said mildly. He motioned for Janice to open her purse.

"This is my wife, Janice," Deal said, trying to ignore the flash of awkwardness that swept over him as he spoke. If Janice noticed, she didn't betray it.

"We were going through some papers in Arch Dolan's office," Deal continued, "we came across something interesting."

Janice gave Deal a look, handed over the folded stop order. Deal held it up in one hand, spread it open for Rosenhaus, who shook his head. "What's that supposed to be?" he said, still surly. His face was puffy from sleep, and there was a cross-hatching of lines on his cheek where he'd lain too long against some bunched sheets.

"It's a stop order issued by Gables Building and Zoning," Deal said. "It says they found asbestos shot through the Trailways building you all were planning to make into a bookstore."

"A media retail center," Janice said wryly. "Bookstore sounds a little quaint these days."

"I don't know what you're talking about," Rosenhaus said, glaring at Deal.

"Of course I don't know exactly what you ran into," Deal continued, "but judging by the way everything went to dead stop over there, I'd gather you've got yourselves a doozy of a problem. Kind of thing that could double, even triple a cost estimate, real quick, not to mention the down time. It's the sort of thing that makes stockholders nervous, the kind of problem building inspectors sometimes get paid to reconsider." Deal paused, letting the implication hang for a moment before going on. "I tried to ask this Kendricks about it, but he wasn't in the mood to be sociable…"

"You called Carver Construction?" Rosenhaus said, shaking his head in amazement. He looked more closely at Deal. "You want money, is that what this is about?"

Deal folded the stop order, handed it back to Janice. "No, Mr. Rosenhaus, I'm not here looking for money. What I'd like to know is what passed between you and Arch Dolan when he told you he'd found out about your little problem."

"You must be crazy," Rosenhaus said, "force yourself into my room and accuse me of some ridiculous…" Rosenhaus stopped then, stood staring at them, his jaw working. "I want you out of here," he said, gesturing at the open elevator.

When Deal didn't move, Rosenhaus reached for a phone resting on a narrow vestibule table. Before he could lift the receiver, Deal clamped his hand atop Rosenhaus's. Deal was close enough now to smell him—a hint of cologne, the sour musk of night sweat.

"Deal…" Janice called, but he did not turn.

"I didn't accuse you of anything. But somebody killed my good friend and I'd like to find out who that somebody was. If you talked to Arch Dolan about this matter before he died, I'd like to know about it, it's as simple as that."

Rosenhaus stared back at him, his eyes just inches away. Deal felt the man's grip on the phone relent, and he relaxed his own grip in turn, stepped back. Janice stood staring at the two of them, her face pale.

"I didn't talk to Arch Dolan about this or anything else," Rosenhaus said, straightening his robe.

"You think he was just saving that stop order for his scrapbook?"

"I don't have any idea what he was doing with it," Rosenhaus said warily. "As I understand it, there was a misunderstanding on the building inspector's part. The matter's been resolved. Or it's in the process thereof."

"In the process thereof," Deal repeated. "You mean the bag man's on his way to Clyde Custer's office? Or maybe you and he haven't arrived on an exact figure yet?"

"I've been very patient with you, Mr. Deal..." Rosenhaus began, his eyes darting toward the phone, the door. There was a sheen of perspiration on the man's upper lip.

"The fact is," Deal said, waving him off, "I can believe Arch Dolan might hesitate about confronting you with this. Even facing the prospect of losing his livelihood, it just wasn't his style. But obviously he knew about your little problem, and maybe someone knew he knew. Maybe this someone got nervous, went over to have a talk with Arch, things got out of hand..."

Rosenhaus laughed mirthlessly. "I think you need to take a pill, my friend."

"Don't worry, Rosenhaus. I know that's not your style either. But people who work for people, sometimes a problem comes up, they worry their job's on the line, they take matters into their own hands..."

"Carver Construction doesn't have to worry about some minor impediment on a single building project, Mr. Deal. It's a multibillion-dollar operation. They're building highways in Mongolia, a communications complex on the polar cap. They've got bigger problems on their minds. A thing like this wouldn't stop them or seriously affect my plans."

"So you've talked to them about the matter," Deal said.

Rosenhaus stared at him, his mouth clamped, his eyes narrowing. "I'm sorry about what happened to Arch Dolan, Mr. Deal. I can understand your being upset. But the implication that I had anything to do with his death is outrageous, *and* offensive." He glanced down at the intricately knotted Persian carpet at their feet, gathering himself. When he met Deal's gaze again, his voice was the modulated, self-assured purr that he probably used for stockholder presentations. "You insinuated yourself in here under false pretenses and I've answered your questions, outlandish as they are. Now I am asking you to leave. Or I'm going to call the police."

Deal felt Janice's hand on his arm. "Come on, Deal. Let's leave Mr. Rosenhaus to his outrage."

Deal turned, saw the spots of color high on her cheeks, felt the intense pressure of her grip. She was as angry as he was, he knew, just being more politic. And there wasn't any more to be gained from Rosenhaus, not now.

He took a breath and relented, following her pull toward the open elevator doors. The eastern sky was a welter of pinks and purples fighting out from a brawl of clouds above the distant Gulf Stream. Boats were already headed out there, he thought, sailors and fishermen on deck, at the wheel, keen to the wind and the salt spray like sea hounds, full of expectation and the simple pleasure of being alive. He could remember feeling that way.

"Just pray you're telling me the truth, Rosenhaus," he said. "I find out otherwise, you'll never want to see me again."

"That's exactly what I'm intending," Rosenhaus replied. And then, the elevator doors slid closed.

"You can forget about going into PR, Deal," Janice said. They were watching the numbers fall on the brass plate above them.

"Yeah, I'm going to cancel all those job interviews I had set up," he said.

"You think there'll be somebody waiting for us at the bottom?" She nodded at the burnished doors.

He shrugged. "The valet?" he said.

She gave him a speculative look. "You do this kind of chat pretty well. I'd forgotten that about you."

He turned to her. "It could be I've changed. You ever think about that?"

She held his gaze. "They say it happens."

They stayed that way for a moment until finally Deal turned away. "Slow elevator," he said, feeling the tightness in his muscles. He reached to massage the back of his neck. "I wonder how Driscoll would have handled it," he said.

"Maybe that's what it is," she said. "The two of you hanging around together."

He turned to stare at her in disbelief. "You're saying I remind you of Driscoll?"

She was about to respond when the elevator car settled to a stop and the doors jittered open. There were three of them standing there: a man in a dark blue suit, styled similarly to the one Mette of the desk had been wearing; a larger man in a plaid sport coat, gray slacks, and scuffed brogans just behind him, and finally the valet.

"Your car is ready, Mr. Deal," the first man said. His hands were folded in front of him, his face as carefully composed as an undertaker's.

The valet stepped forward, handed Deal his key. The Hog was visible, parked just outside the entry doors. The big man—Driscoll's poorer cousin, Deal thought—kept his flat gaze fixed on Deal as he reached to take the key from the valet's hand.

"This place is great, isn't it," he said to Janice. "We ought to come here every vacation."

"Service with a snarl," Janice said, urging him toward the door.

The covers had come off the birdcages, Deal noticed. Loud whistles now. Raucous squawks. A strangled voice, "Come again soon, come again." He gave the menacing trio behind them a last glance and ushered Janice out.

Chapter 15

"Maid service!"

Rosenhaus heard the voice, turned from the windows where he'd stood watching with a mixture of relief and satisfaction as Deal's odd-looking vehicle, toy-sized from this vantage point, inched out onto the sprinkler-glazed street below and disappeared beneath the thick canopy of trees.

Deal had nerve, he'd have to grant him that. But the encounter was another suggestion to Rosenhaus that he'd made a mistake: he'd underestimated either his new associate's stupidity or his capacity for chicanery. Rosenhaus considered himself a ruthless businessman, but these developments had gone far beyond anything he'd condone. He'd been willing to accept Arch Dolan's death as a tragic accident, but now, with what had seemingly happened to Lightner, he had to stop kidding himself. Here he was living in a gangster's penthouse, fending off amateur detectives…it was a far cry from what he was accustomed to. Changes would have to be made, and if his new partner didn't like it, well, there would be other opportunities, other sources of capital for ventures he could now outline to others with certainty.

He turned with a sigh, found a frumpy-looking woman in her fifties guiding a mop bucket off the elevator and into his foyer. What idiot had he to thank for *this* intrusion, he wondered. The place looked wonderful—despite its origins, where else was there to be found a suite like this, for instance?—and they *acted* like hoteliers, but there was something just a notch off-kilter. The entire staff needed a month's in-service at the Ritz, he thought; but then again, maybe it wouldn't do any good. Maybe it was the effect of the tropics—the heat, the humidity, this weird, overwhelming light, the lassitude, the *attitude* it seemed to engender. Bring in a brigade of Swiss Guards and inside of a month they'd be slouching around like natives, toothpicks in their mouths.

"No one called for service here," Rosenhaus said.

The woman couldn't be bothered to look at him. She had her foot on the bucket pedal, was squeezing water from her mop back into the pail. "Told *me* was a mess made in this room," she said, employing an Oakie accent that rattled the mirrors in the entryway. She yanked the mop out of her bucket, splatted it down on the gleaming parquet, made a swipe.

The mop cords lashed around a leg of the Queen Anne side table that held the phone, jerked the receiver off the hook.

"*I'm* telling you…" Rosenhaus began, mustering his most officious tone. He strode briskly into the entryway, reached to pull the mop handle from her grasp.

He was a step away when she spun around, her movements so lithe, so out of keeping with her dowdy appearance, that he was unprepared for what happened next. She had her left hand atop the mop handle, guiding it forward, her right hand gripping it low, giving it the astounding speed.

The wooden point caught him just beneath his breastbone, sending his breath from him in a *whoosh*. He staggered backwards, his feet straining to keep up with the frantic commands from his brain. He felt his back slam against some sharp projection, felt a strange sensation, as if a section of the wall behind him had broken, was sliding away. There was the sound of glass shattering, and he gazed down stupidly as shards of the mirror he'd dislodged burst about his feet.

He'd also stepped out of his slippers, he realized. He could see them on the rug just there, poised perfectly together where he'd left them, empty as the wicked witch's pumps. His feet felt oddly cold and wet, and he glanced down to see them sliding and slicing through the splintered glass. He caught a glimpse of redness reflected in a chunk of mirror, and then a flash of white, and he looked up to find her advancing upon him.

His mouth worked helplessly, popping open and shut, and though he willed himself to scream, what came was a pathetic wheeze that he suspected only he could hear.

"Spend a *life* cleaning people's messes up," she said. She tossed her mop handle aside, stepped forward, swung her open palms toward him like someone about to clap a mosquito out of the air. "You think because you're rich, you're immune? This is our job, mister. This is what we do. You talk to the wrong people, we have to clean up the mess before it gets any worse."

Rosenhaus's hands clutched his gut as tightly as if they'd been sewn there. He might have been able to fend this second blow off, if he'd been given about an hour to arrange his bodily responses. Instead, he could only stare, wondering who this "we" was, stupid as some aquarium fish, watching her hands fly to the sides of his head, clap soundly against his ears…and then there was an explosion of pain like nothing he had felt before.

"Speak no evil, hear no evil…"

…hard to believe he'd heard her utter the familiar refrain, given the roaring in his ears. But just as unlikely that he'd thought it, given the mad jumble in his brain: sheets of red, split by jagged bolts of light—synapses, neural cables shorn, left to snap about, spewing lava-hot sparks of pain, their ghostly afterimages.

He felt himself bounce backward off the wall again, felt his feet find an improbable balance and carry him out of the foyer, away, away. He was moving purely on instinct now, his vision returning in momentary, skewed flashes:

...the tall windows, the distant ball of sun, a golf course somewhere far below...

He blinked, fixed his wobbling vision on the staircase before him. If he could get up there, there was a door, maybe a lock, he could call downstairs...

He'd made the second step when he felt the hand clamp on the fabric of his robe, gather folds of it between his shoulder blades...

...he was going down then, brightly polished wood rushing up to meet his shoulder, his cheek. He was beyond pain now, as if his brain, overwhelmed by all the signals, had simply thrown up its mental hands and cried, "Enough!"

He'd also tossed aside the thought that this was some random, irrational assault, one more manifestation of unmerited terror visited on an unsuspecting Florida visitor. He knew, as he rolled across the thick carpet and came up on his hands and knees, what was to account for it, and the knowledge filled him with a despair that was almost the equal of his physical distress. He had underestimated his new partner, terribly.

He was gasping now, little gulps of air that reluctantly evened out into breaths. He blinked again, this time in surprise. The foyer, littered with glass shards and the streaks of blood his feet had left, was empty. No murderous charwoman advancing upon him, nor standing over him, ready to deliver the *coup de grace*, beat him to death with her Windex bottle...

He felt a wave of irrational gratitude sweep over him. Maybe just a warning, he thought. A wakeup call. Sure. He could understand that. He'd misread his new associate, he knew that, should have realized, given the sums of money involved. He had aligned himself with mobsters unwittingly.

He'd spoken out of turn, and someone had been sent. It was the way they did things, was it not?

He reached out, caught the arm of an aged, solid-looking chair, pulled himself to his feet. The roaring in his ears was unabated, and he felt warm fluid trickling down the sides of his neck, but that didn't necessarily mean irreparable harm. Such people knew how to do these things. Inflict pain but not lasting pain. The idea was to inflict fear. The willingness to obey.

No problem there, Rosenhaus thought. He'd make some phone calls, make amends, smooth the ruffled feathers. The sort of thing he could do better than anyone...

...get a fucking gun, a machete, a baseball bat and...

He forced himself to stop, as if such thoughts might somehow communicate themselves to his new partner. Plenty of time for that later. Right now, get up those stairs, get a lock secured, get a doctor over here...

He took one unsteady step toward the stairs, then another, and another...and wondered for a moment why he found himself running.

He didn't *want* to run, he told himself. He hadn't *willed* himself to run...and still here he was, picking up speed even as he puzzled over it, and might not have understood, right up until the last, had he not glanced aside, passing that great, gilt-framed mirror above the fireplace in the room where Al Capone himself had lounged and likely laughed over scenes not unlike such as this:

Rosenhaus saw himself in the mirror, smears of blood at his ears, his neck, staining the top of his robe scarlet. His mirror self stared back helpless, shocked, as he was propelled faster and faster across the room by the woman who had come to give him service, one of her powerful hands at the scruff of his neck, another at the small of his back.

He was gone from the mirror, then, from the thought of Capone, from the thought of anything, really. Rosenhaus felt her release him, turned in time to see a bank of paned and shining glass rush forward to return his upflung embrace.

He felt the conditioned air give way to the bite of Florida fall, all the cooler at this height. All the angles and reflections and distorted images had melted away, and he soared out over the canopy of trees, over early-morning golfers in their tiny carts, over tennis players and linen trucks, a grocer's van, over squawking courtyard birds, early risers at their coffee, and lap swimmers, and one woman wrapped in a long robe, her hair trussed turban-fashion in a towel…

…who one looked up from her book—which, as she would later marvel, had come from one of Rosenhaus's own stores far to the north—just as he flew down upon her screaming, to meet pool water as gray and unforgiving as steel.

Chapter 16

"Mommy's home," Isabel told him, her voice excited but contained, just above a whisper.

Deal stood in the doorway to the guest bedroom, trying to massage the fatigue he felt from his face, staring at his daughter. Isabel was sitting up in the bed beside Janice's sleeping form, her face radiant.

Isabel had been asleep in her own room when he and Janice had come back to the fourplex, both of them exhausted. Deal had convinced Janice to crash in the guest room, had left her at the doorway with a smile, a clasp of hands. Tired as he was, it had still taken him an hour to fall asleep, thinking about his own wife, sleeping down the hallway in their house.

He found a smile for Isabel, beckoned toward her. "Come on, Mommy's sleeping."

Isabel gave him a doubtful look, and he motioned again. He was sure she'd found Janice by instinct, and it both amazed and pained him. As often as not this past year, he'd awaken to find Isabel had sneaked out of her bed in the night to join him. She was a champion snorer, was wont to kick the bedclothes off, or pull them all from him, and it usually meant a less-than-full-night's sleep whenever it happened. And still, he stared at her now, feeling the pang of the dispossessed parent.

"Come on, Isabel," he said, trying to keep his voice to a whisper.

Isabel stared back at him mildly, not so much in defiance, but as if what he was saying simply did not carry meaning. "Mommy's home," she repeated. She burrowed down into the covers, nestling against Janice, who was face down against the pillows.

Deal was about to go for his daughter when one of Janice's arms snaked up from the bedclothes and wrapped about their daughter. Isabel's smile grew as she burrowed in tighter. *See, Daddy*, the look on her face said. Deal nodded, gave her a smile. He waved and padded back down the hallway to the kitchen, where he'd put the coffee on.

He stood at the open kitchen window as the machine wheezed and burbled through its last phases, watching the dog nose around the lawn, savoring the cool tang of the air, the aroma of the fresh ground beans, the moment's illusion of normalcy. They'd have to give the dog a name, he thought: Flash? Slick? Maybe he'd ask Janice what the Thin Couple called their pooch.

He flipped on the tiny countertop TV, found a local weather update, reveled in the news that it was fifty-eight degrees outside, that a front was on the way that would keep highs in the sixties, drop the temperature to a veritable bone-chilling forty-five in the night to come.

"Still watching the weather?" he heard, and turned as Janice leaned across the pass-through into the dining nook. Her face was still puffy from sleep, her hair tousled. She was wearing one of his T-shirts and the bottoms to an old jogging suit he'd hung in the guest room closet.

"Only in the winter," he said, "when there really is weather." He reached to flick the sound off, left the flickering image alive.

She nodded, giving him a grudging smile. She'd chided him about the habit all the way through their marriage. Her father, farmer to the core, had listened almost as passionately to weather forecasts as he had to grain and livestock reports. "Anything to keep conversation at bay," was Janice's assessment of her father's practice—and anything he did to remind her of the man was dicey.

"It does feel good," she said, coming to join him at the window. She stretched and yawned mightily, arching her back, thrusting her breasts against the fabric of the T-shirt, and, once again, Deal felt the odd, conflicting sensations. He wanted to take her in his arms, pull her close…and yet something held him back. Was he afraid she'd rebuff him, was that it? Or was it that he was afraid that she wouldn't? That whatever might happen then would lead to even greater heartache than what he'd felt to date?

He shook off the questions, irritated at himself for letting his thoughts twist into such impossible spirals. Janice, for her part, was leaning on the sink counter, her chin on her hands, staring sleepily out into the crisp Florida morning.

"That's some dog," she said, watching as the thing snuffed amidst a bed of impatiens.

"It needs a name," he said.

"It probably has one."

"Probably," he agreed. "What'd Mr. and Mrs. Thin call theirs?"

She turned, gave him a look. "Asta," she said. "They called it Asta."

Deal glanced out into the yard. "Doesn't seem to fit," he said. "What do you think of Shark Bait?"

She followed his gaze, shook her head. "Too sentimental."

Deal nodded. He'd be happy to do this for a hundred years or so.

"Where's Isabel?" he said after a moment.

She turned, gave him a real smile this time. "Back asleep," she said. "And snoring." She paused. "I'd forgotten how much I missed that."

Deal smiled back. "She's sure happy to see you."

Janice rolled about, hip cocked on the counter, regarded him. Deal fought the urge to check his own appearance. He was wearing a "We Will Rebuild" T-shirt left over from Hurricane Andrew's aftermath, a pair of rumpled sweatpants with a panther's head emblazoned on one leg, along with the logo of the Miami branch of the state university. He hadn't shaved, hadn't even combed his hair.

"Is she the only one?" Janice said.

Deal wasn't sure if he'd heard her tone correctly, took another look at the expression on her face. The smile was gone, but her gaze was unwavering, and, it seemed to him, inviting.

The same nagging questions were forming in his brain, but he dismissed them this time, no missed chances this time around. He leaned into her, bending to her upturned mouth. He heard her gasp involuntarily as their hips interlocked and he pressed himself into her.

Her mouth met his, her tongue probing, her breath harsh and driving his to a matching pace. He wasn't sure how long the kiss lasted, nor how long it took for him to get the drawstring to the jogging pants undone. It seemed to take only an instant, and on the other hand, it seemed to go on forever.

He had gotten his own sweatpants halfway down his legs when Janice raised one foot to the balky waistband and stamped down, jamming the pants into a wad about his ankles. He raised her onto the counter, noted vaguely that though the tile seemed almost frigid to his touch, she made no sound of complaint, gave only a groan of pleasure as he drove himself into her.

She fell back, throwing her hands apart to brace herself, to meet his thrusts with lunges of her own. One of her hands sent the blender cup bouncing off the still-glowing TV, the other knocking the still-open bag of coffee beans flying to the floor. Deal got one foot out of his wadded sweats, kicked vaguely to clear beans for a place to stand, though he was moving rapidly to a place where he could have done what he was doing while dancing on nails.

Janice had slid down, her head pressing against the counter's back-splash, pressing first the switch for the overhead lamp, then the other that started the disposal grinding. Outside, the dog had begun to bark at something, and a jet roared overhead, inbound, outbound, who the hell knew. Deal heard it all as a kind of music that counterpointed the growing white frenzy in his head.

Janice had twisted onto her stomach now, her toes barely touching the floor. Deal was behind her, his hands cupping her breasts, his feet crushing coffee beans against the tiles. Vaguely, he realized that the faucet had somehow gotten turned on in the sink, that the spigot was pushed too far sideways, that water was gushing freely onto the counter.

Outside, the dog's barking was an unbroken clamor. The jet seemed as loud as a rocket, the disposal an earth mover.

"The water," Janice gasped, her hands splayed flat, sliding about the slick tile countertop.

"Right," Deal said, and drove himself to bliss.

Janice might have started to say something else, but it dissolved into wordless cries. He was holding tightly about her waist with one arm, fighting a sudden weakness in his knees that threatened to send him down. Finally, without leaving her, he lunged for the faucet lever, managed to turn the thing off.

"I like that move," Janice murmured. She had her head resting against one crooked arm, was smiling, though her eyes were closed. "Can we try it again?" she said, wiggling back against him.

"The water's off," Deal said, still trying to catch his breath. He felt like he'd been back on the practice field, running gassers.

"We could fix that," Janice said, still moving against him.

"Maybe we could," Deal said, grinning down at her. He was actually thinking about reaching for the water faucet again, when he heard a new sound and lifted his gaze out the window to find Mrs. Suarez rounding the top of the outdoor stairwell, moving onto the breezeway landing not five feet away from him, her netted grocery bag in her arms.

It was only for a second that their gaze met, but the old woman had eyes a satellite sensor could use. Deal had no idea what expression he might have been wearing, but an impressive array swept rapidly over Mrs. Suarez's features: surprise, shock, even a hint of a smile as she turned away.

"What is it, Deal?" Janice said. She'd sensed something, popped her head up over the windowsill before he could say a word.

"Oh my God," she said. "Mrs. Suarez!"

"*Buenos días*, Señora Deal," Mrs. Suarez said without hesitation, still moving, her gaze still averted. She tossed one hand up in a kind of a wave, scuttling off toward her own apartment. And this time, Deal was certain he'd seen the smile on the old lady's face.

◎ ◎ ◎

"I suppose it could have been worse," Janice said, dumping another dustpan full of coffee beans into the trash. "It could have been Isabel."

Deal nodded absently, watching the way the fabric of the running pants molded her as she stooped to gather a stray bean or two. He'd mopped up the spilled water with a couple of towels, tossed them in the tub to drain, poured them both mugs of coffee—heavy stoneware, "CUP OF JOE TO GO" their logo, things he'd found in a supply-house bin a few weeks ago. He liked them: their weight, the old-fashioned language, the sort of objects that helped anchor a person, he supposed. Janice's coffee was still steaming on the counter while he savored his own, savored the simple pleasure of watching her move.

He supposed there had been other times he'd felt as good, but it didn't seem important to try and remember exactly when. "I liked the part where you turned on the disposal with the top of your head," he said. "Something we've missed all these years."

"Along with a barking dog." She gave him a smile, straightened to toss the last of the beans into the sink. She wiped her hands on her hips, picked up her coffee, regarded him over the cup as she sipped.

"There was an airplane in there, too," he said. "Or a rocket ship."

"Oh, there was a rocket, all right."

They laughed together, and then Janice grew quiet, sipping at her coffee thoughtfully.

"It was good sex, Deal," she said finally. She was staring out the kitchen window as she said it, her gaze fixed on something he could spend a lifetime looking for and never see.

"That it was," he said. He could hear the wariness in his voice, felt himself tightening, girding for...what? Carefree as he'd felt a moment ago, he sensed any calamity was suddenly possible.

She turned to him then, her gaze back in focus. "That's all we're going to call it right now," she said, as if she could read the dials trembling on his internal seismograph. She put out a hand, touched his arm.

"We agreed we were going to take this a step at a time, right?"

He nodded, let out his breath. "Any time you want to try that step over, make sure we got it right..." He trailed off, letting the suggestion linger.

She gave him a tolerant smile, finished her coffee. "So what's next?" she said, putting her mug back into the sink.

"With us?" he said.

She gave him a look. "I don't think that's a question we need to ask, Deal. Not right now." Her gaze held steady on his. "I think we just find out."

"Make it up as we go along?"

"See what happens," she said, nodding. "What do you think?"

"Fair enough," he said. He noticed the tightness in his gut had relented again, his breath had evened out. He reached out to touch her cheek and she squeezed his hand momentarily in return.

"More coffee?" she asked then.

He nodded, handed her the cup. She turned, poured for him. How long since anybody'd done that, he wondered.

"New mugs, huh?" she said, handing the cup back.

He shrugged. "I broke the last of those Matisse ones you bought."

She raised her brows in acknowledgment. "These look like they came from some diner in Bowling Green."

"They still have diners in Bowling Green?"

"If they have them anywhere," she said, shrugging. "I'm not going back to find out."

He thought a moment before he spoke. "You ever talk to the shrink about your folks?"

Her eyebrows came up again. He wondered for a moment if he'd transgressed again, shifted the conversation to forbidden ground, but she seemed relatively unbothered by it. "Some," she said finally. "We've been working more on the day-to-day stuff, mostly. We're leaving the Freudian matters for the major excavation team."

He had another sip of his coffee. "I never finished telling you about me seeing the shrink, you know."

She nodded. "The therapist probably had to go for therapy after you left."

"It went fine," he insisted.

"Yeah?" she said. "What'd you talk about?"

"Stuff," he said. He massaged his neck, checked the floor, the ceiling, came back to find her still staring at him.

"That it's hard, us being apart," he said, relenting. He took a breath. "About how to talk to Isabel, that sort of thing."

She nodded. "Well, I think it's great, your doing that, if it helps you feel better, I mean."

"Oh yeah," he said, nodding. He was remembering the confrontation with the meter reader cop, but decided to keep it to himself. Instead, he thought, he would tell her about the difference between carpentry and therapy. He was about to begin when first he noticed the news bulletin logo flashing on the TV screen and then he saw the familiar shape of the Biltmore swimming up to take its place.

❀ ❀ ❀

They watched in silence as the announcer passed along what few details had been released: Martin Rosenhaus, founder and CEO of Mega-Media, the nation's largest chain of media outlet stores, had plunged to his death, falling fourteen stories from the balcony of the palatial suite once regularly occupied by Alphonse Capone into the pool of the fabled hotel where Esther Williams herself had performed aqua ballet. Police were tight-lipped, but unidentified sources reported that a cleaning woman, herself unidentified, had stumbled into the suite only moments after the incident to discover a suicide note.

Deal switched off the set as a white-robed woman wearing something that looked like a turban on her head began to explain for the second time how big the splash was when Rosenhaus hit the water.

"Suicide..." Janice said, shaking her head in disbelief. She glanced at Deal in alarm. "We couldn't have frightened him that badly..."

"Rosenhaus was right about the asbestos problem," he said, shaking his head. "It may have slowed him down a bit, but it's not the sort of thing that could stop him, not all by itself."

"But if he killed himself..."

"It was suicide all right," Deal said grimly. "The assisted kind."

"I knew he was hiding something," she said, still stunned. "But I thought it was *him*, something *he*'d done..." She trailed off, staring helplessly at Deal.

"Well, I wouldn't rule that much out," Deal said, thoughtful.

"But who would want to kill Rosenhaus?" she said.

Deal shook his head, still pondering.

"The police must have learned we were with him last night, Deal. Why haven't they been here?"

He shrugged. "Maybe because Floyd Flynn's in charge," he said. "We were long gone by the time it happened, after all."

Janice walked slowly through the kitchen archway, sank down on one of the barstools on the other side of the pass-through. "First Arch, then Eddie Lightner, now Rosenhaus..."

As she spoke, an image began to form in Deal's mind, something from a kid's primer, a series of ever-larger sea creatures churning a kind of conga line through the depths, each about to swallow the one just in front, each about to be swallowed by the one just behind. "There's always a bigger fish," he said, softly.

"What?" Janice said, staring at him in puzzlement.

"Rosenhaus," he said. "He thought he was the biggest fish, but he was just chum, compared to the thing that got him."

She was about to snap back at him, demand some human terminology here, but then she softened, sat back in her chair.

"But who?" she said. "Who could have more riding on this than Martin Rosenhaus?"

"I don't know," he said. "But I'll bet if Driscoll were here, he'd tell you that was the key."

"If you're not going to talk to me, Deal..."

He saw the threatening look in her eyes, held up his hands. "I'm serious," he said. "That's exactly it. You ask the right question, sooner or later you're bound to find the answer." She still had her hands on her hips, was still glaring at him, when he picked up the phone and began to dial.

Chapter 17

"And such a plan demands a certain way of thinking, the need to take the long view. You can see that, can you not?"

When she hesitated, James Ray Willis's face darkened. Not just a frown or a scowl, but a manifestation of doom incarnate, a massive wave poised on the horizon and about to crash down. It suggested the dismay of the Egyptians, cowering as vast clouds of locusts obliterated their sun, the fear of the fleeing money-changers as the splintering of their tables echoed through the temples and the lash split their backs, the agony of the masses of Sodom as the fire rained down and lit them like tinder as they ran.

It was an expression that the Reverend Willis had spent years perfecting, and it had become effective enough even when viewed from distant rows in vast pavilions, or passed through the cool, filtering lens of the television camera. But viewed up close within the confines of an airless, windowless editing room buried under countless tons of rock and rich Midwestern soil, the effect would be palpable. A reminder that while the promise of the Word was of gentleness and forgiveness and of ultimate transcendence, there was nonetheless no unpleasant measure that would not be undertaken in order to move the benighted toward the light.

"Can you not?" Wills crooned again in his oddly formal speech. No one had ever spoken in such a way in the various places where he'd grown up, but that was part of the point, wasn't it, big Oakie boy with a moon face and the mark of a century's in breeding, overlay a hundred-dollar haircut and an off-kilter Alistair Cooke accent. Throw them off-guard, never give them what they expect.

Along with the odd syntax had come a note of urgency, however, and this time she nodded.

"Good," he said, settling back in his chair. The mask of doom was replaced by an avuncular smile, everything forgiven in an instant, a harbinger of God's gentle rain drifting down in endless bounty. Years of practice, years of preparation. "Of course you understand the plans. You read all these before you sent them off to your brother, didn't you."

He lifted a sheaf of papers from the desk beside him, riffled the pages with a finger, noted the widening of her eyes. "Oh yes, I had to take these papers back, the ones you sent off to your brother, Sara. I had to go to considerable effort and expense, send some of my best people all the way down to Miami to see that these were reclaimed. We just couldn't have knowledge of all these plans floating about, because it's a dog-eat-dog world out there, Sara. One little piece falls out of a great big puzzle like this…" He smiled, tapped the sheaf of papers. "Well, the whole works could get tangled up."

He paused, gave her a fatherly look. "And I want you to remember who sent these documents where they shouldn't have gone in the first place. It wasn't your intention, I know, but everything that's happened, Sara, well, ask yourself who's responsible."

He saw the look of pain and despair in the eyes, knew that if the gag were to be lifted from her lips, he would see the lips tremble, too. It was not his purpose nor his intention to distress her unnecessarily, but he was human, and she had disappointed him mightily.

"I am sorry," he said, and renewed his smile to show that he was sincere. "But you have been meddling in some extremely important matters, Sara." He gave her a sadder version of the smile meant to convey how much he cared, how difficult this was. "And before I decide what we're going to have to do, I thought we would take this opportunity..." He paused, searching for the words. "...to reorient ourselves, to *rededicate*"—he waved his arms in an encompassing circle—"to let you understand fully, once and for all, the importance of this mission."

He sat back in his chair, gazed up at the unpainted concrete ceiling past the blank eyes of half a dozen television monitors as if seeking counsel. He closed his eyes, began to shake his head gently from side to side.

"Lust," he said, clucking his tongue. "Lust," he repeated, the thought penetrating, clearly paining him.

He turned to her, and his eyes roamed her body, seeing, despite the shapeless dress that had been found for her, the mounds and curves and valleys he well knew.

"I cannot tell you what a disappointment it was. 'This person is different,' that is what I told myself when you joined us. And then..." He realized that his voice was rising again, and he forced himself to calm. He reached out, placed a reassuring hand on her inner thigh, patted gently.

"There is lust," he said, "...and there is love." His hand was moving slowly upward. Her eyes flickered at his face, then toward the hand that she could not raise her head high enough to see.

"The distinction is a fine one, of course." He held flesh cupped in his hand now, still smiling wistfully. "...but we have to make it..."

He left off his stroking motion, grasped a fold of flesh and twisted, watched her eyes widen with shock, her body turn rigid with pain and rise off the narrow bed.

He withdrew his hand and sat back in his chair. "I blame myself, of course. I let my own affection for you cloud my better judgment." His lifted his brows as if to countenance the fact that even he had been human.

"And I may have kept too much back from you, kept you from appreciating what I've undertaken." He gave her a chaste pat on the knee this time, waved his hand at the banks of electronic equipment lining the room behind him.

"And so that is why we have to talk now. Maybe we can reach some understanding yet, Sara. We'll just have to wait and see."

He bent forward then, and cupped her cheeks tenderly in his palms. His smile was back, blooming with the force of many suns. Seared by the force of this gaze, the lame might cast away their crutches, the aged turn lithe, the wayward become whole again.

"I know you can do it, sister. I by God *know* you can."

⦿ ⦿ ⦿

No telling what time it was, nor how long she'd been unconscious. A few minutes, a few hours, an entire day. No way to calculate by the nature of the litany above her, either. The fulsome voice recycled itself at intervals, as if the man were not a man at all, but some holographic image plucked out of the ether somewhere between the cameras of the soundstage and the satellites that boosted his image at one time within the cycle of a week to every country in the world.

She was locked in an awful unending nightmare, that was all she knew. Here, in the room where she'd been brought—Willis's private command post, a production room somewhere in the bowels below the subfloors of the deepest paranoiac bunker—James Ray Willis could be fully and finally transformed.

Down here he could blithely throw off whatever vestiges of humility he maintained in his guise of a "normal" life and become the creature he'd always dreamed of being. And it was her role to serve as witness. That much she knew. But for how long she had no idea.

She should have been able to see the signs earlier. His gradual withdrawal from everyday business affairs, from public appearances, his loss of zeal even for his legendary Sunday performances, his growing obsession with the technology that beamed him farther and wider with every week that passed. But instead, she'd unwittingly become a part of things, hadn't she. Computers, Reverend Willis. Let me tell you about some other things they do. Let me tell you about the World Wide Web.

With a sigh that died somewhere between her intention and the gag that bound her tightly, she rolled her head to the side, let her eyes fall open. His clothes looked the same as the last time she'd looked, but then they seldom varied: dark blue suit, perfectly pressed and starched white shirt, expensive silk tie in muted, abstract swirls. A television preacher who'd been to town. No clue there. Yesterday? Today? Tomorrow?

He'd told her the documents she'd sent to Arch had been recovered, that much she remembered. No hope then, no chance discovery, no person to put two and two together, come riding to the rescue. How much longer, then? How much more to endure?

Willis acknowledged her open eyes with a nod, as if he'd been waiting for her to return from some errand, a phone call, some distracting task. "When I began my planning," he said casually, his knee clasped in his hands, "I frankly despaired that all I aspired to could be accomplished, in any earthly lifetime. Hearst, Hapsburg, Holy See, they all had dreams and unlimited resources, and what did it get them?" He shrugged, adjusting his perch on the metal chair.

She was thirsty, and she needed to go to the bathroom, but if she signaled these things to him, there'd be the nearly unbearable show of solicitousness on his part. And there would also be the watching, no chance he'd allow her in that tiny rest room by herself. What might she do, crawl away down the drain? Hang herself with toilet paper? Wouldn't it be better for him if she did manage to kill herself?

Worst of all was the way he looked at her. As if all this pained him, somehow. As if prolonging the matter were some act of mercy. She'd be dead already had she never been intimate with the Reverend James Ray Willis, that much she knew. Never mind that it had lasted all of a month, that she'd meant as much to him as a new shirt. To Willis it meant he had to appear to ponder matters for a while, until he could manufacture some reason why she had to die, just as her brother had had to die, as the others he'd told her about had had to die, for the greater good of his cause.

Remembering how naïve she'd been sent a wave of shame over her, accompanied by a brief surge of anger. She tried to laser her fury toward him, beam it across the few feet that separated them, but Willis was looking elsewhere, and she was so tired, even such a pathetic attempt exhausted her.

"A knowledge of history did not keep me from pointing myself in the right direction, of course," Willis was saying. He seemed to be talking more to the ceiling now, or perhaps to the ages. "As the poet says, 'Ah, but a man's reach should exceed his grasp,/Or what's a heaven for?'" His smile broadened, and he reached to pat her hand, just where the heavy strap crossed her wrist.

This could not last much longer, she thought. Today, tomorrow, he would weary of the charade, worry that someone would find her, soon he'd shift from history to Revelations, show her the fate of the unfaithful.

"But so much has happened in this era, the network expanded so pervasively, I began to think, what if we'd been wrong all along, the way we'd been envisioning the millennium." He waved his hand dismissively. "Forgetting all the old scenarios, the rain of hellfire, the scourging of the unworthy, the ascension of the few, all of that."

He leaned forward, eager, so close she could feel his breath—hot, dry, the scent of mint—on her cheek.

"I see those images of African Bushmen drinking Coca-Cola, of Australian Aborigines wearing Nike ball caps, Mongolian cave dwellers where there's one pair of trousers for an entire family and it's a pair of Guess jeans, and I ask myself, how far away is the day? and what I mean is this"— he was so close to her ear now that his voice had dropped to a whisper—"how far away is the day when we can finally transcend the boundaries of race and nationalism and parochial self-interest and enter the common world, where the goals are made sensible once again, goals within reason. Where there's no longer a need to make a killing, but a simple living...where we have work that matters, modest homes, personal safety, our neighborhoods back...."

He fell back in his seat as if he'd overwhelmed himself with his rhetoric. "You and I know this, Sara, and everyone knows it in their heart of hearts. But no one's able to get the message across any longer. Doesn't it make more sense for me to be in control of the message-making than the godawful demons who are?"

He was no longer talking to her, she knew. The question, if it were a question, was meant for some far greater authority than herself.

There was silence then, and she saw that Willis sat now with his head back, his eyes closed, sweat glistening on his face, the very picture of a fighter collapsed in his corner after an exhausting match. The muscles were still working in his jaws, as if they were part of an unruly machine that simply refused to stop altogether and on command. He worked his shoulders, swung his head about, took great inhalations of breath, which grew more and more regular, until finally he calmed. When he opened his eyes again, she saw that he had become the old James Ray Willis for an instant, at least, a person, a human being who blinked, seemed to register her presence as if for the first time: who has bound this woman to a cot? how did I come to be here with her?

An instant only, and then it was gone. Willis averted his gaze, checked his watch. "There will be one world, sister," he said in a calm voice. "And it's coming soon, much sooner than anyone suspects." He gave her a smile. "Whoever controls the means of distributing the Word will also control the Word itself."

"Martin Rosenhaus understood something of what I'm talking to you about, but he failed, finally, because he took himself to be more important than the aim itself. He was a good businessman, but a poor prophet. His failure was a failure of vision."

Willis checked his watch again. "It will take a patient person and a humble one to bring these plans to fruition." He stood then, came toward her. "I intend to be that person, sister." His eyes swept over her, lingered here, lingered there.

"Who else did you tell about my plans, Sara? You want to tell me that?"

The question struck her like a slap. That's what it was all about, she realized suddenly, the only reason she was still alive. Distract her with all this talk of plans and goals and a better world, wear her down, then spring it on her. Of course. The moment he was sure his tracks were covered, she'd be gone. She stared back at him, her eyes as full of fury as she could make them.

Willis nodded, his expression unflappable. It was as if he'd forgotten he'd even asked the question.

"Well, that's enough for now, isn't it?" he said. His eyes swept over her once again. "You look worn out, sister. You need to rest and reflect." And then he was reaching for her. "Let's first just get you tidied up."

Chapter 18

"What is it?" Janice said, giving Deal a puzzled look. He pulled the receiver away from his ear, held it out to her as a tinny voice droned on.

"Another machine," Deal said. "Inviting me to make a pledge to the Worldwide Church of Light. For any number of good reasons."

She nodded, hardly surprised. He'd already filled her in on what he'd heard when he'd dialed Sara's home number again. This time, a computerized phone mail voice informed him that he had, in fact, reached the number he had dialed. He'd been invited to leave a message, another suggestion he'd passed up.

As the recorded message paused, Deal brought the receiver back, just in time to hear an actual person come on line. "Worldwide Church of Light," cool and professional, not unlike the recorded voice that had urged him to donate.

"Sara Dolan, please."

There was no acknowledgment, just a clicking sound as he was transferred, a couple of chirping rings, then another computer-generated voice. Deal listened in disbelief, then held the phone up for Janice as the message recycled itself:

"We're sorry, but the voice mailbox you have reached is no longer in service. The party you are trying to reach may have been transferred or is no longer with the organization."

Deal hung up, sat staring at Janice.

"You want to call back, try to talk to somebody else?"

"I don't think it would do much good. They don't seem much interested in conversation out there."

"Well, what, then?"

Deal sat thinking for a moment, then noticed movement at the doorway of the kitchen. "Give your daughter a good-morning kiss?" he said, pointing.

Isabel was standing there, her eyes darting back and forth between Deal and her mother. Her hands tugged uncertainly at the hem of her nightgown. When Janice turned to give her a smile, to hold her arms out, it was like watching a dam give way.

Isabel's face lit up, her uneasiness melting away. In an instant, she was running flat out, into her mother's arms.

"Mommy," she said as Janice gathered her up.

"Isabel, Tinker Bell," Janice said, holding her close. Deal felt something slip inside him, had to turn away for a moment. When he looked again, Janice was plopping Isabel onto one of the counter stools.

"You slept a long time," Janice said.

Isabel nodded.

"That's good," Janice said, giving Deal a look. She pulled down a bowl, found a box of Fruit Loops, eyed it suspiciously. "Is this what you have for breakfast these days?"

Isabel nodded. "Are you going to stay home now, Mommy?" she said, her gaze fixed on Janice's every move.

Janice found milk in the refrigerator, turned to add it to the cereal. "Mommy's going to come and see you lots and lots," she said. She gave Deal another glance, this one guarded.

"I want you to stay home," Isabel insisted, her voice rising.

Janice took a breath, looked at Deal again, finally leaned across the counter so that her gaze rested at Isabel's level. "Listen, sweetheart, you know Mommy loves you, don't you?"

Isabel nodded, but her lip was jutting.

"Well," Janice said, reaching out to stroke her cheek, "that's the most important thing right now. Mommy loves you very much and we're going to spend lots of time together, okay?"

Isabel gave another nod, this one somewhat more assured.

"Now, come on," Janice said. "Let's see you eat some breakfast."

Isabel gave her a doubtful look, scooped out a spoonful of cereal. Deal sucked in a breath of his own, turned to open the kitchen door, let the breeze in.

He was standing, staring out into the bright morning, when he felt Janice's presence at his shoulder. He glanced at her. "Pretty tough, huh?"

She nodded. "Nothing I didn't expect."

"At least Daddy wasn't in there singing harmony," he said.

She gave him a pained smile. "It's not a lot of fun, is it?"

He put the back of his hand to her cheek. "I seem to remember some fun."

She managed a laugh, but there wasn't a lot of joy in it. For a moment, they stood quietly.

"So what can we do, Deal?"

"About Sara, you mean."

She nodded.

He ran a hand through his hair. He could forget all this, he thought. Go in to his office, get some bid letters out, let Floyd Flynn and company handle the detective work. Maybe things were just that simple: Arch had been murdered by robbers, Lightner done in by a disgruntled associate, Rosenhaus by his own hand. All the connections between the three simply coincidence, as it was simply a coincidence that Sara Dolan had chosen to take a vacation or quit her job, just vanish without telling anyone in her family where she might be going.

Too much happenstance? So what. What was he supposed to do about it? He had troubles of his own. A half-dozen building projects that needed his attention, a family to put back together, a life. Where did it say this was his responsibility? He paid taxes, his taxes supported a law enforcement system. Let the people who got paid for these things take care of it.

"We can call the police in Omaha," he said to Janice. "Try and file a missing persons report..." He trailed off.

"Or?"

He closed his eyes. What was it inside him that couldn't let things rest? What overweening pride, what egotistical self-centeredness allowed him to even think he ought to get involved? What on earth could he expect to accomplish?

"Deal..." It was Janice's voice, bringing him back.

He opened his eyes, blinking in the bright light. There was a talk show on the television, a young man yanking off articles of clothing while a female guest and female host stared in mock horror and the audience went wild with applause. Isabel was watching in fascination, spooning in her Fruit Loops mechanically.

Deal held up a finger to Janice, went to the television, punched buttons until the reassuring, geeky image of Mr. Rogers swam into view. He gave Isabel a pat on the head, glanced back at Janice.

"If I went out there..." he began before Janice cut him off.

"We," Janice said, her voice calm, but firm.

"Excuse me?"

"You meant to say if *we* went out there."

"No I didn't," Deal said. "I started to say if *I* went out there, maybe I'd stand a better chance of getting someone to look into Sara's disappearance. It'd also give me a chance to check out this Carver Construction business."

She pursed her lips. "You really think there's a connection?"

He shrugged his Driscoll shrug. "Hard to say."

She nodded. "I'm going with you," she said.

Deal shook his head. "Stay here, take care of Isabel."

She glanced into the nook, where Isabel was engrossed in Mr. Rogers's account of how mail got to be delivered, then beckoned Deal out into the hallway. When he had joined her, she turned on him, her voice subdued but fierce.

"Arch Dolan was my friend," she said. "*I* was the only one who was willing to believe what had really happened, and now that it's starting to look like I was right, you want to shuttle me off to the sidelines..."

"Janice..." he began.

"Don't 'Janice' me," she said. "I am sorry that I haven't been here to be with my daughter. It kills me what I've missed. But a couple of more days aren't going to make a whole hell of a lot of difference now." She closed her eyes momentarily, then turned back to him. "I am a functioning, capable human being, Deal. This matters a great deal to me. I'm just as able as you are to light a fire under some disinterested policeman, maybe more so. If you're going to look for a woman, you can use a woman's help."

He stared at her in frustration. "You've seen what's happened already," he said. "There's no telling what might happen..."

"It could happen to me while you're away," she said. It stopped him cold.

"If they're out there, doing what we think, it could happen anytime," she continued. "Unless we do something to stop them."

They turned as one, stared through the kitchen pass-through at their daughter. Deal took a deep breath, finally. "Mrs. Suarez could take her to her relatives in Hialeah," Deal said. "Nobody could find them there."

Janice nodded.

"You ever been to Omaha?" he asked. He gestured out the open doorway, as if it were just over the line of banyan trees that hid the neighboring yards.

She followed his gesture, turned back to him. "Is this an invitation?" she asked.

"Straight to the hotel, a trip to the police station with me, that's it, agreed?"

"If that's what it takes…" she began.

But by that time, Deal was on the phone again.

Chapter 19

"Kinda like riding in the train, isn't it?"

The tall man sat catty-corner opposite Deal and Janice, his legs jutting out into the narrow aisle. There were four of them in an odd little cabin at the back of the half-filled plane, a space between the main cabin and the crew galley that actually did resemble a train compartment.

Strange configuration, strange airline for that matter. No food service, no seat assignments, just pile on and grab a spot. Air America, one he'd never heard of, but the timing was right. They'd had an hour to pack and brief Mrs. Suarez—*no problema, señor*, Isabel is *muy contenta conmigo*, nobody find us, you go with your wife—then they would run by Janice's apartment for a few things on the way to the airport.

Going to Omaha required connections, they had discovered: the next flight out of Miami would have stranded them overnight in St. Louis. They'd just managed to make the flight, had found their way to these seats when they had been joined by the two, another pair of last-minute arrivals.

As Deal nodded absently, the man reached to pat the arm of his wife, who was engrossed in a crossword puzzle on her lap. The pair looked familiar to him somehow, but he couldn't imagine where he'd have met them. It was probably their very typicality, he thought. They just looked like familiar people.

"Iris'd like it a lot better if it was, wouldn't you, hon?"

The woman flicked her eyes up at her husband, held her gaze there a moment, her lips pressed together as if she were considering some annoying stranger. Finally, she went back to her crossword without comment. The tall man leaned toward him, speaking in a nasal Mid-western twang that carried easily above the roaring engines of the plane.

"She hates to fly. I showed her all the statistics, how you could get killed a lot sooner riding in a car, but it doesn't mean anything to her. All she can think about is how far it is to fall."

The woman glanced at her husband again, her eyes widening momentarily. It might have been fear, Deal thought, but the expression could have as easily been a flash of fury.

"Leave the people alone, Dexter," she said. Something in her tone suggested that a death threat lurked just behind the words.

"It's all right," Deal said.

"She's just unhappy to be leaving My-yam-ah," Dexter said. "Had to pack up her bikini and head back to the snow."

Deal stared at the woman, whose eyes were fixed on her crossword. She had a hat pinned to her head, wore a dotted Swiss dress buttoned to the neck, opaque hose, a pair of heavy black shoes. He supposed it was possible she owned a bikini, but he suspected something more on the order of a knee-and elbow-length garment from the 1920s.

"Now me," Dexter said, "I say hold on as long as you can." He pinched fabric at the knees of his slacks, jiggled the pantlegs for Deal to see: white polyester, some kind of design printed in primary colors. Birdie, bogey, par, he read. Red socks. White shoes. Red shirt with white piping around the sleeves and collar.

"You're a golfer?" Janice asked, turning from the window she'd been staring out of.

"He wouldn't know which end of the stick," the man's wife said. She hadn't lifted her eyes from the puzzle.

"Club," Dexter said. "It's club, not stick."

She looked up at him, tapping the puzzle with her pen. "Right here," she said, coolly. "'Duffer's weapon,' forty-two across. Five letters, starts with s, t, those are for sure. You make club work with that, I'll *buy* you a golf course." She turned to Deal. "He's going through a second childhood, you'll have to excuse him."

"I didn't get a chance to play any while I was down," Dexter said, ignoring her, "but I saw plenty of it around the hotel." He nodded pleasantly at his wife. "I told Mama it looked like a heck of a lot of fun. We're about to retire, you see. Man's got to look for things to keep him busy."

"You don't look that old," Janice said.

"Thank you kindly."

Deal glanced at her, then back at Dexter, who was beaming at her comment. It was true, Deal thought: when you looked closely, you realized he couldn't be more than sixty. It was the same with his wife. They simply gave a certain appearance of age.

"Excuse me," Iris said abruptly, snapping her seat belt open. "I've got to get out." She tossed her crossword onto the empty seat across from her, started past her husband.

"It's okay," he said, struggling up from his seat. "Gotta go myself." He stood aside as she brushed past, shooting him a withering glance.

Dexter waited until she had crossed the galley space, made her way into one of the tiny rest rooms at the back of the plane. "I'm sorry about Iris," he said. "She just hates an airplane to death."

"It's okay," Deal said, and watched the man make his own way off.

Janice waited until the second rest-room door had clacked shut to turn to him. "How long is this flight?" she said.

Deal checked his watch. "Another couple of hours to Chicago. We change planes there."

"I say we change seats while they're gone," she said.

Deal smiled. "I thought you were enjoying the old guy."

"Force of habit," she said. "If you grow up in the Midwest you develop this compulsion—you'll take any opportunity to say inane things to perfect strangers."

She was gathering up her things: a newspaper, a package of mints, a *People* magazine she'd found in the gift shop by the gate.

"You mean it? You're really going to move."

She glanced up at him. "Do I mean it? It's like being locked in a room with my parents."

She was bending over now, rummaging under the seat opposite for her purse and carry-on.

"Janice…" Deal was still protesting as she rose and pushed past him.

"Tell them I got claustrophobic," she said. "That's pretty close to the truth."

⊚ ⊚ ⊚

"I can't believe we did this," Deal said. He had followed Janice halfway up the main cabin of the plane, trying not to look back when he heard the rest-room doors clack open behind him.

"Get a grip," Janice said. She'd already arranged herself, had stowed her bags, her reading materials. She offered him a mint from her package. "A train makes a lot of stops, doesn't it? They'll just think we got off somewhere."

"Real funny," he said.

"Let me ask you something," she said. "You'd rather sit there and trade quips with old stoneface than have a conversation with me?"

"We could have had our own conversation," he said stubbornly.

"Deal, I grew up with these people. They are insidious. You cannot ignore them. You clear your throat and they answer you. You cough and they give you the name of their doctor…"

"Okay, okay," he said. He held up his hand, trying not to laugh.

"You don't know them. You don't want to know them. But they want to know you. They're like those pod people. They won't be happy until they've reduced you to the level of cornmeal, until you're sitting there babbling like they are…"

Janice was fighting laughter now and Deal was doubled over in silent guffaws. They went on that way for minutes, like a couple of guilty kids sharing a joke during church service, until finally a stewardess leaned over to ask if she could get them anything.

Deal opened his mouth, trying to find the breath to answer, when Janice could stand it no more. She gave a shriek of laughter and Deal followed suit. "I guess you've already had enough," the stewardess said, turning huffily away.

It only egged them on further, and it was a good five minutes before Deal could turn to Janice without exploding into laughter. His sides ached, and he wiped tears from his eyes.

"Christ," he said, still fighting to get his breathing under control. "I don't know how long it's been since I laughed like that."

"A long time," she said, nodding in agreement. She blew her nose heartily, dabbed at her eyes. The stewardess was moving down the aisle, her gaze studiously averted. Janice reached out, caught her by the arm.

"Could we have something after all—a couple glasses of seltzer, maybe?" She turned to Deal for confirmation and he nodded.

"Of course," the stewardess said, all smiles again.

"She just wanted to be of service," Janice said, watching the woman walk off.

"We have to get off in front of those people, Janice."

Janice nodded absently. "It is a difference between you and me," she said.

"What's that?"

"You do like to please people."

"You say it like it's a fault."

She shrugged. "Not always. But sometimes you have to put yourself first."

Deal wondered if it was bait. Was he supposed to pick up on it, grind on her as if she'd walked out on them…or perhaps give her the chance to explain once more why she'd had to leave? Neither possibility enticed him. "My old man was the champ at that," Deal said. "I guess I just got in the habit of working the other way."

She nodded, gave him the hint of a smile. Maybe he'd passed the test. "That's what it comes down to, isn't it?" she said. "Our parents. Still controlling us, right from the grave."

"Not my old man," he said. "He's got a gin game going somewhere, a drink in one hand, the other on some babe. He couldn't care less what I was up to."

"Keep talking, Deal. You're proving my point."

"You think I'm on my way to Omaha because I want to please somebody?" He stared at her, daring her to rise, this time.

She dropped her gaze. "I think you're doing it because it's the right thing to do," she said quietly.

"Good," Deal said. "That makes two of us, then."

◎◎◎

As it turned out, they were off the plane and lost in the bowels of the Chicago airport without another glimpse of the couple. Deal imagined them making their way along an ever-narrowing route, from airline, to commuter, to rail or bus connections, until they were finally bumping down a gravel road in a round-fendered pickup, Dexter in his golf getup, Iris still working her crossword in the failing light, a Gothic farmhouse looming up ahead.

Meanwhile, he and Janice had to change terminals, ride an underground tram to do it, cruise along an otherworldly conveyor walkway past some kind of neon sculpture on the walls, an assemblage that pulsed and wavered, hidden speakers pumping out random gongs and chimes and unintelligible mutterings as they whisked along.

"And people think Miami is weird?" Deal said. "I thought this was the Midwest, for Chrissakes."

Janice rolled her eyes. "Everywhere is weird, Deal. You've been working too hard."

"What do you think something like that costs?" he said, pointing at the neon sculpture. They'd come to the end of the moving walkway and Janice had to guide him off, pull him toward a steep escalator up ahead.

"It's an example of art in a public place," she said. "Your tax dollars hard at work."

He was still staring over his shoulder when she pulled him onto the escalator.

◎ ◎ ◎

"Well, look who's here," Dexter said. He turned from the boarding counter, pointing as Deal and Janice hurried from the concourse. "Iris, lookee here."

Iris glanced up from a pamphlet she was reading, gave a cursory nod. "You folks headed to Omaha?" Dexter said. "'Fraid we've got one of those puddle-jumpers to ride in," he added. He nodded out a window where a tiny propeller-driven plane sat, old snow and dust kicking up in swirls.

"Might as well hold off a bit," Dexter said as Deal and Janice headed toward the gate, where an attendant was already sending passengers through. "I like to sit in back, case of we go down."

"We don't mind," Deal said, guiding Janice on ahead. "We're not afraid of flying."

@ @ @

He might have spoken too soon, Deal thought as he clutched the armrest of his cramped seat tightly. They were climbing through a bank of solid gray clouds, and he watched in disbelief as ice steadily accreted on the wings outside. It built up to an eight-inch sheet before huge chunks began to shear away, bouncing off the fuselage with heavy thumps.

"Good Lord," Janice hissed, her hand clamping his arm tightly.

Deal could see Dexter at the corner of his vision, one row back and across the aisle, legs and arms jutting from the tiny single seat. No telling where Iris had ended up, though she'd be on a bus if she had any sense.

Dexter grinned and nodded in his direction. If there was any comfort in it, the roar of the engines and the pounding outside made any thought of conversation absurd.

Before the ice could build up appreciably again, they popped out of the clouds and the roar of the engines abated. Janice turned to him, relieved. "I remember now why I moved to Florida," she said.

Deal nodded, clasping her hand in his. She glanced down, and for a moment he wondered if she was going to pull away. Then she gave him a wan smile and settled back in her seat, closing her eyes. It was a picture, he thought—just looking, you'd have to think all was well.

Chapter 20

"Any time you want to take a look at God's country, just come on out to Wahoo," Dexter was saying. Incredibly, the man and his wife had come to stand behind Deal and Janice in the rental car line at the Omaha terminal. "You just ask anybody where the Kittles live, they'll tell you. For that matter, just ask them, where's Dexter and Iris's place. They'll tell you."

"We'll do it," Deal said. "Count on it."

He scooped up the keys from the sales attendant with one hand, urged Janice away with the other. "Enjoy Omaha, now," Dexter said as they hurried off.

◉ ◉ ◉

"I was right, wasn't I," Janice said. She was huddled in the corner of the rental car, her arms wrapped tightly about her, her hands tucked in her armpits, while Deal worked to get the engine started.

"What's that?" he said. He was distracted, trying to remember his cold-weather driving routines, whether one was to pump the accelerator or leave the starter to its own devices.

"That guy. You couldn't get away from him fast enough."

"He was just trying to be friendly," Deal said. "If you lived in someplace like Yeehaw, Nebraska, you'd probably be starved for company, too. Especially if you lived with somebody like Iris."

"Wahoo," Janice said.

"What?" Deal had given up leaving things alone, was pumping the accelerator rapidly now.

"The name of the town," she said. "It was Wahoo."

"Same thing," Deal said, glancing at her.

After they'd retrieved her suitcase from the baggage claim, she'd taken one look outside, dug out a down parka he remembered her wearing on a ski trip a decade ago. She had its fur-fringed hood pulled up over her head, but she was gloveless and shivering in the frigid air. Outside, winter twilight had dimmed the sky and a gritty snow was coming down nearly sideways, driven by a gusting wind strong enough to rock the car periodically.

Deal remembered buying a parka for the same long-ago trip, but his had burned up a few years back, lost in the same accident that had left Janice with the scars that only she could see. *Forget it, Deal,* he thought. Ancient history. Head down, foot forward. They would work their way out of this yet.

For winter gear, he'd found only a pair of ski mittens and a wool scarf in the back of a drawer. He had borrowed a pea coat from Driscoll, who'd also tossed in a watch cap and a Jon-ee hand warmer. "Used that sucker plenty when I worked Shore Patrol in Korea," Driscoll had said. "Nebraska's even worse."

He'd insisted on digging out a can of lighter fluid from under his sink, filling up the gadget, showing Deal how it worked. "It'll fit right inside those mittens of yours," he added, then stopped him on the way out of the apartment. "Call me if you get in over your head, now."

He was *already* in over his head, Deal thought, fighting the urge to hustle Janice out of the freezing car back into the comfort of the tiny airport. If planes were still flying,

they could get as far back as Chicago tonight, take a room
at the Ambassador or the Palmer House, find a decent
restaurant, have some drinks, pretend it was a vacation, a
second honeymoon.

"What's wrong with this car, Deal?" she said, huddling
deeper within herself.

"The winter," he grumbled as the starter ground uselessly
on at his touch.

Deal hadn't bothered to light the hand warmer, but he
was beginning to wish he had. He'd removed his mitten to
get the key in the unfamiliar ignition and his fingers were
turning to ice.

"Shouldn't they check these cars out, have them ready
for people?"

He turned to her, exasperated. "I bet there's a place on
the rental form to write that suggestion down."

"You don't have to get snippy," she said. "I'm cold, that's
all."

"Have the rest of the coffee," he said. They'd stopped at
a kiosk in the airport, picked up a Styrofoam cupful of weak
brew, a dry doughnut, a leaden cookie.

She shook her head. "It's already ice," she said.

Deal turned, twisted the key again. This time the starter
chugged rapidly for a few seconds, then shifted to a much
slower cycle, and finally fell away altogether with a dispiriting
groan.

"Does that mean what I think it does?" she said as another
gust rocked the car.

Deal sank back behind the wheel. "Look," he said. "I'm
going back inside, make them give us another car. You want
to go with me or wait here?"

The wind was howling outside now, the car jiggling
steadily as if it were a rail car being towed across the tundra.
"Will it take long?"

Deal shook his head. "I'll jump the line. I'll drag the guy out myself if I have to."

"I'll wait," she said. "But hurry, okay?"

He gave her a smile, then saw something in her expression that made him lean across the seat, give her a peck on the cheek. "Count on it," he said.

He turned, was about to throw open his door when she called out, "There's something else, Deal. About that couple."

He rolled his eyes, glanced over his shoulder. "What?"

"I was just thinking," she said. "If they live around here, what would they be doing renting a car?"

It stopped him for a moment. "I don't know, Janice. Maybe somebody brought them to the airport, they can't come get them in the storm."

She nodded, but she didn't seem convinced.

"It's getting dark," Deal said, impatient, his hand on the door. "I'll be right back, okay?"

"Okay," she said, and he swung himself out into the bitter wind before he could change his mind.

❀ ❀ ❀

It *was* an interesting question, he thought as he bent his head against the wind, paused to pull the watch cap over his ears. And even if there were a number of reasonable explanations, it was a reminder to him that Janice often picked up on things he was in too big a hurry to notice. She was probably far more suited to detective work than he was. As he pushed himself away from the car toward the terminal, he made a resolution to himself to remember that.

Outside, the lights of the terminal seemed much farther away than he'd realized. His Topsiders slipped and slid, their low-cut tops inviting in the ice and snow. In seconds his feet were soaked and freezing. He'd also been clumsy using the unfamiliar mittens when he'd pulled his cap on, he realized. He'd left half an ear uncovered, hadn't taken a dozen steps and it had already passed through the painful stage, was rapidly turning numb.

He cursed, pulled off a mitten in his teeth, reached up to yank the cap down, stopped when the lights of a boxy-looking vehicle in the row ahead of him popped on, blinding him momentarily in the gloom.

"You got trouble?" he heard the familiar voice call, and lowered his arm to see Dexter Kittle coming around the opened door of the truck-like vehicle toward him. If he was still wearing his golf outfit, there was no way to tell. He'd donned a quilted snowmobiler's outfit, had replaced the white loafers with a pair of lace-up rubberized boots.

"The damned car they gave me wouldn't start," Deal muttered. He saw the passenger door of the Kittles' vehicle swing open, saw Iris Kittle, dressed in a matching camouflage-style getup, moving his way as well.

"That your missus in there?" Dexter said, pointing over Deal's shoulder. Deal turned toward his disabled rental car, saw Janice's huddled shape through the hazy rear window glass.

"That's her..." Deal began, thinking that something good had come out of tolerating Kittle after all. Even Janice wouldn't turn down a cozy ride back to the terminal, that much he was sure of. He was turning back, ready to prevail upon Kittle, when he felt a stunning blow at his face.

At first, blinded by pain, by the suddenness of it, he had no idea what had happened. But in the few seconds it took for him to realize he was on the ground now, he also understood that Kittle had hit him, and that his mouth was full of blood because he'd bitten his tongue, or the inside of his cheek, hard to tell because his entire head had gone numb with the cold and the force of the blow. He was trying to scramble to his feet when he felt another blow at his side, a kick that lifted him off the ground and drove his breath from him.

"She's in the car, hon," he heard Kittle call.

Deal was gasping, rolling over blindly. He felt another kick, but this one was glancing, muffled somewhat by the thick folds of Driscoll's pea coat. Deal used the force of the second kick, kept himself rolling, digging his elbows into a patch of soft snow, managing to scuttle under the overhang of a van as another kick flashed past, inches from his face.

There was a heavy thud and a curse from Kittle as the toe of his boot smashed against the underside of the van's fender.

Deal had his breath back, his vision cleared now, saw one of Kittle's boots doing a little hop step a few inches from his nose while a string of curses whipped away in the wind. Deal spit blood from between his swollen lips, reached out to clutch Kittle's pantleg. He curled his fingers into a death grip on the soft fabric, jerked as hard as he could.

There was another cry as Kittle's foot slid toward him, his shin cracking against the bumper above Deal's head. Deal yanked again, twisting the boot up until Kittle lost his balance altogether. There was a yelp and a satisfying thump as the man went down hard on his back, a groan as his breath left him.

"Deal!" he heard Janice cry somewhere. "Deal!" The sounds seemed pitiful, whipped into quick nothingness by the wind.

He clutched the fabric of Kittle's pantleg all the harder, used the man's weight as leverage to pull himself out from under the van.

Kittle was still groaning, trying to clamber up on his elbow, when Deal caught a fistful of quilted fabric on the man's chest, swung mightily with his other hand.

"Sonofabitch," Deal said as his fist caught Kittle's cheekbone squarely. "Bastard. What is this? What are you doing?"

He was drawing back to swing again when Iris struggled out of the passageway between the van and another car. She had Janice's chin locked under one arm, was using her free hand to pull the two of them along toward the idling truck. When she saw Deal atop her husband, she dropped Janice, moved toward them. Deal saw Janice bounce limply off the side of the van, a life-size doll cast aside.

He opened his mouth to call to her, but the sound never materialized. Iris had spun toward him in a move that seemed a blur. The sole of her boot caught him high on the cheek, numbing him, sending him over hard onto his back, his hands flying above his head as if he were trying to carve an angel in the snow.

Dowdy old Iris, he thought, bells clanging in his head. Starbursts of light. Strange animal voices. A hyena laugh.

Stick-in-the-mud Iris. She probably had a hundred bikinis and she probably looked like a well-oiled machine in every one of them, he thought dreamily. How would she finish him off, he wondered. Crossword puzzle pen plunged through his heart? Sensible-stocking noose around his throat? Who the hell were these people? What did they want?

"Get her in the car." He heard Iris's voice at his ear, managed to get his eyes open as she bent over to grab his coat with one hand, lift his head up off the snow. She had her other hand drawn back, he realized, a mirror image of how he'd looked a moment ago, ready to cold-cock Dexter, knock him six miles beyond Wahoo. Only difference was, Deal thought, there wasn't much hope he could turn things around.

A fluff of her hair had escaped the hood of her camouflage suit. Little ice balls clung there, bouncing off her forehead like a flapper's beads, like tiny beads on a frosted veil...and then he remembered. The spray of tiny berries he'd picked up in Arch's store after the murder. In the next instant he saw the two of them in their shiny Cadillac car, waving him across the street, Ma and Pa Gothic he'd taken them for, typical tourists, harmless geeks. He'd seen them again, in the Grove, at Lightner's: a tall, gaunt man with his dog, a loony woman in garden attire and Audrey Hepburn sunglasses. He and Janice had probably walked right past them at the Biltmore, and they'd been followed by the pair ever since. They'd killed Arch, and Fast Eddie Lightner, and Martin Rosenhaus. And now it was Deal's turn to die.

Good as she seemed to be, he suspected it would be painless. One sharp blow and good night. And then something occurred to him, swimming up out of his hapless daze. Janice. Was that what had happened to her? Was she already gone? The way she'd fallen, limp, crumpling into the snow so lifelessly...?

He saw a sheen of amber light wash over Iris Kittle's face then, thought at first it was a trick of his addled mind. But Iris had in fact glanced up herself, frozen momentarily, her hand drawn back, her fingers twisted into some kind of strange, death-dealing configuration.

The amber light whisked across her features again. And again. A caution flasher, Deal realized. Cop? Airport security?

He felt a tingling in his left arm now, a rush of feeling that extended, along with the sharper sensations of pain, all the way to his fingertips. His right arm was still numb, so the left would have to do. And just as well, for the left mitten was the one he'd left on, the one where the unlit Jon-ee hand warmer still jiggled inside, freezing him with its cold metallic self.

It was like carrying around a frozen flask in there, he thought as he lunged forward, putting his last ounce of strength behind the blow. She was just turning back to him when his fist met her face, the Jon-ee leading the way like a giant-size set of brass knuckles.

He heard a splatting sound, felt maximum resistance, heard her cry out as she fell over backwards. Deal rolled to his side, scrambled onto his hands and knees, shaking his head like an old bull trying to refocus himself as the picadors swarmed. Feeling was returning to his right arm now, to his pulpy lips, but he was still groggy.

One aisle over, behind a double row of cars, a snowplow was grinding swiftly along, a yellow warning flasher whirling atop the cap. A wake of ice and powder soared high into the air behind the machine, lowering the already miserable visibility to nothing.

Deal looked about the gloom for Iris, sure the blow had put her out, but stopped, staring in disbelief, when he found her on her feet, coming unsteadily his way, blood dripping from her smashed nose, from her mouth, a little dribble of it already frozen into an icicle at her chin. Dexter was trying to pull himself up by the bumper of the van, but his boots kept slipping in the bloody ice at his feet. Janice's form still lay crumpled in the snowbank where Iris had dumped her, but Deal thought he saw movement there, her hand and arm fluttering, or maybe it was just a trick of the wind.

Iris paused before him, wiped a gloved hand over her bloody face, stared down at the mess on her glove. Then she started forward again. The fury he'd seen her train on her husband was nothing compared to the expression on her face now.

She will use her feet, Deal thought, and forced his gaze down, watching her stop, shift her weight…he would be ready, this time maybe pull her down as he had Dexter or at the least block the blow. The footing was bad, she'd have to be extra-cautious to hold her balance…

She feinted with her right, and Deal fought to keep from buying the move. Sure enough, she shifted her weight again, driving her left instep toward his temple. He couldn't dodge it—she was too quick for that—but he managed to twist away so that the blow glanced off his shoulder.

He came up out of his crouch then, his feet sliding on the ice. It was like trying to run across a funhouse floor, he thought as he half-slid, half-stumbled toward her. The only thing he had going for him was that she was working at the same disadvantage. She was backpedaling, readying a punch as he came in on her, but she'd strayed close to where Dexter was still trying to find his footing. Her boots tangled in his and her eyes widened as she lost her balance.

Deal fell heavily against her, wrapping his arms about hers, taking them both down against the ice. They hit and rolled, Iris hissing like an angry cat, squirming, kicking, gnashing her teeth, trying for his nose, his face. She was incredibly strong, but he had a good fifty pounds on her, and if he could just keep himself astraddle her, work himself up to his knees...

He heard the awful roaring behind them then, saw the amber lights flashing off the chrome trim and bumpers, wrenched his head around to see it: the behemoth of a snow-plow had made a turn, was roaring down the aisle toward them now. At first Deal thought that he might be saved, but then he realized that the machine hadn't slowed, that if any-thing, it was picking up steam as it bore down upon them.

The headlights of the thing were dim points of light, one of them misaligned, pointing crazily up toward the sky, the other practically blotted out by the thick, driving snow.

Blizzard, whiteout, whatever, the driver couldn't see them. Deal fought to roll them out of the path of the machine, up against the snowbanked nose of a van, but Iris levered her feet against its bumper, shoving them back into the lane.

He didn't even have time to cry out. The big blade rammed Deal's shoulder, sent Iris loose from his grasp in an instant. He was sure they would be crushed in the next instant, reduced to nothingness beneath the wheels of the huge machine, but then he felt another blow, found himself tumbling head over heels.

He came up gasping as the blade stuck him again and he realized he was rolling along in front of the blade, that he and Iris had been scooped up like any other roadway debris and were being pushed forward, for the moment at least, riding a wave of snow and broken ice piled up in front of the giant blade. Trying not to think about those massive wheels churning just a few feet away, he threw himself backwards toward the blade, tried to pull himself up onto the machine itself.

He made one lunge, grabbed some icy projection, an unknown machine thing frigid and wet and coated with grease. He dug his fingers in desperately, felt a nail splinter, felt the flesh of his palm slice open on something sharp. He shook the cumbersome mitten off his other hand, felt the Jon-ee tumble away into the mass below, flailed desperately for another handhold, but there was nothing.

Out of the corner of his eye, he saw Iris attempting the same move, saw her latch onto something solid on the back side of the blade. She steadied herself, her arm tucked over the top of the blade now, and then, staring impassively at him, she reached inside a pocket of her heavy snowmobiler's suit.

He caught a flash of metal as she withdrew her hand, didn't have to look any closer to know she'd drawn a pistol. So this was it, he thought: He was about to be blown away by Killer Ma Kittle in the middle of a Nebraska snowstorm, and worse, he'd end up frozen like some woolly mastodon in the middle of a giant pile of snow, no one would even know it had happened until spring thaw, whenever the hell that might be.

He reached down, caught hold of a tumbling chunk of ice, heaved it toward her. She ducked, watched it sail well wide of her head, shook her head at his pathetic efforts. She was drawing down on him now, trying to steady her aim against the jouncing of the big metal blade. Deal lunged for another chunk of ice…and then she fired.

He saw the muzzle flash, saw a trace of liquid fire along the face of the blade as the slug tore into the metal, then glanced away, scant inches from his cheek. He threw another chunk of ice, backhanding it this time, using the blade as a backboard. The thing skidded along, skipped off the metal, slammed point first against her chest. Her grasp wavered for a moment, and he flailed about, desperate for another piece to throw.

Not bad, he thought. Not a bad idea at all, if it had been a snowball fight. But she'd already regained her purchase, was raising the pistol again...

...when suddenly the big plow screeched to a halt at the edge of an embankment and they were both catapulted out into space, free-falling now, along with the tons of snow and ice and associated road crud that had until moments ago covered the roadway where Deal had been fighting for his life.

Deal felt himself complete one somersault, then turn again, was well into a second before he hit the bank below. He bounced, flew up, his momentum carrying him upright momentarily, flinging him down just as quickly, but not before he'd had a glimpse of what was coming next.

The snowplow operator had done the easiest thing with his load, Deal realized: he'd simply picked up a great head of steam, then shoved everything out over a sheer dropoff that bordered the rental car parking area. Deal couldn't be sure, of course, given the brief glimpse he'd had, the bad light, the speed with which he was moving, but it had looked suspiciously like a riverbed there at the bottom of the cliff.

His legs and arms were spread wide, windmilling, trying to grasp onto anything that might slow his descent. He hit a bank of crusted-up snow chest first, tore on through it like some human cannonball. He caught sight of a spindly tree, reached for it, felt it rip through his hand like a greased rope. He was still skidding out of control, his feet pointed straight downhill in front of him, a luge racer who'd forgotten his little sled.

There was another dropoff up ahead, one he suspected was the bank to the river he'd spotted before. He clawed frantically at the snow at his sides, but he knew it was no use. Fifteen feet, ten...and then he saw it, another sapling twisting up out of the ice-crusted snow...

He would take no chances this time, no lunging, no bad handholds, no peeling off into the abyss. It took every ounce of his will to do it, but he did do it. He opened his feet wide, sighted down his crotch at the tree, and hit it dead on.

The impact drove his breath from him, spun him around toward the edge, but he locked his legs, flung out his arm, caught the slender trunk in the crook of his elbow to keep from going over. The pain was an electric bolt rocketing around the confines of his body, seeking any way out. His teeth ached, his groin was numb. He hung his head out into the darkness and retched.

He was still dangling weakly when he heard a cry behind him, saw a dark shape hurtle past him and fly out over the precipice by his side. She hit the bottom with a sound like shattering glass, skidding off a ways over a flat white surface, and Deal realized that it *was* a river down there, frozen over now in the cold.

He stared dumbly as the woman came to her hands and knees, catching sight of him almost immediately. A machine, he was thinking. A woman who puts Schwarzenegger to shame. She raised her hand, pointing at him, and he realized she still had the gun.

Sure, he thought numbly. Just his luck. So aching cold here the thing had probably frozen to her hand. Another muzzle flash then, a report that echoed off the cliffside above, a scattering of ice chips that burst near his face.

She was on her feet now, bracing herself, taking her time for this one, enough fooling around for one night. She took a step closer, another, then stopped. He couldn't see her face behind her upraised hands, but he'd have bet money she was smiling.

"Go to hell," he muttered, waiting for it to end.

And then there was another sound of shattering glass, a cry, and a final crash as the ice beneath her feet gave way.

She went down as if a greased chute had opened beneath her. One more gunshot straight into the air, a muffled splash as one palm smacked the surface of the water, and then nothing.

Deal stared uncertainly at the round black hole in the water, stunned at first, then gradually able to comprehend what he had just seen. Seemed good, he thought, but any second she could be bouncing back through the ice, sporting a bikini and a flamethrower in each hand. He counted off a minute, then two, and by that time the feeling had returned to his groin, and he could draw a deep breath without setting off a fire everywhere south of his chest.

He pulled himself up by the slender trunk of the tree that had saved his life, took one more look down at the frozen river, then turned and began to climb.

◎ ◎ ◎

By the time he had pulled himself to the top, slipping back one foot for every two he gained, his hands were bleeding, frostbitten wrecks, his lungs were burning, his pants soaked and shredded. He heaved himself over the berm that the snowplow had built up, checked to make sure he was headed down the right row. It was solid dark, but there were scattered vapor lights here and the snow seemed to have abated, the wind fallen off somewhat as well.

The snowplow was working another quadrant of the lot now, its yellow light still whirling, rooster tails of snow still flying off either side of its blade. Deal hurried down the aisle, spotted the Previa van where he'd taken shelter, saw a dark blotch of ice marking the spot where he'd shattered Iris Kittle's nose, where Dexter Kittle had tried to kill him.

He'd known what to expect, of course, had hoped against hope anyway. How long had he been gone from this spot? Five minutes? Ten? Fifteen at the most.

The spot where Dexter Kittle had lain was empty. The space where Kittle's truck had been parked was an open gap in a line of snowbound vehicles. And, worst of all, in the place where Janice had been, there was nothing but a blank and frozen mound of snow.

"Janice!" he cried. Maybe she'd awakened, was making her way toward the distant lights of the terminal. Sure. He turned that way, scanned the mounded tops of cars, the unmoving dark lot. "Janice!" he cried again.

Only the snowplow roared in answer.

Chapter 21

"We've got people looking for your wife, Mr. Deal. You ready to tell me why you assaulted our snowplow driver, now?" The airport chief of security—Delbert Cuddy, according to his nametag—was perched on a desk, staring down at Deal, who was sitting in a wobbly secretary's chair, where a paramedic had patched him up. Cuddy gestured into a corner of the bright, overheated staff lounge, where the same paramedic was pasting a butterfly bandage over a cut on a fat man's cheek.

It was a good-sized room, with several round tables, a couple dozen standard-issue metal chairs, a couple of vending machines in a corner. There was a microwave oven set up on a serving counter just behind the fat man and a colorful poster featuring a bear in hard hat and ear protectors who urged employees to be safe, and never sorry.

"I didn't touch him," Deal said. That was close to the truth. He'd already gone over the story once with a patrolman, a guy Deal had finally found circling the parking lot in a little Japanese pickup topped by an enormous set of flashers. "I didn't have time for a discussion, that's all."

As he'd told the patrolman, Deal had intersected with the snowplow on the dead run toward the terminal, had jumped up to pound on the operator's cab for help. The driver had driven on, oblivious, for a good fifteen seconds, Deal hammering away at the Plexiglas side door all the while, until the big machine finally ground to a halt, and the door swung open violently, loosing a blast of booze-laden air, giving Deal a look at a guy wearing a grimy, waffle-weave undershirt and a westerncut down vest.

"He told me to get the fuck off his machine," Deal repeated evenly, his eyes on the chief. "I told him someone had taken my wife, that I needed help. I left out the part that he'd already almost run over me with his machine. He yelled at me again, then he took a swing and lost his balance." Deal shrugged. "He fell out of his seat and went all the way to the ground."

Deal glanced over to where the fat guy was sitting, his undershirt stained even worse now: snow grit and grease and a bright smear of blood shaped vaguely like a question mark. There was a lump on the side of his face where his bald head had bounced off the ice. The fat guy glowered back at him, but kept his mouth shut. He might have interjected how Deal had sidestepped the haymaker, had helped him out of his seat and into the snow just a little, but he had apparently decided against it this time.

Cuddy, the security chief, was a burly guy, probably carried the same heft as the plow driver, but he looked a lot more solid. He surveyed Deal, glanced back at the driver. "Yeah, well, you probably just startled Everett. He gets into a routine out there, you know."

Deal considered Cuddy's expression. "I really don't care about Everett," Deal said. "I'm sitting here thinking there ought to be an APB out on the truck that guy Kittle was driving."

Cuddy nodded, his eyes half-closing as if to forestall boredom. "I got a call in to the Highway Patrol. Four-wheel-drive type vehicle, make unknown, color hidden by snow, no tag number. Driver resembles farmer character out of Grant Wood painting." He pursed his lips. "That narrows it down to about half the male population of Nebraska."

"That man has my wife," Deal said, gritting his teeth.

"You *assume* he's got your wife, Mr. Deal," Cuddy said, holding up a cautionary finger.

"What are you talking about?" Deal said. "Where else could she be?"

Cuddy eyed him closely. "You said she fell. I hate to say it, but she could be disoriented, she could have wandered off anywhere..."

"She didn't fall, she was assaulted," Deal said, trying to keep from shouting. "When I saw her, she was unconscious..."

Cuddy broke in. "You told me you thought you saw her hand come up, reach out for you."

Deal stopped, fuming. The man wasn't entirely stupid, could remember the least details of Deal's statements, but it seemed as if he were being purposefully obtuse. "What the hell is this?" Deal said finally. "My wife's been kidnapped and we're sitting around here jerking off?"

The cop shifted on the desk, leaned over the chair where Deal was sitting. "Look here, Mr. Deal, I know you're upset, but let me tell you how it might appear from another side. I get a wild man from My-yam-uh come flying through the doors of my airport in the middle of a blizzard, tells me two people followed him into the parking lot, tried to kill him." Cuddy waved his hands about.

"Fistfights. Gunshots fired. Lady assassin falls through the ice into Carter Creek. Man climbs up cliff to discover wife has been abducted by aforementioned male assailant. No witnesses to any of this, of course. Though I do have a snowplow driver, employee of the City of Omaha for fourteen years, says the same wild man jumped up onto his snow removal unit, physically assaulted him without provocation."

"Talk to the clerk at the car rental counter," Deal said, fighting back his anger. "He had to have seen those people. He rented them their car..."

Cuddy shook his head. "We did talk to him. The guy remembers renting you a two-door midsize automobile, damage waiver declined. He remembers you were with your wife cuz she wanted to know if it had snow tires and he told her Hertz didn't rent cars in Nebraska in the winter without snow tires on. But he doesn't remember any tall guy in a golf getup, a wife that looks like Elmer Fudd. And he sure as shitting didn't rent them any four-wheel-drive vehicle because there hasn't been a one to rent in this airport for a day and a half, ever since the bad weather hit."

Deal stared at the man, trying to comprehend it. The counter had been a mob scene, all right. But the pair had been waiting right behind him...He broke off his thoughts, stared at the chief.

"They weren't there to rent a car," Deal said.

"That's what I just told you," Cuddy said.

"They must have followed us into the line, to find out what kind of car we'd be driving, where it would be parked outside. We took our time getting out there. That's why the car wouldn't start, they must have done something to it..." His mind was outstripping itself, hurling fears, assumptions, counterclaims. Kittle had Janice. Kittle had killed others without a thought. How long did Janice have before she joined Arch, Rosenhaus, Eddie Lightner and his hooker, that poor bastard out walking his dog...?

The door to the employees' lounge opened then and the patrolman Deal had flagged down earlier clomped inside, banging his boots on the linoleum floor, dusting snow off the shoulders of his jacket.

The patrolman looked at Deal, then at the chief. "That car of his had a dead battery," he said.

Deal started out of his chair, but Cuddy motioned him back. "You find a purse inside, luggage, anything like that?"

The patrolman shrugged. "Bag with his name on it," he said, nodding at Deal. "Full of his stuff."

Cuddy nodded, gave Deal a glance.

"They must have taken her things..." Deal began, but Cuddy was holding a finger to his lips. After he was sure Deal was going to obey, he turned back to the patrolman.

"Anybody check out the creek?"

The patrolman shrugged. "Snowing too hard to get down right now," he said. "We put a spotlight on it. It could be a break in the ice, but it's hard to say for sure."

Cuddy took it in, nodding. He turned back to Deal for a moment. "I placed a call to my friend Hank Cross. He's the sheriff out in Saunders County. Nobody named Kittle lives in Wahoo, that surprise you?"

Deal shook his head. "Not at all."

"About three thousand people live in that town, most of 'em know what the rest ate for dinner last night. Hank Cross said he never laid eyes on a pair like you describe."

Deal stared in frustration. He'd always taken Kafka's works as exaggeration, but now...

Cuddy, who had been studying him, turned back to the patrolman, who was headed for the coffee machine. "Get yourself a coffee, Russ," the chief called, "then find a rope somewhere, take my Blazer, get Phillips to winch you down the hill off the front end."

Russ spun about, an expression of disbelief on his face. "Hey, Chief..." he protested.

Cuddy held up a meaty hand. "Or you lower Phillips down, I don't care which. Call in on the radio, let me know if you see anything. You got me, Russ?"

"Yeah," Russ said, resigned. He drew his coffee and went out.

Cuddy turned on the corner of the desk, back to Deal. "Now here's what I know for sure, Mr. Deal. You came into this airport with your wife, and now she's missing, purse, hatbox and all. You tell me there's been foul play, but there's nothing that really indicates that. For all I know, you two

..d a couple too many, got into a spat, she walked out when you had your back turned, all the rest of this is some fantasy."

Deal forced himself to be calm. "Why would I do that, make all this up?"

Cuddy shrugged. "That I wouldn't know, Mr. Deal. Maybe it'd help if you told me what brought you here to begin with."

Deal thought about the question for a moment. Suppose he told the chief all about it, start with Arch's death, take it right on through Martin Rosenhaus, maybe a little discussion of American reading habits on the side. Would that help? Or just get him sent out the revolving door that much quicker?

On the other hand, if he didn't convince the man that Janice was in danger, what chance would he ever have of finding her? This much was certain: every minute he sat here trying to be reasonable was costing him dearly.

"Look, Chief, you don't know me from Adam's off ox, I understand that. If I were in your shoes, I'd probably feel the same way you do. But maybe, if I could just make one phone call, *maybe* I could convince you I'm telling the truth."

Cuddy checked his watch. "I don't see what the point of it is, but if it'll make you feel any better..." He broke off, gesturing at the phone, but Deal already had the receiver in his hand.

❀ ❀ ❀

Actually, it took two calls. The first, to Terrence Terrell's home, in Coconut Grove, resulted in a conversation with Terrell's daughter Grace, who told him that Terrell was in Fort Lauderdale, being wined and dined at the waterside mansion of a fellow South Florida mogul who had a hockey team he was trying to sell. The second call was answered by a staffer for the mogul who wanted to take a message for Terrell.

"He can't be disturbed," the staffer said firmly.

"What did you say your name was?" Deal asked, feeling the chief's eyes on him. "Uh-huh, well, listen, Jeffrey, tell him it's John Deal calling from Omaha and that it's an emergency. That's right, Jeffrey. Life and death."

Deal waited, his gaze locked on the security chief's, listening to the sound of footsteps, doors slamming, muffled conversation on the other end. Finally, there was Terrence Terrell's voice, jovial, boat horns in the background, Terrell wanting to know what the hell he was doing in Omaha. Question of the day, Deal thought, then filled him in, sidestepping as much as possible the issue of what he and Janice had intended by making the trip in the first place.

The moment he got the drift of things, Terrell became all business. He got the name of the airport, the number, the name of the chief of security, even a badge number. Deal heard muffled conversation on the other end for a moment, then Terrell was back.

"I've already got someone working this matter on another line," Terrell said, his voice at its most reassuring. "Give us fifteen minutes, tops. You'll get a call. Just one thing I'm asking of you."

"Name it," Deal said.

"You're holding back on me, aren't you?"

"Mr. Terrell..." Deal began.

"Don't 'Mister' me, John," Terrell said. "You can't talk, I understand. Just call me back the moment you're able, let me know what this is all about."

"You've got it," Deal said.

"That's what I thought," Terrell said. "Hang in there now, John. Keep me informed."

The line was dead then, and Deal put the phone back into the chief's outstretched hand. Cuddy replaced the phone in the set, turned back to Deal.

"So now what," Cuddy said mildly. "The mayor's gonna call me, tell me to give you the key to the city?"

Deal shrugged, checked his watch. "I'm not sure."

"That how it works down in Florida?" the chief persisted. "You get your tail in a crack, you call up some goombah politician, they muscle you out?"

"I don't know any politicians," Deal said.

"Uh-huh," Cuddy said. "Well, maybe you ought to."

The big man heaved himself up off the desk, started for the door. "I'm going to go out there, make sure those two don't drop my Blazer into Carter Creek…"

He broke off as the phone began to ring. He gave Deal a look, moved back to answer.

"Delbert Cuddy," he said wearily. His eyes narrowed then, and he shot another glance at Deal.

"Wait a minute," he said, his voice taking on an edge. "Is this some kind of a joke?"

Cuddy listened a minute more, then sat down in his chair, the tone of his voice shifting rapidly—annoyance, dismay, abject groveling—all in the space of seconds.

"Oh no, sir Absolutely not. I didn't mean to suggest that. It's just I never directly spoke to you before. Right, sir. I recognize the voice now, I do."

He had the phone tucked under his chin, moved to straighten his uniform tie, square his jacket on his shoulders. "Oh, you bet," he said, his eyes darting to Deal momentarily. "Sure thing. Of course. Yes, sir. I appreciate the call, sir. I will. Without fail. Right."

Cuddy replaced the receiver, turned to Deal, took a deep breath, started to say something, then stopped, his eyes on Deal's face as if he were searching for some detail that he'd missed earlier.

"That was the governor," Cuddy said, finally. "Was that Terrence Terrell you called? The computer guy? The governor was telling me how many subassembly plants of his we got in Nebraska."

Deal stood up from his chair. "So we can get to work now?"

The security chief was still shaking his head in dis "That we can, Mr. Deal. That we can."

◎ ◎ ◎

Within minutes, Highway Patrol units were on the scene, followed closely by Omaha city police and a pair of detectives from the Douglas County sheriff's office. Deal wasn't a minute into his third recap of the story before his description of Dexter Kittle's car, sketchy as it was, had been transmitted to dispatchers for all three agencies.

Russ the patrolman called in to confirm a fresh break in the ice as well, but even the detectives were less than ecstatic about that news.

"Carter Creek's froze over all the way down to the Missouri," the one named Dalhousie said, shaking his head. He was a short, intense man with a receding hairline. "There won't be any dragging that bad boy until springtime."

"The weather's not exactly on our side," the other one said. He was the taller, more affable half of the pair. "We're going to put a couple teams out on snowmobiles. They'll circle the airport vicinity in an outward spiral, just in case your wife might have wandered off on her own."

"It's a waste of time," Deal said.

The taller detective nodded. "I understand, but we'd rather err on the side of caution, Mr. Deal. We're trying to get a helicopter up, but with this visibility…" He opened his hands in a gesture of helplessness. "Same way on the ground, I'm afraid. We're getting the word out, but the mess the roads are in, our guys are going to be a little distracted, you understand."

Deal nodded grudgingly. The taller cop, Keane was his name, bore a certain resemblance to Bobby Knight, the incendiary Indiana basketball coach. Deal realized he was waiting for the soft-spoken man to explode at any instant.

"What about Kittle?" Deal asked.

ζe'll run the name," Keane said, "but I doubt anything's
ιg to come up. We tried to stop the plane, see if we might
ιd something there, but it's on its way back to Chicago.
We'll get some people in there once it lands at O'Hare, but
there's already been a cleaning crew go through, a whole
new set of passengers…" He gave Deal a doubtful look.

"We'll get you down to the office," Dalhousie chimed
in. "You can go through the mug books, maybe you can
spot one of them."

Deal nodded, feeling a great fatigue overcoming him. The
detectives had their game faces on, but it was beginning to
sink in. No names, no fingerprints, no real ID. The way the
pair had worked, the woman's lightning-quick moves…the
two might have looked like a couple of the Clampetts, but
they obviously knew what they were doing.

So they were pros, unlikely to turn up readily in any cursory records check, or get themselves picked up as chumps.
But that led to the next question: pros hired by whom, for
what purpose?

Keane had been idly scratching behind his ear with a
pencil while gazing out over the now-crowded staff room.
Suddenly, as if he might have a line tapped into Deal's
thoughts, he turned back to him. "Tell me again, Mr. Deal,"
Keane said. "What was it that brought the two of you to
Omaha in the first place?"

Deal was ready for the question this time, but still he felt
discomfort, an unwillingness to lay bare his own sad logic.
And why? Keane was obviously on his side, primed by
whatever Nebraska powers to do what he could. Listening
to Deal's tenuous thread of connections was not going to
deter him from trying to find Janice. No, Deal thought. It
wasn't that so much as having to admit he was responsible
for what had happened, that he had brought them so far,
going on so little.

He forced himself to meet Keane's gaze. "A close fr of ours, a man named Arch Dolan," Deal began, "he owr a bookstore in Coral Gables where my wife works. He wa killed during a robbery recently. That's what the police think, anyway." Deal paused, watching as the snowplow operator was ushered out the door of the lounge. He gave Deal a last surly look before one of the cops slammed the door.

Deal turned back to Keane. "Arch's sister lives in Omaha but no one's been able to reach her…" Deal trailed off, trying to find the way to describe connections that suddenly struck him as having the same consistency as the logic holding dreams together.

"So you came out to try to track her down, deliver the news in person?"

Deal nodded. "That's one thing."

Keane lifted his eyebrows, made a note on a three-by-five card he had in his coat pocket. "Long way to come in weather like this," he said mildly. "What made you think it couldn't wait?"

Deal shrugged. "It wasn't snowing in Miami."

Keane nodded, as if it were something that needed to be explained. "Aside from the weather," the detective said, persisting.

Maybe the guy was more like Bobby Knight than he liked to let on, Deal thought.

"Like I said, my wife worked for Arch, he and I go back a long way. His parents are on some butterfly-hunting safari in Asia, his uncle had a stroke during the so-called robbery and is still in a coma, his younger sister's on bed rest trying to stave off a miscarriage, so her doctors didn't want to tell *her*." Deal paused, taking a breath. "And this sister Sara, who lives in Omaha, took now to go on a vacation without saying where she was going. The long and short of it is, not one member of Arch Dolan's family knows he's been killed. I thought this was the least we could do."

Closer than running off to Asia," Dalhousie nodded, apparently ready to buy it.

Keane was tapping the pencil on top of his head now. "You think there could be some connection between this murder down in Miami and what happened to you and your wife?"

Deal stared at Keane, still wondering how much to say.

"When you said Arch Dolan had been killed during a robbery. You said, 'That's what the police think,'" Keane added. "Meaning maybe you don't agree."

No crackpot theories, Deal. Let the man do his job. Still…

He took a deep breath. "I don't agree," he said. "Neither does Janice."

"So what do you think happened?"

Deal glanced at Dalhousie, who widened his eyes as if to repeat the question. "It's a long story."

"We have plenty of time," Keane said.

And finally, Deal gave in. He told them about Arch, mentioned Janice's suspicions of Mega-Media, his own initial skepticism and gradual, grudging concurrence, the trail that led him from Custer to Eddie Lightner to Martin Rosenhaus, how finally, grasping at straws, they'd come to Omaha.

"I was tired of getting the brush-off about Sara, but I figured the only way to accomplish anything was to come out here myself. I wasn't crazy about the idea of Janice coming along, but she insisted, and I gave in." He gave Keane a look meant to show how much he regretted it. "The other thing, I wanted to get a line on an outfit called Carver Construction, supposed to be headquartered here."

Dalhousie sat up straighter in his chair. "Carver Construction?"

"You know it?" Deal said.

"I know it," Dalhousie said. "What's Carver have to do with anything?"

"They had the contract on the Mega-Media site," said. "If I'm right, they're the ones holding the bag on asbestos matter."

Dalhousie pursed his lips, fell back in his chair.

Deal turned to Keane. "What's going on?"

Keane glanced at his partner, then back at Deal. "Sara Dolan has a job with the Worldwide Church of Light, right?"

Deal nodded. "Until recently, anyway."

"And you're sure Carver Construction was involved in that Mega-Media project."

Deal studied the man's expression. "You want to let me in on this or not?"

"Carver Construction's a subsidiary of the WCL," Dalhousie said.

Deal stared. "The church owns Carver Construction? How does that happen?"

"They don't just own it," Dalhousie said. "They created it. Like the electric company needs somebody to do construction, it's cheaper to spin off a subsidiary, deal with your own people."

Deal nodded. He'd lost jobs bidding against such cozy setups.

"You're not just talking about 'some church,'" Keane added. "The WCL's one of the largest employers in the state. They've got a sound-stage, a TV superstation that goes world wide, a couple of satellites they rent space on, a big printing plant. And all of it, Carver Construction included, does outside work. The printer did the Super Bowl tickets last year, for instance—it was in the papers when a guy tried to rip them off. And Carver Construction just got a huge contract to build a private toll road in North Carolina. It's a big compound, several hundred acres out past Papillion, on the way to Lincoln."

Dalhousie worked at a hangnail with his teeth. "James Ray Willis never missed a trick," he said, spitting away a fleck of skin. "When Tammy and Jim and some of the other

gelicals crashed and burned a few years back, the
erend James Ray stepped in and picked up the pieces for
.1 your dispossessed congregants. He's turned the thing into
a kind of umbrella for your nontraditional, TV-oriented
church person. They service a couple million members
worldwide, or so I hear."

"How is it you guys hear so much?" Deal asked.

Dalhousie looked at him. "I go to Miami, everybody
knows about Wayne Huizenga, Terry Terrell."

"Willis is as big as that?" Deal said.

Keane gave a humorless laugh. "This is the heartland,
Mr. Deal. Maybe he doesn't play as big in Miami, but out
here James Ray Willis is the Ted Turner of the Christian
Right."

"He doesn't work the media like Turner," Dalhousie said.
"Not these days. He still does his turn on Sundays, of course,
but even most of that's on video. Fifteen thousand people
in that monster church, they have to watch him on a big
screen, like it was a heavyweight fight or something. Past
couple of years it's like he's turning into Howard Hughes."

Deal was half-listening by now, his mind busy processing
what he'd learned. So Sara Dolan worked for Willis, a New
Age Billy Graham, a televangelist who'd diversified. One of
the televangelist's companies had been building the Mega-
Media headquarters in Miami, then had run into a snag,
had to pay off the right group of officials before work could
resume…

"Maybe that's it," he said, an sudden urgency overtaking
him.

"What's *it*?" Dalhousie asked.

"Maybe Sara Dolan found out about the problem Carver
ran into at the Mega-Media site in Coral Gables. That's how
Arch found out about it."

"And…?" Keane prompted him.

"And somebody important wanted it all covered up," said. "The kind of person who wouldn't think twice ab doing whatever it took. Arch Dolan, Eddie Lightner, eve Martin Rosenhaus." Deal threw up his hands. "They must have thought I'd already figured it out, the minute I got on the plane."

"That's a pretty big stretch," Dalhousie said. "James Ray Willis bumping a bunch of people off over an asbestos cleanup."

"I didn't say it was Willis," Deal said. "And maybe there's something more important involved than we know about. Still, it explains all the connections."

"In *your* mind, it does," Dalhousie said. "It'd be about like me flying to Miami, claiming Wayne Huizenga knocked off Yitzhak Rabin."

Deal stopped, staring at him. "This isn't some theoretical problem. Two people followed my wife and me all the way from Miami. They tried to kill me out there in that parking lot about an hour ago, and one of them kidnapped my wife."

Keane leaned forward, interposing himself between Deal and his partner. "Nobody doubts what happened to you, Mr. Deal. I want to make that clear. But you have to understand, whatever you've gotten yourself involved in doesn't necessarily lead to Omaha. The pair who trailed you here could just as easily have been sent by someone in Miami."

"With all due respect," Deal said, "these two people did not come from Miami."

"What's most important," Dalhousie said 'we want to find your wife."

"I'm glad we're agreed on one thing " Deal said.

Dalhousie nodded, going on. "And it's more likely that we'll do that by working from the practical end, right now. We find her, catch the guy, then we find out the whys and wherefores."

"But if someone at Carver Construction is involved…"

alhousie held up his hand. "First thing in the morning,
. Deal. We'll talk to some people over there, we'll look
1to Sara Dolan's status with the church."

Deal started to protest, then cut himself off. He wasn't
going to accomplish anything by protesting. The way matters
stood, he was lucky to get that much. "What can I do?" he
said finally.

"Excuse the very thought, Mr. Deal," Keane said. "But if
this guy meant immediate harm to your wife, he'd have
probably done it right out there in that parking lot."

"You think she's being held hostage?" Deal asked. He
stared at Keane, trying to read his cop's mind, gauge Janice's
chances by the expression on the man's face.

Keane shook his head. "I don't know what to think right
now, Mr. Deal. I'm just trying to do the best we can."

"Was there somewhere you were headed?" Dalhousie cut
in. "A place where your wife might try to contact you, make
her way to, given the opportunity."

Deal shrugged. "We had a reservation at some hoop-de-
do Holiday Inn, a place the rental car guy told us about."

"The Convention Center," Dalhousie said, glancing at
Keane. "Out on Kennedy."

Keane nodded. "That's it," Deal said. "I think you ought
to get out there," Keane said. "Get checked in, sit by the
phone. We'll have a plainclothesman stationed there as well.
We'll talk to the tech people, get them out there as soon as
the weather breaks."

Deal stared at him, feeling his indignation rise. "So I just
go sit in a hotel room, hope for the best?"

Keane studied him a moment. "What else did you have
in mind, Mr. Deal? Say your wife makes her way to a phone,
calls the hotel, there's nobody there to answer. Say she's
somewhere trying right now."

Deal stared back at him. He felt utterly depleted, as if
he'd been up for days. Finally he nodded. Keane reached
into his coat pocket, tossed him a set of keys.

"They got you another car," Keane said. "Right this time."

"Terrific," Deal said.

"We can have a man drive you if you'd rather," Ke̶ added.

"That's okay," Deal said. "I should probably have a car. In case something happens." He hoped it sounded as casual as he wanted it to. So long as he had wheels, he could handle things the way he wanted.

Keane shrugged. "Your choice."

"Try and get some rest," Dalhousie said. "We'll get you over to look at some pictures first thing."

"Sure," Deal said, rising stiffly from the chair. He wondered if he would ever rest again.

Chapter 22

What they had found for him, Deal saw, was a Toyota Land
Cruiser. A glowing burgundy model, it sat idling at the curb,
exhaust spewing like dragon's breath into the frigid air, its
paint gleaming as if they'd run it down the de-icing line on
the runway before bringing it around.

A uniformed patrolman who'd been pacing at curbside
snapped to when he saw Deal coming. "Holiday Inn Convention Center, right?" the patrolman said.

Deal noticed a radio hooked to the belt of his quilted
jacket. An efficient operation, he thought, and nodded.

The patrolman gestured at a black-and-white that idled
just in front of the Land Cruiser. "I'll lead the way," he said.

Deal nodded again, moved gingerly around the back of
the Toyota. There was a dull ache in his groin, but he suspected it was nothing compared to what he'd feel later. He
glanced in the cargo bay, saw his suitcase stowed there. All
the little details.

He wondered briefly how it would have all gone down if
he hadn't had Terrence Terrell to call. Small consolation,
though. A shiny new car to drive, a cop to show him the
way. He gave his lone suitcase a forlorn glance, then pulled
himself up into the cabin of the Land Cruiser. There was a
gaily painted packet on the front seat, courtesy of the

...aska Beef Council: maps, tourist brochures, discounts
...anything you'd want. He tossed it aside, found the parking
...ake release, motioned to the cop that he was ready.
Welcome to Omaha, he thought. Sure. Big steaks for
everyone.

It was dark and still snowing, though nowhere near as
badly as it had been. The roads, though cleared of drifts,
were packed solid with snow and ice, and Deal was tentative
behind the wheel at first. It had been years since he'd driven
under conditions like these, the last time being the ski trip
he and Janice had taken a decade before.

But the sedan he'd driven then was nothing like this big
Land Cruiser. It had continuous four-wheel drive, and the
oversized studded tires seemed to grip the road as firmly as
if they were traveling dry pavement. By the time they swung
out of the brightly lit airport complex onto a broad, curving
boulevard, Deal was already feeling more comfortable, at
least able to turn the wheel without the feeling he was going
to tip over, or send the vehicle into an endless spin.

As if he'd sensed Deal's growing confidence, the patrolman
picked up the pace slightly, his taillights leading the way
through a tunnel of whirling snow into the vast Midwestern
darkness. Though it was not quite nine o'clock, the roads
were deserted, leaving Deal with another unfamiliar sensation. He couldn't remember the last time he'd traveled a
major highway when there hadn't been a maddening, horn-
blaring crush of traffic.

The roads, the car, the situation itself...his head was reeling in time to the throb of a headache that grew with every
passing moment. More and more, he felt the sensation of
being gripped by an awful dream, a set of circumstances so
strange and threatening that his life no longer seemed his to
control.

And the thought that he'd carelessly led Janice into this
was nearly overwhelming. He'd had her back and now look

what he had done. The realization was enough to mak
grind his teeth, pound the wheel in frustration. Worst c
was the helplessness. He was on his way to some conve
tioneer's hotel where he was going to sit and hope he'd hea.
from a killer who had taken his wife? But what was the
immediate alternative?

And what if Delbert Cuddy had been right? What if Janice
had simply run from their attackers, had curled up under
one of the many cars in that frozen lot, was lying there right
now, unconscious, slowly freezing in this insane climate…

…he had worked himself into a near-frenzy, and even
though he knew he had lost all sense of reasoned judgment,
he was about to wrench the wheel of the Toyota into a U-
turn, speed back the way they had come, comb that parking
lot himself, dig through the snowplow's drifts, do something,
anything…

…when he glanced ahead, saw the patrol car, a couple
hundred yards ahead now, its brake lights blooming suddenly
bright, two red nova bursts diffused by the blowing snow.
As he watched in concern, the car swerved, its headlamps
jouncing as it veered off the road at a sharp angle.

Deal fought the urge to slam on his brakes, forced himself
into a series of gentle taps that gradually brought the Toyota
down to forty, thirty-five, then thirty. He was close enough
to see what had happened now: a series of spindly-looking
barricades were strung across the highway, one bearing a
sign, "BRIDGE OUT," an arrow pointing off in the direction
the patrol car had taken.

Deal cursed under his breath, brought the Land Cruiser
to a crawl, edging off the pavement in the direction of the
wallowing patrol car. Still a hundred yards or so ahead, the
black and white piled through a fresh drift, sending a mighty
wave of white that obliterated it for a moment. Then, like a
surfer emerging from the aftermath of a wipeout, the patrol
car emerged into view once again, churning up a steep incline

past a massive outcropping of rock and a clutch of
~rable-looking trees, wrenched nearly to the ground by
~eir burden of ice and snow.

Deal felt a chill just seeing it, even though the Toyota's
heater was pumping out a steady blast of hot, dry air. Not
another car, not a street-lamp, not a house light in sight.
Where in God's name were they? Omaha was a *city*, wasn't
it? A few minutes ago he'd been in its airport. Didn't that
mean there had to be people around? Buildings. Houses.

The patrol car topped the rise above just as Deal plowed
through the drift himself. Snow flew up against the windshield as if a blanket had been tossed over it, and he jerked
levers, punched buttons hurriedly until he managed to switch
the wipers on, clearing the mass enough to see. The way
ahead was vacant now, the patrol car disappeared again, over
the rise, nothing but a pair of rutted tracks and an angry
whirl of snow boring at him through his headlights.

He felt a jolt of panic, but the tires of the big Land Cruiser
bit surely into the icy tracks and the big vehicle climbed
steadily up the steep incline as if it were born to such work.
One thing working out right, Deal thought, patting the thick,
leather-wrapped wheel. Maybe when this was over, when they
were back safely in Miami, he'd get rid of the Hog once and
for all, buy a rig like this, sit up high where trouble couldn't
touch you, churn through sand drifts and boggy job sites
without a care. Sure, Deal, sure. Take a pill, quick.

He gave the Toyota a little extra pedal then, held on tightly
as the nose of the big machine bucked up over the rise and
came down with a jolt. He caught a glimpse of the patrol
car, already far down the opposite hillside, and wondered
about it, how quickly the road fell away on the opposite
site, he was thinking…

…and that was when he realized what was happening
and began to pump his own brakes frantically, his hands
clamped to the wheel.

The patrol car was hurtling out of control, caught ⸱ runaway slide down the steep incline, spinning around nc so that its headlights washed briefly across his face. The ca⸱ slid backwards for a second, leveling out, the headlamps revealing a set of guardrails whisking away in its wake.

A bridge, Deal realized, the patrol car now sliding backwards across a frozen bridge. It veered momentarily, a rear fender striking one rail, whipping the front around against the opposite rail, the process repeating itself as if the car were rattling like a marble down a loose track.

He'll stop in a moment, Deal thought, a couple more bounces, friction would eventually take over. He was also thinking how fortunate he'd been, if he hadn't seen the patrol car lose it, he might have ended up in the same skid. As it was, they'd have one workable vehicle, he'd ease on down, get the cop out of his car...they could get the hell out of this miserable place...

...and then he stopped, staring in disbelief as the patrol car skidded out into nothingness, its lights tilting straight up into the snow-swirling sky for a moment, then falling away into an abyss, just as the Toyota leveled out on the bridge approach and slid gently, finally, to a stop.

Stunned, Deal caught a glimpse of ragged concrete up ahead, twisted steel reinforcement rods curling out, tendril-like, into space—there had been a roadway there once, a bridge, but now it was gone, ripped away by who knew what calamity...

"BRIDGE OUT, BRIDGE OUT," the sign he remembered out on the highway now flashing behind his eyes as if his brain had etched it there in neon...and he then began to understand.

He felt more than heard the impact of the patrol car as it struck something far below, rocks, or maybe support pilings. He flung himself out of the Toyota, ran across the slippery surface. He caught hold of the icy railing, glanced down in

.e to see the patrol car, now a ball of orange and yellow ames, catapulting off the side of a rocky gorge. It struck the rocks again and again, then finally came to rest, a burning pyre that cast its glow all the way up the gorge to where he stood.

He stood gaping at the sight for a moment, his mind racing through an explanation—*she is still alive, Deal, they think you know something, one of you has to stay alive until they can be sure of what you know*—another part of himself shouting orders, "*Into the truck, into the truck while you still can...*"

...and finally, he listened to his own commands, and tried to do just that. He half-ran, half-slid back to the Toyota, found reverse, swung the vehicle into a tight arc, dropped the shift into low. He was fighting the urge to floor the accelerator—*you'll dig yourself into a grave that way, Deal*—when he saw him, standing like a specter in the middle of the road, arm upraised. In the same instant, he saw the muzzle flash. He threw up his hand to ward off the spray of glass as the Land Cruiser's windshield exploded, and knew then it was too late to run.

Chapter 23

As he dove beneath the dashboard of the Land Cruiser, Deal heard two more shots ring out, heard the rending of metal, a thudding sound as one slug tore through leather and seat padding somewhere above him. He had only a few seconds, he knew. No return fire, Kittle would realize there was nothing to stop him, he'd move in, finish the job.

Deal reached up, unlatched the driver's-side door, prayed Kittle would choose that side to approach. He grasped the steering wheel, pulled himself into as tight a ball as he could, his knees drawn toward his chest, soles of his shoes poised by the door panel. He reached up, found the key, killed the ignition, slapped his palm about until he saw the dashlights die. All those unfamiliar switches, all the blather from the Driver's Ed manuals—"Take a moment to familiarize yourself with your car's control panel." He could only hope he'd managed to douse the headlamps as well.

He lay quietly, hardly daring to breathe, his ears straining for the slightest sound. He heard the whistling of the wind, the creak of metal as the body of the truck swayed in answer. If there were footsteps out there, they were lost in the storm, in the smothering snow. He might have an instant to react, or he might not, Deal thought. Perhaps one shadowy glimpse before the shots came. And if Kittle approached by the passenger door…then he would die without knowing it had happened.

dark now, he wasn't sure if he could see, or even if the were standing there peering in through the driver's-e window. Maybe he could perceive a vaguely glowing sky out there, maybe not. Maybe it would be best to make a run for it, pull himself out, hope he could find cover...but he knew it was no good to think that way.

Pay your money, take your choice, Deal. Another of his old man's sayings. A million of them. His old man's way of stipulating his authority. He could hear him now, if you'd listened to me, you wouldn't be in the fix you are now.

Right. Deal could be drunk somewhere, in the middle of a card game or urging the ponies to fly, he wouldn't have given a red apple crap if Janice had left him, come back home, or flown to the moon. He could be free as the breeze that threatened to topple the Land Cruiser on its side, send it down the same final plunge the patrol car had taken.

He might have seen a vague shadow then, or it might have been a trick of his eyes, the sort of thing staring hard into darkness could conjure up all on its own, and he hesitated, blinking, because he would have only this one chance.

"Deal!" He heard the scream then. "He's there, Deal." Janice's voice, carrying shrilly over the howling of the storm, and Deal let fly, kicking with everything he had, a death grip on the steering wheel for leverage.

The door rocketed outward, thudding into Kittle before it had swung open a foot. Deal heard a cry, and came up from behind the wheel in the same motion. He threw himself out of the truck, still holding on to the door frame for balance. He glanced around, his eyes finally adjusting to the darkness, saw Kittle's truck a few yards away, backed into a grove of oaks, but strangely, no sign of Janice. He heard scuffling sounds at his feet, looked down to find the dark lump that was Kittle fumbling about in the snow nearby.

The gun, Deal thought, *he's looking for the goddamned gun.* He strode forward, delivering a kick just as Kittle found it, raised his hand to fire. Deal's foot caught Kittle higher than he intended, burrowing into the man's upper arm, but it was a solid blow and the gun soared away into space.

Kittle still had his head turned when Deal hit him, one step forward and a solid right that started low and caught him flush at the hinge of the jaw, the perfect punch that sent him toppling into the snow with a groan. Deal's hand went numb with the shock of the blow and the cold, but he ignored the pain, took another step, aimed a kick at Kittle's ribs, ready to send him over the side, send him to oblivion...

...but Kittle saw it coming, and rolled away. Deal felt his feet fly out from under him, and then the ground came up to meet his back, shoulders, and then his head slammed down with stunning force. He meant to roll over once, get his feet under him, get up, get back to Kittle, but instead of stopping, he was picking up speed, tumbling over and over, head below his feet and launching into the air again. He soared for one second, two, then three or four, stunned, too disoriented even to be afraid, until finally he came back to earth, or something like it, a sideways plunge into a deep drift of snow, where he floundered breathlessly, sucking in nothing but great mouthfuls of feathery, suffocating snow.

Swim, Deal, swim. Swim your way out. The ski instructor's decade-old advice for escaping avalanche filtering vaguely up through his consciousness. Something he'd thought of as terribly incongruous at the time, how in God's name could you swim through frozen water...

Don't try to climb...wiggle out sideways...it's Nebraska for God's sake, how deep could snow be here...

And then he felt his hands strike solid ground, a rock, a tree limb, which he grabbed like a lifeline, one hand, then the other. He wrenched himself out, gasping, saw a shadow of hillside above, a glimpse of clouds and broken sky. Then came the wash of headlights through falling snow, a vehicle up there turning around, the sound of a motor grinding hard, grinding away.

By the time he had struggled back to the Toyota, Kittle's vehicle had topped the rise, headed back toward the highway where the barricades had been switched. Deal caught a brief glimpse of its boxy silhouette, then saw it slide away below the ridgeline. He took a moment to scour the surroundings, check the area where Kittle had hidden his truck.

He cupped his hands, called out her name, bellowing above the wind, "Janice, Janice," twice to each point of the compass. But there was no answer, only the soughing of the wind through the trees and the clatter of ice crystals off the new paint of the Land Cruiser at his side.

He stared about, eyes straining, tearing in the wind. In the Land Cruiser, beneath it. He ran to the end of the bridge, stared out into the abyss where the patrol car had gone down. He'd heard her call to him, warn him, he was certain of it. But there was no place she could have gone. She must have been inside Kittle's truck, maybe she'd only made it to the window, had only enough strength to call to him…

He was already back at the Toyota, up into the seat, glass nuggets crunching beneath his feet, at his seat, the odd sensation of wind in his face, no windshield to stop it anymore.

He found the ignition, turned the engine over. He used the headlights until he was close to the ridgeline, then doused them again, navigating the last fifty feet in darkness, his hand held up against the stinging wind.

He paused as he came over the rise where he'd seen Kittle's truck minutes before. The storm actually seemed to be breaking up. A wan moon slipped out from behind a mountainous cloud, illuminating the countryside for a moment, could have been a scene from Currier & Ives. Below him was the plain they'd crossed following the false detour, a mile or more of desolate country dotted here and there by clumps of trees, broken only by the vague line of their tracks. And there, toward the horizon, one lone vehicle making its way up the embankment toward the place where the, the deserted highway.

Deal saw the truck regain the pavement, saw it stop, th Kittle's figure crossing the path of the headlights, and th man struggling to drag the barricades out of the way. Deal took his foot off the brake, guided the Land Cruiser carefully down the deep ruts in front of him. The moon had ducked behind another cloud bank, but there was a soft glow that was enough to keep the roadway in sight. By the time he reached the bottom of the hill and started up the gradual incline toward the highway, Kittle was back in his truck, fishtailing through the opening he'd made in the barricades.

Deal, his headlights still off, eyes squinting to keep fixed on Kittle's taillights, didn't concern himself with the barricades. He picked up speed, sent one careening sideways off the right fender of the Land Cruiser, blew another into splinters off the front brush cutter. The heavy vehicle didn't veer, didn't wobble. Another mark in its favor, he thought. If they ever got out of this, the Hog's days were numbered.

The highway was curving southward, and even though they had picked up speed, the wind rushing through the gaping hole in the windshield seemed to have abated. That meant they were running downwind now, he thought, grateful for small favors. The lights of Kittle's truck illuminated a large traffic sign that spanned the highway, but it was too far away to read. By the time Deal reached it, the sign was simply a looming shadow overhead, and the direction it seemed to mark was an unbroken ramp of snow leading off into darkness at his right. He could make out a distant glow in the sky in that direction and supposed it marked the lights of Omaha, but they were swinging further southward now, a course that only deepened Deal's anxiety.

He didn't have much in the way of a plan in the first place—keep Kittle in sight until they reached civilization, get help, ram the man's car if he had to, whatever it took—

~~e~~ direction they were headed now did not seem
~~nising~~ and he wondered how long he could withstand
~~e~~ frigid blast through the windshield, and what would
~~h~~appen if Kittle realized he was being followed. Even worse
was the gut-wrenching possibility that he'd left Janice behind,
that she was wandering alone in that frozen landscape...

He commanded himself to stop. She wasn't back there,
he'd heard her, she was up there in that car, Kittle's prisoner,
and the only hope he had of seeing her again rested on his
ability to maintain this chase.

All the rest was fit to worry about another time, Deal
told himself. He was alternating one hand with the other
on the wheel now, jamming one under his armpit, his thigh,
until some semblance of feeling returned to the numbed
flesh of his fingers, repeating the process over and over again,
thirty-second intervals, then twenty, even less.

There was a chunk of windshield still hanging on the
passenger's side, and if he leaned across the console in that
direction, he got some relief from the wind, could massage
some feeling back into his face, though the crazy-quilt web
of fractured glass made the already miserable visibility almost
impossible.

And he'd had the effrontery in the past to have cursed
the Miami heat, he thought. Never again, he vowed. Never
again. A man gets hot in Miami, he can always go jump in
the ocean. Another of his father's aphorisms rattling around
in his head, this one on the mark.

The snow was suddenly thick again, heavy wet flakes that
pasted themselves to his face, melted, then froze before they
could drip away. He swiped his hand across his face, realized
he'd have to hold his free hand up as a shield or his eyes
would simply ice over.

He glanced ahead, felt a surge of panic when he saw he'd
lost sight of Kittle's taillights. A turn up ahead he couldn't
see? A sudden rise? A dip? He fought the urge to flip on his

headlamps, to give the Land Cruiser a bit more ped.
Without headlights, with the road conditions as they wer
and the biting wind nearly blinding him, he was on a suicide
mission as it was.

He saw another road sign flash by, lifted his foot from
the accelerator, heard the whine of the engine as it took on
the force of the big vehicle's momentum. He strained into
the darkness, looking for signs that Kittle had veered off the
highway, but could see nothing.

If he could just chance a few seconds with his headlamps,
he thought, even as hard as the snow was falling, a few
moments of light and he could still see if anyone had taken
that turn…but he knew he could not risk it. His one hope
was that Kittle thought him gone, that sooner or later the
element of surprise would pay off…

He saw movement out of the corner of his eye then, and
glanced up—something flying over his head, for God's
sake?—could not stop himself from hitting the brakes. The
big vehicle hesitated before its rear wheels broke loose and
spun about, leading him in a breathtaking skid down the
highway.

He clung helplessly to the wheel, waiting for the wheels
to drift off the pavement, catch some hidden rift or burrow.
At this speed, the vehicle was sure to flip. And that, he
thought, would be that. He watched the overpass that had
caught his eye slide away behind him, felt the Toyota veer
left, then right as he fought to bring the wheel into line.
How the hell were you supposed to drive backwards, anyway? They'd left that part of driver training out, down in
Miami. He'd write a note about it, somebody could deliver
it to the Florida politicians, "We found this suggestion in a
glacier in Nebraska, guy had it clutched in his mitten…"

Miraculously, though, the Toyota did not veer off the
highway. It continued its slide another fifty yards or so,
gradually slowing with gravity, with Deal's tentative taps at the

akes. They finally came to a halt, the snout of the vehicle till pointed firmly back in the direction they'd come from.

Deal discovered he could breathe again, and peeled his fingers from the wheel. He sat massaging feeling back into his hands, noticed the engine had stalled, noticed the deafening silence that had descended. Snow drifted lazily through the shattered window, threatening his view of the overpass they'd skated under, now a dim line at the horizon. No lights. No sound of Kittle's truck in the distance. Nothing. Where to now, Mr. Deal?

He reached for the ignition, held his breath momentarily, closed his eyes in thanks as the Toyota's engine responded with a growl. He backed gingerly into a tight turn, hesitated, then flipped on his headlights. Snow piling down heavily again, dim ruts of traffic ahead of him, but were those Kittle's tracks, already filling up?

He thought a moment, then pressed the dome light button, found the welcome packet that he'd tossed aside. It had slid to the floor, disgorging its contents, and he had to rummage through the soggy welter of papers for several moments until he found the road map he'd prayed would be there. The Beef Council was nothing if not thorough, he thought as he unfolded it.

He held the wet map up to the light, shook away a crust of dirty ice, found Omaha, the airport, the road they must have taken. He checked the trip odometer, shook his head at the short distance he'd traveled. It seemed he'd been driving forever. He consulted the map scale, did some quick calculations, retraced what he hoped was the route he'd taken.

He found a wavering blue line leading away from the highway at what seemed like the right spot, a state or county road that curled eastward into a bulge of land outlined by a bend in the Missouri River. No towns marked there. No bridge. No reason for a road that he could tell. Big beef ranchland, maybe. A road to a subdivision yet to become.

He checked again. The main highway they'd been trav̶
was some kind of belt road. If he was correct, it would t̶
back west, toward the city, a mile or so up ahead.

He strained to see into the darkness, but it was hopeless.
Even if Kittle had taken that route, the thought of gaining
ground under these conditions was absurd. Kittle would reach
the city long before Deal, there'd be any number of exits, he
could never hope to guess which way Kittle had taken...

Deal bit his lip in decision, spun the Toyota into another
turn, then headed back, down the highway, pressing the
accelerator as fully as he dared. Wasn't this how Janice's
parents had bought it, it occurred to him. Heading the wrong
way down an ice-slick highway? Some irony in that, he
thought, but he'd consider it another day.

He held the accelerator firm, speeding back under the
overpass, past the exit itself, slowing only when he saw the
back side of the exit marker as it loomed up out of the
blowing snow. Gentle taps on the brakes now, Deal. A
controlled skid this time and an easy, controlled power slide,
finishing up with the headlights on the sign, which on this
side he found covered by an impenetrable blanket of frozen
snow.

Deal stared at the sign for a moment, nodding. Nothing
less than he might have expected. Nothing was going to be
easy. He gripped the wheel tightly, aimed the Land Cruiser,
pressed the accelerator down. There was a roar from the
engine, and a series of bumps as they left the pavement and
shot across the shoulder. An instant of clear sailing, then,
and a sudden thud that sent Deal rocking forward as the
Toyota's brush cutter slammed into one of the heavy
aluminum poles supporting the sign.

Snow cascaded down in a mini-avalanche, flurries roiling
into the Toyota's cabin, filling his lungs with a breath-
stopping gulp that was more frozen crystals than air. Chunks
of ice thundered off the Toyota's top and hood, but Deal

already in reverse, churning back over the frozen ulder, dusting snow from his face and shoulders.

"...IDE CHURCH...F...IGHT," he read now, white letters against a green background in gaps where the snow and ice had fallen away, and he found himself wondering if it was a sign the taxpayers had paid for. It didn't really matter, though, did it? He knew now where he had to go. He dropped the Toyota into low and hit the accelerator again, this time following the arrow he'd missed the first time, and the dim outline of Kittle's tracks.

⚙ ⚙ ⚙

Deal risked his lights for a while longer, letting them burn until he had swung about, crossed the overpass himself, and picked up the shadows of a stand of trees up ahead. No way to tell what might lie in there, he thought, flipping the switch that sent the road back into darkness. He held the wheel grimly, pointing himself toward the gloomy smudge that was the grove, waiting impatiently for his eyes to adjust once again.

Once Kittle got where he was going, everything was going to become vastly more complicated. How would he approach the man under such conditions, he wondered? How on earth would Deal reach him without endangering Janice more than she already was...

He forced those questions away, and then he was into the grove of trees, all the light reflected from the vast blanket of snow abruptly cut off, and he found himself driving utterly on faith. There could be a cliff up ahead, a frozen lake, a brick wall, who the hell knew? Hit the brakes, he'd surely slide off the road, keep going it could be even worse.

What a joke, he thought. What a pathetic, sickening joke. Maybe Arch was somewhere where he could appreciate the madness of it all, though Arch would be fretting it was all his fault Deal was in such a fix.

Not your fault at all, good buddy, Deal thought, willing his thoughts into the ether. All you wanted to do was sell good books, turn people on to the things you'd come to love, do a small, decent thing in a bloated, overgrown world, and look what it cost. Not your fault at all.

Deal thought he might have repeated the words out loud this time, wondering if it was about to end, one last tumble into a ditch, a snow-bank, maybe the goddamned Missouri River…

And then he was through, back out into the bright plain again, the snow abated suddenly, the moon breaking through the clouds, the Land Cruiser steady on course. The road was a straight shot along a ridge, then came a long, slow descent, where in the distance the yellow cone of Kittle's truck lights bobbed and ducked like something from an animator's pen.

And there, in a valley below, their apparent destination was laid out: a series of lights marking what seemed at first to be a village. Town hall here, church spires there, a picturesque, tree-lined lake…and on the other side, some sort of arena with a huge parking lot, all of it connected by strings of amber vapor lights marking the winding streets.

He saw a cluster of strange structures on the opposite ridgeline—satellite dishes, he realized, clustered near a microwave relay station. A town into communicating in a big way, he thought. And he might have gone on convincing himself he was headed into some modern version of Duckburg or Appleville or Prettytown if he hadn't just then passed the big building with the massive sign illuminated out front.

He wasn't sure he'd read correctly at first, had to turn in his seat to read the glowing letters on the sign's opposite face. He'd seen such elaborate signage before. Certain builders couldn't help themselves, so seduced by the feelings that come with lives of moving monster machines and leveling mountains and sending steel and glass towers to touch the sky, it seemed only natural to spend a few hundred thousand dollars on a living marble monument to yourself.

"Look what I can do," they say, *it* said. Huge polished slabs rising up from a pedestal of boulders like stone metamorphosed into purpose, two-foot steel letters backlit in light so ghostly, so intense, that it seemed shot out from radium, plutonium, kryptonite.

Carver Construction, Deal read, nodding. His hands seemed frozen to the wheel. He glanced down into the valley that looked so placid and inviting from this vantage point. Forget Duckburg. He was descending to the village of the damned.

Chapter 24

"What you find out, it's how confining such a life is," Willis was saying. "I know it sounds like whining, but that's the truth of it."

He'd dragged a more comfortable chair from one of the sound-mixing consoles, found a portable refrigerator, was sitting where she'd have to look at him any time she opened her eyes, sipping some designer seltzer from what looked like a hand-painted bottle. His clothes were in place, his hair neatly combed, but the flush had not left his cheeks, and his eyes glittered, dancing about the room.

"There's no normal, everyday going out in the world anymore," he said, "because everybody wants something from you, even if it's just to say hello."

He sat back in his seat, shaking his head, then popped forward again almost immediately. "You get sick of saying hello to people that just want to go home and say, 'Guess who said hello to me today,' never mind the ones that really come after you, got a deal, or a bone to pick, or maybe they think I still lay on hands and when I finish supper wouldn't I come out to the Winnebago where Uncle Art's all stove up with bone cancer, see what I might could do."

He drank deeply from his bottle of water, stared up at the ceiling. "That was another lifetime," he mused. "Before I saw the light."

e turned back to her then, leaned forward, forearms on knees. "I'm going to tell you something, Sara." His face as as bland with self-involvement as a schoolboy's, his speech less studied, as if the careful façade he'd worked so hard to build were giving way at last.

"It was you as much as anybody who helped me see where this was headed, you realize that? Seven, eight years ago, I didn't know what a computer was, not really, not till you came along, brought us into the twenty-first century."

She closed her eyes, bit the inside of her lip in despair. *Wonderful*, she thought. She'd helped make a monster even worse.

"Of course I know you were just doing a job for us, didn't have your eyes on the prize, but that's to be expected." He waved his hands about in a gesture of magnanimity. "But I caught your fever. You believed and you made a believer out of me, especially once I saw how important this was going to be. The television's important, of course, but it's no longer the boss. It's just a little part of the big picture. Telephone, television, movies, radio, cable, books, magazines, newspapers, even the computer's a part of it, your World Wide Web." He ticked the items off on his fingers, formed his fingers into fists, which he held up before her face.

"It took all this talk about what was going to go on all these webs and cables and channels to get me thinking, you see. All those people out there fighting amongst themselves about making up programs," he said dismissively. "I understood that's all I used to do, and that's what got me out of the miracle business."

He banged his fists together, then opened up his palms, his face gone from frown to beatific smile in an instant. "I spent a lifetime worrying about getting out the word. Find some dramatic way to get the word out, I thought. Tell the folks how it is. I was worried about the message, you see, and that was all wrong." He shook a thick finger in the air between them. "First thing is, Jimmy Ray, I said, you get yourself hold of the *means* of distribution. Once you have the *means*, then you're in the catbird seat. The means *becomes* the message."

She stared at his beaming face, wondering if, even if there were no tape across her mouth, she'd have the nerve to tell him someone had had the thought a few decades before.

"That's why the networks are hurting. Their programs aren't any different, any worse. They lost their stranglehold on the means of distribution, that's all." He glanced around for his bottle of water, found it, polished it off.

"Same thing applies to books. You don't have to fool around with the publishers and the editors. You get yourself hold of the means of distribution, and then the editors and the publishers—-for that matter the writers themselves— they'll have to fall into line sooner or later. Your brother understood that, God rest his soul." He gave her a look as if Arch's murder were a regrettable but necessary detail.

"Sure, it's going to take a while, and you get your little bumps along the way, fools like Rosenhaus think they're smarter, more important than they are." He shrugged. "But the important thing is to hold fast to a vision." He nodded sagely at her. "You work along in the right direction, that's all that's important. Control the means, then the minds come easy."

He reached out, patted her cheek gently. "But that's enough for now," he said. "It's getting late, and I'm keeping you up." He rose from his chair, adjusted his trousers, smiled down at her.

"I tell myself," he said, and held up his palm before his face, as if it were a book to read, "'James Ray, it's not too late for Sara. She's a bright woman, she's someone special just like you always thought.'" He paused, shook his head sorrowfully, held up his other hand as if it were a facing page. "But there's another part of me says otherwise. Tells me we've run out our string."

He folded his hands together, stared at her sorrowfully. "The saddest thing is, I've got to the point where I understand that it doesn't matter, Sara. It's a concern what happens, I admit it. But it's a small concern compared to all this other." He broke off, waved his hands about the room. "You, your brother, Martin Rosenhaus…" He shook his head again. "You matter, of course…but you just don't matter an awful lot."

He smiled at her, made a gesture. "Would you like to go to the bathroom now?"

She squeezed her eyes shut tightly, fighting tears of fury, of anger, shook her head violently back and forth. She'd burst, she'd die first…and yes, she probably would die, she thought. He would kill her. He would kill her soon.

"Now what the hell do you suppose that is?" she heard Willis say, and opened her eyes to see him moving toward the big control panel behind him.

Willis bent over the board, a puzzled expression coming over his face as lights flashed and meters danced. Willis punched a series of buttons, and a bank of monitors on the wall above the console popped into life: the cavernous convocation center, empty. The reception center lobby, also empty. The vast parking lot where she'd been captured, a vast expanse of snow. Willis moved a switch and the view of the parking lot tightened. Tire tracks there, it seemed. Willis fiddled with a joystick and the camera angle swung up from the parking lot onto the facade of the Convocation Center, the cradle of the Worldwide Church of Light.

A boxy four-wheel drive vehicle had been parked hastily there, two wheels up on the snow-covered sidewalk, a set of foot tracks leading toward the entrance where one set of glass doors yawned open to the gusting wind. Snow drifting inside, a mini-glacier forming in the ever-flowing Stream of Mercy.

Willis flipped another switch and six different angles of the interior of the chapel filled the monitors. Row upon row of empty seats. Vacant aisles. Choir loft big enough to

hold the entire congregation of most churches, also e
A stage so vast the Red Sea could be parted there, also en.
or almost empty.

Another switch, and a zoom-in upon the pulpit. A tall,
gaunt man standing there, his face drawn and battered, a
picture of the country preacher clutching the sides of the
lectern and imploring his congregation soundlessly, what
looked like a bundle of rags on the floor near his feet. She'd
seen him before, she knew she had.

"She says she needs help, hon."

"Why, of course she does."

The two of them, out in the very same parking lot that
had been illuminated on the screens, moments before. She'd
thought she'd been saved then, and look what had happened.

Willis rammed a button with the heel of his hand and
suddenly there was sound issuing from the tall man's lips:

"…if you're down there, wherever you are, there's trouble.
I've lost Dora. I don't know what's happened to her. Maybe
she's come back here, I don't know. We need some direction
here, James Ray, big time." He broke off, gestured at the
lump of rags at his feet. "I brought one of them back, like
you said. I took care of her husband, but we had some
problems. I just don't know what you want to do now."

Willis slammed his hand down, cutting off the audio.
"Lord God Almighty," he said, already on the way toward
the door of the bunker. Though the words were spoken softly,
his expression suggested that wrath was sure to fall. "If the
man wasn't my own flesh and blood, I don't know what the
hell I'd do with him."

Chapter 25

Deal had just rounded the last curve that would send him down toward the cluster of buildings laid out below when he saw the gates. He should have expected something like this, of course. Private road, private compound, after all, you could do whatever you wanted. It could have been worse, though. It could have been guard gates, hurricane fence, armed sentries.

Instead it was a modestly landscaped entry, matching raised mounds on either side of the road, a little traffic circle in the middle where a cluster of boulders and sandstone slabs had been arranged, something that was probably a rock waterfall in the summer. There was another mausoleum-styled sign informing visitors that they had finally reached Mecca, or in this case, the home of the Worldwide Church of Light.

A set of welded pipe gates guarded both sides of the circle, each painted bright yellow and bound to a matching stanchion by a length of chain. Boldly lettered signs affixed to the gates advised Deal that the grounds were closed and invited him to come again.

As he got closer, he saw how Kittle had handled the matter of the gates: a fresh set of tire tracks swung around the right-hand gate between it and the big stone marker. Kittle had taken out one of the floodlights that illuminated the sign, had in fact clipped the edge of the stone, knocking off a chunk at its corner.

Deal would have been happy to take the same route, but there was another problem. Something huge there, in his way, something impossible, an enormous frozen man...

Then he realized, as he wrenched the Land Cruiser back onto the road. Not a man but a statue, a gigantic representation of a man in flowing robes, his arms upraised in a benedictory pose. The thing—a depiction of James Ray Willis, he supposed—was lying on its back in the snow now, its arms reaching toward the heavens. Until recently the statue must have presided over the entrance to the grounds, lending its blessing to everyone who came and went. Until Kittle had clipped its foundation, sent it tumbling down, that is.

Ozymandias, Deal thought. There was a poem that even he could remember. Shelley, wasn't it? "Look on my works, ye Mighty, and despair," some tumbled statue in the desert, its legend proclaiming the enduring magnificence and everlasting power of its subject. He'd written a paper on it, had managed a B in that English class.

He stomped the accelerator flat, hit the gate doing forty, snapped the brittle chain holding it as if it were glass. There'd be time to despair later on, he thought as the gate crashed open before him.

The road had been graded inside the compound, but it was still snow-covered and treacherous, especially on the switchbacks that twisted down toward the valley floor. He was concentrating so hard on the road before him that he wasn't aware of the vehicle behind him until the red flashers caught him in their glare.

He glanced in his rearview mirror, startled. Another four-wheel-drive vehicle, big light bar affixed to its top, flashers spinning, headlights flashing high to dim, high to dim. Cops, he found himself thinking. Cavalry to the rescue. Then remembered where he was.

He'd instinctively taken his foot from the gas, and ⟨vehicle had closed the gap between them. "Pull over!" De⟨ heard the amplified voice cracking from behind him. "Pull over *now*."

Deal glanced ahead. One more turn, then a straight chute downhill past the lake, the big arena-like building and its parking lot beyond. He saw Kittle's truck up there, crossing the snowbound lot.

Hadn't this cop seen Kittle, he wondered? And then a chilling answer occurred to him.

The security vehicle was abreast of him now, a Chevy Blazer, he saw. The two oversized vehicles were taking the last curve in a precarious ballet. One slipup, Deal thought, one nudge, and he'd be over the side.

He saw the passenger window of the Blazer slide down, caught sight of a man in a parka turned toward him.

"Pull over!" The voice crackling again, echoing off the frozen hillside. Deal felt a thud, felt the wheel of the Toyota shudder in his hands. He stole a quick glance at the sheer drop-off on his right, glanced back at the man beside him. Were the bastards trying to kill him? He clutched the wheel with one freezing hand, sent his window down with the other, opening the perfect slipstream for the frigid blast outside.

"Hey!" he shouted, struggling to make himself heard over the wind, over the straining engines. "Back off…" he added, then stopped.

The man across from him had a pistol raised, had brought his other hand up to steady his aim. Deal didn't wait to see what his intentions were.

He slammed on the brakes of the Toyota and the Blazer hurtled forward. There was a muzzle flash and the popping sound of a pistol shot. He saw the brake lamps of the Blazer ignite, felt the wheels of the Toyota lock on the ice beneath him.

The Blazer had slewed diagonally across the road in front f him and Deal ducked as another muzzle flash erupted from the passenger window. He still had his head down when the two vehicles collided.

He came up in time to see the Blazer skid on the ice, then go over the side, barreling down the steep slope toward the frozen lake. The Toyota slid in the other direction, slammed off a projection of rock that jutted where the road had been cut, then spun to a halt a few feet downhill from where the Blazer had gone over.

He watched the Blazer roll over once, then come up on its wheels again, skidding wildly out across the icy surface of the lake. It came to a stop finally, and for a moment, everything was still. Deal set the Toyota's parking brake, stepped shakily down, stared out at the silent Blazer.

A break, he was thinking. He'd finally caught a break.

Then there was a blinding eruption of flashes from the Blazer and a hail of automatic fire that chewed into the Toyota's grill. Deal dove for cover behind the fender, covering his head as metal screamed and hoses burst above him. He smelled brake fluid, antifreeze, scorched oil, all the fluids a dying car could leak.

The firing abated, and he heard the whine of the Blazer's engine come to life. He glanced around the Toyota's fender, saw the Blazer, its top crushed down, its windows shattered, grinding inexorably toward him. Another blast of fire sent him down again.

No point in trying to run, he thought. And even if the Toyota was still drivable, they'd cut him down before he got a hundred yards. But what to do? Fire some snowballs their way? Start an avalanche?

Which led him to consider the next best thing, something he'd already learned in his brief time in frozen landscape. Not much, of course, but what were his options? He stood up cautiously, opened the door of the Toyota. He released the parking brake, slid the shift into neutral. Another hail of fire tore through what was left of the windshield, blew on through the back windows this time.

He leaned heavily against the door frame and tried to find some decent purchase on the snowy ground. He felt the Toyota give slightly, and found a crevice where the pavement ended that he could dig both feet into. He gritted his teeth, felt a fire in his groin as he pushed with everything he had. *Sorry, car*, he thought. *Last chance, it's either you or me.* And finally, the car gave way.

He rolled aside, dodging another burst of fire as the Toyota slammed down onto the ice. He glanced up to see muzzle flashes erupting from both windows of the Blazer as the Land Cruiser slid crazily toward it.

Slugs caromed off the Land Cruiser like tracer fire. Then there was a bright ball of flame as the gas tank went up. The Blazer swerved, would avoid this rolling fireball easily. And it would have. Would have dodged Deal's last toss easily if that's all he'd had in mind.

The Blazer circled slowly toward the smoldering Land Cruiser, and a spotlight beam shot out, playing across the ruined carcass. Twenty feet, ten feet, five. Another hail of fire chewing into the already shattered driver's side, they'd have to be sure...

...and then he heard it, what he'd hoped for when he sent the heavy Land Cruiser out on the ice, a crack that echoed off the hillside at his back, then another, and another. The Land Cruiser went first. Its rear wheels seemed to drop a foot or so as though some giant hand had jerked its axle from below. Then, abruptly, its snout pitched forward and disappeared beneath the water.

Inside the Blazer, they must have realized what was happening, Deal thought. He heard the big engine roar, the wheels whining furiously. It teetered on the edge of the sudden dark slash that was open water, the tires locked in a

less spin on the fractured ice. And then, as if the driver
inexplicably thrown the vehicle into reverse, as if the
eels had found purchase at last, the Blazer shot backwards,
nishing into the dark water.

◎ ◎ ◎

here might have been screams from that broken place, but
eal, who was already up and running toward the big arena,
villed himself not to hear them. By the time he'd crossed
the huge parking lot and was edging along the shadows in
front of the building where Kittle's truck was parked, he
had convinced himself it had been nothing more than the
keening of the bitter wind.

Though the snow had stopped, the wind had picked up
and it seemed very nearly as bitter as when he'd been driving the windowless Land Cruiser. He longed to be inside,
anywhere, no matter what the danger, so long as he could
be warm again. Still, he approached the entrance slowly,
cautiously, staying close to the thick shrubbery, praying no
one was watching from the brightly lit foyer. With the vast
bank of windows steamed as thickly as they were, it was
hard to tell, but then, he told himself, it would be just as
difficult for anyone to see out.

He broke out of the shadows finally, headed for the open
set of doors on a dead run, trying to keep his thoughts under
control, praying he wouldn't squander whatever chance he had.

He stopped briefly at Kittle's truck, glanced through the
windshield, felt a surge of hope when he saw Janice's bag
tossed carelessly on the floorboards. He flung open the door
to check the back, recoiled when an alarm Klaxon began to
sound.

Deal cursed, slamming the truck door, racing on toward
the foyer of the building. He slid inside, wrenching the glass
doors closed behind him, fighting against the drifted snow
until they clicked shut and the wail of the truck's alarm
dimmed.

A killer with an alarm on his goddamned pickup tru Deal thought, leaning with his back against the glass to catc his breath. The guy probably had life and health insurance, a pension plan, too.

He glanced around, hoping to see a coatroom entrance, a bank of phones, but he'd stepped into something that looked more like an arboretum than a foyer: He heard the sound of running water, glanced across the room at a sculpted rock formation, a tumbling waterfall that fed a meandering artificial stream, little signs posted here and there: FOUNTAIN OF EVERLASTING HOPE. ETERNAL STREAM OF MERCY. GLADE OF PEACE AND BROTHERHOOD. The water was steaming in the blast of cold air that Kittle had let in, and the place had the surreal look of a movie set or some theme area out of Disney World. He didn't have to look to know that the fountains and the waterways would be lined with the glittering coins of the faithful.

He pushed away from the glass then, hearing muffled sounds from inside the chapel, the heavy bass rumble and echo of a PA system. He approached one pair of the inner doors, thick wood slabs with little portal windows, checked inside, tried the latch. The first set was locked, but he moved aside and found another set where the latch gave with a soft click. He pushed inside, found himself in a short passage that led to an inner set of doors.

Good architecture, he thought, the sort of anteroom quality movie houses used to have but had thrown over years ago. The Reverend James Ray Willis wanted to make sure nothing would disturb the assembled parishioners, apparently.

Deal moved on to the second set of doors, glanced through the tiny window, was startled at the immensity of what he saw inside. "Church" was a misnomer, certainly. "Arena" was more like it. Maybe "coliseum." The place, a sea of empty seats, dimly lit in the reflection of exit lights and row markers, could hold thousands.

far down an aisle wide enough to have driven the Land Cruiser along was a nearly darkened stage, illuminated only at a pulpit raised off to one side. Someone was standing at the lectern there, bellowing into a microphone. Deal couldn't make out the face, but the form was unmistakable, even at this distance. Kittle, his gaunt frame bent over the top of the lectern, one hand clutching the microphone, his voice booming. There was a dark form on the floor of the stage beside him. Anyone else might have taken it for stage property, might have missed the shape altogether, but not Deal. He felt his heart give, felt gratitude, and fury, and desperation.

"Reverend!" Deal heard as he slipped inside the cavernous hall. "Reverend!"

Deal thought he saw Janice stirring groggily on the stage floor at Kittle's feet, had to hold himself back from a mad rush down the long aisle. He gazed over the bank of seats at his right, glimpsed another aisle running between the last bank of seats and the building's wall. The seats themselves were the type that folded up when no one was sitting, and that would give him a clear track, he thought. He dropped to his hands and knees, scurrying off over the concrete surface like a theater rat toward the far aisle, Kittle's pleas booming through the air above him.

When he felt his palms reach the carpet of the far aisle, he straightened a bit, began an awkward crab walk that would take him down to the stage, opposite the end where Kittle stood, craning his neck, looking out into the darkness for his blessed reverend to save him.

If he could just make it up into the wings without being seen, Deal thought. Make his way directly behind Kittle, surprise him with a rush...

But Deal hadn't gone a dozen yards when he froze, his heart thudding in his chest. Someone was standing in an alcove, he realized, close enough to reach out and touch.

Someone with a weapon raised, about to put an end to this, a burly, bearded man wearing sandals. And a tunic?

In the next moment, as his eyes adjusted to the dim light, Deal felt his breath release. His gaze traveled on up the lifelike statue, to another of the little plaques mounted above the alcove.

"SOLDIER OF THE CROSS," he read. Further down the aisle, another alcove, a beseeching Madonna, her hands lifted toward the heavens in supplication. A series of the things all over the hall, he saw now. Seven deadly sins, Christ bearing his Cross, all the iconography of his childhood Bible class, and then some.

He stood carefully, ducked into the soldier's nook, reached out to the sword. A short blade, and carefully dulled, but a seemingly authentic reproduction otherwise. He tugged on the blade, but the statue's hand held fast. He jiggled the thing a bit, felt some give. He waited for Kittle to repeat his call, and then, as the sound echoed across the great room, he grasped the blade firmly and twisted with all he had.

There was a puff of plaster as several of the soldier's fingers flew away into the darkness, and suddenly Deal was holding a freely swinging sword by its blade. He turned the thing around, slipped his hand inside the guard. As he'd hoped, the thing had a heft to it. It might not cut butter, but it would have to do. Just holding it made him feel better, almost a soldier himself. He ducked out of the alcove past the shattered arm of the statue, hurried on down the plaster-strewn aisle toward the stage.

He found a set of stairs there, blocked by a low gate that he simply stepped over, a hurdler's move, but in slow motion. He ducked back down, came up the steps on his hands and knees, pausing when his gaze cleared stage level. He glanced at Kittle, whose gaze was directed straight ahead, then turned, gauging the distance across the neck of stage before him until he'd reach the cover of the curtains.

When Kittle bent to the microphone once again, Deal made his break. One step, two steps, three…no more than a dozen feet, but it seemed endless…

He dropped to his knees, grasped the weighted bottom of the heavy drapery, was rolling under its protective hem, when there was a sudden blaze of light that enveloped him, enveloped everything. Deal tumbled on beneath the curtain, on his back and gasping. He found himself in a fly gallery now, staring up into the upper recesses above the stage, where ropes and guys twined crazily, where banks of lights had suddenly sprung into life.

Had Kittle spotted him, thrown these lights on? he wondered. He urged himself up, turned toward center stage, holding his dull sword at the ready, waiting for Kittle to burst through the drapes, make his final charge. But the moments passed and still no one came.

"What in God's name are you doing, buddy?" Deal heard then. The voice boomed about the arena, echoing even louder than Kittle's had, sending the stage curtains them-selves into a tremble. Deal gave an involuntary glance up into the flies.

Deal waited a moment, but heard no further sounds. He edged quickly along the backside of the curtains, until he thought he'd reached a spot behind the podium. He found a gap where two sections overlapped, glanced quickly out, caught sight of a figure out there bathed in bright light now, a light so bright it nearly blinded him.

But there was no time to hesitate, Deal thought, already making his charge. If Kittle chanced to turn, his butter knife of a sword wasn't going to do much good against a gun.

He was up over the back of the pulpit, still fighting the incredible glare from the stage lights, and thank God Kittle hadn't seemed to hear him still, though that seemed rather strange, didn't it? And even odder, Deal thought, as he dove for the man who stood motionless at the podium, staring

out over the empty auditorium, his arms raised in th
familiar pose of benediction, it wasn't Kittle standing there a
all. It was Willis, he realized, in that brief fraction of a second
that he left his feet. Willis, who'd come to take Kittle's place.

Deal's arms reached out to close about the neck of the
Reverend James Ray Willis, then, but somehow, impossibly,
he caught nothing but air. Deal sailed off the edge of the
pulpit and crashed to the floor of the stage below, his
shoulder crumpling painfully beneath him. He came up on
his hands and knees, groggy, the sword still clutched in his
hand. He stared up dumbstruck at the unwavering image
above him. It was James Ray Willis, all right, down to the
last glittering detail, but there was something wrong with
that picture.

"Wait for me right where you are, buddy."

Willis's voice boomed off the walls about them, and the
lips of the image moved. But the facial movement was
generic, devoid of expression, that of a ventriloquist's dummy.
The realization came slowly to Deal, partly because it seemed
so bizarre, so impossible.

A hologram, he thought. He'd tried to tackle a goddamned hologram.

"Deal?" he heard. And turned, still dazed, to see Janice a
dozen yards away. She had struggled to one elbow, was
reaching out for him...then she collapsed again. Deal pushed
himself to his feet, started for her.

He might have taken two strides, no more, when he
sensed movement behind him. He turned, caught a glimpse
of Kittle advancing upon him, already too close, he thought.

Deal felt a stunning blow at the base of his skull, felt
himself tumbling forward, his chin bouncing off the wooden
surface of the stage. Odd that there wasn't more pain, he
was thinking. His dull sword spun away across the black-
painted wood, its phony jewels and golden paint firing off
glints and glitter as it went.

He felt Kittle's hands on him now, cupping his chin roughly, felt the man's knee dig into his spine. There'd be one sudden movement, Deal knew, one electric bolt of pain despite any effort he could make, no matter how hard he fought to hold his chin steady…and his neck would snap and all this would end.

What he felt was not fear. Only sadness and despair. Arch, he thought. And Janice. Some soldier he'd been. Kittle's grip tightened. Deal's jaw rose a fraction…

And then he heard the explosion and simultaneously he felt release. Kittle's hands fell away, his knee slid off Deal's spine. He heard a soft sighing sound, as if Kittle were stirring in his sleep, and then he felt the man slump atop him. There was another shot, the force of it striking Kittle, then burning into Deal as well.

Deal managed to turn his head aside, saw a very real James Ray Willis standing above him, pistol in hand. "I'm deeply sorry," Willis said. "My brother was an idiot. You should never have gotten this far." He shook his head sorrowfully, nudged Kittle's body aside. "This isn't personal, you understand. There is something so much larger at stake…"

Deal's vision was going in and out now, full of glittering pinpoints. Hard to tell if the Willis talking to him was the real Willis or the hologram of Willis.

"Not personal," Deal repeated. His head was spinning, he could taste blood in his mouth. Janice was a few feet away. She was alive. But this man would kill him, and then he would kill her.

"I'm going to remember that," Deal said, trying to get his feet under him. "I'll tell Arch Dolan when I see him. He'll feel better. And Rosenhaus and Eddie Lightner, too, if they're in the same place, that is."

"It's over with now," Willis was saying. He took a step back. "There doesn't have to be any more killing. It should never have happened in the first place. But there wasn't a choice."

"And Sara Dolan," Deal said. "I suppose there wasn't a choice for her, either?"

Willis shook his head. "She's alive," he said, glancing over his shoulder nervously. "...but she's not important."

Deal felt it like a blow. "Then what *is* so goddamned important?" Deal said. He was on his hands and knees again. He saw blood dripping steadily from somewhere onto the stage floor beneath him. He felt a wave of nausea, clenched his gut tight. "Why would you have to kill some poor guy who just wanted to run a bookstore?"

Willis wiped his forehead with his sleeve. Not the hologram, Deal thought. Holograms didn't sweat, didn't come unglued. One thing to play God talking long distance to your button man, another thing to look at a person, put him away yourself.

"We'll be more careful," Willis said, the words pinwheeling out, now. "The stakes, after all. Time itself, that's what we're fighting for. To spread the word, the right word." His eyes were glittering. "It's not power. It's not money. It's to be used the proper way." He swept his hand about the auditorium. "I'm not some politician. The world's gone to greedy hell, I don't have to tell you that. But what self-centered politician could turn such a complex mess around? But if a person, the right person, could control the *way* the word got out, then you'd control *what* got out. A worldwide web, all right: but a web in fact, orchestrated together with books, magazines, newspapers, television, and radio, as it is in fact today, but finally in the proper hands. Not buy time, but control time..."

"You want to go out over the Internet, dance on every desk in the world, is that it? A little homunculus, going to tell us how to behave?"

Deal laughed, despite the pain it caused him. "The worst of it is being killed by a lunatic," he said. He coughed, felt a gurgle in his chest, knew where the blood was coming from now.

Willis snorted. "Look what the real lunatics did, Mr. Deal. In Germany, in Russia, in China. And what about us? The United States of Make a Killing Quick. You think our leaders are the sane ones?"

Deal felt his vision going black around the edges. He wanted to rise up, take a swing, do something, *any*thing, but there was nothing left. No strength. Only will. He stared up at Willis. "Keep in mind what my old man used to say," Deal managed. "You can't make chicken salad out of chicken shit."

Willis face darkened.

"Pull the trigger, you dickwad. Get it over with."

Willis raised the pistol. "What must be..." he began sorrowfully, and then there was a deep thudding sound, and he stopped midsentence, his eyes going sightless, his body suddenly rigid, his hands splaying out at his sides as if he'd stepped on a high-tension line. The pistol tumbled to the stage, bouncing near Deal's cheek.

Willis crumpled, blood spraying from the crown of his perfectly coiffed head, as he fell atop his brother. Deal saw her there, realized what had happened, saw her lift the heavy blade again.

"Janice," he called, not sure if he were actually speaking the words, not sure if she could hear. "It's enough, Janice."

Still sobbing, her face gone wild, she brought the blade down again.

Chapter 26

Miami, Six Weeks Later

The image on the television screen was of James Ray Willis, in all his holographic glory, his arms spread over the flock of his faithful, thousands of them gathered in their temple, faces rapt as their leader spoke of reclaiming their lives from the modern-day forces of Moloch. The scene shifted rapidly then, cutting away to the stoic visage of Ted Koppel behind his desk on the *Night-line* set.

"And so they still gather at the Church of the Worldwide Light, to pay homage to their fallen leader," Koppel intoned, "and to a person they will tell you that James Ray Willis was a man maligned by the media and done in by a cabal formulated by an international consortium of bond traders and powermongers.

"As for allegations that Willis himself had engaged in a ruthless plot to engineer his own media empire, they will respond by shaking their heads in dismay." Here Koppel's visage dissolved, to be replaced by a montage of images: a bank of satellite dishes and microwave relay towers; a series of foreign-language newspapers and magazines tumbling atop one another; a shot of Martin Rosenhaus, from sunnier days, his foot atop a silver shovel at the groundbreaking of a

Mega-Media store; and, of course, the shot that had appeared in nearly every newspaper and current events magazine the world around: it was a view outside the convocation center of the Church of the Worldwide Light, where an armada of police cars and emergency vehicles had converged—in the foreground were John and Janice Deal, faces haggard and blood-streaked, struggling away from the carnage inside with Sara Dolan propped up between them.

Koppel's image was back then. "All of that merely more proof for the true believer that the international cabal is in full swing, capable of making anything happen…or seem to have." Koppel smiled his patented smile, as if to acknowledge the absurdity of the notion. After a moment, he bent to shuffle some papers in front of him and turned back to the camera brightly.

"As a footnote, we can report that as of this day, the House of Books in Coral Gables, Florida, where the unfolding of this tragedy began, is once again open for business under the stewardship of new managers Sara Dolan and Janice Deal. We'd like to wish them the best of luck."

There was a cheer then as the scene cut away to commercial. Deal snapped off the power on the big-screen TV, then turned with his glass held high, toasting the crowd that was still assembled in the book-store's reading room, despite the late hour. Terrence Terrell, who'd donated the TV in honor of the event, had gone home. But Driscoll was still there, of course, and Sara, and Janice. All of them cheering, along with the crowd. For books, and everything else.

⊚ ⊚ ⊚

"Pretty good champagne, Driscoll," Deal said a little later. He held his plastic glass up to the light. What was it supposed to be, anyway? Lots of big bubbles? A few little ones? It tasted good, that much he knew.

Driscoll looked around the room, the crowd long gone, shrugged his characteristic shrug. "Must have been a mistake," he said. "The guy that owns the Zaragosa Drive-ins gave it to me, a little bonus on account of I caught the scumwad who was knocking over his stores."

Deal nodded. "Did you do like you said, hand over the money, wait 'til he drove away to call the cops?"

"That's what I wanted to do," Driscoll said. "But when he pointed his gun at me, it pissed me off. I made out like I was scared, dumped a milkshake in his lap. By the time he looked up to complain, he had my boot in his face."

"Through the drive-in window?" Deal asked.

"Took the frame with me, going out," Driscoll said.

"I'm sorry I missed it," Deal said.

Driscoll waved it away. "Another bad guy bites the dust. Wasn't as spectacular as what you two managed."

Deal glanced over at Janice, who was leaning against the reading room counter, talking with Sara Dolan. "I'd have traded bad guys with you, that's for sure," Deal said. "And to think I dismissed Willis as a nutcase...a guy who wants to tell the world how to think claims there's this big conspiracy to tell us all how to think..." He trailed off, shaking his head.

"Don't feel so bad," Driscoll said. "There were plenty of folks who felt the same way when this German house painter had pretty much the same idea. The sad thing is"—he gestured at the darkened TV screen—"there's still all these people out there ready to believe what Willis wanted to feed 'em. If he'd ever gotten it all in place, if *someone* ever does, who knows what could happen..." He broke off, giving his Driscoll shrug, the one that acknowledged everything and anything.

Driscoll smiled then, and lifted his glass. "Anyway, here's to you, Johnny Deal. You did good." He turned to the others, raised his gravelly voice. "And here's to books."

Janice, who'd gone to toss another log into the fireplace, turned to join the toast. It was a balmy March night, and the temperature outside was hovering in the mid-sixties. Still,

Deal had thought it only appropriate to build a fire. Arch would have gone for it. Turn the AC down to frigid, stoke the fire. Controlled cold weather. And what better way to mark the grand reopening?

It had all begun with a reading in the big room earlier in the night, a huge, Russian-styled marathon of a program: poets, fiction writers, a couple of playwrights, two dozen or more, all from South Florida, and the audience well into the hundreds, spilling out of the reading room, through art and architecture and philosophy, all the way into the children's section, where they'd rigged up the intercom so people could listen even if they couldn't see.

Later in the evening, one of the readers, a performance poet from somewhere in the Caribbean, had led a conga line out the front door of the place, snaking across the street and past the still-shuttered Mega-Media site, the whole crowd chanting, "Hell no, we won't go," and tying up traffic for a good twenty minutes. A couple of squad cars had come by to check out the disturbance, but the cops, one of whom resembled the guy who'd nearly ticketed Deal the day he'd left Dr. Goodwin's office, had gotten in the spirit, used their cars to block off the street, redirect traffic until the line was back inside the House of Books.

"To books," Janice agreed. She lifted her glass, her eyes meeting Deal's momentarily. She turned away to the counter, where Sara Dolan leaned back on her elbows, a wistful smile on her face, tear tracks tracing her cheeks. "And to the beginning of a long and successful partnership," Janice added.

She paused, took a breath. "Despite everything that's happened, we all know someone's going to come in and open up that big store across the street." She gestured out the window behind them. "And I've heard it said that little shops like this one are going to become footnotes to history, as doomed as the neighborhood hardware store when Home Depot comes to town.

"But"—and here her chin jutted out, her eyes narrowing—"I say there are some battles that have to be fought. This is different. It seems a lot more important than hammers and nails."

"Fact is," Deal said, "when we had all those little hardware stores, there used to be a lot more brands of hammers to choose from."

Janice shook her head. "Leave it to you, Deal. Somebody to get sentimental over hammers."

Sara's smile broadened a bit as she pushed away from the counter, lifted her glass, too. "I'll drink to that," she said, banging Deal's glass hard enough to slosh champagne over both their upraised hands. "And to good friends," she said.

She paused then, glancing about their surroundings. Burning fireplace, stacks and shelves of books, magazines with strange names and some in foreign print. The familiar smell of paper, and glue, and woodsmoke.

"And here's to my brother..." she added. "I'm not going to get weepy, I promise. But he would have loved this night."

"Of course he would have," Janice said. The two women embraced then, champagne spilling from their glasses as they clutched one another tightly.

Deal looked on, feeling teary himself. He glanced at Driscoll, who harrumphed a strangled cough and turned away.

Deal found himself smiling as his old friend continued his pretense of coughing. Driscoll would rather spend a day in the dentist's chair than admit his feelings, he mused. But he had them, all right. And he'd step in front of a train to save someone he cared about.

Deal took a sip of his drink, thinking how fortunate he was, how fortunate they all were, really. Terrible things had happened, and yet they'd survived and more. Janice and Sara partners now, he and Janice at least working in that same direction, life might just be slipping everyone a little payback yet...

He broke off then when he realized who was missing. "Els," he cried, and everyone turned to look at him, their expressions frozen in concern. "What's happened to Els?"

He led the dash through philosophy, architecture, art, out through hardcover fiction and past the small bestseller rack by the circular stairwell in the main room, where they found Els's wheelchair tipped over on its side.

Deal cursed under his breath, jumped over the wheelchair, grasped the rails of the staircase, taking the steps two at a time, spiraling his way upward as fast as he could manage, the others thundering behind him.

He found Els in the inner room, the place he had always referred to as his "inner sanctum." The mess had been erased, the broken table repaired, a new easy chair brought up, the lamp replaced.

The doors of the glass case that housed Els's most prized volumes were hanging open, two books teetering precariously at the edge of an upper shelf. Els himself was slumped in the easy chair, his eyes closed, the light burning at his shoulder. A copy of *Huckleberry Finn* lay spineout and open against his chest.

How he'd made it up here by himself, Deal would never know. The man had been making progress the doctors would never have dared hope for, but he still couldn't speak, and he hadn't been out of his chair without assistance since they'd brought him home last week.

Sara was at Deal's shoulder then, her hand flying to her mouth when she saw what Deal was looking at.

"Oh, Els," she cried.

El's eyes came open at the words, his expression that of a man who'd been snatched from a dream, or caught in some compromising act.

His hands went to his chest, clutched the copy of *Huckleberry Finn*. His mouth popped open once or twice, his face contorted in the painful fashion Deal had come to recognize when Els was trying to speak.

"You scared us, Els," Deal said, moving carefully toward him.

Els held up one hand, kept the other pressed to his chest. "Book," he said, the sound bursting finally from his lips.

His hand stroked the cover as if a pet lay there. "Good book," he added.

And there was no one to disagree.

🐚🐚🐚

It must have been near six when Deal awoke. No real light outside, but there was the hint of light to come. He'd been sleeping far less soundly the past year or so, often finding himself sitting up, swinging his legs out of bed without knowing why, then hearing Isabel's cough or bad-dream moanings, and realizing, and padding down the hallway to her room. Mr. Mom Deal.

It wasn't Isabel this time, though. He lay listening, heard the dog—Flash, or Shark Bait, or Rover, they would have to decide one of these days soon—shifting on the floor below. He heard the sounds of his own heart, of his breathing, and then the rustle of Janice's breathing at his side. He reached out, felt the warmth of her back, felt the slow rise and fall beneath his touch, life moving on.

"You're awake," she said after a moment.

"Yeah," he said. "You okay?"

"I was dreaming again," she said, her voice controlled, emotionless.

He moved closer to her, circled her waist with his arm, drew her into him.

"Willis?" he asked. "You were dreaming about Willis?"

She lay quietly for a few moments, took a deep, shuddering breath. "I killed a man, Deal. I killed him."

He reached up, pressed his palm against her cheek, drew her hair back, felt the dampness of tears. He felt the familiar helpless ache in his chest, the one that came each time he sensed her grappling with those demons that only she could know. He could brave gunfire for her sake, he could go hand to hand with any real-life monster that lurked out there...but against these forces, he felt so powerless.

"You did something you had to do, Janice," he said. "But you did the right thing. And it's going to pass. You're going to get over it." The words rang so pitifully in his own ears.

She took his hand in both of hers, squeezed, drew it to her chest. Another bone-rattling breath. "I hope not, Deal," she said, finally. "I really do hope not."

They lay quietly for a moment, Deal considering the somber wisdom of her response, and fighting that familiar sensation of guilt, that once again he'd been the cause of Janice's pain. But that was wasted thought, wasn't it? What happened was over now. Things had happened, she had reacted, he'd have done the same in her place, anyone would have.

"Twice," he said finally. "You saved me twice. From Willis, and from Kittle, too."

There was a pause. "What are you talking about?" she said after a moment. "Willis shot his own brother. I didn't have anything to do with that."

"I'm talking about earlier, out in the snowstorm, when Kittle was about to blow me away. When you called out to warn me."

She raised up on her elbow, turned to him. "I really don't know what you mean, Deal. I don't remember anything from the time that woman grabbed me in the parking lot until I woke up and found myself on the stage of that awful building."

He shook his head, just as disbelieving. "Kittle was standing outside the door of the truck, he was about to shoot. I couldn't see him, but you could, I guess. I heard you scream. 'He's there, Deal.' If I hadn't heard you..." He broke off, staring at her. There was enough light now, he could see the same stunned expression on her face.

"You think I imagined it?" he said. He knew he hadn't. He could still hear her voice, its urgent echo across that frigid landscape. He'd heard it all right. No question about it.

She shook her head. "I don't know what I think, Deal."

They stayed that way for a moment, both frozen, both in wonder. Finally, she bent to him and took his face in her hands. She kissed him and slid down to press herself against him. At first he could feel the heat of her flesh against his, but that sensation quickly disappeared. It was as though they'd fused together, he thought. It was as though they'd never part.

Les Standiford is author of the novels *Spill* (released as a feature film), *Done Deal, Raw Deal, Deal to Die For, Deal on Ice, Presidential Deal, Deal With the Dead,* and *Bone Key* (April of 2002). In the Fall of 2002, Crown will publish a work of non-fiction, *The Last Train to Paradise—Henry Flagler and the Building of the Railroad that Crossed an Ocean.* He wrote the pictorial history *Coral Gables: The City Beautiful Story,* and has contributed the text for the photographic essay collection *Miami: City of Dreams.* His articles and stories have appeared in numerous anthologies and magazines, including the *New York Times* best-seller, *Naked Came the Manatee* and *The Putt at the End of the World.* He is a recipient of the Barnes & Noble Discover Great New Writers Award, the Frank O'Connor Award for Short Fiction, a Florida Individual Artist Fellowship, and a National Endowment for the Arts Fellowship in Fiction. His books have been reprinted in Great Britain, France, Holland, Germany, Spain, and Japan. He is currently Professor of English and Director of the Creative Writing Program at Florida International University in Miami, where he has lived since 1981, with his wife Kimberly, a psychotherapist, and their three children, Jeremy, Hannah, and Alexander.

To receive a free catalog of other Poisoned Pen Press titles, please contact us in one of the following ways:

Phone: 1-800-421-3976
Facsimile: 1-480-949-1707
Email: info@poisonedpenpress.com
Website: www.poisonedpenpress.com

Poisoned Pen Press
6962 E. First Ave. Ste 103
Scottsdale, AZ 85251